The Summoning:

Book Three of the Trencit Legacy

The Summoning

Paul Melniczek

King's Way Press
Atlanta 2017

King's Way Press

3721 New Macland Rd.
Suite 200-141
Powder Springs, GA 30157
http://www.kwp-books.com

This is a work of fiction. Names, characters, places, and events portrayed in this book are fictitious and are products of the author's imagination. Any similarity to real persons, living or deceased, is coincidental and not intended by the author.

ISBN-13: 978-0-9988367-7-5
ISBN-10: 099883677X

Artwork Copyright © 2017 by Wayne Miller

The Summoning

The Summoning

The company arrived at the rim of a wide valley, looking down at a heavily forested depression where strands of evening mist trailed upwards like transparent serpents. Sarion held up one hand, calling for a temporary halt, and the hunters from Nighton rested for a moment, a few taking the chance to drink water from their pouches, while the lead and rear guard remained vigilant. They were in dangerous country.

"What do you think? Keep moving and camp somewhere down there or stay on higher ground for the night?" Valadire spoke as he pulled off one of his riding gloves and smacked it lightly against his thigh.

Sarion was silent for a moment, lost in thought. They had left the western gate a number of days ago, and were now heading deeper into the southern reaches of the borderlands, the wilderness growing denser, the villages and outposts more infrequent. They had failed to see a single traveler in the past two days. Entering a veritable no-man's land, they had journeyed into a wide region of thick forests and hills which sat between the Ridgeline and the high mountain range which buffeted the southern city of Sharield, the most isolated province under Trencit's dominion, although it was primarily an independent territory itself, lacking any steady flow of communication or trade. Ruled by Lord Berillon, it was a beautiful city built on a plateau next to a deep lake, constructed to maximize the natural geography surrounding it, as were all the major cities of Trencit. Sarion had never been there, and knew of few who had. There had always existed a strong sense of loyalty between Nighton and Sharield, but since the threat from the Glefins had been eliminated, there was little need for war strategy, so both had gone their separate ways; Nighton maintaining its role as protector of Trencit's western entrance, Sharield going about its business as a small but thriving city in the south, content with its own independent affairs.

"The woods have been quiet, and we've seen no sign of marauders. I think we should press on. In my heart I feel that time moves against us. Our victory against the Dark Mage will be shortlived. Once he learns of his failure at Nighton, he'll try something else," Sarion answered.

"Perhaps he's already doing that. We just don't know it yet." Chertron entered the conversation, the reliable fighter handling a small apple as if debating whether he would take a bite.

"Your ideas are always sound, my friend. I fear the truth in your words. Our enemy has been plotting our defeat for a long time, I think. We've been reacting to his attacks. That's exactly why *we* need to be the ones on the offensive. We must find Gar-kiln. And soon."

Valadire spoked. "And when we find this village, we must be extremely cautious. Who knows if it even exists yet, or if any remain there? But that leads us to another question, Sarion. One which you've been reluctant to talk about. Do we try Sharield first, or seek Gar-kiln ourselves?"

In truth, Sarion hadn't made any decision yet. He believed that someone from the large city had to have been at the village in the past, or knew its location at the very least. But to reach Sharield would take additional time, a few days. Time they might not necessarily have. Sarion had deliberately taken them on a path due south, keeping between the opposing mountain ranges in an effort to forestall this decision in case they found information concerning the whereabouts of the village. He'd been looking for travelers from the area, but so far they'd had no success, and very soon they would have to turn east if they were to gain the reaches of Sharield.

Sarion looked at the newly-appointed Captain of Nighton, his second in command for this mission. "I haven't decided. I hoped that circumstances would make the choice for us, but it appears this is not so. We'll continue in this direction for another day, and if we still can't find anyone to question, then we'll make for Sharield. It would be foolish to search in the wilderness for this village without any notion of its location. We could be out here for weeks, and little is known about the deep south. *And*...there's always the possibility that the prisoner lied."

It was an unpleasant thought, but one they needed to consider. They could trust no one, especially an emissary of their enemy.

"Very well," Valadire said. "There's little more we can do. Not until we come across valuable information."

Sarion agreed and he dismounted, stretching his arms and legs. The air was damp, and he pulled his cloak tighter, moving forward. The group rode in typical Nighton hunting fashion -- two abreast, their leaders protected in the middle. Men nodded as he passed, and the company numbered fifteen strong, handpicked by Chensel, the Nighton leader, to accompany Sarion and Valadire on their mission. Walking through their ranks, his eyes matched those of Lassel, the young woman who had surprised him back at the western fortress where they had battled the Killworm. It was unheard of for a woman to be a member of the Western Watch, yet here she was, chosen as one of the hunters on the venture from Nighton. Sarion had hardly spoken to her since their departure from the valley of Nighton, but he noticed her gaze whenever they passed close, her eyes following him, although she said nothing. The first time she'd taken off her war helm, he'd seen what lay beneath -- fair skin, warm, intense blue eyes, and that shock of golden hair. She was smaller and leaner than her comrades, but the hunters treated her as an equal, her reputation known throughout the Western Watch. She handled her horse with exceptional ability, and had fearlessly struck against the terrible Killworm where other riders had fallen, a good number unable to control their steeds, the war animals frightened by the deadly predator. Dressed in a cloak of forest green, a long bow was strapped to her back, a brace of knives at her waist, and a long sword waited in its sheath on her belt. She looked as formidable as any of the other hunters, and the girl had left an impression on Sarion. He wondered as to her background, but knew this wasn't the time or place for curiosity. They were on a dangerous venture, and he couldn't afford to wonder about who she really was. His only thought was to lead them safely in the wilderness and find the answers they searched for.

He soon reached the front, where a veteran named Huyargal watched his advance. Alongside of him was Geld Rinn, who led the hunting party, a young man who had climbed the ranks of Nighton quickly, his reputation as tracker and swordsman gaining the approval of several Foresters. He remained on horseback, his keen eyes peering ahead into the valley which waited below.

Sarion joined them, Chertron and Valadire

following close, Piril and Bertilik spread out several yards to either side, ever vigilant as personal guard to their charge.

"The forest seems quiet, Captain Sarion." Geld Rinn spoke, but he continued looking forward into the growing gloom.

"This part of the borderlands is strange to me." Valadire gestured with both arms for emphasis. "I've never been this far south."

Sarion replied. "I've never been to Sharield myself, or to this country, and our maps give little detail. No markings for town, hill, or dale. One large expanse of white, describing nothing. It's my belief that few dwell here now, if ever. We're beyond the power of Trencit. King Gregor has no sway over this hinterland." Sarion crouched down on one knee. "Wait...I see tracks in the dirt."

Geld Rinn eased off his mount, and Sarion motioned the others to back off while he examined the ground. The younger tracker joined him, and both men pointed, searching for additional signs.

"Yes, something passed here," said Sarion, Geld Rinn nodding. "These are certainly not boot prints, or made by a horse." Sarion stiffened, his eyes flashing. "These tracks were made by some type of creature."

"A large one at that," said Geld Rinn.

Now Sarion straightened, moving forwards. "And whatever it is, it went down *there*."

All eyes followed his hand, which pointed directly ahead of them.

"Into the valley."

"I'm sure we haven't been followed by anything," said Sarion.

"Most likely it's a chance encounter," offered Valadire. "Something prowling this area."

"And something *not* native as well," Sarion added. "It could be a predator from the Lowlands. A creature which has wandered past the Ridgeline -- or was driven here by our enemy." He folded his arms. "We've seen no signs of anything from Grammore since leaving the western gate. Heard rumors and stories, yes. So it's not improbable that we've come across something now, and we're not that far from the Ridgeline. The entire borderlands is under a silent invasion. We know this."

Chertron came forward. "The question now is, what is our plan? Enter the valley, knowing that something unknown is down there, probably dangerous? Or take another course."

"*Definitely* dangerous..." Valadire added. "We've yet to see anything from Grammore which was friendly and harmless."

Sarion frowned with the man's attempt at dark humor. "Well, you're not *entirely* correct, Valadire." A vision of Alayian's dazzling smile went through his mind. "But there can be no doubt that something deadly has come this way. I think it best that we change our direction and avoid whatever passed through here. I fear there will be enough confrontations in the near future to challenge us. Let's move west. The forest grows somewhat thinner in that direction."

Geld Rinn nodded, turning his horse sideways, but everyone stopped in their tracks as a bloodcurdling howl erupted from behind them, a good distance off by the sound.

Sarion pivoted, and the hunters looked to the trees, searching for signs of an impending attack.

"Predators from Grammore, coming out for the evening hunt."

"Do you think they came across our path?" Chertron asked.

"No way of knowing," answered Valadire. As he spoke, more howls erupted from the north. "But they might soon. It sounds as if a pack is making its way from where we came. And they're not wolves..."

"No. We heard similar cries in Grammore, and encountered several creatures. If they catch wind of our scent, we'll have no option but to fight a pitched battle. The air is dead now, but they may come across our trail." Sarion went back towards his horse. "Get ready to move off, Geld."

Several of the surrounding men had grim looks on their faces, but they were a competent group, purposefully chosen to accompany Sarion on the mission. They would not give in to fear.

Every few moments another howl echoed through the woods, although none of them seemed any closer. Sarion spoke to the rearguard, warning them of what they might expect. He then returned to the front of the company, telling Chertron to remain at the back where his sharp eyes and ears would prove helpful. The durable warrior agreed, and Sarion made the company close ranks, still keeping two abreast.

"We're going into the valley. With luck, we can avoid the creatures prowling to the north, but we also know that something has entered the hollow, most likely from Grammore. Perhaps it's already left. Everyone be alert to our surroundings. Many of these predators have great abilities of concealment. Keep your eyes and ears open. Let's be off."

Valadire approached, his voice low. "Sarion, wouldn't it be wise for you to stay in the middle?"

"My skills are needed where they may. We can't

afford to miss something."

"Geld is one of our finest trackers."

"That may well be, and someday he'll have my experience. But he missed *these* signs, although I don't blame him. It's near impossible to track while riding, you know." Sarion grinned, and slapped his companion on the shoulder. He now rode in the lead with Geld Rinn, while Valadire muttered beneath his breath at Sarion's decision to place himself at highest risk in the front. The company moved forward, the horses finding their way on solid ground which now sloped downwards. The trees were less dense on the incline, and the footing was sure. The forest behind them was silent, and Sarion hoped the pack of creatures was moving away from them. He kept them at a slow pace, making sure not to lose sight of the creature's tracks. From what he saw, he believed the unknown creature walked low to the ground, clearly on four legs. By the stride, he determined that it wasn't necessarily something which could move quickly, but he wouldn't underestimate its abilities.

The company rode on quietly for a few minutes, gradually descending. Soon they reached the floor of the valley, and the visibility was poor here. Some of the hunters took out their lanterns, an invaluable tool for traveling in the wild. They continued forward, and at one point Sarion dismounted, signaling for the others to follow, as it was growing more difficult to see the footprints. They appeared very fresh, and Sarion guessed that their quarry had entered the hollow within the past day. It was an unpleasant situation, but he would rather be tracking the unknown creature then have it tracking *them*.

The woods were thick, and heavy brush strangled the mossy trunks. Mist rose from the ground, further obscuring their view. Several squirrels darted away, disturbed by their intrusion. Sarion realized that soon it might prove impossible to track the creature, and they were barely moving along at all now. They were getting nowhere.

Piril and Bertilik rode immediately behind, silent and ever vigilant in protecting their charge. Geld Rinn kept his eyes ahead, leaving the tracking to Sarion now. The air was still, and a few night birds called in the distance, but there had been no cries from outside the valley since they'd entered. Sarion hoped they had avoided whatever hunted the forest.

Sarion walked along, stooping low to the ground, when he heard the trickle of water. Following the trail, it led directly to a small stream, maybe ten feet wide. Here the tracks ended. Sarion paused.

"They lead into the water?" Geld Rinn asked.

He nodded. "We'll pause for a moment. I want to cross *first* and see if I can find where the tracks come out again."

Sarion jumped on his horse, signaling for everyone to remain in place while he moved ahead, under the watchful eyes of Piril who shadowed him. He then dismounted, leading the horse as he went upstream, scanning the ground for signs. After a few short minutes they returned, now heading downstream. Finding nothing, the pair returned to the company, Sarion shaking his head.

"The trail ends here. The creature must have stayed in the water for a while, maybe looking for fish to eat. There's a flat outcropping of rock that continues on for a ways. It's possible the creature moved over it and left no trace. I saw no mark of its passing, and the rocks are broad. But in this light, I could have missed something."

Valadire spoke. "I like it not, losing the beast's trail. There's still a good chance that it will continue moving, seeking prey. And no sound of pursuit from behind. We might be in luck."

Sarion shrugged. "Perhaps. I think it best if we find a suitable spot to camp for the night. Let's follow the water downstream and see what we can find."

Valadire nodded, and the company was again on the move. They crept forwards, the lanterns casting enough illumination even in the mist and twilight. Sarion had certainly experienced much worse conditions while in the Grammore Lowlands, where night travel usually proved to be impossible. The watercourse meandered along, cutting a swath through the trees, and after several minutes it widened, the bottom growing deeper and softer. It soon ended and the company stopped in front of a marsh, haze lifting off the surface like the spirits of the dead.

Sarion immediately felt a strong dislike of the place, although he couldn't find any source of his unrest.

"Now what?" Valadire asked, and both men stared out at the sluggish water.

"I think this answers our dilemma. We rest here for the night. It's senseless to push on anymore, as the ground is uncertain, and we can't risk having any of the horses getting trapped in the muck. We'll have the water at our backs, and won't have to defend every direction from possible attack. Hopefully the morning will shed light on our situation, and if something trails us, the stream will have washed away signs of our own passing. I don't know of anything else we can do for now."

Valadire agreed, signaling the fighters to make camp, two men already serving as sentries.

The Nighton hunters kept to strict routine, preparing for the evening rest, with Valadire making arrangements for the watch shifts. The air was humid and insects buzzed around them, the horses flicking their tails to chase the bothersome things away. Sarion sat on an old stump, gazing out at the still water.

Chertron slumped down next to him, handing Sarion some fruit and dried meat. "The air has been turning warmer. We're getting deeper into the south."

Sarion nodded but said nothing.

"What's on your mind?"

"Hmm. Everything, I guess."

"Worried about where that creature might be? I'm concerned too, but the valley is wide, and the borderlands are vast." Chertron shrugged. "What more can we do?"

"Nothing, I would say." Sarion sighed. "This journey has been uneventful, and that's a *good* thing. But we need to find someone with knowledge of the village, or we have no choice but to make for Sharield and seek help. I was hoping to have come across some information by now, but we've come up empty."

"Sarion, you can't solve every problem Trencit faces. You've done more than your share in the past few weeks. By the Seven...Led us into Grammore, and returned. Helped Nighton find victory against attack, and been promoted to one of the highest ranks in the westland. And Edward is now safe behind the walls of the fortress. I think these things should bring some measure of accomplishment to your heart."

Sarion listened to Chertron's words, and was thankful for the fighter's companionship. He represented the finest qualities of a Trencit warrior. It was not the first time Sarion understood the shrewdness of Charadan's choice. How he missed the General...

"My thanks for your words of comfort, my friend. You have a genuine ability to reassure me when all I see is darkness. True, we've made strides, you're right -- but without knowing the entirety of what we face, there can be no rest for us."

Chertron disagreed. "We've been fighting a war

in the east for so long that none can remember how it even started anymore...But we don't dwell on it. We go out, serve our kingdom, try to protect the family we have left behind, and hope fortune is with us on the battlefield. Did you ever think that this war in the westland might be the same as what is going on in the east?"

"What do you mean?"

"We may never see the end of it, that's what...We're only two men, after all. This battle might far surpass our own lives. If you only ever look into the darkness, you'll never see the light. I take comfort in the world around me; my family safe in Trencit, my companions and fellow warriors vigilant in the field. The sunlight shining on a new day. There is much beauty in the world, my friend. If you can keep this in your heart, then it makes the burdens of our life much more bearable. In the end, there is only so much we can do. Try not to be so hard on yourself."

Sarion stared at him.

"How else do you think I can stay away from my wife and children for so long? 'Tis a terrible burden. Have faith." Chertron clapped him on the shoulder, and for the first time in a while, a genuine smile crossed Sarion's face.

Sarion slept for a time, his dreams peaceful for once, the nightmare wings keeping their distance. But he came awake with a start when he felt hands shaking him.

"Sarion, awaken. Something comes."

He immediately came to his senses, his eyes scanning his surroundings. Valadire had awakened him, the Nighton Captain's eyes wide and piercing. The hunters were on alert, several of them rustled from sleep.

"What is it?" Sarion whispered, a knife already in his hand.

Valadire pointed, but to Sarion's surprise, his focus was towards the lake, and not the dark forest which loomed on all sides. But the lake? Visions of the Grammore Lowlands chased through his mind, when the company of warriors had been attacked by a muck dweller, a huge beast which lived in the swamp at which they'd camped for the night. Was the same thing happening to them now, while still in the borderlands?

His instincts were in full play, and he listened as gentle splashing came from the water, invisible in the night and mist. The noise was soft, but there could be no mistake. Something was approaching...

Sarion signaled for the fighters to retreat from the water's edge, pointing to Valadire and Bertilik for them to remain with him. The lanterns were hung on low tree boughs, and they reached into the murk, but the shadows held greater reign in the denseness of the wild. Long moments passed and the sound drew near as something headed directly for them. Sarion knew whatever it was had seen their dim light but they had no choice. They couldn't go blindly wandering the forest at night. Although it could alert nearby predators as to their presence, the light also served as their protection.

He knew they had little time before the intruder revealed itself, so he notched an arrow to his bow, eyes fixed on whatever showed. Another minute passed and the sound was clear now, but it made Sarion pause as he now recognized it. This was no creature that approached, but a boat. The sound was one of gentle rowing. His eyes widened in surprise.

Seconds later a form took shape from the gloom, light gleaming dully against the fog. A small watercraft appeared with a hooded figure seated inside, steering right for them.

"Reveal yourself, stranger, if your purpose is true. If not, you'll have that paddle knocked from your hands by a Nighton arrow." Valadire challenged the newcomer, his own bow held ready.

"Fools..." The person spoke, the voice low and raspy. "Is this how you treat a harmless old man?"

"Even someone old can be a servant of evil," replied Sarion. "In these dark days, we trust none. What is your name?"

The man lifted his paddle from the water, letting the boat drift closer, and pulled back his hood. True to his word, he looked old, his hair white with a long beard. He appeared groomed, at least, Sarion thought.

"I'll give mine if you give yours."

"Fair enough," he answered. "My name is Sarion from Nighton, and with me is Valadire."

The man nodded. "You can call me Ereck. Rare to see travelers in these parts, and never a patrol from Nighton. You're heading south yet. Must have got lost a while ago...Unfriendly woods you're in now, fighter. Best turn around and find your way back home."

"That's not possible, at least until our mission is done. And we could tell you the same." Valadire had lowered his bow, but one hand rested on the hilt of his knife. "You're lucky to still be alive, and danger is near. A large creature has entered this valley, possibly from Grammore."

Now the old man laughed, a harsh cackle more than anything. Sarion remembered the treacherous Mugil and the trap which had been laid for them while searching for Jerol. He wasn't about to fall for the same thing, although this man did seem to be more open with his tongue than the Dark Mage's servant.

"That's a hoot for sure." He smiled. "You telling *me* that it's dangerous here?"

He laughed so hard he nearly fell out of the boat, and Sarion shook his head, trying to figure out if Ereck was either an enemy or just a half-crazed old man. Valadire scowled, clearly unamused. Some of the other hunters approached, including Chertron and Geld Rinn.

"We're trying to help, but it seems you haven't the wits to understand." Valadire pressed him further, growing angry, but Ereck only laughed harder.

The old man finally settled down after several moments. "Nothing wrong with a good laugh, especially living a life in the wilderness. Ah, well. When you live beneath the shadow of the Ridgeline for as long as I have, *then* you can warn others about it. Not until...Try it for a few score years. There are things living there that would freeze your blood, fighter. Chew you up and spit out the bones." His expression turned grave.

"We're aware of the danger," Sarion replied, realizing that Valadire was getting nowhere. "Our offer is genuine, and if you know anything about the Western Watch, then you know our word is true. If you need aid, we'll give it."

Ereck shook his head, pursing his lips. "Don't need it."

"Very well," answered Sarion. "Then perhaps you can aid *us* instead."

Ereck shrugged.

"We're looking for a village in the south. It's not on any of our maps. We left Nighton days ago and have been searching for clues as to its whereabouts."

The old man replied. "I know the area pretty well. If there's any village within a week's ride of here, I've been there before."

Sarion glanced at Valadire. Was this the opportunity they'd been looking for?

"The village is called Gar-kiln. Do you know of it?" Valadire asked the question first.

The Summoning

Sarion stared at Ereck for a reaction, and from what he saw in the old man's eyes, he knew beyond the shadow of a doubt that the horror of the prisoner's tale was all true...

"You don't want to go there, fighter. It's a place of death now. Go back to your fortress and forget whatever madness brought you this far."

"How do you know this?" Sarion asked.

"I know a lot of things. I have ears and eyes. How do you think I survive out here? By luck? Gar-kiln is home to the dead, and I know that you'll go to your graves if you enter that cursed village. You want to find death? You'll meet it there, sure enough." Ereck stared at him, his gaze unflinching.

"Regardless, that is our destination. The westland is under siege and our need is great. We've been warned already." Sarion was firm. "Do you know then of the Dark Mage?"

Ereck twisted his face, as if he'd eaten something sour. "I know enough to avoid him and his monsters." He spat. "And you should too. I see it in your eyes."

"Old man, we seek the village. Can you tell us where it is or not?" Valadire snapped at him, his patience gone.

Ereck wrinkled his nose. "Fine by me. Are you so eager to meet your doom, fighter? That's what you'll find there." He was clearly not intimidated by the Nighton hunters.

"That is our road, no matter what waits for us." Valadire responded, unwilling to be put off.

"Won't listen to reason then? Well, if you're so determined to find it, then I'll tell you where it is." Ereck sighed, shaking his head. "Seems to me you'll keep looking anyway." He muttered to himself for a few moments. "Listen. I have a map at my house. I can show you how to get there."

"My thanks for your help. Where is your house? Here in the valley?" Sarion looked around, wondering where -- and how -- this old man could live in the wild.

Ereck cackled. "Back yonder." He pointed to the lake.

"Are you part fish then?" Valadire said.

"As much a fish as you are wise..."

The Forester moved forward, an angry retort on his lips, but Sarion held up a hand. "Peace, Valadire. We need his help."

The old man nodded. "That you do, although you'll wish it were otherwise once you get to Gar-kiln, mark my words. I live on an island. Keeps me safe from these cursed beasts that hunt the woods lately. Things weren't always this bad. True enough, once in a while something crosses the Ridgeline looking for new hunting grounds and fresh prey, but nothing like this..."

Sarion nodded in understanding. Yes, an island might offer a safe haven from predators.

"I'll take you there. But my boat can only hold three at most. Otherwise we'll all end up in the mud. Some nasty things live in here."

Sarion looked over at Valadire and Chertron, both of them with questioning eyes.

"Very well. I'll go along and take Geld Rinn with me."

"Captain Sarion..." Piril started to object, but he waved him off with one hand.

He turned, whispering to the guard. "It's all right, Piril. It won't be long, and I think we can trust Ereck. We'll be careful. Stay here until we return, and watch the forest for signs of the creature."

Piril looked unconvinced, but Sarion's orders were final.

Ereck spoke. "You said there was something in the valley earlier?"

"Yes, I tracked it to the stream, and then lost the trail. There's a large outcropping of rocks on the far side, and it might have gone that way." Sarion shook his head. "In the dark it was difficult to be sure."

"Hmm." Ereck rubbed his beard. "That sounds like trouble. It's not safe here with something like that around, not that it's ever *entirely* safe in these parts. I don't like it at all. What did the tracks look like?"

Sarion described them.

"It's big for sure. Anything which can make its way alone through the wild is dangerous. Your men are not safe here."

"No less so than anywhere else. Marauders prowl the rim of the valley as well." Valadire said.

"I've been hearing them the last few nights. Didn't see one yet, though." Ereck paused for a moment, then reached into a bag at his waist. "This might help a bit."

Sarion looked at him suspiciously. "What do you have in there?"

The old man pulled out a small sack. "Ha. Something which can disguise the smell of the men and horses. Herbs, roots. Have a look, although you won't know what any of it is."

He handed it to Sarion, who sniffed at the contents, and then named several plants he immediately recognized.

Ereck's eyes widened in surprise, and he smiled. "A tracker...was one myself years ago. That explains much. Have the men throw it around the camp. Use it all. Might protect them until we get back. Might..." He shrugged. "Once you get too confident in the wild, you're already dead. Let's go."

Sarion looked at Chertron and Valadire, shaking his head slightly. He handed the pack to Chertron. "Take care of this and await our return. If anything happens, signal with the horn."

"Have a care," said Valadire. "If he tries anything, I'll tie him to a line and use him for bait."

Sarion grinned, then walked away, waving for Geld Rinn to accompany him.

The three of them entered the boat, which looked and felt unsteady. Sarion knew that Ereck had made it himself, but hopefully it would hold them all. He wondered again as to how long the man had lived here. There were settlements and small outposts throughout the borderlands, but for someone to live by themselves this close to the Ridgeline was rare indeed. Sarion had the feeling that there was a lot more to Ereck than his outwards appearance.

Geld Rinn offered to paddle, but Ereck just laughed at him. "These old bones do fine enough. Don't be fooled."

They glided off into the lake, Sarion looking behind as the men watched, while Chertron spread the contents of the pack around the perimeter of their camp. The night was getting long, but daylight was still hours away, the fog maintaining its damp grip. The shore soon disappeared, and Sarion felt as if they were floating in the air like phantoms, visibility diminished to a few feet in every direction. Bullfrogs bellowed out their call, and moths fluttered around their lantern. He heard fish splashing in the shallows, and to Sarion it all appeared natural, nothing out of place. Geld's narrow eyes were like slits of black as he gazed about, trying to see where they were going. Sarion admired the younger man, seeing much of himself in the tracker's lean form. He had quickly risen in the Western Watch, hailed as perhaps their finest tracker, his skill-at-arms widely recognized. He would be considered for a higher position in the future, maybe even achieving the prestigious rank of Forester one day. Chensel had chosen wisely, but as always with the Nighton leader, there were other motives hidden away. Sarion realized that this mission would prove to be a turning point for Geld Rinn -- either proving his maturity as someone suitable for higher standing, or a confirmation of the opposite -- that he would still need years of seasoning in the field.

Sarion didn't know which it was, and he figured Geld Rinn had probably never even considered this to begin with.

Minutes passed by as Ereck led them deeper into the water, then suddenly he broke the silence. "Up ahead, we're here."

As he spoke the last word, a shoreline appeared directly before them, a wooden dock coming into view. The old man steered them perfectly into the pier, hopping out with surprising agility. Geld Rinn followed quickly and then Sarion, while Ereck picked up a length of rope and secured the craft.

"Up the steps and we're there. I don't get much company, so don't complain about the mess."

Geld Rinn lifted an eyebrow, but Sarion could only shrug. They went in single file up a steep set of stairs, and trees surrounded them, long branches dipping wearily towards the water as if to quench their eternal thirst. The vegetation was thick, but a path formed of flat rock had been made into the ground, and they stayed on this for several dozen feet until a small building rose out of the gloom before them. The place was dark, the door closed.

"Did you make this yourself?" Geld Rinn asked.

"Ha." Ereck chuckled, but would say no more. "Let's go in, your men will grow impatient, thinking I've taken you hostage." He winked, and gave Sarion a sly look which looked more disarming then anything.

He pulled the door open, the hinges creaking

eerily. They all went inside into a small room which held a single table in the middle with a bright lantern sitting on top. Shelves were tucked against each wall, the fixtures packed with a variety of items, including jars, dried leaves, and an assortment of things which Ereck had most likely accumulated over years of living in the wilderness.

"Only got one seat...Be right back."

The old man moved into the next room, and Sarion watched his shadow, knowing there was another lantern inside somewhere. He locked eyes with Geld, nodding for the other man to stay alert while he examined the chamber, looking around for anything which might reveal more about their strange host. Sarion heard Ereck rummaging about, clearly searching for something.

"Ha. Got it."

Moments later Ereck reappeared with a large parchment. "I think you'll find this interesting, fighter." He handed it to Sarion.

"What is it?" Geld Rinn asked.

"A map of the westland."

Sarion placed it on the table, moving the lantern close. A look of surprise crossed his face at what he saw. The map showed the area around Nighton and western Trencit, and there was the Ridgeline, flowing down the entire length. It continued further south, including the names of places Sarion didn't even know about. A large X was marked on a crudely-drawn diagram of a lake, and next to it was written *home*. And as he scanned lower, another mark caught his eye.

Gar-kiln...

"There it is. And only a few days march judging from what I can make of this. Who made this?" Sarion turned to Ereck.

"Me, of course. And it's three days from where

we stand, to be exact."

"This is accurate?" Geld Rinn questioned him.

The old man shook his head, muttering. "No, I like to draw false maps when I'm bored. You should see my collection."

Geld Rinn grimaced.

Sarion continued browsing over the map, and then his eyes went to the western edge where *Grammore* was written on a huge expanse of space until there was no more room. "Seems you don't have any more knowledge of the Lowlands than we do..."

Ereck gave him a curious look. "Don't be so quick to make conclusions, fighter."

"What else do you know?" Sarion straightened, looking at him.

"More than you think. I know where the Black One lives."

Sarion and Geld Rinn stared at him in surprise.
"Murkvale."

"You know of this place?" Sarion couldn't believe it. Could Ereck confirm the prisoner's tale, give them information that could help lead them to their enemy?

"Yes, I do. And a great many things besides."

"How did you come by all this knowledge? Do you possess magic?" Sarion knew the old man held secrets, that much was clear. Although he didn't appear to be a threat of any sort, there was something different about him, something special...

"Don't be so hasty for what I know. Have some caution." He then paused for a moment, his face darkening. "I see it in your eyes, fighter." Ereck said.

"Do not think to seek out the black sorcerer. You'll be destroyed!"

"That is ultimately for King Gregor and the leaders of Trencit to decide. We are assailed from the west, and it's time to take the battle to *him* now..."

"Foolish words!" Ereck spat. "What makes you think you stand a chance against him? Have you seen the creatures under his power? Blacker than the night and more terrible that your worst nightmares."

Sarion nodded, speaking quietly. "Yes, I have seen them, and even fought them for the past few weeks. At Nighton we were assaulted by a Killworm before venturing south."

Now it was Ereck's turn to show surprise. "A Killworm? Shades..." His hands trembled in reaction.

"We faced it, and destroyed it." Sarion quickly added, shaking his fist in emphasis. "We're not without our *own* weapons."

The old man was silent for a few moments before replying. "You defeated a Killworm? How is that possible? Every legend says they were unable to be destroyed by fire, iron or axe. Unless..." He paused, looking at Sarion as if seeing him for the first time. "Yes, you must have magic -- and strong magic indeed." Ereck nodded to himself. "Hmm, it seems there is more to you than meets the eye as well." He smiled crookedly.

"Come," said Sarion. "Our need is great, and you may have much to offer. Will you let me have the map?"

Ereck sighed. "Take it, I have another. And I guess you'll want to know how I came by it."

Sarion said nothing.

"I made it myself, as I mentioned." He winked at them. "From my years of travel, although I don't get too far anymore. Up and down the westland. Now, I stay here most of the time. Bones are too old. I know a few trappers who pass through the area, and I barter with them and catch news of the borderlands. They have ears everywhere, them folks."

Sarion nodded, and Ereck slumped into the chair.

"There was a time when I even went into the edge of the Lowlands as well. I was younger then, like you -- and probably just as foolish."

"I've gone there twice, but the need was great. Once on a mission against the Glefins, and recently in pursuit of an ogre." Sarion's eyes grew clouded.

Ereck rubbed his beard. "Shades. Seems we both have many stories to tell. Tales indeed, but not the time." He chuckled.

Sarion leaned on the table. "My tales are sad, and ones which are best left alone."

Ereck answered. "I won't bother you with them, have no fear. But what I told you is true about my travels. And there is more to say. Your companion asked about my house before."

"Yes," said Geld Rinn.

"And the answer is no, I did not build it."

Sarion wondered what this had to do with anything. Time was slipping, and the men were waiting for their return.

"Someone else lived here before I came across it, quite by accident." There was a glimmer in Ereck's eye.

"And who was that?" Sarion asked.

Ereck stared at them both. "A servant of the Dark Mage."

❁ ❁

Forlern yawned, staring out the window of his quarters in the great hold which housed the Gran Barshara, the electorate of the free city of Lastrad. The young fighter reflected on the events of the past several days, or rather, the lack of events. The trip south had been quiet, traveling with the caravan which protected the powerful leader. Forlern had opted to ride on horseback with the two Homeguard chosen to accompany him, denying the offer to remain within the Gran Barshara's private wagon. Forlern would have been extremely uncomfortable inside the garish quarters, and believed the arrangement was more suitable for himself and the strange electorate alike. Little word had been said since they had left Daregil Keep, but all that would be changing this day. It was time to pursue their quarry, the unknown thing which stalked the streets of Lastrad, murdering the people.

Forlern heard movement behind him and he turned, already knowing that it was Erlang, one of his escorts.

"Kirlat will be back shortly. The Gran Barshara's household lacks for nothing."

"No indeed," Forlern replied. He looked at Erlang for a moment, measuring him. A seasoned fighter in Trencit's elite, he was cautious in everything he approached, not given into acts of brashness or risk. Exactly why he was picked by Galivon, of course. His face was criss-crossed with scars, and he'd seen much battle in the east against the Devlents. His countenance always serious, the fighter appeared to be a bulwark of granite, clearly showing that he was not someone to be intimidated by anything.

Forlern liked him.

"So, today we go on the hunt?"

Forlern nodded. "We'll meet up with Questron this afternoon and go from there. The city is large, with many places to hide. Since we have no idea what it is we're even looking for, we might as well start narrowing down locations. Unfortunately, I think we're going to be here a while." Forlern shrugged, feeling the weight of what had been placed on his shoulders. To search a city as large as Lastrad for a mysterious creature which had eluded capture from the sizable army housed inside seemed an impossible task. There had yet to be any confirmed sightings of what was responsible. It seemed ludicrous to think he would be the one to succeed where an army had failed...

"I know what you're thinking," said Erlang. "But we'll do our best. King Gregor and Captain Galivon chose you for this mission, and they chose wisely. You have returned from Grammore unscathed while General Charadan fell. We will suffice. Are we not the Homeguard?"

Forlern nodded. They were the finest fighters in Trencit, trained in all arts of warfare and subterfuge. If they failed, who else could accomplish the task?

"That we are, my friend." He stood. "Let's look over these maps again and double-check our plan."

They walked over to a large table in his quarters, one which was shaped in a rectangle carved from the finest oak, the top covered in parchments and maps, accompanied by bowls of fruit, meat, cheese, and goblets of wine. True to the Gran Barshara's word, all their needs had been taken care of.

Forlern had thought long and hard about what he would do once they reached Lastrad. He had asked for diagrams and maps showing the entire city, including the barracks and military quarters, the expansive housing area for the citizens, and even the Daj-Yartel, the palace which held the Gran Barshara, his family, and councilors. Forlern had studied the maps intensely the past two days, poring over everything, leaving nothing out. He had met yesterday with the Captain of the Lastrad Guard, Questron, and spoken about what the man knew of the murders.

Paul Melniczek

There had been little to tell...

Nothing was certain about the attacker's identity, or what it even looked like. Only the rumors of something disappearing into the night, black and elusive. None who had been assaulted had lived to tell about it. So all they could go on was reports seen by people in the city or guards, a few who had seen *something*. The odds of finding this thing were not good, and Forlern knew it.

And worse yet, six more people had been killed last night.

They sat at the table, Erlang scanning a detailed map of the city.

Forlern was lost in thought, and he rubbed one hand across his chin. He had been idle for long days, and he felt restless. He was not one for plans and schemes, but a man who thirsted for action. Tonight they would be going out in search of the elusive thing stalking the city. Tonight and every night until they found and killed it, or were killed themselves...

There would be no other resolution. Forlern knew this in his soul.

And so he could only do the best he could, rely on his training and instincts and the resources given to him. Although things looked desperate, he was still a determined man, and whenever he felt such, the results were the same.

In the end, he would prevail.

Nodding to himself, he picked up a map of the inner city, where barracks and storerooms backed up to the palace itself. The home of the Gran Barshara was lavish, but paled in comparison to Daregil Keep in size and scope. It was built to house royalty, and to intimidate those who found themselves on the opposite side of its immense wealth. Forlenr immediately disliked it and everything else about the Lastrad leadership, and felt they were not to be trusted, but what was he to do...

36

The Summoning

Focusing on the task at hand, Forlern knew this creature struck only at night, and although the attacks appeared random, at times specific people had been killed, leaders of the city itself. In conclusion, several things could be deduced from its actions...

Firstly, it possessed intelligence, even cunning. The attacks were premeditated, not just the random assaults of a predator killing for food. No, this thing had a purpose, which clearly was to undermine the leadership of Lastrad, place a veil of fear over its population.

And it was succeeding.

Another thing was the creature attacked at night. This certainly made sense, as it was obviously comfortable in the dark, moving about unhindered. Forlern had a plan to turn the advantage their way, and was ready to implement a strategy when he met with Questron. In fact, he had already made up his mind on what their actions would be, and was confident that it was a good start.

His mind was turning about, analyzing his plans, when a knock at the door interrupted his line of thought. Before he could even reply, a deep voice boomed in from outside.

"Forlern, it's Captain Questron. May I come in?"

"Yes," he answered, signaling Erlang to stand and leave his place for the officer. The door opened wide and a tall man entered, wearing light chain armor and dressed as if ready to do battle. Although they had only met yesterday, Forlern already felt he had the measure of this man. Questron was fairly young for such a high position, but his reputation was widely known. Captain of the elite Lastrad Guard, he commanded a large force of the finest fighters in the southland, some of them former Trencit warriors, others brought in from beyond the kingdom's borders. The Lastrad army was under his direct command as well, and Forlern was certain he was paid extravagantly for his services, the most powerful man in Lastrad besides the Gran Barshara himself. Despite the trappings of his office, he was a man of action and discipline, and suffered no lax in the men under his sway. His long nose and narrow eyes gave him the look of a wolf after prey, and his gaze was made of steel. He was both feared and respected, and awarded all behavior suitable as to what he saw fit, whether by promotion or severe discipline. Lastrad was a large city which thrived on trade, and it attracted both the best and the worst. Only someone with an iron hand could keep the law in place, and the combination of the Gran Barshara and the Captain of the Lastrad Guard was a successful partnership.

"Greetings, Captain Questron. I was expecting you later, but this will do fine."

Forlern signaled Erlang to leave them. "Go see if you can find Kirlat and see if he needs anything else. I'll talk to you later."

Erlang nodded, bowing in deference to Questron, who acknowledged him. Forlern compared his attitude to the Ja-Ravel assassin, who he had not seen since their encounter in the Grip. It was not the first time he wondered about the man's whereabouts. To Forlern, the assassin was almost as worrisome as the unknown thing which stalked the city...He had been arrogant, supremely overconfident, dismissing Forlern immediately. Furious at the incident, Forlern had kept his temper in check that day, refusing to be baited by the deadly fighter. And Forlern had been warned more than once about confronting the man. Sure of his own skills, Forlern was quite uncertain of sparring with a Ja-Ravel assassin.

Questron sat down and helped himself to a goblet of ale. "I wanted to stick with our later time, but things have changed." He peered at Forlern over the rim of the mug.

"That's fine. I'm eager to start with our preparations anyway." He returned the man's stare, wondering how much he could trust him with. "Everything all right?" Forlern prodded gently, feeling him out.

"Not since the killings started, I'm afraid. Klellan returned today, and he'll be helping directly with our hunt."

"Hmm, do I know him? I can't recall hearing the name." Forlern asked.

Questron shrugged. "I thought you met him at Daregil Keep. He's the personal bodyguard of the Gran Barshara."

Forlern nodded, inwardly wincing. "Ah yes, now I remember." He wondered how far he could press. "I haven't seen him in a while, actually. Met up with him in the Grip, but never saw him inside the Keep."

At this, Questron paused, and Forlern saw something in his eyes, but as to what it meant, he had no idea.

"Strange, he rarely leaves the side of the Gran Barshara these days."

"I don't wonder, as he fears for his own life." Forlern decided to pursue the matter as far as possible, despite the danger. Had he caught a glimmer of uncertainty from the Lastrad Captain?

"True enough. I don't need to play coy with you. You're here for a reason, and we need all the help we can get." Questron looked down at the maps scattered in front of him.

Forlern knew that such a statement from the leader had profound repercussions, an admittance to being ineffective against the predator which stalked the city. Was this man in fear of his position?

"I'll do whatever I can to aid you. King Gregor

wants peace in Lastrad. But we fear there is much more to it than the killings."

"The trouble in Grammore?" Questron asked. "Trencit is besieged on both sides, it would seem. And the loss of Charadan will have a ripple effect. There's talk that the leadership in Daregil Keep has been reduced."

Forlern wanted to frown, but controlled himself, maintaining his composure before answering. "We lost our finest leader, there is no question. But there are others who have taken the reins of what he left behind. The Homeguard is as strong as ever, I can *assure* you."

Questron met his gaze, and neither man flinched. After several tense moments, the Lastrad Captain grinned. "That's exactly what I wanted to hear. If you would have said anything less, then I would have seriously doubted your determination."

Forlern nodded, feeling relieved. "You have my word to hunt this creature until it's found. I don't make such talk lightly." He held out his hand, and Questron returned the grip, Forlern feeling the man's resolve in the power of his gesture.

"Tonight we start the hunt." Forlern leaned forward, and he felt excitement coursing through his veins. What they would find -- if anything -- was uncertain, but he felt confident that he would have Questron's full support in his actions, whatever they might be.

And this fact was a tremendous factor in boosting his own confidence, something which had been unusually lacking in recent days.

The Summoning

The sun had already set over the city of Lastrad, but Forlern had not been outside to see the last orange rays. He stood in one of the three massive granaries owned by the government of Lastrad. It was filled with stores of wheat, grain, and corn, some purchased by the city, and some of it given as levy by the farmers living within the surrounding region as payment for their protection.

Forlern looked around at the mounds of grain and huge containers filled with corn. There were tons of it here, enough to sustain the entire city in case of a siege. The threat of war had been a very real possibility for a long time in Lastrad, being so close to the eastern front. Buttressed in the back by deep forests, a cluster of high foothills, and behind them a small mountain range, it offered some security, but it still lay only a few short day's ride from the unpredictable eastland. The only thing standing between Lastrad and the marauding Devlents was the mighty fortress of South Watch, the most southerly stronghold controlled by Trencit. The citadel was constantly being assaulted by the enemy forces, and Forlern had served there for a span, but it had been a period of relative quiet, both sides relying on subterfuge and raiding rather than open warfare. The area directly to the south of Lastrad was rich in farming, but lacked any major towns and no fortresses. If South Watch ever failed, so would the rest of the south, and Lastrad would be isolated from central Trencit. And so it had remained a protectorate of Trencit, but for all intents and purpose it was a free city, not paying homage to Daregil Keep, but maintaining close ties nevertheless.

Forlern pulled out a small map from his pocket, nodding to himself. Erlang and Kirlat were both several feet away, watching the proceedings, but more so being vigilant for their charge; the newest Captain in the Homeguard.

41

Questron appeared from behind a huge container of wheat. "They're making a last sweep on the north side, and then checking the roof for openings as well as securing all windows."

Forlern stared at the roof, which was dozens of yards overhead. "So there is no sign that anything has been here?"

The Lastrad Captain shook his head.

Forlern looked at the map again. His plan was now moving into action. With the help of Questron's men, they were making large sweeps in certain parts of the city, areas where there were places to hide, and few people on watch. He figured that the unknown creature must have a lair somewhere, and since it killed every night now, it had to be in the city. Lastrad was protected on all sides by a huge wall that was manned heavily by guards, day and night, and since the killings had begun, watches had been doubled. Forlern had also told Questron to have all the fires increased in the case the creature possessed the ability of flight. The Lastrad Captain had given Forlern a strange look, but after the fighter told him of the pursuit from Grammore, he understood. It was clearly an alternative that Questron had never even thought about, and he appreciated the suggestion. He also had not thought to check the large storehouses, and Forlern had the feeling that the man was giving him as much headway as possible, respecting his plan.

Forlern still wondered if the powerful officer was concerned for his own position. If the Gran Barshara had eluded to his own vulnerability back at Daregil Keep, refusing King Gregor's offer of asylum, then none in Lastrad could boast that their office was immune to change. The longer Forlern stayed in Lastrad, the more he understood the hierarchy of its leadership. Elected and appointed leaders had much more to lose than someone actually *born* into power.

Waving Erlang over, Forlern discussed a part of their plan he was uncertain about, and they talked for several minutes while Questron commanded his men. In the end, they were at the granary for another half hour, until Questron was convinced it was secure.

Now it time for the next one...

They repeated the process, although a new patrol was in place, waiting for their orders. The second warehouse was similar to the other one, but not as high. The men swept through this one now, checking for signs that anything had stayed there. Again, nothing turned up, and Questron ordered the men to fasten all windows, check for openings in the side, and make certain nothing could enter from outside.

When they headed for the third building, nightfall was upon them, the sky clear and the air warm. The weather had been pleasant since Forlern's arrival in Lastrad, and the good visibility helped their search. One thing that continued to bother Forlern, though, was the Ja-Ravel assassin, or his absence, rather.

As he entered the guardroom of the last warehouse, Forlern was taken aback when a familiar face loomed from within, coming straight towards him.

It was Klellan...

"We meet again, fighter."

Forlern caught himself, not wanting to show his surprise. "Ah, yes. We met in the Grip."

"Seems you're more valuable to King Gregor than I expected."

There was a lot of meaning behind those words, Forlern thought to himself. More valuable? It was no vote of confidence concerning his ability. He had to be very careful with this one, at least until he found out more about him.

"I was sent to help rid Lastrad of the evil killing

its people. I hope we can work together in finding whatever is responsible." It was as true a statement as he could muster. The last thing Forlern wanted to do was to antagonize the assassin.

"If you're successful, then you will have improved upon what a standing army could *not* do." Klellan leaned lazily against the wall.

Questron came towards them, and clearly the remarks were a barb aimed at the Lastrad Captain.

Klellan continued. "The third warehouse is clear. I checked it myself."

His statement had all the sounds of something not to be challenged.

Questron nodded, accepting the answer. "Very well. With the granaries secure, we move on. Night is upon us."

"And more killings will come with the darkness..." The assassin sneered, shaking his head. "You think this plan has any chance of success?"

Questron answered, his voice neutral, but Forlern immediately knew there was animosity between the two men. It was astonishing to look at, considering the power and influence Questron commanded.

"We will succeed in the end, Klellan. With or without *your* help..."

He left it at that, and gestured for Forlern to follow him.

The assassin spoke as they left. "I'll join up with you later. The Gran Barshara wants to be kept informed on your progress."

Questron never turned to acknowledge the man, and the company moved off into the night.

The Summoning

That evening found Forlern and the others making a sweep of the immediate palace grounds. The area was ablaze with light, tiny moths fluttering all about, some of them flying voicelessly into the killing flames.

Guards were all over, and every single door and window to the palace was heavily protected. Forlern checked his map and consulted with Questron on the structure.

"Are there any hidden tunnels beneath the palace?"

Questron gave him an odd look. "An old dungeon, a few storerooms. Only a few have access. And there are none that lead out of the building. This is it."

Forlern considered. "What about the vents?"

"Hmm, never thought about that," Questron admitted. "If the thing is lean in size, it could move within."

Forlern nodded. "It's something we need to consider."

"A moment." Questron went over to one of his men, briefing him quickly. Satisfied, he returned. "I'm impressed, Forlern. You've suggested things I never even thought about. I guess that my routine of dealing with cutthroats, thieves, and the Lastrad Council has found me unprepared for this situation."

Forlern grinned. "Perhaps if you had entered Grammore and fought with some of its native beasts, you might think the way I do. After we finish this business, why don't we take a trip together and I'll show you around the Lowlands?"

The Lastrad Captain actually laughed. "I'll keep

it in mind."

They both appreciated the moment, releasing some of the tension. Then Forlern turned serious, and looked around carefully. His men and Questron's always placed a respectful distance between themselves, drawing close only when summoned. His voice was low.

"Klellan. It seems you two don't see eye to eye..."

Questron frowned. "He's a thorn in my side, but he has the Gran Barshara's favor. He can say what he wants without fear of repercussion."

"And do what he wishes too, I see." Forlern finished.

The Lastrad Captain shrugged. "No one likes him, but he's the best fighter I've ever seen. He killed three of my men last year in one of the taverns."

Forlern was surprised. "Why wasn't he thrown in prison? Are there no laws in Lastrad anymore?"

Questron snorted. "Claimed it was self-defense. The Gran Barshara was so impressed when he heard that he made him his personal bodyguard, winning him over completely. He challenged my top men in hand-to-hand combat in exhibition, and bested them all. No one has ever spoken against him since."

Forlern was silent. Klellan had clearly set himself up, and he was certain Questron already knew this. But was there more to it?

"You don't believe his story, do you?"

The Lastrad Captain stared at him, and Forlern knew he was being measured again. After a few moments, Questron shook his head. "No, I do not. He schemed to secure his place. It's common knowledge that the Gran Barshara is always looking to place top fighters in his guard, no matter their background. It's no secret."

"What about assassins?"

The Summoning

This time Forlern caught the man off-guard. "What do you mean?" Questron's eyes narrowed.

"You *don't* know then..." Forlern lowered his voice even more.

Questron remained silent.

"This needs to be kept between us both. No one else. Do I have your word?" Forlern asked.

"Yes." Questron never hesitated.

"Klellan is a Ja-Ravel assassin."

The Lastrad Captain pursed his lips. "Theirs is a dead cult, gone for long years. None remain of their evil legacy."

"Not true." Forlern looked around at the men, who were vigilant. They couldn't hear the conversation. "We have some knowledge in the Homeguard of a sect in the deep south, resurrecting the old ways. He wears a ring, and I know of this talisman. There can be no mistaking this. Only a member of the Ja-Ravel would bear such. Klellan is a Ja-Ravel assassin without a doubt. I thought you might have been aware of this, but obviously not."

Questron put a hand to his face, rubbing the light growth of beard there.

"I wonder if the Gran Barshara realized this." Forlern wondered aloud.

"It wouldn't matter. He doesn't care who he hires, as long as they're the best. He pays them handsomely for their skills. But this concerns me greatly. I don't trust him to begin with, and if what you say is true, then it must be taken into consideration."

Forlern questioned. "Such as?"

Questron's face turned grim. "He might know something about these killings. Maybe even have a hand in it..."

His response sent chills up Forlern's spine, knowing that if Questron's assumption was true, the game they played had just turned even deadlier.

The next several nights proved uneventful for
Forlern and his group of hunters. They searched out all
the large buildings where something could remain
concealed; armories, warehouses, and the largest homes
of the leading citizens, but they came up empty.
Companies of armed men were sent out into the city,
commanded to go into every house and search every
floor from top to bottom, looking for signs of the
unknown predator. Forlern also suggested that the night
patrols be increased to no less than twenty men. With a
group of this size, they could either fight off the creature
or at least see what it was they were dealing with.

And their action had some effect.

Lastrad fighters had not been attacked in the past
few days, but individual people were still being killed.
The citizens of Lastrad went through with their business
during the daylight hours, but once dusk arrived, people
scurried off to the supposed protection of their homes.
Families were now staying together overnight, hoping
for safety in numbers. The Lastrad Council put out a call
for a generous reward to anyone with information
concerning the assaults. Klellan appeared when he
wished, helping sparingly, usually showing up only to
criticize their efforts. Forlern tried his best to ignore the
assassin, but it was becoming increasingly difficult. In
the past, his fiery temper would have flared to the point
of taking action, but not now. He was learning self-
restraint, something he had been taught in the
Homeguard but had only revealed itself in the past few
weeks. Worse yet, he started to wonder if the Ja-Ravel

assassin was deliberately trying to provoke him into a confrontation, one which he wanted no part of...

So time passed, and Forlern spent nearly all his waking hours either in conference with Questron, both men either drawing up plans to bring their adversary into the light, or venturing out in the city on the hunt.

It went on like this for days, and then one night, over a week after their arrival of their own assault against the invisible predator, they finally received a stroke of good fortune...

Forlern's company stood in the midst of the impressive Vanyair Market, finishing a sweep of the area, the night sky clear and expansive, when they heard footsteps approach from around the corner. The guards were prepared for anything, and weapons were raised. Suddenly a man came into view, breathing heavily, and he nearly ran into one of Questron's personal bodyguards.

"Halt. Give us your name and rank."

"I seek either Captain Questron or Forlern. My name is Mikhul from the Third Ground Company. We've spotted something on one of the roofs down the next street."

Forlern and Questron stared at each other for one brief moment...

"No time to waste. Take us there now!" Forlern exclaimed, hoping this was the opportunity they were looking for. The company hurried off, Questron signaling for them to be quiet as possible. The man led them down a wide street, then turned left into a narrow alleyway, finally stopping at the end, where a group of men waited. They had been watching the alley, and gestured in recognition. One of the men, their lieutenant, motioned for Questron and Forlern to approach. He put a hand to his lips, and pointed to the corner. The others on watch gave way, nodding.

Forlern and the Lastrad Captain peered around the corner, both men silent as the night. Street lamps illuminated a square-shaped area, a popular section where linens and precious carpets were traded. Forlern hardly dared to breathe as he gazed into the gloom, but he immediately saw something which should not be there...

Dozens of yards away, on the side of one of the holding buildings, something black was clinging to the wall, and Forlern thought he could make out a head, body, and tail.

A creature was perched against the stone, like a spider on a web. He caught his breath.

They had found it...

At last, through a stroke of random luck, here it was.

But *what* was it?

The thing lifted its head from the wall, moving it to either side as if sniffing the air. Forlern noticed the air was coming towards them. The creature was searching for a scent -- their scent. If the wind had been behind them, it would surely have been alerted as to their presence.

He watched it, unwilling to take his eyes off the beast for fear that it would slip away. Just by seeing how it was able to attach itself to the side of the wall answered many questions. It was a thing of incredible agility, with the capability of moving wherever it wanted to, climbing buildings with ease, coming at its victims from any possible angle, silent and deadly.

But what should they do now? If they approached with a large group, most likely it would flee before they could get near. Now, it faced the interior of the square, as if waiting for something. Yes, Forlern realized. It waited for prey, for an unsuspecting person to walk close, or a small group on patrol.

The Summoning

That quickly his mind raced, trying to think of some way to gain the advantage, set a snare for the creature. He backed away, making no sound, signaling for Questron to follow. Forlern led him deeper into the alley, far enough that no sound would carry. He already knew the thing probably had exceptional hearing, so he couldn't take any chances. When he was satisfied, only then did he speak, barely a whisper.

"Now is our chance. We must act swiftly."

"Agreed." Questron nodded. "Do you know what this is? I've never seen the like."

"Nor I. But I'm certain this is what we seek."

"You have a plan?"

Forlern nodded...

Minutes later Forlern, Erlang, and Kirlat entered the square where the creature waited, but from the opposite side. The plan was simple -- they were the bait.

When the creature made its move, Questron and his men were to come at it from where they watched. Several men had scattered, climbing on the surrounding roofs, setting a snare for the beast if it tried to escape. Forlern knew their plan depended heavily on good fortune to have any success. He didn't want to fight it directly, but there was little choice.

The three of them walked ahead, Erlang carrying a lantern which threw back the shadows. Even without their own light, the square was fairly illuminated from the large posts which were lit every night throughout the city. And with the clear sky overhead, the conditions were ideal for their mission.

Forlern had one hand on the dagger given to him

from Barimon, but he wasn't convinced the creature possessed any magic, so he debated whether to use the weapon or not if it came down to it.

His hand slipped away from the pommel, instead falling on the hilt of his short sword.

The men deliberately acted casual, looking around as if on a normal patrol, not anticipating an attack from the deadly predator. Forlern's skin prickled with excitement as well as trepidation. It was impossible to know what this thing was capable of. For all he knew, they could be walking right into a death trap. His fighting instincts kept down the feeling of dread which threatened to rise up, knowing that the slightest mistake would be fatal.

Moments later they reached the center of the square. There was no way that the lurking creature could not have seen them already. His two escorts walked beside him, and he heard their breathing grow heavy. What must they be thinking, he wondered? But they were experienced Homeguard, weapons masters in their own right. They were ready for whatever happened.

Forlern led them down the middle, not wanting to let the creature think they knew of its presence. He paused for a moment, and pointed in the opposite direction of where it waited. Not wanting to give the predator too much opportunity, he continued walking, easing gradually towards where it lurked.

Closer they got, and he knew it *must* strike soon.

Two dozen yards away, and still no movement. Forlern glanced at where it perched, but saw only shadows. It was well-concealed, with a better visual position than anything approaching from the square.

Only a dozen yards away now, and nothing. Erlang placed one hand on his own sword, and Kirlat did the same. Both men were breathing heavier, anticipating the attack.

The Summoning

Forlern gritted his teeth. Come on, he thought. What are you waiting for?

And then, like that, the creature exploded from hiding in a flurry of claws and teeth. Forlern had never expected anything to move so quickly, and he ducked, barely in time to avoid being decapitated.

Erlang wasn't so lucky...

The creature's momentum drove it right into the hapless warrior, one talon slitting his throat before the man could bring his weapon to bay. In the same fraction of a second Kirlat stabbed at the beast, but found only empty air. The creature lashed out with its left foreleg and dealt a killing blow, leaving the fighter standing with mouth wide open, staring into the dark then collapsing forwards, a gaping hole in his own throat.

Shouts rang out all around as Questron and his men erupted into the fray. The Lastrad leader was first and ran directly to Forlern, trying to distract the beast. Swarming behind him were the other men from the patrol and some from his chosen guard, several of them with bows ready.

The creature was taken by surprise now, realizing too late that it had become the hunted. Stealth and darkness were its allies, not a large force of prepared fighters.

Forlern saw the creature's hesitation and cut it open in the side with a flash of steel. The beast hissed in pain and leaped to the right, bounding on four legs. Now that he had a chance to view it in better light, Forlern saw that it was reptilian, with a scaled hide and four wicked talons at the end of each long limb. They were shaped oddly, padded underneath, and Forlern knew that it possessed some kind of special ability making it agile enough to climb even a sheer wall. There was no time to think though, and he scrambled after it, the monster clearly looking to escape. On the far building a pair of figures appeared, some of Questron's men wielding bows, and they rained a hail of arrows onto the beast, several striking it. The men rushed to both sides and the creature drew up, knowing that it was surrounded. Despite its quickness, the unexpected assault had worked, the men on the roof slowing it just enough for the snare to be complete.

They now had it encircled...

Forlern never took his eyes off it. The thing hissed and spat, while more of the fighters hit it with dart and dagger.

"Don't get too close!" Forlern yelled a warning, as several men engaged it only a few feet away, thinking it finished.

The creature huddled to the ground, avoiding most of the missiles thrown at it. It crouched down, its head nearly touching the earth. Forlern didn't trust it, and encouraged the men to keep pounding it.

Without warning the beast flung itself forward in a last desperate attempt, knocking several of the men over on the far side. Two of them were severely slashed by the lightning fast claws, and it made good its escape, scuttling down an alley on the far side.

"After it!" Questron screamed, and men took up the chase. But none had been set to guard that area. There hadn't been enough time to cover the entire square.

The creature was gone...

"Are you all right?" Questron came over to Forlern, who had gone down on one knee.

"Yes." He sighed. "It didn't get me. But Erlang and Kirlat are dead."

It was true. Forlern had known from the instant the creature struck that neither men had a chance. It had been too swift in its attack. Too quick and too deadly.

"Forlern, there was nothing you could have done.

I'm sorry about your men." He paused. "And you'll find out that being in a position of leadership like yourself, many more deaths will follow."

Forlern looked at him, his eyes smoldering. "They're both dead, and we've failed. The creature is gone."

Questron looked around the square, several men milling about, helping the wounded, others on guard. Most of them had fled in pursuit of the creature. The Lastrad Captain looked down at the ground.

"Not so. We injured the thing badly. It *has* left us a trail."

He pointed.

Trickles of blood led straight into the alley and beyond where the creature had fled.

Forlern stood up, pulling out his knife...

"What?" Sarion exclaimed, in disbelief. "A servant of our enemy?"

Ereck nodded, his weathered face deadly serious.

"How did you come by this knowledge?"

The old man yawned, stretching scarecrow thin arms behind his head. "Quite a night you've made for me here, fighter. A stroke of luck too, that you found me. Or rather, that *I* found your company."

Sarion was silent, impatient to hear what Ereck had to say. From the corner of his eye he saw Geld Rinn staring at him, and he knew the young tracker was brimming with excitement.

"Another stroke of fortune that I came across this little house, built on an island in the middle of the great westland forest. I wandered about in those days." His voice grew wistful. "I was young, and adventurous. Like you, fighter." He pointed at Sarion. "Traveling through this valley, I was amazed, when one clear morning I looked out at the water, and saw something reflecting off a ray of sunshine in the distance. Curious, I made a small raft and paddled out, eager to see what was out here."

He paused.

"The sun had thrown a glimmer of light off glass. And I found this." Ereck spread his arms. "I know, it doesn't look like much, does it?" He cackled. "But then, appearances deceive, don't they?"

"So what did you find?" Geld Rinn asked.

"Ah, much. Some I could understand, the rest, no. Seems he traveled the borderlands, much like myself. Listening, watching, learning." Ereck scratched his beard.

"And who was this person you talk about? How do you know he served the Dark Mage?" Sarion questioned, feeling the need for urgency, yet fascinated about what this find could mean to their mission.

"He left behind a journal, that's how I know. Part of one, at least. Pages were missing, but I learned enough. Early on he wrote of his findings. He was an alchemist of some type. Never had any true power, no magic. But he searched for it. It was his passion..." His voice trailed off.

"And he found it, didn't he?" Sarion finished for him.

Ereck gave him a sharp look. "That he did."

"The Dark Mage. He must have encountered him in his travels." Geld Rinn said.

The old man nodded. "One found the other, most likely. And this is where I guessed about the rest of the story. His last entry spoke about meeting someone of great power, one who could teach him what he was seeking. His stronghold was in the Grammore Lowlands itself. A terrible place called Murkvale. He left behind enough information so that I could figure this out."

"How long ago do you think he left here?" Sarion asked.

"A very long time, I think. Yes." Ereck paused for a moment. "I believe this sorcerer has been around for a great while, making plans. And seeking those who would serve him."

"Enslaving some by their thirst for power and knowledge." Sarion said.

"You hit the mark, fighter. That's exactly what I think happened. And if someone gets in his way, you know the rest. He's an evil one all right. He wants the westland for himself, and Trencit next, most likely. Seems like his plan is no great secret."

"We captured one of his servants after the assault on Nighton. This is how we came by our knowledge, and the search for Gar-kiln. What you're saying confirms our suspicions, and what we learned from the prisoner. He was corrupted by the Dark Mage, forced to serve him, and was given the magic to control several of his creatures. The village was taken over by a tribe of ogres, the people either tortured or made to serve him."

Ereck rubbed a hand wearily across his forehead. "That's a terrible story, fighter. I met the people who lived there. They were good to me, always friendly, exchanging stories and willing to barter. Strong people, living in the wilderness. To come to such an end..."

"A curse fell upon them in the guise of the Dark Mage and his enemies. In his last breath the prisoner asked us to go to the village and end the terror. And Lord Chensel, who now leads the fortress of Nighton, has commanded me to pursue this mission. So you see, I have no other options." Sarion stared hard at him.

Ereck inclined his head, then pulled out a

parchment from beneath his cloak. "Take this then. It shows some minor detail of Grammore and hints at other things. I know not how he came to it, or why it was left behind. Maybe he intended to return here one day, maybe not. In the end, he found what he was looking for regardless."

Sarion took the parchment, putting it in one of his pockets until he had a chance to look over it. "The time has come and we must depart. You have given us much, and we're in your debt."

Ereck stood, muttering. "Thanking me for sending you to your graves? A poor choice of words, fighter."

He took the lantern and gestured for them to follow as he left the building. It was still dark outside, and the mist clung to their garments like the hands of the dead. Night birds cried in the distance, and something splashed in the unseen waters. They retraced their entrance and went back down the path and moments later to the dock.

"All right, your men will be restless. You should leave the valley at dawn."

The three of them entered the boat, and within seconds were paddling off again, vanishing into the gloom which was eager to claim their forms. The lake permitted their passage, the small craft gliding forward with little sound. The water was still, with an occasional splash from a fish or bullfrog, in pursuit of prey in whatever form it took.

Sarion didn't want to break the silence, but questions demanded answers, and when they left, they would leave behind any chance to press Ereck for more information. The old man had already revealed insight on many things, and the shadow of the Dark Mage loomed menacingly behind every query.

"Do you know of a creature called the Ravenor?"

Sarion asked.

"Ravenor? Never heard of such a thing. Why do you ask?" Ereck continued paddling, his lean arms easily meeting the challenge of exertion.

"The prisoner told us that it was brought to Gar-kiln by the ogres in an attempt to force their servitude. Some were fed to it," Sarion said, gazing out at the lake, wondering what they would find once they reached the elusive village.

The old man spat. "Curse that one. Those poor people never had a chance. I understand your determination, fighter. But be warned -- the black sorcerer has many servants at his disposal. They've been scouring the borderlands for years now, and Trencit too, I imagine. His mark is everywhere. I don't think there's a way to defeat him." He turned about, staring directly at Sarion. "And don't think you're the one who can do it, magic or not..."

He muttered to himself, paddling even faster.

Sarion didn't feel like pursuing the matter, so he focused on the coming days, and what their plan would be. The village was not far off, and they had been traveling in the right direction at least. If accurate, the map might very well prove to be invaluable. Meeting Ereck had been a stroke of good fortune, something they had experienced very little of in the past few weeks. But it would take a combination of luck and skill to protect them against the Dark Mage and his powerful servants.

Peering ahead towards the shoreline, Sarion saw several pinpricks of light, which could only mean they were drawing close to the company of Nighton hunters. A sense of relief washed over him as they glided along, knowing that the men were safe. The valley was silent around them, and a soft whistle echoed across the waters as someone signaled their arrival. Within seconds, figures loomed ahead in the mist, men standing watch as they closed in on them.

"Hail Sarion."

He recognized Valadire's voice, and one of the figures waved.

"See? Looks like my protection worked." Ereck said, pushing his paddle into the soft mud, steering them for the company of fighters.

"How large are the fish in this lake?" Geld Rinn asked, the question sounding odd to Sarion, and he turned to see what the young tracker was talking about.

"Some big ones, for sure." Ereck answered, and they were scant feet from the shoreline now.

To their left, waves lapped against the small rocks that bordered the water as something disturbed the surface.

"Very large, it would seem." Sarion stood, trying to see what the source was.

Now Ereck looked in that direction, his face showing surprise. "Hmm, I don't know what kind of fish can do that. Not in these waters."

The fighters came towards them, but Sarion suddenly waved them off, pointing towards the lake. The men appeared uncertain, and he shouted a warning. "Get back! Something comes!" He bounded from the craft, pulling Ereck and shoving Geld Rinn forward at the same time, both men surprised by his actions. Sarion's instincts had warned him in time but it was too late, as the water erupted in fury as something huge thrashed to the surface, and he knew immediately where the unknown predator had been hiding...

Shouts rang out in the night and steel clashed in preparation for the confrontation. The beast charged directly into the waiting men, taking down two fighters as it rammed its bulk into their midst. Sarion was several yards away with men between him and the creature, including Chertron and Valadire, both of them turned about with swords drawn.

Sarion caught a quick glimpse of the thing, which moved on four legs, its body squat and long, giving it a deadly combination of power and leverage. The head was narrow and pointed with a long beak for a mouth, and with this it attacked the men. Chertron struck it on the back, and sparks showered from the blade as it bounced off the hardened scales which covered most of its body. The durable fighter shouted in pain, grabbing his arm which was jarred by the blow. He backed away as the creature whipped its long tail, narrowly missing his legs from a crippling assault.

Shouting orders, Sarion knew that his words were meaningless. In the close confines of the forest, the hunters had to rely on their skill and training to survive, it was that simple. There was no room for arrows, and the predator had them at a disadvantage with its ferocity and ground-hugging form.

"Aim for its eyes!" Sarion screamed a warning, trying to get close, but Valadire and Bertilik were in front, shielding him in case it turned their way. Piril helped Chertron move from the fray, the lean fighter looking stunned, carrying his arm in pain.

The creature continued driving its way forward like a battering ram. It carried a lot of weight and used its bulk to knock aside anything in its path. Another fighter named Sordag was in its way and the man moved to his right, trying to avoid the raging beast, but it proved to be disastrous, as the creature turned in that direction and trampled the man to death. Lassel slashed at it with a pair of knives, striking its right leg, and the creature snorted in pain, but it never stopped. Instead of pressing the attack, it crashed ahead in the foliage, vanishing into the trees and mist. Within moments it was gone, the sound of its passing dying into the waning night.

"Let it go." Sarion yelled to the men, as a pair of hunters started after it. "Guard against its return, but I think it's gone for good." Sarion sighed, looking at the men who had fallen. Two of the fighters had been crushed beneath its bulk on the shoreline and never had a chance to flee. A third hunter had made the fateful choice to turn directly in its path, and the creature had killed him instantly.

Valadire came over to him. "Three men gone, just like that. It happened so fast, we never had time to defend." He shook his head.

Ereck had been ushered behind them when the creature emerged from the lake, and now he spoke. "I'm sorry fighter, it's partly my fault. I held you up too long."

Sarion said nothing. "It was ill fortune that the beast came at us. I don't think it even meant to attack."

"What do you mean?" Valadire asked.

"It came out of the water and we were in its path. We probably surprised it as much as it did us. It fled straight into the forest without trying to kill us all."

Valadire nodded slowly in understanding. "I think you're right, Sarion. It attacked us on instinct. It uses its bulk and strength as means to defend itself, and it probably went in the water to feed. Its beak is not made for killing fresh prey on land. For all we know, it might eat only plants."

Sarion waved to the hunters, several of them still in fighting stances. "Give the men a proper burial," he ordered. "We'll leave at dawn."

His face grim, he stared out at the dark waters which had hidden the dangerous creature. And only minutes ago he had been thinking them fortunate for stumbling upon Ereck and his island home. It had been a foolish and short-lived notion...

The Summoning

"I'm coming with you."

Sarion looked at Ereck in surprise. "What?"

"I said I'm coming along. I might be of help. And I feel partly responsible for the loss of your men."

Dawn was breaking through the foliage overhead, and the Nighton hunters prepared to leave, their numbers reduced by three.

Chertron stood next to Sarion, rubbing his shoulder, a puzzled look on his face. "We're all experienced in the field. We can't afford to protect you in a pitched battle. Stay here where you live."

Ereck coughed. "I'm more able than you care to think. You won't have to worry. I can take care of myself. And you have an extra horse as well now."

Valadire approached. "It's time to go, Sarion. Let's leave this valley behind us."

Sarion nodded, still silent.

"Well, what is it? If you leave without me, I'll follow regardless. If not, give me a few minutes to get my things." Ereck walked away, moving towards his small boat. Moments later, he paddling into the thinning mist, soon disappearing from sight.

"Are you debating whether he comes with us or not?" Valadire shook his head.

Sarion finally spoke. "He's shown us much information. He also has some knowledge of the borderlands and even Grammore. I haven't mentioned it yet, but he knows of Murkvale as well."

"How do you know if he speaks the truth?" Chertron questioned.

"Some of what he talked about corresponds with the prisoner's tale. He might prove useful." Sarion stared at them both for a moment. "He comes with us."

Chertron frowned, but then nodded. Valadire, appearing much more skeptical, merely shrugged, then went over to help Geld Rinn with the riderless horses.

The company finished their preparation, and now awaited the return of Ereck. He reappeared shortly in the craft, maneuvering it between a copse of cattails, and then left the boat, carrying a small sack over one shoulder. He motioned for a nearby hunter to help as he hid the boat in a thicket of tall grass.

"Never know who might stumble by." Ereck said.

"Out here, in the middle of nowhere?" Valadire raised his hands in disbelief.

"Well *you* did, now didn't you?" Ereck returned, making the other man scowl. "Since you waited, that means I'm coming along. Let me ride in the lead. I can get us to Gar-kiln quicker than any of your men."

Geld Rinn glanced over at Sarion, and he nodded. Within moments, the company was off making their way around the shoreline, moving to their right. Sarion conferred with Ereck, and he rode behind the two of them, the vigilant Piril at his side. Directly behind was Valadire and Bertilik, and Chertron brought up the rear after the others, Lassel riding next to him. The durable fighter had taken a liking to the young girl, amazed at her skill in weaponry. Sarion was amused at the pairing, and secretly took comfort that someone as seasoned as Chertron could be close by to aid her, although so far she'd proven her capabilities, and none would question her presence in the hunting party.

Hours passed, and they moved through the thick undergrowth of the valley, the ground sloping gradually upwards until they breached the edge, soon leaving it behind. Ereck kept them on a southwest course, and Sarion instinctively knew that they were drawing ever closer to the Ridgeline, the formidable mountain range scarcely a day's ride away, a natural boundary separating the westland from the vast and dangerous Grammore Lowlands. The terrain here was level, and heavily forested, like much of the westland. The day grew old and they still rode on, pausing only twice. Ereck spoke to Sarion frequently, making comments about their surroundings, but there was little to tell. They were deep into a hinterland where few ever traveled, even the sturdy trappers who made their living by foraging into the wilderness. Gar-kiln was the only known village in the region, and there were no other towns except for ones within a few hour's ride from Sharield. Ereck told him that if they struck due east now and somewhat south, they would find the large southern city in a few days.

Evening eventually fell upon them and they halted for the night, Sarion grateful for the uneventful day. They made a small fire, Ereck offering scant advice, talking only when asked. Sarion decided they were at little risk here from prying eyes. The Dark Mage's servants were abroad, but he didn't think there was any chance of direct pursuit since leaving Nighton. After the watch was set and the men settled, Sarion sat down, leaning against a tree stump, Valadire and Chertron at his side. Ereck hunkered across from them only a few yards away, munching on some salted meat. A few moments later he approached.

"We'll reach the village by sunset the following day, or close to it. Whatever caused the death of that place will still be there, fighter. If you insist on going, be warned."

"Yet you come with us." Sarion said.

The old man spat. "I never said I would *enter* the village. I'll get you there, maybe convince you to change your mind. Go inside? Never."

His words troubled Sarion. They had no idea

what they would find in Gar-kiln, if anything. Perhaps people were still alive there, held captive by the emissaries of the Dark Mage. Or maybe it was abandoned now, of no use to the Black Sorcerer.

Either way, they would soon find out...

They had come this far, and there would be no turning back. They needed information about their enemy, and they would not discover anything behind the walls of Nighton, or sequestered away in central Trencit and Daregil Keep. No, their only hope was to remain on the offensive, learn what they could about the Dark Mage and the nature of the threat, and try and react. Sarion was convinced that if the leaders of Trencit chose to wait, the answer would show up on their doorstep, sooner or later. He had always been someone of action, enjoying the challenge of weaponry and tracking, honing his skills as he pushed himself to the limit, almost obsessively. His service of Nighton years back had kept him constantly in the field, and it was normal for the Foresters to travel the borderlands, keeping in touch with the people and anything which threatened. This fluid level of command was the best course of defense for such a large area, and one of the things which he so admired about the Western Watch. They were the eyes and ears of Trencit's western province, and had always proven to be a match for any task which came their way. He felt a surge of pride now, knowing that he was once again within their midst, promoted to no less than Second Forester. It was a heavy command, demanding an incredible amount of responsibility, and Chensel had placed his trust in him. He could not let him or the men of Nighton down.

Valadire was speaking to Ereck, and Sarion came out of his reverie. "We'll be ready for whatever we find, mark my words. We need to approach with utmost caution, and be prepared for flight if necessary."

Ereck shook his head. "A poor plan if I ever heard one."

Sarion spoke. "I'm not debating the matter with you. Tell us what you may, but I've already told you our mission and the threat to Trencit. What is your suggestion then, to abandon our plans and admit defeat? Retreat into Nighton and Trencit while our enemy's forces ravage our lands?"

"That is exactly my suggestion." Ereck matched his gaze, his eyes unblinking.

"Enough of this." Sarion stood. "My men need their rest. And remember one thing." He pointed at Ereck. "We are fighters of Trencit, sworn to protect its people and uphold our laws. We do so willingly, and wherever our duty leads us. Good men have fallen because of our enemy. Brave fighters and leaders of our land. People I would call friends, although our time spent together was fleeting. The Dark Mage *will* be made to answer for his actions."

Sarion stalked away and none of them spoke, the conviction in his stride enough to discourage any further argument. They soon drifted off, going to their separate areas to sleep and leaving Ereck alone, the old man rubbing his beard and whispering beneath his breath before he found his own spot for the night.

The following day greeted them with a dull glow as dark clouds had rolled in overnight from the Ridgeline, the air heavy with the threat of rain. The men moved about restlessly, breaking camp and preparing for the day's travel. Sarion walked through their ranks, smiling at times and speaking words of encouragement.

Their destination was near, and he needed everyone on full alert. From the corner of his eye he felt someone staring at him and he turned, gazing into Lassel's warm blue orbs. Her intense look was startling, and he again found himself wondering as to the young woman's background.

"Captain Sarion, it looks to be a dreary day for our journey. When will we reach the village?"

He walked over to her, matching her stare. "Most likely by tomorrow, nightfall or later."

"And what do you expect to find there?" Lassel asked, her gaze unflinching.

The fighters had been told about their mission, and potential hazards along the way. Everyone was well aware of the threat to Nighton and the westland, but only a few knew the full extent facing them, the faceless entity known as the Dark Mage. Chensel had not ordered Sarion to keep them ignorant about the menace, nor would Sarion have chosen to do so.

"You know that we seek information concerning our enemy, the Dark Mage."

She nodded.

"Our hope is to find some clue at Gar-kiln that can aid us in our battle. The prisoner said that his people were enslaved, forced into servitude or killed. Perhaps some are still there yet."

"And perhaps servants of our enemy as well."

"That's a possibility. We must be careful when we arrive there."

"We are Nighton hunters and will do our best. It grieves me that we lost companions at the lake. We had no warning."

Her eyes were fierce, and Sarion saw the loss in those blue orbs. He felt it keenly himself. "It saddens me greatly, and these men were under my command. Every choice leaves open the door for danger to find us. I've seen too many good men fall these past few weeks. Sometimes it seems that our enemy expects our every move, and it's been extremely difficult for me in recent days. I find myself questioning everything I do lately..." His voice trailed off, and he was surprised by his own honesty. Was her presence alone this disarming?

"Captain Sarion, have faith. Your name was spoken highly of before your return to Nighton. None would question your decisions. And you're now Second Captain of the Western Watch. If you weren't the most capable man for the position, you surely wouldn't be that now."

He heard emotion behind her words, but it was hard to know the source. Regardless, he felt encouraged by her conviction. He lowered his voice, down to barely a whisper. "There might be great danger waiting for us ahead. Be careful and trust your instincts. I don't want anything to happen..." He didn't finish the sentence for good reason, not knowing where it might lead.

She smiled. "And take care of *yourself*. But that's one of the reasons I'm here as well." Lassel pivoted effortlessly, the movement one of remarkable grace and agility.

He remained staring at her back as Valadire approached. "I find myself enchanted with her as well, my friend. The men are ready."

Sarion had nothing else to say.

Minutes later the group was mounted and off again, plunging into the thick forests, moving ever southward. The terrain was unchanging, an endless ocean of tree and shrub, broken by small hills, streams, and the occasional fen. Geld Rinn rode with Sarion in the lead now, Huyargal and Piril directly after them. In the rear was Chertron and Lassel, the pair of them making a formidable team, and Sarion was keeping it that way. Ereck rode behind them, a change from the previous day. A growing dread had come over Sarion since last evening, a feeling that danger was lurking in the trees ahead, nameless and hidden. It could very well be the presence of Gar-kiln, he knew, but he always followed his instincts, trusting to nothing else. They knew that the Dark Mage's servants had been nearby, and might still be. Their past encounters had been deadly, facing creatures of terrible power and violence. There was no way of knowing what lay ahead, but Sarion wanted to meet it first, relying on his own skills over anyone else in the company. There were some very capable people in the group, seasoned warriors like Chertron and Valadire, expert trackers like Geld Rinn, and deadly fighters like Lassel, yet he knew that none were his equal. He did not think so out of overconfidence or arrogance, but Sarion realized this regardless. He also seemed to possess an uncanny instinct for survival, which had proven itself time and again, and it was *this* which kept him alive while others fell. He was not so foolish as to think that fortune had not played a hand in this as well, but still, the fate of their mission might be on his own shoulders in the end, and he needed to pull from all his personal resources, no matter what they be. He had avoided death countless times, and the feeling always hovered over him that the next encounter would finally spell his own destruction.

He rode on silently, knowing that there was still another factor which existed in this maelstrom of chaos, and that was the undeniable presence of the magical talisman, the rod which General Charadan had found in the lair of the Killworm, and subsequently had been entrusted into his care after the brave leader had entered the terrible city of Gorothagled and fallen there. The shades of the dead reared up before him now, taunting him with warnings of doom. Banishing the vision, he put his mind to the immediate task, trying to avoid pitfalls and remain vigilant against danger. His real foes were formed of flesh and blood, although he knew there was the possibility that other enemies existed of an unknown nature. Gorothagled had shown him things which he'd never dreamed about, and wouldn't want to otherwise...

Morning passed, and then afternoon, the forest cloaked in a mantle of gray. Deer sprang away from them, startled by their presence, and other small woodland creatures shuffled about, but nothing else. Birds fluttered about overhead, and as in the rest of the westland, wildlife abounded here. Ereck kept them on a southerly course, but also veering westwards at times, drawing ever closer to the formidable Ridgeline. At one point after midday they ascended a small hillock, and when they crested the top they caught a glimpse of the barrier mountain range, scarcely a day's ride to the west. Sarion paused, examining the terrain, but all he saw was a canopy of trees going endlessly in all directions, carpeting the feet of the Ridgeline before disappearing into the haze of the high places.

"It's hard to believe anyone can live out this deep in the wilderness," Geld Rinn said. "This is a no-man's land, and we're trespassing."

Sarion said nothing, but knew the truth behind the young tracker's words.

"You could wander forever in here and never see another person."

Sarion turned to him. "Let's hope that you never have to enter Grammore then."

He urged his mount forward, and the party resumed, Ereck muttering behind him. The ground angled downwards, but the descent was gradual, just one of countless hills that formed the spine of the westland. They halted once for a brief rest, taking fruit and drink, but Sarion soon had them off again, eager to find their destination. They traveled late into the evening before finding a suitable site to set camp, a small clearing sliced in two by a bubbling creek lined with high grass and flat stone. Sarion had not come across signs of anything which might threaten since leaving Ereck's valley, and he was greatly relieved. The fighters prepared for the night, guards vigilant at the perimeters.

Sarion sat with Chertron for a while, discussing plans for the next day, but there was little to talk about. Their knowledge was limited, and they had no idea what to expect.

"When we reach Gar-kiln, we should split into two groups," Chertron offered. "That way we can't be taken entirely by surprise."

"Hmm. Your plan has merit, although it also separates our strength. I don't like the notion of having my men out of sight."

"Who would, but it's a necessary risk. In the end, our mission needs to carry word back to Nighton and King Gregor. If something happens, we must be prepared." Chertron's gaze was intense.

"What do you fear?" Sarion asked.

"Nothing; you know me by now, my friend."

"All too well. But I see it in your eyes. What bothers you?" Sarion pressed him.

Chertron looked at the ground, his voice low. "This village. Gar-kiln. In my heart I feel that it's not abandoned. It's cursed. I don't know what lurks there now, but I like it not. And I don't trust the words of the prisoner."

Sarion was silent. "What would you have me do? Return without gaining any further knowledge? After coming this far?"

The fighter shook his head. "I know we can't do that."

"Then let's be vigilant, as much as possible. What I *do* trust is your wisdom and strong arm at my side. The Nighton fighters. My own weaponry skill. It must suffice."

"But will it be enough, I wonder." Chertron sighed, lying back on the grass, closing his eyes.

Sarion stared at him for long moments, haunted by his friend's words and somber tone.

The night was kind to the company of fighters, nothing threatening over the late hours, and they awakened once again to a gloomy dawn, the clouds looming even darker and heavier than the previous day. Sarion knew that rain would find them soon enough, and he prepared the group for another long ride in the dense westland forests.

Consulting with Ereck throughout the day, Sarion kept them on a course which would soon bring them to the village of Gar-kiln. He was amazed that the place could be found by anyone, but Ereck had assured him that it was fairly well-known in this region of the borderlands, inhospitable though it seemed. There existed other villages as well, but these were much closer to Sharield's protective arms.

Halting only once in the morning and again in the afternoon, they continued on, making good time in the thick woods. Rain began to fall in heavy drops, and the fighters took out their sturdy cloaks, no voice raised in complaint. These were some of Nighton's finest fighters and could bear any weather conditions, no matter how adverse. Conversation grew muted as the day waned, and everyone was on edge as they drew ever closer to the mysterious village. They had not seen anything but gray the entire day, and now the light faded even more as a premature nightfall fell upon the westland. The rain remained steady, and they brought out their lanterns to pick their way. They came to an area where the trees thinned out, and it was here that Ereck called to Sarion, urging them to halt.

Sarion guided his mount back towards Ereck, and the old man gestured. "Not far ahead now. There's an area of high grass, and from there you can see the village."

Sarion nodded. "We'll leave the horses here." He rode through the group until he reached Jurit, choosing the veteran fighter to remain with the animals.

Ereck dismounted, muttering beneath his breath. "If you insist on going, then I wish you good fortune. I'll try one last time to convince you to do otherwise." The old man stared up at Sarion, who merely shook his head.

"You've proven invaluable with your information. But you know I cannot change the course of my mission now. If we can gain knowledge of our enemy's plans, then the risk is necessary. We all realize this, and none come along unwillingly."

Ereck spat. "Loyalty only goes so far, fighter. And it can lead you right to the grave."

Sarion turned his horse, ignoring the comment. He then also dismounted, handing the reins to Jurit, who tied the horse to a fallen tree. The rest of the company followed his lead, and a few minutes later Sarion gathered them together.

"Here's what we will do. I'll lead the first group, with Chertron, Piril, Bertilik, and Lassel. The second group of seven will be led by Valadire, and the rest of you go with him, Jurit the only one staying behind to ward the horses. We'll encircle the village, making our way from the outside, using as much cover as possible. The darkness will hide our movements as well." He came over to Geld Rinn. "Use all your ability to avoid detection. Take them safely into the village. Your skills are exceptional, and trust yourself."

It was an important moment, Sarion realized, deliberately drawing the young tracker out in an effort to boost his confidence. Valadire and the others had more seasons beneath their cloaks, but Geld Rinn was one of those rare fighters who possessed an uncanny ability in the field, both with tracking and weapons mastery. Sarion knew it was time for the young man to take his prowess into an active, hostile environment, and his skills could mean the difference between life and death.

Geld Rinn nodded.

"All right. We don't know what we'll find here. It might very well be abandoned, and we can find clues as to the purpose of our enemy. It may also harbor dangerous creatures, waiting for exactly this kind of action. Regardless, our mission is paramount. Whatever we find, word must be taken back to Nighton and Lord Chensel. If something happens, find Jurit and flee with great haste."

His words were grim, but he was their leader, Second Forester of the Western Watch now. His days of being a farmer were long past, and he knew that it was something he could never recapture again. For the sake of the westland and even Trencit -- the men and women who lived there, going about their own peaceful lives -- he had been entrusted to protect, and all his decisions must be to the greater benefit of the citizens. Edward's youthful face appeared in his mind's eye, and he felt an incredible determination to find and defeat the enemy, no matter the cost to himself. He felt the presence of the powerful wand, and he knew that he was its bearer, and the talisman must not fall into the hands of the Dark Mage and his emissaries. On his broad shoulders rested an uncomfortable balance of hope and doom, and he felt the burden as a physical weight. And he also felt an urge, subtle but strong, to wield the rod and lay waste to any creature which might wait ahead somewhere...

It was a feeling which he must *not* succumb to, even if their need was desperate.

"Two hours, no more. Return here with news of what you found." He stared hard at Valadire." If Gar-kiln is indeed abandoned, then we meet within its center, but only if you're absolutely certain that nothing remains there. Understood?"

Valadire spoke. "Yes. And be careful yourself, Sarion. We don't know what we'll find."

"Good luck." Sarion gripped his hand, and nodded to the others going with his group.

The men tightened their cloaks, patted their weapons, and were off into the growing mist, Geld Rinn leading them, Huyargal at his side. In seconds they vanished like tormented spirits doomed to roam the world until the end of time itself.

"We'll give them a few minutes lead, as they need to make their way around the edge." Sarion spoke to Chertron, but his companion was silent.

Checking his own weapons, Sarion moved around the group, speaking words of encouragement. Piril guarded the way in front, his watchful eyes never leaving the darkness. Several minutes later Sarion knew it was time, and he motioned them all together. "Not a word is to be spoken unless our safety is at risk."

The fighters looked at him, their faces resolute and respectful. Lassel nodded, a gesture of complete trust.

Sarion only hoped that it was well-placed.

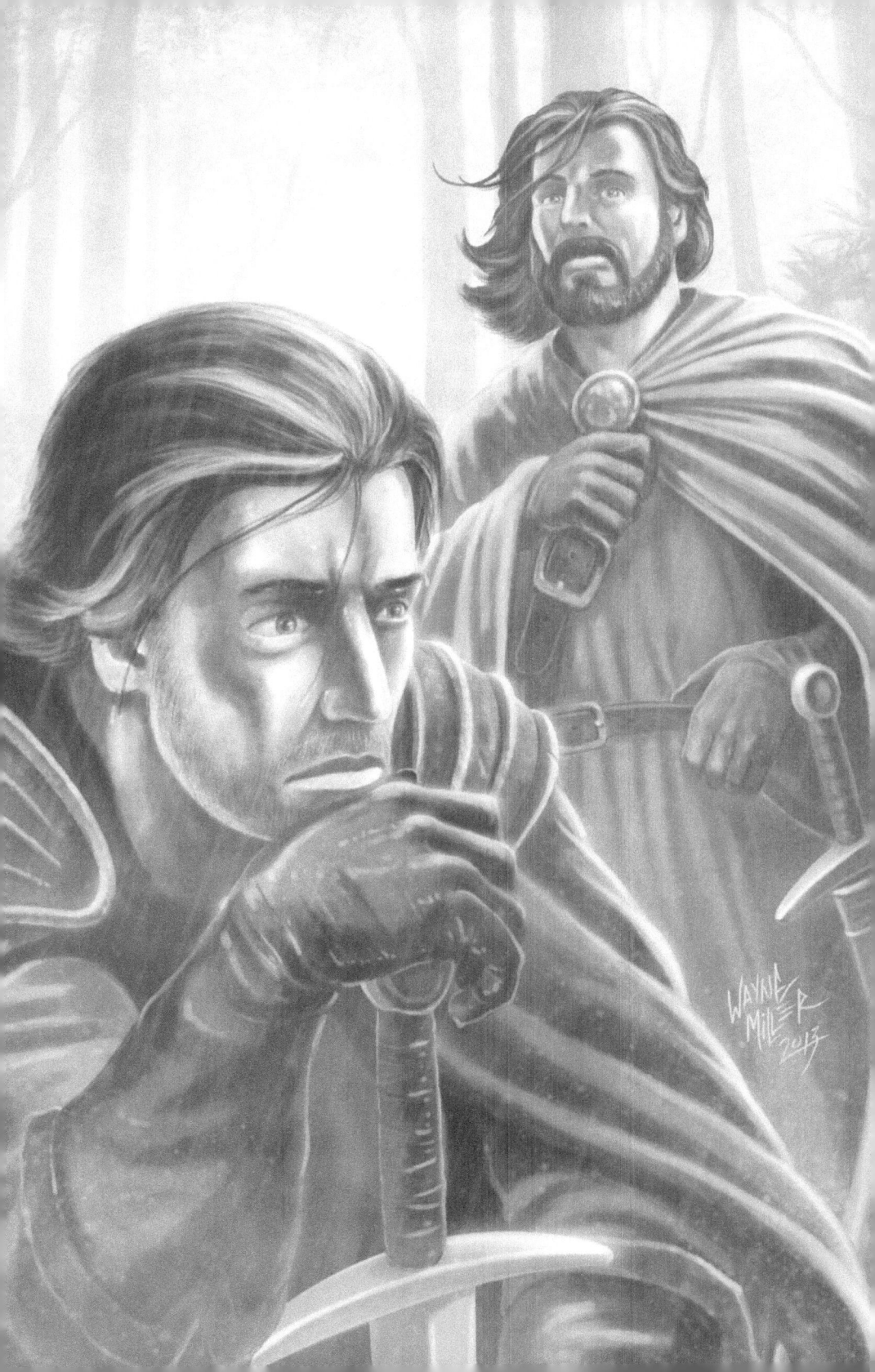

Paul Melniczek

Sarion and the fighters made their way through the tall grass, concealed by darkness and mist. The rain fell down in small droplets, steady and showing no sign of letting up anytime soon. Faceless wraiths they were, making their way stealthily between the undergrowth, and soon the grass fell away on both sides, revealing a stretch of open field, a large building looming several dozen yards from where they stood.

Scanning the landscape, Sarion could make out little detail. Nothing moved, and the structure appeared to be a storehouse of sorts. He gestured to Chertron and the fighters, signaling for them to fan out in hunting formation. Seconds later they made their way forward, half-crouching and hurrying through the night trying to avoid notice from any watchful eyes. They reached the side of the building and halted, Chertron moving down one end and Piril the other. They shortly signaled back that nothing was nearby, and Sarion examined the building, staring up at a pair of windows a few yards off the ground. Most likely they were secured from trespassing creatures, with the villagers living in an area where unfriendly things prowled. Debating on whether he should see what was inside, he quickly made up his mind, motioning for them to go to his left and enter at the front entrance. Chertron was already in place, and Piril stayed where he was to guard against anything approaching their flank.

Chertron never moved, his lean form missing nothing. Sarion reached his side, and peered around the corner. Several wagons lay scattered about, the kind used to move stores around, able to carry much weight. They appeared intact, and of little importance to them. Pointing ahead, Chertron glided along the edge, stopping before a wide door that was open. Right behind him came Sarion, Lassel and Bertilik on his heels. Piril came closer, but stayed at the corner now, watching their back.

Chertron entered first, Sarion following silently. The interior was large and dark, countless shapes looming before them. The smell of hay was strong, and Sarion knew that light was needed if they were to search the inside. He brought out his lantern and lit it, keeping the flame low. With Chertron next to him, they moved slowly, examining the crates and piles of hay. The others stayed behind, and within moments, Sarion decided that nothing useful would be found here, so he returned to the entrance, shaking his head.

"Time moves swiftly, and there is no cause to linger."

Chertron nodded in agreement, and the company was again off. A dirt road led south, and they stayed off it, moving parallel. Sarion risked the lantern, bending to the ground at times as he looked for tracks. There were wheel marks going in both directions, and his heart sank as he noticed large booted prints made from something of which he knew all too well.

Ogres...

...and they appeared fresh.

Cursing to himself he pulled up, the others looking at him curiously. He immediately doused the flame, gathering them close, Piril still in the rear, Chertron with an eye forward.

Sarion whispered. "These tracks are recent. And from the size, there were two ogres that came this way and left."

Chertron muttered beneath his breath. "Ogres. Just as the prisoner said. This is evil news for certain. They're still here somewhere."

Sarion nodded. "We can't know how many

others, or how long ago they were in this place, but the tracks are clearly recent. My guess is that they maintain a presence here yet, with a guard of sorts."

He stared at them, looking for signs of fear, but saw none. Not in this group...

He continued. "Well, this is ill news, but perhaps it might be meaningful to us."

"What do you mean?" Lassel asked.

Sarion replied. "They remain here for a reason. Something of importance could yet be found in Gar-kiln. And that is why we're here now...regardless of the risk."

Chertron spoke, looking warily into the night as if expecting a host of monsters to appear at any moment. "That may well be, but this place worries me. I feel it conceals secrets...and danger."

"It concerns me too, my friend, but there is nothing to be done about it except to see this mission to its end. Chensel knew the truth of this." Sarion straightened. "If any wish to stay behind and wait, you may do so without shame." He stared at them all, and several frowns returned his gaze.

"You know we all follow willingly," Lassel said, shaking her head. "We are fighters of the Western Watch, and danger is the meat and bread of our livelihood, especially in these troubled times. We won't abandon you for any reason."

Although it was too dark to see clearly, Sarion knew there was a sparkle of determination in the girl's eyes which matched her words. She was a firebrand of fortitude, and again he wondered as to who she really was. He felt proud to be among them as their companion and Captain, but with the sense of pride came an overwhelming feeling of foreboding. Chertron was right. *Ereck* was right. Gar-kiln was a place of evil and dread. The tracks from the ogres proved this much; that it was somewhere to be avoided at all cost. His instincts buzzed inside, warning him of another trap.

Like in Sprechyd Wood...

Their miscalculation had cost the lives of a number of men, including the brave Karrol. Sarion had befriended the man quickly, and had only known him for a few scant days as they traveled together in search of the missing Jerol. The expedition had ended in disaster, almost claiming Sarion's life as well. Only the intervention of the mysterious creature calling itself the Keeper of Sprechyd Wood had managed to save him as it sensed the presence of powerful magic from the talisman he bore. It had been a desperate time for him.

Was it the same now?

He paused, knowing the others waited for his action. In that moment a chill went down his spine as he felt a terrible certainty that not all of them would return from Gar-kiln. Stunned by both the horror and power of it, he couldn't speak for a moment.

Still they waited...

Recovering, Sarion shook off the feeling of doom and spoke. "Let's go further. No talking for any reason. Use our signals. Chertron, I want you to stay in the back as rear guard. Your ears and eyes are sharp. Warn us if anything follows. I'll lead, Piril and Bertilik behind, Lassel behind them. We stay in this formation until we meet up with the others. Keep all your senses focused to our surroundings. We can't afford to be taken by surprise."

None of them answered, and he didn't expect it regardless, and with that he moved ahead, the rest of them following his lead. He kept to the right of the path, making his way quietly through the light undergrowth. Bushes and trees edged the causeway, and their boots were muted by the wet ground. Rain fell upon their cloaks, but they continued with fixed purpose, Sarion gliding ahead smoothly as only the most seasoned of trackers could move while on the hunt. They went this way for several minutes, encountering nothing, hearing nothing. The only sound was the soft patter of rainfall tapping against the leaves and ground. It was a dismal night, and the world around them was hushed, permitting their passage.

Sarion wondered again what they would find here. Their journey south had enabled them to uncover valuable information, and at last they had reached Gar-kiln with Ereck's help, although several of their company would not be returning, waylaid by the creature hiding in the lake. Losing comrades would never become an easy thing for Sarion, especially now that he was a Captain of the Western Watch once more, but he could not afford to dwell on their losses. Men under his command had been killed years earlier, and he knew their faces would haunt him forever.

Yet he also knew he wasn't to blame. Evil walked the world then, as it did now. It was up to people like him to protect those who could not do it themselves, and he constantly placed his own life at risk in the effort, even going into Grammore at the request of the now slain General Charadan.

He wanted so badly to defeat the Dark Mage and his emissaries, pushing himself to his limits, and at times thinking his strength and will alone would be enough. But no, that path was a dangerous one and the day would come when he found himself unaided and surrounded, a victim of his own pride. This battle would only find victory if they all worked together, finding a way in which to destroy their enemy. He must not blindly forge ahead, although the desire was strong even now to leave his companions behind and go himself.

Minutes passed and they still moved stealthily along the trail, remaining concealed from prying eyes. Without warning the forest opened up and the path

ended at a tall wooden gate which curved off to either
side. Sarion immediately knew that this was a protective
barrier against creatures prowling in the wild. He
signaled for them to move east, and the company melted
into the trees. There was no way he would chance that
entrance, for it might be guarded. He led them on for
another minute, and then he moved forward again. The
great fence loomed before them, at least fifteen feet
high. Gathering the fighters together momentarily, he
had Piril take out a length of rope, and they approached
the barrier. With Piril on the bottom, and Chertron on
his shoulders, Sarion moved over their forms like a cat
at prey, easily gaining the top with rope in hand. He
peered cautiously over the rim, and he now looked down
at the main village itself. Rain and mist obscured nearly
everything, but he could make out the rooftops of the
closest homes, all of them oddly shaped, crafted by their
own unique owners. Trees circled the buildings, and
some of these had large yards to go with them while
others huddled together as if to fend off the wilderness.
There seemed to be no order to them, and he scanned his
surroundings, making sure nothing threatened. Satisfied,
he looked for a way to get his companions over the
fence. He spotted a hole in the structure to his left, and
there were others as well, the fence showing its age and
wear from the elements. He scuttled over that way,
careful not to lose his balance, and took the rope
through, knotting it in the middle. He tugged to make
sure, and then dangled half the length behind him for the
others to ascend. Taking the other half, he lowered
himself into the village, his boots slowing his descent.
As soon as he hit the ground, his sword was in hand and
he crouched into a fighting stance, ready for anything.
Moments later the others followed, Piril first, Bertilik,
Lassel, and finally the sturdy Chertron. They halted,
examining their situation.

Sarion lowered his sword, analyzing their next move. The village appeared large, based on the size of the fence alone and what he could make out from his previous vantage point. There would be countless buildings and homes, and they could not afford to waste time searching each one for clues. The best thing would be to head for the middle and meet up with Valadire and the others, and stick to the plan. Hopefully they would come across useful information as they moved forward. They lacked any real knowledge of the village save the name, so there was little else to go on.

Giving a hand signal, they proceeded as before, staying in hunting formation. Sarion had Piril and Bertilik fan out a bit, to either side, relying on their moving position to protect against any assault. They hurried forward, Sarion leading them between homes and outbuildings, missing nothing. Gar-kiln looked deserted, and there was no movement in any direction. Darkness claimed all, and visibility remained poor. There was no way he could risk a light, so he relied entirely on his senses and limited vision. But the village was silent, keeping close its secrets. Sarion felt as if they walked in a tomb, and couldn't shake the feeling. The prisoner had told them to free his people, but Sarion feared it was too late.

He knew instinctively that the only ones left here would be servants of the Dark Mage.

The Nighton hunters continued in this manner for several minutes, passing quietly like forsaken wraiths intent on their own secretive purpose. The buildings grew denser as they approached the center of the village making them close ranks, and still nothing appeared. No sound reached their ears, and the rain fell in a steady sheet, splattering on muddy paths and soaking everything.

They walked along the side of an old building

formed from sections of long wood, and Sarion paused, crouching down as he neared a shuttered window. They had passed by a number of windows, keeping their distance each time, hurrying by and doing their best to avoid being seen. It would have been extremely difficult for them to be spotted with the obscuring night and mist, but Sarion was taking no chances. This time he wanted to try a different approach though, so he pressed his ear close while the others watched him, never letting down their guard.

Surprised, his eyes narrowed when he heard something, a low noise.

Movement. From inside.

He tried to peer between the boarded shutters, but only darkness greeted him.

Listening with strained ears, he waited for more. Long seconds passed, but there was no other sound. Turning, he gestured to Piril directly behind him and pointed. The fighter shook his head. He hadn't heard anything.

Sarion bit his lip, concentrating. He was certain that something had moved inside the building, but what?

They had come this far, encountering nothing. Tracks from ogres, but no other signs. Although the village appeared deserted, he feared the worst, that guards still remained here, their purpose unknown. The absolutely last thing he wanted was for them to fight a pitched battle, and he had enough experience with ogres to know that they were ferocious combatants, cunning and possessing brute strength, a match for twenty normal men. Of course, they were all excellent fighters here, but still, they might find themselves severely outmatched. He also knew that they could not afford to be seen and pursued, so if something inside the building spotted them, then it needed to be dispatched immediately and quickly.

Paul Melniczek

Signaling by hand, he motioned for Piril and Bertilik to follow him around the front while Chertron and Lassel would find entrance in the back. Weapons ready, they moved into action, crouching and hurrying to gain access. Slipping onto the porch, Sarion went to the front door, carefully trying the handle.

It was open.

Gritting his teeth, Sarion pushed the sturdy door inwards, knife held before him. The place smelled of mold and disuse, abandoned to shadows and death. His two guards were right on his heels, but he waved Bertilik to stop and guard the front. He fervently hoped that whatever waited inside would not require all their strength. Sarion signaled for Piril to light his lantern, and they hesitated, the flames licking out and chasing back the darkness, revealing chairs, furniture, and small dust devils tumbling about, stirred from their passing. The room was small and appeared empty. He knew the others would have gained the back entrance by now, and that left only one or two rooms between them. Creeping ahead, they went through a narrow alcove and moved deeper into the home, and it was here that Sarion believed the sound to have come from. The chamber was larger than the previous one, and crates filled the room, piled on top of each other.

Here there was space for something to remain hidden...

Light greeted him from the opposite direction as Chertron and the Nighton hunters advanced. There was no time to waste, so Sarion decided on a direct approach.

"We're from the Western Watch. We're here to help."

His question had an immediate response. First, a whimper, and then movement. A figure loomed upwards from the right wall, and all eyes fixed on what appeared to be a man, his clothes torn and soiled. He raised his hands in the air, sobbing.

"I thought…you were one of them. What are you doing here?"

He came forward, and the hunters circled him warily.

"We've faced treachery before, so forgive us if we are overly cautious." Sarion motioned for Piril to move closer to the man. The Nighton hunter looked him over, with a watchful Lassel at his side. After several moments, the fighters lowered their weapons, but Sarion knew they would react to anything if the man threatened.

"I thought I would never see one of my kinsmen again. You're from Nighton, you say?"

"Yes. We've come here to give aid, and to find answers."

"You'll only find death here."

Sarion frowned. "Nevertheless. What can you tell us? Are there any others?"

The man shook his head. "If there are, then they're like me. Hiding, living in constant fear of being found. Korlig and Seffrel hid with me for weeks. They both decided to take a chance and leave the village."

"Did they make it?" Chertron asked.

"I don't know. I chose to remain rather than risk sure death from the beast that guards the woods."

A chill went down Sarion's spine at his words. "What do you mean?"

"You were lucky in avoiding it, or else you would not have made it this far. They made a gap in the fence so it can come and go. It's a terrible creature." His hands trembled. "Do you have food? Please, I'm starving."

Chertron took some salted meat from his pouch which the man eagerly accepted. He ate it quickly, and

Lassel offered more.

"We've no time to spare. We need to know anything you can tell us about what happened here, and what still remains. What's your name?"

"Fortisel." He chewed some more before answering. "But you must leave now."

"We'll take you with us. We have horses tied up to the north. We climbed the fence, not willing to risk that entrance. Is it guarded?" Sarion questioned him.

"It might be. I think there's only a few of them left in Gar-kiln. Most of them have gone."

"Do you know where they went? Were there ogres as well?"

Fortisel nodded. "Ten that I saw."

Chertron cursed. "We cannot overcome such numbers."

"And where do the guards stay that remain here?" Sarion pressed him.

"There's a large barn near the center of the village. It was our main place for trade and barter, standing on its own with no adjoining buildings. It is there they have taken up, so they can see in all directions. I know a few of them are still here; they keep it lighted and make their patrols from the barn. I've gone alone at night to spy, hoping they'll all leave Gar-kiln soon and I can chance my own escape."

"What else is in there besides the ogres?" Chertron now asked.

"There's a man who leads them. I don't know anything about him except his name -- Chardoom. He serves the black one and was sent here to enslave us all. It is he who controls the mighty creature."

Sarion matched stares with Chertron and then continued. "Is this the beast called the Ravenor?"

Fortisel's eyes grew wide with fear. "I know not its name, only what it can do. The creature is terrible!

I've never seen anything like it in my darkest dreams.
Our people were fed to it as an example..."

"And some were taken away from here?"

He nodded vigorously. "You know something
then of our fate?"

"We do." Sarion looked to the front, knowing
that they needed to find Geld Rinn and the others soon.
But there *were* answers to be found in Gar-kiln. The
question was how to get them...

"I can't explain this to you now. We need to act.
Another group with us approached from the south. Do
you know if this area is being guarded?"

Fortisel shook his head.

Sarion bit his lip. "What about the creature's
whereabouts?"

"It comes and goes. It stays in the forest most of
the time, searching for prey, I would guess, perhaps
sleeping as well. It's larger than you can imagine."

"We would have heard it coming when we
entered. Maybe we can continue to avoid it."

"I've watched it from a distance. It think it
moves by scent and sound. I've seen it leaving the
village as well."

"Does it come into here at all?" Chertron asked.

"No."

"What about the ogres? Do they search for
villagers yet?" Sarion asked.

Fortisel shook his head, his bearded face
growing angry. "They made some of our own people go
around at night, looking for others. We had to kill
several. I think the ogres forced them for their own
enjoyment. They probably think we've all slain each
other by now, or that the creature eventually found us."

"Sarion, we need to go now and find the others.
Time is against us." Chertron grabbed his shoulder.

"I know. We need to find out one more thing

about the beast." He turned to Fortisel. "If this creature is so powerful, how do they control it?"

The man answered, his eyes smoldering. "Chardoom is its master. When he summons it with his horn, the monster comes."

It was as Sarion feared then. The Dark Mage had sent another of his personal servants here, and that could only mean one thing -- the Ravenor was most likely a creature of magical origin, and they had no idea of what it was capable of...

"All right. We go now in search of Geld Rinn and the others. The odds are stacked too highly against us here. Fortisel, I want you to return now with Bertilik and Lassel the way we came. Chertron, Piril, and myself will meet with the others before we're discovered. The last thing..."

But he never finished his sentence as an eerie wailing echoed through the night. A terrible call rang out in the cursed village, one promising certain death.

Fortisel grabbed Sarion's arm.

"He summons the Ravenor..."

Sarion's heart sank.

Too late!

The beast was coming back to Gar-kiln. There was no time to waste now. If the monster caught them they might all be killed...

"Bertilik! You and Lassel backtrack and leave with Fortisel. Take the horses deeper into the woods and we'll rendezvous as soon as possible. We must not all become trapped here."

The fighter nodded, but Lassel's eyes were wide

with dismay. She started to protest but Sarion dismissed her with a wave of his hand.

"Those are your orders. Hurry now and be careful."

He grabbed Chertron by the shoulder and Piril was on his heels immediately as he rushed towards the front entrance and into the night. Behind him Fortisel shouted words of warning. "Beware the creature! Don't go near it..."

And with that they were outside once more, heading directly for the heart of the village and the deadly things which lurked there, the last place any of them wanted to go...They moved forward, crouching low and staying close to cover as they ran through deserted backyards and alongside looming buildings which had once housed the villagers of Gar-kiln. They kept along the edge of a dense hedgerow, the tops of it growing out of control, and a stray dog startled them as they reached the end, the animal sniffing them once before vanishing into the thicket.

Directly before them sat a row of buildings varying in size, appearing like crooked teeth in a massive mouth, all of them connecting together in a long curving line which disappeared into the gloom to either side. Sarion knew that they were near the center of the village, and they needed to pass through these somehow, realizing what might lay behind them, dangerous and unrevealed. Motioning with one hand for them to follow, he moved straight ahead, knowing that a direct approach would be the quickest. They reached the back of an old stone structure, which might have been someone's home, or even a trading store. Sarion scanned the building, his head angling upwards. A large oak squatted against it to their left, the hoary branches struggling for purchase along the aged stone.

Sarion approached it, grabbing the lowest branch

and lifting himself up. Behind him Chertron grumbled, but that was the only sound they'd heard since the dreadful call. The climb was fairly easy, the limbs thick and rough, and shortly Sarion was able to propel himself higher, finding a branch which rubbed against the building's edge. He followed it to the wall where he placed his boots on a narrow ledge, then he lifted himself to the roof, moving catlike along the top, the others having more difficulty. The footing was uneven, the roof carpeted with moss and weathered against the elements, the rainfall making it slick. Sarion moved cautiously ahead now, keeping his profile low, and within moments made it to the far side. Flattening entirely, he peered over the edge, taking in the landscape. Buildings trailed off on both sides, and across a wide dirt street were more buildings, roughly the same size, most of them similar in appearance and condition. This was the heart of Gar-kiln where villagers once bartered and traded their wares amongst themselves and occasional travelers and merchants. There was nothing unique about the town except for its close proximity to the Ridgeline, and that in itself spoke volumes of the toughness these people possessed, and one which had ultimately contributed to their demise...

Looking to his left while the other two joined him, he saw where the buildings ended and a large, solitary structure stood on its own. He knew this had to be the barn which Fortisel had spoken of, and even if he had not been forewarned, the beams of light which issued forth from the ponderous front doors would have been convincing enough. Whatever lived there waited without any fear of discovery, making no secret of its presence. It spoke of confidence and power, and that worried Sarion. The road was silent and he gazed across, looking for signs of the other group led by Valadire and Geld Rinn. Surely they would have heard the call and been alerted of danger. But he felt a shiver of trepidation, wondering if an alarm had been made because their presence had been detected, or was it for an entirely different reason? He had no idea which one it was.

Nothing stirred, and Sarion wondered if any of the enemy was out, even now patrolling the village. Worse yet, where was the creature known as the Ravenor?

But his second question now found an answer as something huge approached the barn from the far side, a monstrous shadow materializing from the rain and mist like a behemoth awakened from the deepest bowels of the earth. The creature was tall and broad, impossibly large, and Sarion's mouth opened in astonishment at the sheer size of the beast. It towered over the barn, lumbering directly before it and halting motionless. The three companions waited there breathlessly, the same question on all their minds as to what was taking place. It appeared that their presence still remained a secret, as the monster made no move in their direction, not looking anywhere in particular. They were dozens of yards away from it, but it was frighteningly close due to its size and nature. The massive head was as high as the building they perched on, and this fact was not lost on Sarion. Then light flared brighter from within the barn and a pair of shadows emerged, heavily armed and large in their own right, although greatly dwarfed by the imposing bulk of the Ravenor.

Ogres...

Yes, he thought, just as the tracks told him earlier. And Fortisel...

Following directly behind them came another figure now, draped in a black robe, the head cowled over by a hood. It looked to be a man, and Sarion knew immediately that this must be the one known as

Chardoom, an emissary of the Dark Mage and the one in control of the Ravenor. In his hands he carried a long staff, and he approached the terrible creature without hesitation. Waving the rod before him, the Ravenor bowed its massive head, and Sarion could see now that the creature was eyeless, its face black as the night with a jaw wide enough which could swallow man or horse whole. From what nameless pit this thing had been spawned in was beyond Sarion's comprehension, and he could only guess that it was a monster from the old world, akin to things like the Killworm, bred in magic and malice by the ancient race of giants. It was terrifying to behold.

The air shimmered between Chardoom and the Ravenor, and seconds later the great beast turned its neck and moved away in the direction it had come, lumbering off in the darkness before vanishing completely. The ogres went inside, closing the door behind them, flanking the black-robed servant of the Dark Mage and disappearing once more.

The three of them waited long moments before Sarion retreated to the middle of the roof, signaling Piril to keep watch.

"What do you make of that?" Chertron whispered, shaking his head in amazement. "By the Seven, what a monster. Like unto the Jurvech itself, something I had wished never to lay eyes upon again in my life."

Sarion nodded. "I'm as bewildered as you, I'm afraid. Clearly this Chardoom maintains control of the beast, while the ogres are here to protect him from harm."

"What do you think he did to it? That staff he bears must contain magic given to him by the enemy."

"My exact thought as well. But the question is this -- what does it all mean to *us*?"

The Summoning

He stared at Chertron, but his companion had no answer, crouching there in silence. Finally he quietly answered. "I know not."

"Hmm," was all Sarion managed to say, his mind trying to fathom what it all meant. He knew there was a purpose for Chardoom to still be in Gar-kiln; that was certain. And…he was determined to find out what it was. Unwilling to speak just yet and alarm Chertron further, he pulled his cloak tighter against the rain, taking out his flask and drinking water from it, his companion shrugging and doing the same.

He glanced towards Piril but the fighter was a statue, all attention focused on the barn and what lay beyond.

"Eh, no sign of the others yet." Chertron said. "Let's hope that they can stay hidden from the enemy and make their return. If they caught a glimpse of the Ravenor, they know as much as we do. Avoid it at all cost. The old man was right. This village is cursed, and death waits here for any who trespass."

Sarion nodded, deep in his own thoughts. He remembered the meeting with Chensel where he'd argued his point with the Nighton leader, saying that all roads led to Gar-kiln, convincing him to give Sarion permission to embark on a quest for knowledge. Well, here they were now…They had searched the forsaken village, finding only one survivor. Confirmed the presence of ogres there, and even caught a glimpse of another servant of the Dark Mage, someone called Chardoom, and worse yet, seen the creature called the Ravenor up close. Much too close…The prisoner's tale was confirmed, the facts leading to the truth. But what was the greater truth? What was really going on here? Sarion bit his lip, trying desperately to make sense of things. They could return now, claiming success for the mission, but he knew it would prove little, gaining them no additional knowledge. And in reality he did not dare to go back himself to Nighton. Chensel had ordered him to stay in the field indefinitely, choosing to help where he could, in an effort to keep from being taken to Daregil Keep and King Gregor. The decision had been made for Sarion to act as protector of the rod, and not let it enter Trencit. This was surely against the king's wishes, and both he and Chensel understood what a dangerous game they played here.

But they had agreed upon it, and if Sarion knew anything about Chensel, it was that the man possessed strong talents and would not willingly be maneuvered against his will. He was an incredibly capable leader, both shrewd and far-sighted. Nighton was in good hands, but all of that was inconsequential at the moment. He was in Gar-kiln *now*, a haven of death, nightmares, and monstrous creatures. And also secrets…How best could he use his situation to their advantage? They'd come so far, but had failed to learn any new information that would help them fight the Dark Mage, and men under his command had already been lost. Sacrifices had been made to get them here.

An idea crossed his mind then, one perilous, even foolhardy. He was close to discovering something important, of that he was certain. Nighton was many miles away, and for them to have traveled this far and return with nothing more than a confirmation of the prisoner's tale would be a shallow victory, or none at all. No, that was unacceptable, and Sarion knew it.

So where did that leave him…

He stared at his surroundings, formulating a plan. Dangerous? Absolutely. But he'd already made his decision.

"Chertron?" His companion eyed him curiously.

Sarion hesitated for only a moment. "I need to enter that building, find out what purpose this Chardoom has for remaining in Gar-kiln."

The fighter looked shocked, actually gasping. "My friend, are you *mad*? Haven't we both seen the Ravenor?" He was at a loss for words, then he quickly continued. "You tempt fate too much, Sarion. Shades, to pursue this plan is as reckless as anything I've heard in my life."

Sarion shook his head. "We've learned nothing to help our cause on this journey. At best, we know the prisoner spoke the truth. Would you have me send word or return to Nighton now, lacking further knowledge of our enemy and his schemes?"

Chertron never hesitated. "Yes. And we can leave here whole and intact if we're fortunate."

"Then we disagree, although I greatly value your judgement."

"One which you never bother taking, I'll add."

"That's not true." Sarion sighed. "But I won't be persuaded otherwise. I'm going into the barn."

Chertron's face looked stricken with pain. "How can you overcome the ogres, no less the servant of the Dark Mage? You can't have forgotten our trek through Grammore and what it cost us to defeat *one* such beast?"

"I'll never forget; we both know that. But I'm not seeking to do battle. Just search for answers. Enter unseen, then leave without them knowing I was ever there."

His companion lowered his head, rubbing his brow. "You continue to surprise me, Sarion. I should know better by now. And…your bravery is unsurpassed. Where you find the courage for such action is a mystery. In the face of such odds, against creatures which easily overwhelm our strength. Ah, what's the use? You'll do as you deem fit, no matter my arguments to dissuade you. Then I'll go along and we'll both meet our fate together," he muttered. "A fitting end to all of our adventures together, foolish or not. So the tales will tell."

Sarion gently shook his head. "My friend, you don't have the skills as I to move as quickly and quietly as needed. You must stay behind."

Chertron bristled in anger. "Sarion, how many times will you take such risk upon yourself? If you're captured, we haven't the strength to set you free. We would all be slain."

"No one is to come after me. Those are my orders for the entire company. If I don't return, you're to find Valadire and the others and leave the town immediately. Avoid detection by the Ravenor, remain split into two groups."

"You realize that if you're captured, then it won't be long until they figure out that you weren't acting alone. It might very well doom us all."

Sarion clapped him on the shoulder. "I certainly won't be captured then, will I? Have faith in me. I have much of it in your own ability to escape, even if I am caught." A mischievous grin crossed his face, although he was filled with reservations, his heart heavy. It was an extremely daring scheme, and few could undertake it with any hope of success.

But Sarion also knew that he was one of those few...

To leave Gar-kiln now, when the answers were so near, was simply not an option for him. Too much was at stake. Yes, the risk was enormous. But so were the other possibilities, and the consequences of having a lack of knowledge. They needed to stay on the offensive, and not let the Dark Mage manipulate them at his leisure.

Chertron spoke. "And also remember Chensel's warning. You can't let the rod fall into enemy hands at any cost."

Sarion nodded. "I understand. That's part of my dilemma now. While I carry the talisman, I'm under whatever protection it has to give. However, if I leave it with you in the chance I *am* captured, then I also lose that protection."

"Shades. Then it's an easy decision. Don't go."

Sarion frowned. "No, my mind is made up. I go alone and with the rod. Take Piril and leave immediately. Meet up with others back at the horses. Cross the street further down to avoid detection. Go nowhere near the barn. Valadire should be returning soon as well. Wait an hour for my return, then leave. No questions."

Sarion slipped back, signaling Piril to follow. He quickly told Piril his plan, the strong fighter shaking his head to no avail. Soon, they made their way back down the building and were shortly on the ground again. The rain was a consistent sheet, blending the elements into one shrouded landscape broken by the dim figures of homes, trees, and hedgerows.

"Good luck, my friend." Chertron whispered. "Return safe and soon."

Sarion clapped him on the arm and then left, the others staring at him for a moment before moving off into the opposite direction. He hurried along using the natural cover around him, noiseless and surefooted. The task before him required stealth and speed. His mastery of arms would be of no use to him, and there wasn't the slightest doubt in his mind of this fact. Yes, he'd battled ferocious creatures in the past few weeks, overcoming traps laid before him, and escaping unscathed, for the most part. The ogre had been slain by the remaining members of his company, weakened when he finally arrived. The defeat of the winged gargoyles had also been a combined assault, from his companions and the northerners. The giant brute in Sprechyd Forest had won the fight though, Sarion barely escaping with his life, and only through the intervention of the Keeper of the Wood. And at Nighton, they had all destroyed the Killworm in the end, aided by the protective power of the rod. Sarion had battled the huge bear-like creature outside the walls, injuring it, but even then he needed the help of others to finally kill it off. There had been other skirmishes against nameless creatures, and many times Sarion and his companions had avoided them. As he thought about these past confrontations, more times than less, finding a way of escape had meant securing another day to live and fight. The monsters facing them were extraordinary in nature, possessed of unique skills, inherent talents, and unsurpassed violence.

They had been outmatched in nearly every instance.

Sarion paused, the gravity of all the recent conflicts coming to bear down on him. It was daunting, terrifying. Men were simply no challenge against these beasts unless they were grouped in superior numbers, and even that did not always hold true.

The Jurvech, Ravenor, and Killworm were all proof.

And what lay before him now was yet another such scenario. If he was spotted by the enemy, he was done for…

There were at least two ogres that they already knew of. More could be lurking elsewhere. And he'd seen enough of the Ravenor to realize that magical or not, there wasn't a man alive who could hope to defeat such a monster in hand-to-hand combat.

In a pitched battle he might be able to fend off a single ogre for a period of time.

Maybe…

But the creatures of Gar-kiln? Never.

He had to be extremely careful.

The Summoning

Shortly, he was past the building from which they'd hidden. He glided by the others, making himself one with the night. No light shone from any window or opening, and the darkness was nearly complete. Gar-kiln was a graveyard for the dead, and would quickly welcome the foolish or unwary into its treacherous embrace.

Sarion needed to make sure he avoided that welcome himself...

He carried on, moving parallel with the barn on the other side of the row of structures. Some had gaps in them, and he caught an occasional glimpse, shards of light piercing the gloom like dull swords. The end of the buildings sat before him now, and he slowed. Here was the moment of greatest danger, as the barn stood in isolation, and he needed to get close to it without being seen.

Sarion slunk further away to the left, using all the natural cover he could find, relying on the distance and elements as concealment. Rain continued to fall, and the wind had picked up. His plan was to go behind the building and search for an opening, hoping it wasn't guarded in the rear. It was not a hope that he counted entirely upon, however, but it was his immediate plan. There was a chance that the guardians had no fear of assault, with their greater strength and nearby presence of the dread Ravenor.

Giving the barn a wide berth, he now approached from the far side where the Ravenor had left from, and he scanned the road for any sign of movement. The town looked deserted, although he knew that was false. His greatest fear was that the enemy had hidden away more creatures or ogres, waiting just for this type of act. Shrugging aside his reservation, Sarion moved on, crouching down, flattening to the ground at times. As he drew nearer, he saw that unlike the front part, the barn's back windows were all shuttered, light leaking outwards between the cracks. Gritting his teeth he waited there, for well over a minute, watching and listening. He caught snatches of sound from within the building which sounded like voices, low and muffled. It came from somewhere inside the first level, and he knew immediately it had to be from the ogres, communicating in their own guttural language. They were a tribal race from what little he knew, or had read about. Truthfully, they had been considered to be a *legendary* race until Sarion and Charadan had encountered one near Hawker Peak, the event which had served as a catalyst for everything else which followed.

Sarion tried to think things through, formulating his plan of entry. The ogres were large, and would have to stay on the lower level of the building, which was sizable. That meant it was to be avoided. If he could gain access to the second story, there lay his greatest chance of entering unseen. Still he waited, every sense straining to hear or see more, but the darkness was complete. The combination of mist and rain was too effective, concealing nearly anything outdoors, whether they be man or beast. Convinced he was alone, Sarion hurried to the back wall, merging with the structure like just another shadow, and that night, he was...He took off his sword and placed it in the high grass which edged the building, not daring to take it inside and risk the slightest noise.

He'd already spotted his means of entry. A window opened almost directly over his head, nearly twenty feet high. The barn was made up of long, thick pieces of wood, placed tightly together, but not so tight that he couldn't find a grip between the sections and climb, and that was his plan. Wasting no time, he started working his way upwards, fighting the slick wood and making certain his grip was sure before ascending further. Slowly he made progress, hardly daring to breathe as he went higher. It took him only a minute until he reached the side of the window, and he paused, out of options now except to chance looking inside. Careful not to make any sound, he glimpsed between the shutters, his eyes adjusting to the dim light coming from within. He was able to make out a small room with a closed wooden door, a rough-looking bed of sorts sitting inside, composed of straw and blankets. A lantern lay on top of a large crate, and there was a mixture of items alongside it. Sarion saw plates and utensils, scraps of food, and other items which didn't look too important. For all appearances, it was someone's bedroom, scantily furnished, but unquestionably one which was being used.

But by who? The mysterious man known as Chardoom? Could this be his resting area? It made sense. Upstairs, out of the way. There would be little reason for him to stay below with the ogres, whose presence was one of purely violence, acting as guardians and protectors at Chardoom's beck and call.

There was a latch on the window but it was already partially open. He pushed lightly, and the panel slid smoothly. Well, it would be an easy thing for him to enter soundlessly but he paused, debating his next course of action, to somehow find out who occupied the room.

Sarion stiffened then as he heard a noise from within.

Someone was coming. He would soon discover the answer to his question…

The door opened slowly and a figure materialized from the inner gloom.

But… it was a woman!

Sarion's eyes widened in surprise, and he watched as she moved over to the bed and sat, one hand rubbing her brow. Long black hair cascaded down her shoulders, and she was dressed in riding leathers.

What was a woman doing here of all places? And she appeared fairly young at that…Frowning, ideas about her presence flashed through Sarion's mind, and he immediately reached the conclusion that she was *not* staying here out of her own free will. In fact, it seemed highly likely that Chardoom kept her for his own purposes, none of which would be good. It seemed the most probable explanation under the circumstances. Sarion hesitated, trying to figure out his next move. The girl slumped into the bed, pulling the blankets across her body as she turned on her side, facing the wall. She appeared tired, ready to sleep, and Sarion thought her posture might just present himself with an opening. He waited long moments, knowing that the longer he stayed, the more perilous it became. Two minutes passed, another, and still he remained, patiently observing her.

Finally, it was time. Gritting his teeth, he moved the window open further, relying on his skills to remain quiet, the wind and rain helping to dampen any noise. In a moment he had the window fully opened, and he never hesitated, pushing himself through and quickly entering. It was a daring move, but soon he found himself inside, with the woman resting on the bed only a dozen feet away. She shifted, and Sarion froze, crouching to the floor catlike. Holding his breath, he remained in position, his eyes never leaving the arch of her back.

He couldn't chance her letting out a cry of surprise, as there was no way of knowing how near the enemies lurked. There could easily be someone right outside the door, guarding the level, or even resting themselves.

Sarion moved towards her, using his fingertips to balance himself. He stopped right next to the bed, and still she lay there, unmoving. He inched his way higher, never making a sound. A moment later and he was close enough to hear her breathing, slow and steady. She was on the verge of sleep, perhaps in the early stages. But he couldn't take any chances.

He had to move...

Quick and virtually noiseless he pounced, slapping one hand over her mouth, pulling her body toward him with his other arm. She flinched and then struggled, coming fully aware instantly as Sarion pressed himself against her to prevent movement, bringing his face directly before her own.

Her eyes opened wide in surprise and fright, Sarion stared hard into a pair of strikingly gray orbs, smoky and intense. Her features were beautiful, the skin pale and flawless, the shock of hair black as coal, long and tied behind her neck. He held her fast but not hard enough to hurt her. Sarion wanted her to see who he was first, hoping she would realize his motives.

She struggled for only a moment, going limp then, her face still showing amazement.

"Shh." Sarion whispered. "I'm here to help you."

She looked confused, and shook her head. "How..."

"I'm from Nighton. We must leave now." Sarion nodded towards the window. "You can't make a sound. Can I take my hand away?"

She moved her head in response as Sarion released his grip and backed away. He pointed toward the door. "Are they out there?"

She shook her head. "Across the hall," she

whispered. "But you're in grave danger. You must flee now, whoever you are."

"Come with me." Sarion took her hand, helping her from the bed and grabbing her cloak sitting next to the crate. "Out the window. I'll go first, you follow. Trust me to get you down."

She looked at the window fearfully, resisting, and then turned towards him. Sarion smiled, nodding as he edged her on. "I won't let you fall."

He went first, moving himself outside. Satisfied, he urged her forward, but she still hesitated, looking behind her at the door, then back at Sarion, indecisive.

"The Ravenor is in the woods somewhere." Sarion said.

She nodded. "I know. It won't be back yet."

"Let's go." Sarion lowered himself, making room for her. She followed tentatively, but he was right there, lending support while maintaining his own balance. It wasn't an easy task with the rain and wind, but he guided her down, using every inch of the wood beams to give him the leverage he needed. Their pace was slow, but she was physically capable of the action, which helped him tremendously. After what seemed like long minutes, they made it to the ground, Sarion finally breathing a huge sigh of relief.

But they were far from being out of danger, and he grabbed her hand, pulling her across the slick grass and toward the cover of other buildings. Never looking back, he didn't stop until they were out of view from any unfriendly eyes. He hoped that if there was something keeping watch, that she would already know of it and warn him, but she was silent. They passed through Gar-kiln, two with the night, Sarion keeping the pace brisk, his hand locked with hers. They continued this way for several minutes, and he knew they were finally past the immediate danger of the barn, at least.

Only then did he pause, turning to look at her.

"My name is Sarion. First Captain of Nighton."

She stood straight before him, her lean body appearing fit and untested by their flight. "I'm Wharla. But what brought you to Gar-kiln? Surely you know the death that waits here."

"I led a company of fighters from Nighton to seek out answers. Some I've found, but I think you'll be able to answer the rest for me. Were you taken prisoner? Are you all right?"

Wharla stared at him hard for a moment, and Sarion could imagine those smoky eyes boring into his own. She nodded. "I haven't been harmed, if that's what you mean."

"Good. But you were captured when your village was invaded?"

"No."

He stiffened. "No?"

Her answer startled him, and Sarion knew there was something odd with her response. Not taken prisoner by the ogres? But what then? There was nothing else that made sense, unless…

"You don't live here then?"

Wharla shook her head.

"You were here by chance? Traveling?"

"No."

"How did you get here? Captured from somewhere else?"

She said nothing, instead shaking her head again.

Sarion gripped her arm, hoping that he hadn't made a terrible mistake. "You came with the ogres. You're with them…" His heart dropped at his own revelation.

"Yes."

Immediately Sarion's knife slipped into his hand, and his mind raced at the implications that he had been foolishly trapped by the enemy. He looked around, searching for the direction of attack, but Wharla shook her head, staring hard at him.

"I will not betray you."

"How can I trust someone who walks beneath the shadow of the Dark Mage, in the company of evil?" Sarion was conceding nothing.

"You can't. But you'll understand when I tell you who I really am."

Sarion waited there, knowing he must do something. *Soon...*

"Chardoom is my father."

❈ ❈

Chensel sat in the high-backed wooden chair which was reserved for the Captain of Nighton, and at the moment, the entire weight of his position fell heavily upon his shoulders.

"Where is Sarion?"

Barimon was direct, not even bothering to sit. Their company had just arrived at the fortress, Chensel scarcely having time to prepare himself for the expected confrontation. They had all known that King Gregor would demand answers, and the sudden appearance of Thustan, his son, along with the mage himself, had now elevated the situation to an even higher level. Chensel knew it was a dangerous game that Sarion and himself were playing, realizing that the king would not just sit back and wait until Sarion eventually found his way to Daregil Keep. With Trencit in turmoil after the loss of Charadan, and the possibility of a war on both fronts, King Gregor would be under tremendous strain in advancing a strategy, and Chensel fully understood the importance of Sarion and the talisman he now carried with him.

"Is he here?"

Thustan spoke, his voice low, the man's face conceding nothing. Chensel knew he was well-respected and even tempered, popular himself along with the king. But the mage was a different story – a mysterious and elusive figure who was held in close regard by Gregor, sitting on the High Council, with virtually nothing else known about him, but only a fool would be ignorant of the man's position and power. Chensel stared at one and then the other, steeling himself for what could very well be a combative meeting. There was no point in steering them away from the truth. These men were much too shrewd to be misled, and his loyalty demanded otherwise...

Chensel took a deep breath before responding. "Sarion has departed from Nighton."

Barimon's eyes narrowed, the mage clearly angered by his answer. "Where has he gone and for what reason? King Gregor insisted that he come straight to Daregil Keep. We are here to bring him back."

"That's not possible at the moment," Chensel replied.

"What?" The mage leaned close, his arms gripping the table.

"Sarion is now Second Forester of Nighton, and I've sent him on a mission."

Thustan sat down on the chair directly at Chensel's right side, but Barimon remained standing.

"You've promoted him?" Thustan asked.

"Yes. He held a high ranking some years back, and with the loss of Jerol and others, I saw fit to enlist his aid once more. He is a leader of men."

The answer was true enough, but Chensel had no illusions that it would temper their attitudes.

"You had to know we need him in Daregil, yet you still advanced him?" The mage's eyes flashed.

"I did. We were assaulted at the western gate by a Killworm, and in the battle we managed to capture a prisoner who possessed information about our adversary."

By the expressions on both their faces, Chensel knew this was the first these men had heard of the attack, but Barimon's face only hardened more.

"And where is this prisoner now?" The mage pressed him.

"Dead. There was powerful magic involved."

Thustan looked over at Barimon, and they locked gazes for a long moment.

Thustan spoke. "This is ill news, Lord Chensel. We must hear of this attack on Nighton and Sarion's whereabouts. What happened to the Killworm?"

"We fought it in a terrible battle and many fighters were lost. In the end, we slew the beast."

"What? That's impossible." Barimon approached him, the cloak around him only adding to the mage's intimidating presence. "Every legend and story is clear in one thing – that the Killworm is magical in nature. You must be mistaken. Perhaps the creature fled on its own."

Chensel folded his hands together. "No, there is no mistake. It is our belief that the rod Sarion carries negated the creature's power, making it susceptible to our weapons. Even so, it was mighty in strength, and it took all of our efforts to defeat it. I've never seen anything so destructive."

He stopped there, unwilling to go further. Like Sarion, he thought the talisman possessed tremendous power, and now that he understood the primary focus for their arrival from Daregil Keep, it only bolstered his determination to prevent the rod's use. If Sarion felt it was too dangerous, then he was willing to place his entire faith in that conclusion, even though it would present a direct opposition to the royal command...and jeopardize his own position as well.

Thustan nodded. "Charadan made a rare find indeed, then. We must seek out Sarion and bring the rod to Daregil Keep at once."

"Sarion was the one wielding it in battle. What does he know about it?" Barimon's eyes bore into his own, and Chensel felt that the man was trying to probe the deepest recesses of his mind, attempting to unlock his most guarded thoughts.

He matched the man's gaze without flinching. "Only that it possessed strong magic, and might be able to help us fight the servants of our enemy, who we only know as the Dark Mage."

The room was silent, and Thustan rubbed the light growth of beard across his face, lost in thought, while Barimon's expression refused to soften, the man staring intently at him. Chensel felt the tension in the room, but he remained calm, his composure intact. He had not achieved his own position without reason, although he disliked the internal workings of the kingdom, and like the other fighters of Nighton he preferred the vast, unpredictable borderlands over the formal rigidity of greater Trencit and its unassailable capital.

"And you sent him away...to where?" Barimon finally broke the silence.

"To a remote village in the south called Gar-Kiln. The prisoner spoke of this before he died. The town was overcome by our enemy, and it is our belief that answers remain there yet. A hunting party was sent out, led by Sarion. They left days ago."

The scowl on Barimon's face clearly conveyed his disbelief and anger with Chensel's decision. Thustan frowned, but didn't appear to share the mage's forcefulness.

"While I understand your decisions, I don't agree with them," said Thustan. "Nighton's need is great, and we will do what we can to reinforce the westland. But concerning Sarion, there can be no further delay. My father's command is clear, and must not be disobeyed. We must seek him out immediately and take him back with us."

Barimon paced around the table, his arms stuffed inside the folds of his robe. "We'll never find him in the wilderness. A small hunting party can travel more swiftly and quietly than our company, plus we're unfamiliar with the territory, even with help from Nighton."

"Then what is your suggestion? We cannot abandon him." Thustan said.

"And we won't...Chensel, if he returns to Nighton during our absence, you are commanded to have him taken to Daregil Keep."

The First Forester nodded but said nothing, knowing that he had to follow direct orders from King Gregor.

"He could be anywhere by now, but still, we must pursue him." The mage paced back and forth, Chensel unable to feel the slightest amount of comfort in the man's presence.

"Well," he finally spoke, ceasing his movement. "We will try and rendezvous with Sarion after we hear more of this tale, as I'm sure there is much we need to learn first. I do have an idea of where our next destination lies. Have some food and wine brought to us. We'll be here for a while..."

The mage finally sat down and Chensel inwardly winced, knowing that at least concerning *this* statement, he was in total agreement...

The Summoning

Forlern's eyes glittered, sensing the chance to finally put an end to the savage creature that had killed so many, including his own two men, good and reliable fighters; his kindred in the Homeguard. They had injured the beast, and now it had left them a clear trail to follow. His pulse raced from the heat of recent battle and he was weary, but these things he could put aside. He had been trained well, by some of the finest weapons masters to be found anywhere, but this harsh routine was a secondary factor in Forlern's overall capabilities as his confidence and determination reared up. Forlern had quickly risen above others who had received identical training, and his superiors had not been blind to his talent, including General Charadan, although Forlern had been ignorant of this observation up until the leader's death in Grammore. Even then, it had not come to him immediately.

But after his arrival at Daregil Keep and subsequent promotion, his perspective had changed drastically...

He looked at Questron, nodding.

"We've no time to waste. Like any other creature, it will seek shelter to escape from us and nurse its wounds. When we track it down, we can finally put an end to it, and seek revenge for our fallen comrades."

Questron signaled to his men, but some had already broken off, wasting no time in pursuing their deadly prey. Joining the Lastrad Captain, Forlern hurried alongside of him, the pair surrounded in both front and back to ward off any surprise assault. Forlern knew how capable these guards were, but none of them had a chance against such a monster in hand-to-hand combat. No, their hope was in numbers and strategy, and so far it had paid off, although the price in blood had been high. They raced down the wide streets of the city, soon leaving the Vanyair Market proper, gradually heading deeper into Lastrad and into the residential area. There were thousands of places where this creature could be hiding, Forlern knew. Even with the Lastradian army at his disposal, Questron had failed to discover the creature's lair, or anything else about its nature. The man was shrewd and cunning, and Forlern fully realized his precarious position. Anyone could be replaced...The Gran Barshara had made a direct appeal to King Gregor, who had sent Forlern to Lastrad in order to hunt the creature and put an end to its reign of terror. And although Forlern had added his own perspective to the dangerous situation, it had been a stroke of luck for them to have caught up with it. Sooner or later Questron's men would have confronted it, he was certain.

But that wasn't the extent of it. Forlern knew that his own presence might end up giving them just enough of an advantage to tip the scales in their balance, and he couldn't forget the blade which he now carried, one that could ultimately prove the final difference if the monster was indeed magical in nature. As they swept along through the night, Forlern wrestled with this very notion. From what he'd seen of the beast, it had failed to display any capabilities which could only be explained by something of magical origin, the strongest argument being the fact that they had wounded it badly, perhaps enough to kill it. So this meant that the beast was of normal flesh and blood, and although it was assuredly a deadly predator from Grammore, it was able to be killed with their weapons.

They hurried onwards, one of Questron's men

signaling back that the trail was still fresh. At times Forlern saw dark splotches on the stone, blood stains left from the fleeing predator. It was wounded badly, and must be getting weak. It was only a matter of time, probably minutes, when they would catch up to it. Forlern's greatest concern was that it would climb over the walls of the city at some point and try to make good its escape, and after another ten minutes of pursuit, his fear came to light.

The company halted before one of the inner barracks which housed soldiers from the inner guard and Questron moved forward, demanding answers. One of the lead fighters rushed back to him.

"Captain Questron, the trail has disappeared. Our trackers have lost the trail."

Questron's face darkened, and Forlern knew it was an unacceptable answer. Before he could speak, Questron pointed to the buildings surrounding them.

"I want men on both sides of the street. We already know that the beast can scale walls..."

Before he could finish his sentence, a warning horn blared from their right, behind the barracks and coming from the great wall which enclosed Lastrad. Battlements and guard houses were scattered evenly around the entire girth of the large city, and Forlern knew immediately that the creature was trying to escape.

"Hurry!" Questron shouted. "Through the building and up the walls. We can't let the monster leave the city!" He gave several orders, including for men on horseback to ride to the front gates and cut off the fleeing monster. The company passed the guards at the entranceway to the barracks, Questron mobilizing all the men to aid in the pursuit of the predator, some accompanying them, others rushing to the main gates. It was chaotic for several minutes, Forlern frustrated at not knowing where the creature was and what exactly it was doing. They bounded up the stairwells which led to the wall, soon exiting the building through its upper reaches and entering the cooler night air once more.

It didn't take long for Forlern to discover the creature's whereabouts. Men were positioned along the great wall, bows bent and arrows singing in the night. He pointed, his keen eyes immediately spotting the strange beast as it made its way higher, only a dozen yards from the top. A set of stairs led to the ramparts, and Questron signaled for them to move, already bounding up the first steps. In a rush, the company plunged upwards, Forlern finding himself in the middle, the creature blocked by the Lastrad Guard. Cursing beneath his breath, he didn't want the creature out of his sight, not even for a second. They had come this far in tracking and pursuing it. If the monster somehow managed to avoid death or capture, then it could slip away in the night into the vast lands bordering the city.

Determined that it would not happen, Forlern pushed ahead, shoving aside a pair of men before him and gaining the upper causeway with the lead, Questron at his side.

"There!" The Lastrad captain shouted. "Don't let it escape!"

Volley after volley was launched at the thing, but it weaved back and forth, avoiding most of the deadly darts. Several struck it, and Forlern saw the trail of blood staining the wall. It had to be severely injured, he knew, but he was still amazed at its endurance and dexterity, even in its weakened condition. Still, they had no idea what manner of beast it was, and it could possess abilities beyond their knowledge. It had already killed hundreds of citizens from Lastrad, and what bothered Forlen even more was the systematic way in which this had been achieved. It was not just some mindless beast from the Lowlands, but something which

116

had a deadly purpose behind its actions, and certainly intelligence.

The creature now reached the top of the wall, where several guards immediately engaged it. Questron shouted a warning but the company watched helplessly as the monster struck first, using its speed to behead two of the men. More fighters came at it from both sides, but the creature had no intention of prolonging the battle. Instead, it now disappeared over the edge, clambering down the outer side and vanishing from view. Cursing in frustration, Questron bounded up the stairs and moments later the party reached the wall, all of them staring warily into the night as they saw the creature's lean form crawling headfirst down the side. In a few seconds it would be on the ground, with nothing between it and the surrounding trees and plains.

"Can nothing stop it?" Questron smacked the wall with one hand, his men continuing to rein arrows at the beast, which would soon be out of their reach.

"There's nothing left to do here," said Forlern. "We must track it from outside the city now."

Questron nodded, gesturing to one of his commanders. "We move in a minute. I need to coordinate our defense."

Nodding, Forlern stared into the darkness, watching as the creature moved deeper into the shadows, knowing that the hunting party would be on its way shortly. Questron's men were already moving to track it down, while they would follow after with a larger company. He knew that once they managed to catch up with it, they would have the final advantage, and it should prove enough. Still...he knew these creatures fairly well by now, and realized that they were capable of anything. He would certainly be taking no chances. Standing there impatiently, he waited for a few long minutes until Questron returned.

"We'll take horses with us and a company of fighters with supplies. It's not going to escape."

His voice was low and deadly serious. Forlern knew that the Lastrad captain had been under tremendous pressure as the killings continued unabated, and the man had a personal score to settle with it. His position might very well depend on it. The Gran Barshara had enormous resources to spend in providing for protection of the city, but if someone could not perform their job, then they were replaced. Yes, Questron had many reasons to succeed in putting an end to the monster at last.

And Forlern had his own score to settle as well...

❋ ❋

"What?"

Sarion was stunned by her answer as he held her arm, keeping the woman at bay. Had he heard her right? Chardoom was her father? Then what did that make her, except for someone under the cloak of evil that was the Dark Mage?

"He is my father. I travel with him because I have no choice in the matter."

"Despite all these terrible things he's done while serving his cowardly master? How could you?" Sarion felt his anger stemming hotly to the surface, outraged as to how anyone could keep such company, father or not. Instinctively he mistrusted her, and woman or not, could not let down his guard. He knew nothing of her, whether she was being truthful or otherwise, and he'd walked into enough traps to realize that this could very well be yet another. And the more he thought about it, he also understood something else...She might prove invaluable to them, especially if she knew some of the dark one's plans to move against the westland and Trencit. Yes, he thought. If anyone had answers to the secrets of Garkiln, she would hold them.

"Let's go. We're getting out of here now."

Wharla pushed against him. "Wait, I can't leave."

"You can and you will."

"My father will come after you with the Ravenor. He'll be furious. Do you know what that creature can do?"

"I have a pretty good idea." Sarion pulled her along, and she reluctantly followed. "Quiet. If you give us away, there will be no further doubt as to where your loyalty lies."

"But I don't want to see anyone else hurt."

Sarion stared at her for a moment, shaking his head, holding her by the arm. "Let's go."

He hurried across the grass, moving towards the closest buildings and the deeper shadows. The rain had dwindled to a relentless mist, but this time he was grateful for its presence, wispy trailers seeping between tree and shrub, clinging to the sides of the homes, enveloping all in its fold. Sarion never paused, towing his reluctant captive along, keeping one eye on his surroundings, the other on her. She remained silent, her face expressionless. He had no idea what her motives were, if any, but she was by far the most important find which had fallen his way against the manipulations of the Dark Mage and his minions. Distasteful as it was because she was a woman, he couldn't let that fact overshadow their need for useful information.

The minutes passed as they wound their way through the village, Sarion never slowing, wondering how long it would take for Chardoom to discover that Wharla was missing. With any luck, it might be overnight, and that could give them all the time they needed to make good their escape. He then thought of Fortisel, and wondered if the man knew anything about Wharla. Yes, he thought. He would be able to confirm what she'd told him, which was little so far. But it might prove to be enough.

For now...

Answers would be forthcoming. Or so he hoped. He glanced over at her, but she continued staring ahead, moving fluidly and having little difficulty. She possessed an air of confidence about her, and Sarion wondered what else they would discover. He knew she could turn out to be as evil as any of the other servants of the Dark Mage, and this was the strongest possibility. Yet the optimistic side of him considered the alternative. Perhaps she was telling the truth, and was not involved in any of her father's atrocities.

He shook his head, finding it hard to imagine that she was guiltless in all of this. Well, he wasn't able to think about it further. Time pressed against him, and he worried about the other group led by Valadire and Geld Rinn. Most likely they had seen the Ravenor as well, and were even now making good their escape from Gar-kiln. If fortune was on their side, they would be free of the dread village soon and into the surrounding wilderness. Chardoom would discover his missing daughter, and the chase would be on. Nighton was many miles and long days away, and the country was difficult, but no less difficult for the emissaries of the Dark Mage. At least on horseback, they could hope to outrun them. The ogres could travel through wilderness, but would take time, and the Ravenor was a monstrous beast, lumbering and vast. He doubted whether it would even be sent to pursue them. Sarion would question Wharla more after he rejoined the others, and find out what he could about their enemies. It seemed as good a plan as any at the moment.

The minutes slipped past and at last they found themselves nearing the edge of the village, the wooden fence rearing up before them. He paused, gathering his bearings for a second, then moved to the left, where he quickly found the rope. Peering cautiously about, he made sure they were alone, and then he pulled on the rope, making sure it was secure. He finally released Wharla's arm, whispering.

"It is here that we came in. My men will be waiting past the barn with our horses. Can you make it up by yourself?"

"I'll ask you again. Leave me here. I can distract my father enough so that his attention stays focused on the village and give you enough time to escape."

"What about the Ravenor?"

She shook her head. "It will find your trail; sooner or later, but by then you'll be long gone. I don't think he'll be able to come after you. His master has other plans in store for him from what I know. But if I'm missing, he'll send the monster after you. He won't let me be taken, regardless of his master's wishes."

Sarion hesitated, indecisive. "Doesn't he have to be near the beast to control it?"

Wharla seemed to consider his question for a moment, and then nodded. "Yes. But I don't know how far his power reaches with the staff. It's a terrible risk to take. You have no chance of defeating the Ravenor." She stared at him.

Sarion felt the urgency of his situation, but he refused to make a move yet. He still needed more information. Or rather, he needed to hear what she had to say. There was no way of knowing the truth of her words.

"Do you know what Chardoom's orders are? What the Dark Mage commands him to do?"

"I've asked him, although he tells me little. I'm a prisoner, with no place else to go. Please leave me here to my fate."

Sarion waited, then pressed her further. "Tell me anything you know."

"My father mentioned something about going to the east soon. That's all I know."

"East? That's not much help," Sarion muttered. "So you claim that Chardoom will come after us once he finds you missing. Even if the Dark Mage commands otherwise?"

Wharla appeared confused. "I don't know for sure, but it's what I feel in my heart…" She started to speak further, then stopped. She had a dusky loveliness about her, and Sarion found himself both alarmed and appalled at the same time. She was a paradox, and he had no way to unravel the truth of who she really was. He felt both an aversion and a strange attraction to this enigmatic woman…

"You're going with me. That's my decision. Friend or enemy, I can't afford to leave you behind. Up you go. I'll carry you myself if you refuse."

Wharla stared at him for a moment, as if measuring his resolve, and then conceded, saying nothing more. Sarion helped her up the first few feet before finding out that it was an easy task for her, an observation that he made a mental note of for later. He followed right behind, scrambling up quickly, then he waited until she was safely on the ground. Sarion then cut the rope with his dagger, gathering the coils, and jumped down the remaining few feet.

Holding her arm, he motioned her forward, and they hurried down the pathway, moving silently through the hushed forest. The rain had finally ended, and the earth was soft and yielding beneath their feet. Sarion gazed ahead, looking for danger, and then he grabbed

Wharla by the arm, clamping one hand over her mouth. Startled, she looked over at him, but Sarion was already creeping into the trees.

Something had moved ahead of them, down the trail and near the barn. He saw the building looming eerily in the distance, and again he saw movement, coming straight towards them now. A figure approached, unaware of their presence. Closer it moved, nearly on top of their hiding spot in the bushes. As it came alongside of them, Sarion placed a hand on his sword, uncertain for a moment, and then he relaxed.

It was Piril.

Sarion emerged from the tree line with Wharla at his side. His sudden appearance took the fighter by surprise and the man pivoted in a flash, weapon pointed at them both.

"Hail Piril."

After a moment's hesitation, the fighter lowered his sword. "Captain Sarion. You surprised me, and I'm glad you've returned. But who is this with you? Yet another villager?"

"I'm glad as well, but we're not out of danger. Look after her. She's a prisoner."

Piril never questioned his orders, and immediately went to her side.

"It's time we return and find the others. I'm sure Chertron will be anxious."

"Indeed."

The three of them hurried along the path, the night quiet and hunkered down around them. Sarion wondered about Chardoom and where the Ravenor might be, but he had no time to dwell on it. They glided along, entering the high grass, and Sarion knew they were only a short distance from where he'd left the others. Only a minute passed when he saw someone crouched ahead, keeping guard. It was Birtilik, and the three joined the Nighton hunter.

"Hail, Captain Sarion."

Nodding to the fighter, Sarion paused. "Any word from Valadire's group?"

"Nothing yet. They're still in Gar-kiln."

Frowning, Sarion turned around, looking back where they had come from.

Then Wharla spoke, undisguised urgency in her words. "Did you send other men into the village?"

He nodded, a feeling of uneasiness coming over him from her tone and the expression on her face.

"Where are they?" She demanded.

"On the far side of the village. They were to make their way around and rendezvous with us at the center."

"They are in great peril then."

Sarion felt as if he'd been struck. "They know about the Ravenor."

"The Ravenor isn't what they need to fear. It's the Crage, Chardoom's messenger."

Sarion's blood went cold at her words...

❀ ❀

After they heard the call, Valadire froze in place, signaling the others to back away. They were near the center of the village, and had neither seen or heard anything unusual, nothing to give the impression that anything remained in Gar-kiln, alive or dead.

Nothing, until now...

They moved between a pair of homes on their side of the street, burying themselves within the shadows. Whatever had sounded that horn was nothing they wanted to meet. Indecisive about his next move,

The Summoning

Valadire knew that their presence might very well have been compromised. He wished fervently that Sarion and his men had not been discovered, but it was impossible to know. He peered around the edge of the building, but nothing moved within the mist and haze, but as he looked, he saw a faint glow beyond his vision, where the street curved off to the right, something which had to be from a light source.

He needed to know what was out there before deciding on what to do next.

Turning, he signaled for Garlis to come forward, a veteran hunter who had lived near Hawker Peak for years, and knew the dangers of living beneath the shadow of the Ridgeline as well as anyone.

Pointing ahead, the fighter knew what was being asked without having to question. Nighton hunters were well-trained and disciplined, and seldom needed to ask about their orders. Hurrying off, he made his way down the street, heading for the source of the glimmer. Geld Rinn came near, nodding as he followed the man's progress. Valadire tapped him on the shoulder, cutting at the air with one hand. Knowing what to do, the young fighter followed after Garlis, who was nearly out of view.

Geld Rinn moved wraithlike in the mist, picking a spot where he could pause. He caught sight of Garlis as the man ducked between two buildings, and then he reemerged moments later, his head darting about in both directions, making ready to continue. Geld Rinn's keen eyes watched his comrade, waiting until there was more distance separating them; a routine part of their hunt to minimize danger to the group. Satisified, Geld Rinn was ready to follow after, when something huge materialized from the shadows of the building where Garlis had paused, and with frightening speed it lunged after the unsuspecting man, seizing him in his place. Geld Rinn felt a cry lodge in his throat, watching as Garlis was crushed where he stood, his attacker silent and deadly. His instincts screamed at him in warning, and the young fighter moved, dodging into a narrow corridor between a pair of ramshackle buildings, then running to the back, feeling the sweat already soaking his shirt. Garlis was dead, there was no question, and if he had been any closer, he would be as well. Whatever it was that had killed the fighter had been swift and efficient, wasting no time in disposing its prey.

Geld Rinn prayed that Valadire had seen his action. Garlis had been out of Valadire's vision, but he wasn't certain if the Nighton Forester could still see *him*.

He had to return to the others and get them out of there, but he had no idea if the creature had seen him before he left. It had given no indication, at least. As he ran, he looked over his shoulder, listening for signs of pursuit. Whatever lurked back there was a dangerous predator, something from the lowlands, and most likely under the power of the Dark Mage and his servants. Geld Rinn had seen enough of it in those few short moments to realize that their best hope was to flee, and not have to fight it in a pitched battle. He was convinced that it would prove too much for them. He didn't need to see more...

Geld Rinn reached the back of the property, finding it enclosed within a high fence made of wood. He knifed his way between high grass and scattered bushes, searching for a path through. Although in disrepair, the fence was solid, and he went into the far corner, hoisting himself up by placing his boots between several loose gaps. Agile and quick, the fence proved no obstacle for the young fighter, and he was over in moments, finding himself in a grassway of sorts, with buildings in every direction. Gar-kiln was a sizable village, without any real design in its makeup. Outlying homes sat near the encircling wall, with scattered properties leading in towards the main road at its center. The properties were all different, with some having large plots of land including hedgerows and trees, while others huddled together, connected or built on top of each other as if to fend off the wilderness outside and the looming shadow of the Ridgeline. He hastened back towards where the others would be waiting, hoping they had already fled, but knowing he must reach them, not leaving it to chance. He moved cautiously through the darkness, eyes and ears keen to anything out of place, and he went past several more buildings, trying to regain their previous vantage point. He pulled up then, hearing something in the distance from the center of the village. There were two quick shouts, and he felt fingers of ice claim his back and neck.

There could only be one reason for such cries, he knew. The creature had found Valadire and the others…

Geld Rinn kept going behind the buildings, thinking to return the way they had come. He didn't know what had happened, but knew the best plan for his own survival as well as the others was to elude the creature, and try and help his companions later. Hurrying along, he weaved in and out of the mist like a comrade to the night himself, noiseless and unseen. A thick copse of woods appeared before him, a section of trees within the village which had never been cut down. He made for it, plunging directly inside and beneath the overhanging branches which were dripping with moisture from the rain. Keeping near the edge, he kept looking towards the center of the village, hoping to see something which might shed some light on what was happening with Valadire and the others, but all he could see was the endless gloom and the silhouettes of the various structures enshrouded in the mist, like a half-imagined vision of a forbidden landscape.

Another sound reached him which sounded like a muffled cry, but he couldn't be sure. Biting his lip, the only thing he could do was to keep moving. The creature had been quick and deadly, and he held no false hopes that he could have stood against it. Accomplished with sword and bow, he was a skilled fighter in his own right, but the predators from Grammore were an enemy that far outmatched the hunters of Nighton. Only in greater numbers did they have a chance, and even then it was no certainty.

He wished Sarion were here now. *He* was an equalizer against these monsters, his weapons mastery uncanny, his confidence unshakable. Sarion was someone who Geld Rinn looked up too, and hoped he could someday imitate, or at least try to…

But Sarion wasn't here, and Geld Rinn had no time for regrets. Not if he were to stay alive.

Gliding through the trees for what seemed like an endless amount of time, it was only minutes later when he came out the other side where he paused for a moment, examining the landscape. Nothing moved, and he left the cover of the small woods, hurtling towards a line of buildings that he recognized from earlier. Quickly gaining the corridor between the nearest pair, he hurried to the front, peering around the corner. The street in front was empty, the night soundless. He went to his left, back in the direction from where they had entered, knowing that the gate would be near.

Running in a crouch, he kept to the side of the homes, darting behind everything that offered concealment, wondering again what had happened to Valadire and the others, when a figure appeared from across the street, materializing from the mist and dark. Geld Rinn ducked beneath a cluster of bushes, flattening to the earth and staring in the distance. He made out the shape of a man, who was also attempting to remain as obscure as possible, but moving steadily towards the outer gate. Geld Rinn was certain it was one of his companions, and he lifted off the ground, hurrying along from his own side of the street. After several moments, the man disappeared, vanishing into an alley between a pair of two story homes. Geld Rinn looked down the street towards the middle of Gar-kiln, weighing the dangers of attempting a crossing. Although nothing moved, there were too many shadowed corners, too many hiding places for him to take the risk. Instead, he continued down his side, deciding to wait until there was more cover. Whoever was out there had the same goal in mind, he knew; to escape from the creature which pursued somewhere behind. Better that they both do their best in trying to leave the village, where they could meet up later.

It was a harrowing flight, and Geld Rinn used all his skill to remain silent and out of sight, hoping that the Grammore predator was elsewhere. Several more minutes passed, and the homes broke up now, fewer with larger spans of property separating them. Without warning, the outer fence reared up in the night, and he looked about to see if it was where they had entered. It looked unfamiliar, and his sense of urgency grew frantic. If the creature caught up with him here, he would be trapped. He moved along the fence, looking for a way of access. He had no rope with him, and his only option was to find a place where he could get a foothold and climb up. But nothing offered a way for him, and he found himself following the fence further. It had been built to keep out creatures both big and small, and overall was solidly built. After several tense minutes of searching, he found a spot where an old tree sat nearby, one of its branches leaning against the fence after having been split by age or a chance lightning strike. Gazing over his shoulder, the night remained quiet, and he scrambled upwards, his hands and boots finding sure footing in the damp, mossy bark. Quick, quick, he told himself. Soon he had reached the spot where the branch hung over the fence, and he used it as a bridge to advance. The limb swayed beneath his weight, and he had to stop several times, making sure he didn't fall to the ground. He was able to gain the fence, and he skirted the top, looking down the other side, hoping something was there to shorten his fall. Trees loomed close, and he stared at the closest. A large, hooked shaped branch hung only a few feet away, and without pausing, he adjusted himself, angling towards it. After hesitating only a second, he pushed off from the fence, grabbing the branch with both arms, hanging there for a moment before working his way inwards. It easily held his weight, and shortly he was climbing down the thick trunk and on the ground once more. Garkiln was behind him, and he moved quickly away. Even without the fence to guide him, his own tracking ability soon led him to where they had entered. He didn't want to risk using his lantern, so he worked his way through the woods and brush, passing into a gap that looked familiar. He looked around, making sure it was empty before going into it, never seeing the figure that waited there to one side. He was almost upon it when he discovered he wasn't alone in the clearing, his sword instantly in his hand.

"Wait." A voice hissed in the night, and his fear turned to relief, as he recognized Valadire's tall form looming before him.

"It's me, Valadire. I thought you had been lost with Garlis."

"I'm glad to see you. I didn't know what happened back there after the creature took him."

Valadire shook his head. "We saw you run, and I knew there would be only one reason for you to act like that without a word. I realized that something had attacked Garlis and you had no choice but to flee yourself. Shades, what a monster."

"There was nothing I could have done to save him." Geld Rinn lowered his head for a moment." The creature attacked so swiftly. It looked huge. So what happened?"

"Listen, we can't stay. It's not safe anywhere near this cursed village." He grabbed Geld Rinn's shoulder, moving him forward.

"The others..." Geld Rinn started.

"Gone."

"Gone?"

"All of them. The beast hunted us through the streets and we separated. I knew it was too much for us and our only hope was to split up and escape. It nearly had me behind one house. I saw it pass in the dark, quiet and deadly. I heard it take the others..." He faltered for a moment.

"The men. Taken like that, without a chance? If we would have fought it together we would all be dead."

Geld Rinn felt the emptiness like a black void in the pit of his stomach. Valadire and himself were the only ones left. Their group had been decimated, and he had not even lifted a weapon in their defense. And what did that mean for Sarion and his group? How had they fared?

Were *any* of them still alive?

Sarion finally made his way back to their makeshift camp, with Piril and Wharla in tow, Bertilik remaining on guard. Chertron was the first to see him, the tough fighter exhaling a deep sigh of relief.

"Sarion, my friend. You've returned at last, and with someone else now. I was worried."

"Me too." Sarion clapped him on the shoulder. He looked around, spotting Lassel and Erek approach, the latter muttering something beneath his breath. There was no sign of anyone else. Understanding his look immediately, Chertron shook his head.

"Still not back."

Sarion felt the coldness moving along his body, his concern for the others bearing down on him like a numbing weight. "There's another creature lurking in the village where Valadire and his men were to go. I only hope they managed to escape before it found them. What can you tell me about this beast?"

He turned to Wharla, who now was at the center of everyone's focus. Fortisel then came forward, holding a piece of dried meat in one hand. Sarion stared at the villager, searching for some sign of recognition, but the man was expressionless. Seizing the opportunity himself, he pointed to him.

"Fortisel, do you know of this woman?"

The man shook his head. "Who is she? I know everyone from Gar-kiln. I've never seen her before."

Sarion nodded, thinking the matter over for a moment, but time was something he didn't have. Not with Valadire still in the cursed village...

"What of the Crage?"

Wharla matched his gaze. "It is Chardoom's messenger. It brings back orders from his master. It's a monstrous creature, large and cunning. Too deadly for your men."

"Who is this woman, Sarion? And how does she know such things?" Chertron stepped forward a pace, as if seeing her for the first time.

Sarion waved him off for a moment, his hand

gripping the hilt of his sword. "All that matters right now is that Valadire and the others are still back there, with no idea that this thing is waiting on the other side of the village. I'm going back for them."

"Wait." Chertron leaned close. "We don't know if we can even believe her. But regardless, it's too late to warn them. Once they heard the Ravenor, they surely would have fled. And it grieves me to say this, but I must..." His voice trailed off, and Sarion already knew what the fighter was going to say next. "If this beast found them, they would have already fought it by now." He shook his head sadly. "That battle would be over, and you know it. How many more risks can you afford to keep taking?"

Sarion was silent, gritting his teeth. Chertron moved to his side, pulling him away from the others, his voice low.

"You lead this company, and are now a Captain of Nighton as well. We all knew the risks we faced coming here. We're all fighters, struggling against the forces massed against us. It's our chosen path, and we do so willingly. None of us can be sure we'll return from any mission. But you can't always insist on placing yourself at the forefront of danger, Sarion. What happens to Nighton if you are lost? And to Trencit? You cannot defeat the Dark Mage single-handedly. Think of these things before returning to the village."

Sarion hesitated, his eyes boring into those of his companion.

And however distasteful the logic, he knew that Chertron was right. In the past few weeks, he had led many battles against the minions of their enemy, at times taking the entire risk upon his own shoulders, and barely escaping with his life more than once. It had been a dangerous move going into the barn, the very heart of the enemy stronghold in Gar-kiln, as he tried to find information that could help their cause. Yes, he had escaped unharmed, and with someone who might yet prove to be invaluable, but again, it had been extremely perilous. What would Chensel have said about his act?

He thought he knew the answer to that question without asking…

Sarion looked over at the seasoned fighter, someone who had proven his own worth numerous times over, and found that there was no reasonable argument to again risk himself by going back into the village. As a Captain of Nighton, he had responsibilities that demanded sounder action.

"All right." Sarion nodded. "I can't argue with you, although it pains me to wait here until they return."

"I know, my friend. I feel the same way. It's a bitter life we lead, but it's our choice, and one that I have never regretted. Not once. Every turn could be my last, and my wife might find herself widowed, my children orphaned. But it is for my family that I do what I must. Them, and the innocent people of Trencit who rely on our strength and courage."

Sarion clapped him on the arm, then turned around, looking at the others, who had given them a respectful distance. He waved for Lassel to approach, and bent close to her.

"Lassel, you're in charge of guarding Wharla. Until I say otherwise, she is not to be left alone for any reason. I want you to search her. Hidden weapons, belongings, strange markings, anything that looks out of the ordinary. The servant of the Dark Mage at Nighton had a piece of metal fused into his skin. If she bears something unusual, you will be able to recognize it."

She nodded to him, her face displaying her normal look of confidence and determination. Sarion returned to the others.

"Wharla, you'll be treated as our prisoner until I

decide otherwise. Lassel will ward you for now. You're to be searched. Cooperate with her."

Wharla stared at him, frowning, but said nothing. Lassel held her by the arm, then pointed toward the other side of the clearing. Sarion made out Jurit's form several dozen paces away, the fighter still warding the horses.

"The rest of you prepare to leave immediately. If the creatures of Gar-kiln discover our presence, we will strike east and put as much distance as possible between us and them. The ogres move on foot, and although they travel quickly, they are no match for us on horseback. I don't know about the Ravenor. The beast is enormous, but I can't imagine that it can outrun us. As soon as Valadire and the others return, we depart."

He walked past them, going towards his own horse and pack. His stomach rumbled with hunger and he was thirsty, his throat dry. Piril shadowed him, and Chertron followed after, Ereck a step behind. Sarion gestured to Piril, pointing to Lassel and Wharla as they moved towards the surrounding treeline.

"Stay close. Keep them within sight."

Piril nodded and hurried off. Ereck came forward now, rubbing his hands together.

"Well, fighter? Was it as I told you?"

Sarion didn't answer, eager for some food and water before circumstances might have them racing away once more. After finding what he was looking for, he slumped to the ground and leaned back against a tree, sighing heavily.

"Gar-kiln is a haven for monsters and nightmares. Ogres remain, and we saw the beast known as the Ravenor. We also found out that the one who controls it is called Chardoom, a servant of the Dark Mage. He carries a staff of some type from which he directs it. Although we escaped detection, I entered a barn where they keep quarters, where I found Wharla."

"She was with the ogres?" Chertron asked in surprise.

Sarion nodded, hesitating for a moment. "She told me that Chardoom is her father."

"What? Shades…" Ereck muttered. "She can't be trusted, fighter!"

"I know. I'm undecided about how much I can believe her. She didn't resist being taken, although she pleaded with me to leave her there, claiming that Chardoom will follow us with the Ravenor. But she seemed uncertain of it as well. I really don't know what to make of her. She says that she has no part in all the terrible acts committed by her father, but travels with them against her will. Wharla says she has no other family, and nowhere to go regardless."

"You would think she would have been overjoyed to escape. I don't like this at all." Chertron rubbed his chin. "It could very well be some kind of a trap."

"I thought the same from the beginning. But I couldn't leave her behind, either. Friend or foe, she has knowledge of our enemy, and that's the most important thing we need right now. Besides, I don't think she poses any risk by herself. Although she seems capable enough, she still is only one woman against a company of fighters."

"Unless she carries magic." Ereck added. "Dark magic."

"If she does, then Lassel will discover its nature. She'll know if something looks important, or out of place. From what we've already learned, the servants of our enemy bear distinct markings or talismans. We know what to look for."

"You hope," Ereck muttered. "Many assumptions, fighter. Ones filled with grave danger."

The Summoning

"And I need no reminder from you or anyone else," Sarion snapped back. "I make choices for the defense of the westland and Trencit. Many have fallen to the Dark Mage and his servants. I take none of this lightly. If you want to be of help, go question her yourself."

They all looked over in her direction, Piril staying at the edge of the trees, giving the two some privacy, but not enough that he would be too far to help if necessary. In the middle of the clearing, Fortisel paced about, looking nervously back toward the village. Sarion shook his head, wondering about him as well. He had seemed genuine enough, but treachery had been reaked against them before, and could certainly happen again. Chertron followed his gaze, nodding.

"I've been watching him as well since we left the village. I think it goes without saying that we all keep our eyes open to them both."

"I think he's had ample time to betray us while we were back there. And it would have been a stroke of incredible fortune for us to have searched his particular house. No one could have known that we were coming."

Sarion was confident in his statement. They had left Nighton almost immediately, and had not been tracked all those miles in the wilderness. No, the Dark Mage might have suspected that they would eventually find Gar-kiln, but not have knowledge of where and when they would arrive, if ever. His power was great, but the distance between Nighton and Grammore was not easily overcome. Of course, the winged beasts might travel swifter than a man on horseback. Still...

"Chertron, I want you to question Fortisel, and search him as well. Explain that we've faced treachery from our enemy. He should give you no trouble."

The lean fighter nodded, moving away.

Sarion finished eating, feeling more uneasy with

Valadire still missing. Restless, it was all he could do to restrain himself and head off back to the cursed village, but his mind told him otherwise. Every minute they remained there increased the chance that their presence would be discovered, especially with Wharla missing. Feeling the weariness in his body and limbs, Sarion closed his eyes, his mind unable to find peace, still lost in a vortex of emotions. The minutes passed, but he was unaware of the passage of time, his heart filled with a slow rush of anxiety over what to do next. He could not leave without the others, barring an outright attack, which was entirely possible this close to the village. Weary or not, he would have no real rest until his men were back, and they had put a safe distance between themselves and Gar-kiln.

Sarion then heard a commotion coming from the far side of the small clearing, and he opened his eyes. Raising himself up, he spotted several figures approach as they emerged from the gloom.

It was Valadire at last! Following directly behind was Geld Rinn.

But they were alone...

His heart sinking, Sarion looked about for any of the others, but as Valadire came towards him, the fighter shook his head, speaking first.

"We were attacked. Geld Rinn and I were the only ones to make it out."

Stunned, Sarion closed his eyes. He instantly knew they had been attacked by the creature called the Crage. Wharla had been right. More of his men killed, the original hunting party which had set out from Nighton now dwindled down to a fraction of its starting strength.

"I'm sorry, Sarion. There was nothing we could do but flee, or else we would have shared the same fate."

Geld Rinn approached. Valadire continued. "We

heard the great call of the beast, and I sent Garlis ahead to scout. He was taken by something swift and deadly, and Geld escaped into the backyards as I ordered the rest of the men to retreat. I knew we had no chance in a fight with any of the Grammore predators, but we were hunted and found. By design or misfortune, I know not. My men are gone."

Gone, Sarion thought, horrified. Four men, strong and seasoned fighters from Nighton, protectors of the westland. Four more families that would never see their loved ones again...

"I'm sorry," Valadire repeated. "They were under my guard, and I've failed to keep them safe."

"Enough of that," Sarion snapped. "This entire group is mine to command, so the responsibility falls on my shoulders alone. Chensel knew the risk as did the rest of us."

Valadire was silent, and Sarion continued, fighting down the feeling of rage he felt building deep inside. "It's time we make good our own escape as well. Everything is ready to go. Gar-kiln holds nothing more for us, so let's hope that the sacrifice of our comrades will help Nighton against the evil of the Dark Mage. The sorcerer has more blood on his hands, and he *will* be made to answer for it."

No one challenged his statement.

"We must flee this evil place. Our presence is no longer hidden. The beast will warn its master."

Sarion pointed towards Lassel and Wharla as they materialized from the treeline, Piril bringing up the rear. Gesturing to the horses, Sarion ordered everyone to gather up the few remaining belongings and mount their steeds. Time pressed sorely against them, and he didn't want to stay in that cursed place a moment longer than necessary. Chertron went for Bertilik, and Jurit ushered Wharla and Fortisel to their own horses.

And then they all heard the horn echoing in the night, a faint, chilling blast that had them all scurrying.

"Hurry! We've been discovered!"

Sarion leaped astride his own horse, and he knew the chase was finally on. He had to get them out of the immediate area surrounding Gar-Kiln. He had no idea how swiftly the Ravenor could move, and he certainly had no desire to force the issue. The company members grabbed the last of their belongings, and Sarion ordered Geld Rinn into the lead, Ereck next to him. Sarion was directly behind them, Piril and Bertilik following, the two newcomers after them, with the vigilant Lassel keeping a watchful eye on their backs. The durable Chertron brought up the rear, with Jurit at his side.

As they rode off into the trees, Sarion wondered how it had all come to this…They had set out from Nighton fifteen strong. A group of skilled fighters and talented huntsmen, striking into the great westland forests on a quest for a village which was known only by name, nothing more. Their chance meeting with Ereck had proven fruitful, the old man guiding them steadily towards the southwest where Gar-kiln lay waiting. Sarion had split the company into two, and while his group had emerged unscathed, Valadire's charge had met with disaster, all of his men slain except for himself and Geld Rinn.

Had it been a mistake on his part, letting them separate?

He understood that such decisions needed to be made, and were never easy. They were a part of leadership, most especially in these dangerous times. In his earlier service men had also died. It had affected him then as well, made him question his own role as a leader, reminding him that every choice must be carefully and wisely taken, as people's lives depended on it.

And now more men were dead.

The Summoning

Tree branches and tangled thickets scattered in their wake, the night at last slipping into its latest hour as dawn would soon be arriving. A light rain still fell, and the mist clung to everything. It had been a long and arduous night, not to be forgotten anytime soon. A herd of stag broke to their left, frightened by their intrusion, but the fighters never slowed, knowing what pursued somewhere behind them, deadly and focused.

Sarion tried not to dwell on the lost men, but found it impossible. He had been promoted by Chensel, reinstated into the Western Watch once again as a high ranking Forester, second in command only to Chensel himself. Promoted, although he had not sought the position. He was still amazed at the circumstances which had led him here. How his life had changed only within the span of a few weeks...it was stunning. And it was something he had no desire for. His life back at his farm, with Edward and his servants, had been everything he could have wanted. Despite his fighting background, Sarion had always been low-keyed, not one to seek out adventure. And now, his entire world had been cruelly rearranged, turned and thrown about until little of his previous existence remained, and worse yet, had undertaken terrible risks on multiple occasions, barely escaping with his life. All around him the vortex swirled; unrelenting and unforgiving.

He must *not* lose himself within all this...

Regardless of the horror, the responsibility, the violence and death, he must be the person he had been before. Someone with a sound mind, a compassionate heart, who made thoughtful decisions filled with discretion.

But it was so hard to do, incredibly so...

Time passed as they drove onwards through the great forestland, no landmarks breaking the monotony of green and brown. Although it was wilderness, still it remained part of the great westland, and despite the advance of terrible creatures from the Grammore Lowlands, Sarion refused to believe that their enemy would have the advantage here. His monsters were formidable, cunning and deadly, but the Dark Mage's powers had to have their limits. Their victory over the Killworm and the other beast at Nighton's western wall was proof of this fact. These creatures could be evaded, and even killed. Sarion told himself to remember this, and not lose hope. And Wharla, although an enigma, might prove to be invaluable once they discovered her secrets.

And Sarion was convinced that she indeed held them...

The minutes passed by swiftly, giving away to hours, the dawn finally arriving, although it was merely a lessening of the darkness, the surrounding forest gloomy and grey. The rain stopped, and the air was damp and heavy, the threat of additional storms remaining with them. Morning came and went but Sarion never slowed, eager to put as much distance between themselves and the cursed village as possible. They were all tired and weary, but there was no help for it. At times he conversed with Geld Rinn and Chertron, picking a path that would steer them due east. The countryside was unchanging around them, a dense hinterland of wood and valley, pocked in places by small streams and scattered hillocks. Maps would prove useless here. To Sarion's knowledge, there had never been an organized effort to search and track this region of the westland. And if it had been done, there were not enough men to patrol the area. Even Sharield had always kept their scouting parties close, fearing clashes with roaming predators from beyond the Ridgeline. Further to the south was a region which few knew anything about. Sarion had been told about the existence of several towns, but virtually nothing else was known about them. Rarely would any travelers venture as far north as Sharield from the deeper south. The country was too difficult to traverse for the purposes of trade or the exchange of news. People tended to their own lives, and the challenge of staying alive and protecting one's family and holdings were more than enough to deter any thought of straying past the next day. The westland was huge and formidable, and Sarion fully believed that the southern reaches were not much different, except with less people, and no organized structure and monarchy like Trencit. The curious part of his mind had wondered about the area over the years, but he had never considered going there on his own. There was simply no purpose to it with his own responsibilities.

He thought back to his farm and lands, content that Edward was safe in Nighton, but the lad had been the only one who had left. The others from his homestead had stayed, telling the couriers that it was their home, and they would remain there, regardless of the risk. Sarion hoped that wandering marauders would not roam close, but there was no guarantee of such fortune. Other outlying towns had been attacked, and some much deeper inside the westland, like Fledge Rae, which lay disturbingly close to Nighton itself. They had lost men from Karrol's charge there, to a creature lurking among the rooftops. Again, Sarion wondered as to how these monsters had been placed so strategically throughout the westland. The Dark Mage had given magical power to his main servants, people like Chardoom, and they commanded dreadful beasts, waiting on the orders of their foul master. But not all of the predators were magical in nature, like the Killworm. It was possible that someone like Chardoom had led the monster to a certain area, and then left it there to terrorize whatever was unfortunate enough to come across it. Sarion didn't believe there were many such powerful servants, but there were some, and wherever they were now was of grave concern. The Dark Mage had been calculating his move for a long time, and these events had not come about quickly. It was a somber thought, and one that left the door open to the possibility that the evil one's hand was far-reaching, past the westland and into Trencit itself...

He wondered about Forlern, and how he had fared with his own unenviable task – bringing news of Charadan's fall to King Gregor. Surely, it had been an extremely trying situation. By now, news must have rippled through the central kingdom and beyond, but as to what the consequences would be, he could not tell. Troubles enough lay before Sarion's feet, and every road he traveled was perilous and fraught with uncertainty. Men were dying in frightening numbers, and there appeared to be no end in sight. The words of the Keeper of Sprechyd Wood haunted him, telling him that the Dark Mage would be victorious if he chose. It was an unnerving prediction, and a paradox as well. If he chose? Why would he not? His goal was clear – to destroy Trencit's defenses and undermine its leadership. There could be only one eventual goal to such a strategy, and that was to conquer the kingdom and claim it for his own. Whomever their adversary was, his endgame was plain enough.

Sarion pushed them forward, horse and riders, until the afternoon found them in a lightly wooded region, the mist and rain left behind as the sky brightened overhead. A small stream tumbled over rocks before them, and Sarion at last called for a halt, thinking that any pursuit was far behind them. They had ridden many miles since leaving Gar-kiln, without any hint of their enemy. Sarion refused to believe that Chardoom could send the Ravenor after them without his own presence, and although durable and fierce, the ogres could never match the pace of the westland war horses. He then thought back to the original hunt for the ogre into Grammore, reminding himself that their quarry had been extremely difficult to find in the wilderness. It was probably best not to assume too much when it came to their enemies…

The riders stretched weary limbs and immediately fell into routine, setting watch and tending to the horses. The air was humid from the persistent moisture, but the breaking cloud cover promised that a new front was pushing its way through, emerging from the menacing heights of the Ridgeline and gathering into the greater westland.

Sarion drank deeply from his water pouch, splashing cool liquid against his face from the stream. Piril did the same while Bertilik watched, the two fighters forever vigilant in protecting Nighton's Second Forester.

"Ah, 'tis a terrible thing, facing the troubles before us. Will it ever end?"

Chertron came alongside him, sitting down and munching on dried meat.

"I'm sure you sorely miss your family." Sarion replied, without looking at the noble fighter. They had been through so much already, and Chertron's simple remark needed no elaboration. When *would* it all end? Was it a question that even had an answer? Or perhaps the war with the Dark Mage would be like the one on Trencit's eastern front against the Devlents, which had spanned countless years with no respite. Both sides had suffered losses which numbered in the thousands, fighting relentlessly against the other for reasons which none could probably remember. Sarion wondered if any efforts had been made to end the conflict, by either side.

Chertron nodded his head at Sarion's reply, and

continued sitting there, looking weary.

"Let me ask you something. Your knowledge of Trencit politics surpasses my own. I'm curious about the ongoing war with the Devlents. Has anyone ever tried to end it?"

"End it? What do you mean? Through a treaty?"

"Yes."

"I've heard that talks were tried, many years ago. Envoys were sent to the Devlent chieftains, but none ever came back."

Sarion shook his head. It might well be true. They were a savage race, and although he had never actually seen a Devlent, Chertron's answer was consistent with everything else he'd been told. But it was such a waste of life for both sides. Why couldn't different races of people live together, work together? Unfortunately, history told that it had always been this way, and Sarion knew it wasn't going to change any time soon.

"Well, we have enough problems facing us here for the moment. Nothing we can do about solving that problem as well, so don't get any ideas, my friend."

Sarion frowned, but was silent.

"And so that leads me to my next question. What exactly are we going to do next?" Cherton leaned closer, although no one else approached.

"I have a plan, but it's not anything complex. For now, we make for Sharield and talk to Lord Berillon. He needs to be convinced of the threat from Grammore and what type of danger his people face."

"Surely Chensel has sent emissaries by now to warn him?" Chertron responded.

"Yes. We discussed all this when I left. But that was before our visit to Gar-kiln and learning about Chardoom. I'm the best person to adequately describe our enemy, and what options we have to defend the westland. I've never met Berillon, but he's well-spoken about by the few people who have traveled there."

The fighter nodded, angling his head as two figures approached. The shadows were lengthening, the surrounding forest filled with the comforting sounds of evening insects as they emerged from hidden holes and the deep grass.

Sarion followed his gaze as both Ereck and Fortisel drew near.

"Well, fighter, it seems we've both got our answers from the cursed village. You didn't heed my warning, but I can't blame you. I think I know you well enough now that although you're stubborn, you also bear a great responsibility in protecting the westland. I don't envy you that."

Sarion nodded. "There are many of us who share this burden. Members of the Western Watch place their own lives first in defense of family and friend. It's our vow when we join. All know the danger, whether it be in time of war or peace. Unfortunately, we now live in grim times."

"I'll wish you the best of luck in whatever you do then."

Sarion looked at him curiously.

Ereck squinted his eyes, glancing at Chertron. "My time with you is done. I helped do what you asked me, but this is as far as I go. I'm an old man, and have long given up the sword or bow. I survive on my wits." He tapped his head, chuckling. "And something that one back there needs to do more of..." He pointed at Valadire in the distance, but Sarion merely shook his head at the verbal jab, knowing it was better to leave the small rivalry alone.

Ereck continued. "I'm leaving now, and would like to have a pair of horses to take."

"Two?" Chertron questioned.

"My friend here is going with me. We spoke for a few minutes, but I'll let him explain."

Fortisel came forward, inclining his head. "I can't begin to thank you and your men enough, Captain Sarion. But I have no desire to travel further with your company. I'm also not a fighter, but a peddler and craftsman. I've lost everything in Gar-kiln. My family, my people..." He stopped, looking close to sobbing. "I don't want to face those creatures again."

"I understand." Sarion said. "We're heading east, and will find villages and larger towns soon enough. You're welcome to stay as long as you wish under our protection, but it's your choice."

Fortisel nodded, his face creased with worry. "My thanks, but I wish to leave now. Your company has stirred the evil in Gar-kiln, and I fear they will come after you."

"They may, but will not match our speed. And we will find greater numbers of men who may help us as we move onward."

"It's not only that." Fortisel lowered his voice. "It's you."

"Hmm?" Sarion asked.

"There's something special about you, something dangerous. My intuition is that wherever you go, you will meet great danger. Whether it's your intention or not, you'll meet it. You seem to fear nothing, and that terrifies me. I don't have that type of courage, and don't want to have it, I'm ashamed to say. But I want to leave you now, while I still can. Thank you and good fortune."

With that, he bowed deeply, then turned his back, walking away. Sarion felt Chertron staring hard at him, but he ignored his companion's look, following the outline of Fortisel's back until he melded with the other shadows of fighters at various forms of rest or work.

"I told him he can come to my place and stay. I could use the extra set of hands, and companionship, truth be told." Ereck shrugged. "And like him, I have no wish to see this through. I won't survive whatever ordeals wait for you, Sarion. I only hope that *you* do."

"Is there anything you need from us?"

"No. I can find my way around good enough, by sun and star. A few days and we'll be back at my home."

"Good fortune to you then, Ereck. Perhaps we'll meet again somewhere." Sarion shook the other's callused hand.

"I don't think so, fighter. Our paths are as different as the ends of the universe. Farewell."

Ereck nodded to Chertron and walked off towards the others, where Fortisel had already mounted a horse.

"Do you think it wise to let Fortisel go without further questioning?" Chertron asked.

"I think we've heard all the answers he could give us already. You spoke with him and found nothing more of interest through his words or on anything he carries with him. His tale has been validated by what we saw in Gar-kiln. And in a pitched battle, he would be of little or no use. We would end up protecting him and Ereck as well. I think it's best, and they knew this. They'll be much safer if they leave our company." Sarion pondered his own words, realizing how chilling they actually sounded.

Indeed, anyone who traveled with him was risking their own life, and that lurid fact didn't seem to be changing anytime soon.

It took a long while for Forlern to reach the main gates of Lastrad, as the city was expansive and the going slow through the paved streets. The night was growing deep, the coming dawn several hours away. There was little conversation as the party galloped onwards, Questron just before him, surrounded by his personal bodyguard on every side. The company's numbers had swollen since leaving the wall where the creature had escaped from, as the Lastrad Captain's orders were followed through, the plans put into place. By now, word had spread throughout the city that the guard had fought with the creature and wounded it, and were now in fast pursuit. Hunting parties had rendezvoused at the spot where the beast had fled from, and Forlern knew it would be several more minutes until they gained the area.

As to what exactly they would find, it was anyone's guess...

The night sky was clear overhead, and that was a good thing, at least. Any additional light would be helpful, and the party of fighters brandished torches to ward against the outer darkness. Within the city limits, streets and walkways were lighted every night, although many alleys and back areas were shadowed. It was in these parts where the roughest and vilest of Lastrad's citizens did their work. Any large and prosperous city was a natural breeding ground for villains and other opportunists, and Lastrad was both...

The minutes passed, the horses moving faster now as they could run on the open grass. Immediately outside the city lay farms and villages, normally a safe area this close beneath Lastrad's mighty arm. The killings had taken place only inside the city itself, and Forlern was not overlooking this fact. He knew that the creature had been deliberately set there to undermine the Lastrad leadership, make the citizens and its officials realize that they were not invulnerable to the monster's invisible reach, and the plan had been greatly effective. They needed to capture or kill it. Soon...Even if the beast had been seriously injured and driven off, there would always be doubt as to whether it might return again. Questron could not come back to the Gran Barshara emptyhanded. It would seal his own fate and guarantee the loss of his position.

No, a man in his ranking had none other to blame than himself. Forlern knew it might not necessarily be fair, but politics rarely were. Daregil Keep wasn't much different, he knew. You rose or fell within the ranks based on your accomplishments, or lack thereof. It was part of a fighter's life as well if you proved fortunate (or unfortunate enough) to achieve any position of importance.

He knew that it included himself too, especially after having been so recently promoted...

Members of the Homeguard were the elite of the land, and the Lords of Trencit expected nothing less than superior results.

Passing the high wall of Lastrad on their left, Forlern could make out the figures of guards perched above, torches flickering at intervals to illuminate the area, the men looking spectral and menacing from this distance. Since the attacks had started, the watch had been greatly increased but to no avail. Forlern believed that the deadly creature had remained hidden somewhere within the large city, and it bothered him more than a little that despite their efforts, they had yet to discover its lair.

Galloping ahead without pause, the company reached the spot where the creature had fled. Questron called for a quick halt as several men approached, the smaller party now merging into a larger group of armed men who had set up a watch perimeter. Fires blazed in every direction, and Forlern knew there were at least a hundred guards within eyesight. Taking advantage of the brief respite, he grabbed his water pouch, drinking deeply. Sweating from the ride and the early battle, he felt energized, his mind clear and body ready for action. His training allowed for nothing else, and he scanned the night warily, knowing that dawn was still some time off.

It had been a long night, and he wondered how events would play out.

Several moments later Questron signaled him to draw near.

"Gastrale has led a hunting party into the woods yonder. He has the lead on us, but hopefully that has also kept him on the trail of the beast. With its injuries, I can't imagine that it can still move quickly."

Forlern shrugged. "We can only hope, but I know enough not to underestimate these Grammore predators."

"We'll follow straight behind them. I have a pair of trackers in the lead. My men will also fan out to either side, in case of an ambush. We won't be taken by surprise."

Nodding, Forlern was eager to move forward. "Let's be off then and claim the head of this monster. No one will sleep too well unless we bring it back."

Questron gestured to his men and they were again in motion, their numbers greater. Additional fighters were arriving even now, and Forlern knew that the Lastrad Captain would not be taking any risks. There would be hundreds more within a short time.

The forest in this area was not too thick, grass springing up in numerous clearings. The horses made good time and the light from dozens of torches illuminated the woods, the company breaching the trunks like a spectral garrison of fighters resurrected from the grave. The men thundered ahead, Forlern's keen eyes focused on their surroundings, but his vision was cloudy, obscured by the smoky torches and the rapidly changing landscape. He felt the need for urgency, wishing to capture the creature and put an end to it for good. His life had been swept from under him the past few weeks, and he missed the companionship of Sarion and Chertron. Confident as he was, he'd come to rely on the talents of his friends, and knew they made a great team together. He took more than a little measure of pride in his own skills, but he also recognized the same in others. And he had never met someone quite like Sarion before, barring maybe Charadan himself...If Sarion had come to Daregil Keep and come under the attention of the Homeguard Captains, there was no telling how high he would be within their ranks. He also realized that the Lords of Trencit had been aware of Sarion for quite some time, and had wondered about where he had gone to after his service at Nighton.

Forlern missed Sarion, there was no question, and he regretted the circumstances which had necessitated their separation. He missed the reliable Chertron as well, along with his healthy dose of dark cynicism, which was usually directed at himself. It made Forlern smile, thinking of the stalwart fighter, someone whom he had grown to respect and admire. He wondered how long it would be until the man could return to his family, who lived somewhere in the middle of Trencit. A great many fighters were away in the field, sometimes for long months without reprieve. Rotations were getting fewer and shorter, and the mighty arms of Trencit had been calling in its fighting force for a long time, asking them to give the ultimate sacrifice of life and limb in defense of their homeland.

When and how would it all end?

Well, he had his own part to play in the greater scheme of things, and was not one to take his responsibilities lightly, especially with his new ranking. In the past, the consequences of his decisions had not always gone beyond his own immediate scope, but now, they had major repercussions. Possibly for the first time, Forlern began to understand what Sarion had been going through, and it was not a pleasant thought.

They rode onward, with still no sign of either their quarry or Questron's hunting party. Forlern hadn't expected to see anyone soon, but as the miles and minutes dragged on, he became increasingly anxious, with still no indication of what had transpired ahead of them. Almost within the frame of that foreboding notion, a shout from the front drew the men up short, the ranks closing. He pushed forward, watching Questron advance, his horse only a few strides behind. The trackers had called for a halt, but even in the dim lighting, Forlern didn't need their skill to see what had caused the delay. Bodies lay scattered on the ground, Forlern recognizing their uniforms immediately.

They were Lastradian guards, all of them dead...

Questron dismounted, along with several members of his bodyguard, other fighters cautiously scouting ahead and to both sides.

"Seems as if they caught up with the creature and fought a quick battle," said Questron.

"And lost." Forlern added.

There were at least a dozen figures lying crumpled on the ground. The trackers moved through the slaughter, one of them coming towards Questron. "Most likely the creature ambushed them from the heavier brush." He pointed ahead to the left.

"I wonder if it was a desperate ploy, having been slowed by its injuries?" Questron shook his head, talking more to himself than anyone in particular. "All right, let's be off all the quicker. The beast has some fight in it yet, and the sooner we reach our men the better we can aid them."

The war party headed off once more, faces appearing more anxious than only moments earlier. Forlern could almost read their minds, and knew what situations like these could do to even the most highly trained men. The terror of this Grammore predator had worked its way into their collective minds, killing off the citizens of Lastrad, unseen and deadly, and even now, against superior numbers, it still seemed capable of having the upper hand and causing more chaos. Forlern again wondered if it did indeed possess a latent magical ability of regeneration, and if so, would he need to strike directly at it with the knife given to him by Barimon and King Gregor.

Several minutes passed and again the trackers paused, one of them moving back to confer with Questron. Not to be left in the dark, Forlern positioned himself between two of the Lastrad Captain's personal guards, eager to hear any news.

"Shouts in the distance, Captain Questron."

"You're sure?"

"There can be no doubt. We're closing in on them."

Forlern frowned. Something was clearly taking place, and it could very well be another skirmish with the beast. Visions of slain fighters passed before his eyes, and he shook this off, focusing on their situation.

"Proceed cautiously. We don't know what's going on ahead of us, but we're about to find out. No more pauses until we reach the hunting party."

The tracker nodded and pulled away, rejoining his companion. The fighters moved forward, Questron giving a hand signal which Forlern recognized would tighten their formation and give notice for a coming attack. The Lastrad men looked grim, their faces pale from the flickering torch light. Ahead of them the trees began to give way and a field opened up, the fading night sky in its last celestial garment before the arrival of dawn. The horses broke through the last trunks of the forest, and Forlern gazed at the dim horizon, seeing a flat landscape filled with fields of grain, darker shadows representing small copses and contours in the terrain. They had breached an outlying farm, one of many which surrounded the great city. Questron whistled and the company urged their mounts onward at a greater pace, now that the path was clear. Almost immediately Forlern saw pinpricks of light in the distance, and he called to Questron, but the warrior had already spotted them. Forlern knew they were torches, and he caught snatches of shouting now as well. A battle was being fought, and the Lastrad company kicked at their steeds for speed.

Forlern had a strong sense of foreboding that their hunt was finally at its end, and this would also spell out the end of the creature, and probably more men as well. His mission to Lastrad was nearing its own fruition, and all his time and effort, along with the sacrifice of lives, would reach its endgame. Kirlat and Erlang were both dead, and their murder demanded justice…

As they drew closer, the sounds of fighting became louder, and Forlern saw silhouettes in the fields, waving and moving about. They must have the creature surrounded, he thought. Eyes fixed on the sight ahead, he heard the clash of steel on steel, and he shook his head. What was going on there?

The foremost of Questron's scouts were already there, some of them pivoting about and returning. Forlern had his own sword in hand, and he could now identify the shapes of men as they fought in the gloom, torches cast to the ground and given up as their bearers were in a struggle to survive.

But something was wrong here. Something…

Words echoed back to them from the scouts, and Forlern watched the fray, now only dozens of yards from them. A terrible battle was taking place, and there seemed to be more men that he had thought possible. He knew the hunting party was large, but this many?

And then he noticed something even stranger...There appeared to be a separation within the ranks of fighting men, one which resembled something familiar to him.

He gasped in recognition, dread filling his heart, as realization dawned on him, one of the scouts shouting clearly, the word cutting like a sabre of ice in the pre-dawn gloom.

"Devlents! Beware!"

Forlern shouted to himself. "Devlents? Shades!"

Questron's men were fighting against their age-old enemies from the east, the crafty and treacherous race known as the Devlents, who were engaged in a war which had started long before any of them had been born. But what were they doing this far *west*? The Trencit Royal Armies held the fortresses of Southwatch and Northwatch, and patrolled the lands for many miles in several directions. A chill went down his spine as he wondered about the implications. But there was no time for speculation, as Questron's new company was now working its way into the fray, hailing their comrades and cursing at the unexpected sight of their enemy, sword and bow raised in greeting.

Forlern quickly tried to analyze their predicament, estimating numbers for either side. Even from their closer vantage point, it was impossible to see everything, but the original hunting party numbered several dozen, with the new fighters swelling their ranks. The Devlents were on his left, on the eastern side, and the company was sizable. It was definitely a strong patrol, and outnumbered the first party. A combination of warriors both on foot and horseback, they were using their normal mode of field battle against the Lastrad fighters. In appearance, the Devlents were smaller than men by a foot or more, but were bulky and muscular, their face and skin a darker complexion, their heads protected under helms of steel. At first glance they looked human, but with spots on their face and all over their skin; mottled patches which gave them natural camouflage in cover if they chose not to be fully clothed. Their hands were thicker and larger than human hands, and they possessed great strength of arms, moreso than their human counterparts. They spoke their own tongue, but it was suspected that they completely knew the common language of men as well, although there was no clear knowledge of this.

All these things raced through Forlern's mind in a fraction of a second, his instincts taking over in sizing up this surprising new threat and formulating the best plan of attack. The Devlents turned to meet this other onslaught, holding their lines and showing no sign of emotion. They were a species of warlike creatures, never asking or giving quarter, and would sooner kill themselves on the battlefield before surrendering. They were a shocking contrast to the people of Trencit, who placed more value in their own lives. Forlern had seen Devlents slice their own throats to avoid capture. They were a heartless enemy, and if someone was unlucky enough to be taken alive by the Devlents, they were never seen again.

Forlern now charged into the fray, Questron and his men closing ranks and trying to split the Devlents down the middle. Several minutes of intense combat took place, Forlern slashing at the enemy from his horse, trying to both keep astride his animal while doing as much damage as possible. Darts flew over his head, and he knew that behind the foremost ranks were other Devlents who were trying to influence the outcome of the battle despite being in the back rows. But the Lastrad men also had bows, and countless arrows rained down upon the Devlent ranks, many finding targets. The battle waged to and fro, and Questron rallied his men around him, plunging directly into the foremost guard of the enemy and creating a gap. Others followed after including Forlern, who was looking for the

Davish-tar, the Devlent captain. Like any organized fighting force, their warlord would direct the events of the conflict, and if you could take them out of the battle, it would undermine the Devlent hunting party. Following after the Lastrad captain, Forlern struck the neck of a Devlent who came too close, its body slipping to the ground as life seeped from the dark form.

Questron shouted from a few yards ahead, and Forlern caught sight of a tight ring of Devlent warriors all on foot, surrounding a figure within their midst. Clearly Questron had been thinking the same thing, and was now engaging the bodyguard of the Davish-tar, his men fighting courageously at his flanks, one of them going down beneath a black pike. Forlern grabbed a knife from his side, whipping it through the air and killing the Devlent instantly as it pierced its throat. Two more of the bodyguards fell beneath the Lastrad swords, and the Devlent captain waved its own sword in the air, daring any who would draw near. Questron met the challenge, leaping from his horse to engage the rival captain, and the pair fought a heated battle, both of them slashing and weaving, the Lastradians looking on but not wanting to interfere lest they cause Questron to lose focus. The remaining Devlent guards lay dead or dying, and Forlern looked around, sensing that the tide of battle was now in their favor, and would soon be over. Watching Questron in one-on-one action for the first time, Forlern was immediately impressed at the man's swordplay. He was quick and confident, clearly a master of steel in his own right. Pressing the warlord ruthlessly, he seized upon an opening as the Davish-tar stumbled, moving swiftly in and dealing a death blow through the Devlent's chest.

The enemy leader faltered, then slumped to the ground.

"Well done, Captain Questron."

One of his men spoke, but Questron never paused,

scanning the scene around him, and signaling men to move into places where he saw fit. There was really nothing that Forlern could add to the combat, as clearly Questron was efficient in directing his men, sizing up the situation and reacting instantly. Shouts and screams echoed around them, almost all coming from the guttural throats of the enemy.

Just when it seemed the battle was finished, a new cry rang out in the night, and heads turned to look northward, Forlern trying to discern the cause for this new distraction.

"Captain Questron!" A man rushed towards them. "Another hunting party of Devlents draws near."

Shaking his head, Questron pointed with his sword. "More of these devils? Where did they come from?"

"The forest behind us. Our rear scouts had to flee for their lives. We were not taken by surprise, but their greater numbers would have slain us all."

Forlern came forward. "How many are they?"

The man's face looked grim. "Greater than this other hunting party."

Forlern felt a knot in the pit of his stomach. It seemed they were not out of the woods yet. They were now in another fight for their lives, and he wondered about the appearance of this second hunting party. He didn't believe in coincidences.

"This is a trap." He drew close to Questron, who said nothing.

"We've been led here by the creature. I think there can be no doubt as to that. Our enemies have allied themselves with each other. As to what degree, there is no way of knowing."

"And what about the King's legions at Southwatch?"

"That will have to wait. We first need to get out of here alive."

Forlern and Questron both looked to the north,

where they watched as a large smudge hurried towards them as the new group of Devlents approached. Forlern knew immediately that they were outnumbered. He also knew that more of Questron's men would soon arrive as well, unless they too were now delayed.

"I don't know if we can defeat this new company." Questron stated it matter-of-factly, without any hint of regret or frustration.

Forlern replied. "I think we can outrun them if we have to. Our company is all on horseback, while they are evenly split, if they're following their normal hunting tactics."

"Hmm. I would hate to rely on past behavior, especially if my own neck is on the line," Questron answered. "It looks like you're right, though."

They both watched as several dozen of his men moved to engage them, and there was a mixture of both mounted Devlents and ones on foot. The fighting around them had all but ceased, and the weary and injured men closed ranks to defend and engage the new company. Forlern waited for Questron's decision, whatever it was to be, and it only took a few seconds for the Lastrad Captain to decide.

"Give them no quarter. Let's go."

His words were menacing, filled with the promise of more death. Whatever Forlern's impression had been of the man before, he was completely convinced now of one thing -- on the battlefield, Questron was a man of great skill and swift decision making, and Forlern would certainly not relish the thought of facing him on *opposite* sides of a conflict...

They were moving again, everyone mounted on their steeds, weapons brandished. Some of them took out bows, quickly searching for targets and letting their arrows fly, while others formed a protective wedge around their captain, ensuring that they would not be outflanked.

Devlent faces appeared before them now, grim and unforgiving. Shouts and death cries were raised all about them, and Forlern found himself freshly immersed into battle once again. Many of the Devlents slashed at the Lastradian war beasts, trying to cripple them and unhorse their riders, but Forlern had seen enough of the Lastradians to respect their ability in the field. They were well-trained and disciplined, and both of these things gave them a strong showing while in battle. Things had changed now, as just a few minutes ago they had the advantage of greater numbers, and the reversal of this factor weighed heavily on their current situation. And they were not necessarily superior fighters when compared evenly with the Devlents, who were born and bred as a warlike race. Despite the fact that Questron commanded a capable enough army, they lacked the seasoned experience which both the Devlents and Royal Legions possessed. From the beginning, Forlern had predicted this, and he was sure Questron knew it as well. Forlern thought that if the Lastrad captain was set on winning this battle, then the difference might very well come down to the stronger fighting prowess of Questron and his personal guard, along with Forlern's own presence. It was an intimidating thought, with no certainties. After all, he was only one Homeguard fighter. The outcome was unclear, and Forlern knew that both he and Questron were in a battle for their own skins…

It was a terrible struggle, the sky above turning a faded red with the coming of dawn, the blood from two races staining the fields below in a splattering of crimson. Scavenging birds circled above, greedily sensing the feast of flesh which would shortly come. Forlern's mind had a singular focus though, the fight, as he slashed his sword before him, dodging dart and shaft, and trying to take down as many of the enemy as possible. A blow from behind nearly unseated him and he shrugged it off, realizing that he had narrowly missed being thrust from his horse.

The Summoning

Questron and his guard were close, again trying to force their way into the heart of the Devlent patrol and find their leader, but this time things were much different, his men growing weary from the protracted hunt and earlier skirmish, now drawing on reserves to sustain them. Time was meaningless, and Forlern soon noticed that the number of active fighters on the Lastrad side were alarmingly low. The Devlents had also suffered terribly, but their superior numbers gave them a steady advantage, one which led Forlern to the realization that they had no chance of winning this battle...

Questron fought on as if a man possessed by a demon of war, striking down any that came forward to challenge him, the Devlents approaching more cautiously. Although they had no fear of dying, their own strategy was simple enough; to completely eradicate the enemy, and any action that increased the chances of this outcome would be attempted. Forlern knew that they would never retreat from a fight when they had a clear advantage. He again wondered if more of the Lastrad fighters would arrive. They could make the difference here, and still lead them to victory. Was this Questron's plan? There was no way to tell, as the man was a score of yards to his right now, two guards separating them. Forlern felt beads of sweat soaking his tunic, and his throat was parched. He had lost count of how many Devlents he'd killed, and like Questron, saw that the enemy now approached him differently as well, recognizing his skill. Several darts came his way and he swatted them out of the air, urging his horse to the right as a Devlent reared up from nowhere, cutting the animal across the neck with a wicked pike. Seeing his danger, Forlern leaped from the dying beast, landing on his feet with sword singing as he cut down the guilty enemy with a flash of his blade. Without a horse, it was a different kind of fight now, but one he was even more comfortable with. Two Devlents rushed him, and he feinted to the left, right, and back again, ducking beneath a blow which would have severed his head, striking upwards and killing the enemy who had taken a fraction too long in recovering.

One of the Lastrad fighters came to his side, offering some protection. Aware of his presence, Forlern was unable to pause as more of the Devlents surged ahead, eager to finish him off. Grabbing a spear from the ground, he blocked the first attempt, knocking one of the Devlents to the ground. The fighter next to him put a sword through his throat, and Forlern engaged another of the relentless creatures. It was some of the fiercest fighting that Forlern had ever seen, and it seemed as if he was surrounded on every side by the enemy. He never stopped moving, unwilling to give the Devlents an easy target, instead butting the Devlents with the spear while slashing with his blade. The minutes dragged by agonizingly, and he was weary, pushing his body to its limits. A stab of pain came from his arm as a dart finally caught him, embedding partially in his flesh. It only took him a moment to pull it out, muffling a gasp as he did so. The fighter next to him went down in a flurry of limbs and weapons, and two Devlents were on him, one of them thrusting a pike through his abdomen. The creature paid for it with his own life though as Forlern brought his blade up too fast for the Devlent to defend, cutting it to the ground.

His situation looking desperate, he shouted for Questron, knowing that this was an unwinnable battle. Off to his right, one of the guards heard him, urging his horse over.

"I lost Captain Questron. I don't know where he is."

Both men fought off attackers, thrusting them back, one of them severely wounded.

"We have to flee. If we stay here, we'll all be dead," Forlern said, his breath coming in ragged gasps.

The man nodded, his face grim.

"The same goes for Questron." Forlern stared at

him for any hint of hesitation. "This isn't worth sacrificing your life."

The fighter held one hand down, helping to lift Forlern behind him. Looking around for an opening, Forlern saw a gap behind them and to their left. "There!" he grabbed the man's shoulder, pointing. The fighter maneuvered the horse, kicking in his boots and giving the beast the command to flee. The bulky animal bowled over a Devlent blocking their escape, and they weaved in and out of openings, leaping over fallen bodies and leaving them in its wake. In moments they reached the perimeter of the battle scene, the horse picking up speed and galloping away. Forlern noticed other fighters fleeing the battlefield as well, heading to the north and west. Scores of Devlents were still fighting, but Forlern couldn't make out a single Lastrad fighter. Anyone still in there was either dead or soon to be...

The Devlents were finishing off any remaining adversaries, and although it goaded him to be leaving the fray, Forlern had learned long ago that it was better to live and fight another day as opposed to holding ground on the battlefield against hopeless numbers. During the journey into Grammore, it had been the only way the three of them had managed to survive, as himself, Sarion, and Chertron had emerged from the dreaded lowlands after escaping from creatures beyond their power.

"Keep to the fields and the open sky," Forlern said. "We can't trust the woods."

The fighter nodded, but said nothing.

"What's your name?" Forlern asked.

"Criel. One of Captain Questron's personal guards."

"I hope he made it out as well," Forlern said.

"In the heat of battle I became separated from the others. I lost sight of them."

They raced ahead for long minutes, Forlern peering behind them but he saw no pursuit. He wondered as to their motives, and then with chilling certainty decided that their plan had been to get Questron all along. It had all been a trap, carefully laid out, an attempt to draw the Lastrad captain from the city and destroy him and his guard. The creature had led them along, pursued by the hunting party, and naturally Questron would be leading the chase. Forlern shook his head. The implications were all bad. The Devlents aligning themselves with the Dark Mage, a hunting patrol this far east, and the undermining of Lastrad's leadership. It was a plan which showed cunning and depth, and by all indications had been long in the creation. Frowning, he scanned the horizon, fields stretching to three sides. A small building loomed to their left, probably a storage area for tools and harvesting. Forlern was about to dismiss it when he noticed something moving. He'd seen a shadow, the new light revealing the presence of someone, or something there.

Something that had seen them coming, and hidden because of it...

It might have been a worker, fearful of dangerous events nearby and secreting themselves from prying eyes. Or possibly someone else. A Lastrad fighter, or a Devlent scout. Either way, he had to find out.

"Criel, over to that building." The fighter slowed the horse. "I saw something move into the bushes, or enter. Let's go see, but have a care."

They cautiously approached, stopping a dozen yards from the entrance. Bushes ringed the building on three sides, and it appeared to have only one door; a wide, latched, wooden panel, which was now closed.

Forlern dismounted, and it saved his life as a pike whipped out from the shadows, one which would have pierced them both in a deathgrip...

The horse panicked, kicking and neighing, galloping away with a dead rider and leaving Forlern exposed in the fields, where he rolled to the ground, using the high grain as camouflage. A figure crouched next to the building, using the brush as cover.

Forlern moved forward, half-bent over, a dagger in one hand, his sword in the other. The figure in the bush reacted to his approach, exactly as Forlern knew he would. With effortless grace, he let the knife fly, finding a target as a muffled shout escaped from the attacker's throat, but Forlern wasn't about to let up. A second knife was immediately in his hand, and now he had a better view of his assailant, who appeared to be a man and not a Devlent.

"Speak your last breath before I send you to the grave." Forlern threw the weapon, embedding it in the man's chest. The figure crumpled to the ground, and Forlern drew close, wary of any other hidden enemies. He stopped, crouching low, as something growled from inside the building, and then he noticed something near the entrance.

Something dark was on the ground, a liquid.

It was a trail of blood…

Leading directly into the building.

His mind raced, possibilities emerging quicker than he could embrace them. Someone wounded had entered the building, someone who had lost a lot of blood.

Someone, or *something*.

And then he suspected more. The creature! Was it inside and had it taken refuge, escaping from the Lastrad hunting party? It had been gravely wounded, and now was holed up, either to die there, or find help. He gritted his teeth. He would help it, all right…

The man moaned, bent over and holding his side.

"What do you have to say?" Forlern asked, his sword before him, pointing at the man's throat. "Do you wish to reveal your allegiance with the Dark Mage? Perhaps you can make amends for your treachery."

A low, pained laugh escaped from the man's throat. "You'll never have the satisfaction of hearing that,

Forlern."

He knows me?

"Who are you, villain?"

The man lifted his face, and the dark eyes met Forlern's own orbs.

Klellan!

"You!" Forlern shouted. "You were behind the killings!"

"How cunning of you to figure that out now, as I'm dying." In obvious pain, the Ja-Ravel assassin leaned back against the building, the dagger still in the side of his right chest. Forlern had been accurate with his aim. He had wanted to cripple the man, but had not dealt a fatal blow, he knew. Still, he might bleed to death…

They locked eyes, both hearing a low, pain-filled groan from inside the building.

"The beast…" Forlern started.

"…is nearly dead now. And with it, my fate is sealed."

"Sealed?" Forlern asked, keeping his distance, knowing that Klellan could not be underestimated, even this close to apparent death. The man looked terrible, his face pale, his body shaking uncontrollably.

"Such is my end."

He held up one arm, pulling the sleeve, a cautious Forlern looking on as he saw a strange band of metal around it, appearing as almost a part of his flesh.

"The mark of the master." He tried to laugh, but it only caused him to double over, coughing up blood. Long moments passed, and Forlern thought the man was done, Klellan's eyes closed.

"Tell me why. You have nothing to lose now. Why did you do this? Are there more Ja-Ravel involved?"

"You know who I am, Forlern. And you must also realize that I will never give you the information you seek."

Forlern spat. "Then leave our world all the more

swiftly. Your legacy will die with you."

"No, no it won't...you don't know what you face yet, do you? Ah, you'll find out. You and your petty king and his counselors. Let puppets like yourself fight their battles, make their sacrifice...I don't relish your fate. Your time will come, and it won't be pretty."

Klellan's words were chilling, but Forlern shrugged them off. "And what do you have to show after all this? You've been a pawn yourself at your foul master's bidding. Well?"

The assassin coughed, answered by another groan coming from inside the building.

"I chose my own destiny and knew the risks. The Ja-Ravel never ask to be forgiven...I lived by my code. And will die by it. But I always served myself. What about you?"

He coughed once more, his eyes fluttering, and Forlern knew that he was finally gone.

Forlern left the small building, convinced that the creature was finally dead. Huddled in a corner, it had looked weak and harmless in its last seconds, although nothing could have been further from the truth. The beast had been responsible for the deaths of hundreds of people, and ultimately would have slain the Gran Barshara himself. The Dark Mage had chosen his assassins wisely. It had been a deadly beast from Grammore, some unknown species, which had possessed great abilities of stealth and camouflage, while being controlled by a predator no less deadly or cunning than itself; the Ja-Ravel assassin Klellan. In the end it was a victory for them, but a costly one indeed, with some questions answered and new ones brought to light. Forlern wanted to know how the Ja-Ravel had become allied with the Dark Mage, and how strong his involvement with the Devlents was. It seemed now that their greatest fear had come to life after all; an alliance of evil on both the eastern and western fronts of Trencit. Countless miles separated the frontiers, but Trencit was a vast and open land, where people had the ability to travel almost anywhere unhindered. It was not that far-fetched to imagine that emissaries of the Dark Mage had spent time coordinating events and enlisting the aid of discontents. Still, it was no small outreach to bring the Devlents into the fold, as they despised all other races; but that only strengthened the notion that the Dark Mage had great resources at his disposal.

Forlern saw the horse several dozen yards in the field and he whistled it over, feeling a pang of regret that Criel had become yet another victim of Klellan's treachery. The animal quietly approached, its rider now gone. Forlern lifted himself onto the horse, wincing in pain. He had his own injuries which needed tending, and he needed to get back into the city. It was too dangerous to stay in the area with roaming Devlents, and he could only hope that Questron had been reunited with the following hunting party and was also on the move once more. Forlern looked across the horizon to the east, but the earlier battlefield was too far off in the distance to see, partially obscured by the sloping land which he had traveled across. Lastrad would be easy to find, and he wanted to steer clear of the forest and find a wider and more open path. Galloping along, he drank from his water pouch, wary of anything out of the ordinary, but all he saw were long fields of grain and scattered farms. He kept in the same direction for a while, eventually spotting a road in the distance, already marked by figures moving both on foot and by wagon, undoubtedly heading for the great city and the Vanyair marketplace. Not wishing to bring unwanted attention to himself, Forlern led his horse into a small copse, waiting for the road to empty before entering. Convinced it was clear in both directions, he urged his steed forward and set a good pace to reach Lastrad. The path wound about, avoiding deeper woods, and Forlern realized that the people who lived in the surrounding countryside were at great risk from marauding Devlents. He didn't know the patrol routines from Lastrad, but knew there had to be regular hunting parties guaranteeing the safety of both merchant and farmer. These people were the lifeblood of the great trading city, and the leaders of Lastrad had always looked after them, but now, this protection would be set to the challenge...

The land passed by quickly, great fields to either side broken by small hills and forests, at times broken up by meandering streams which bubbled beneath small, stone bridges which carried him above. It was a pleasant country, temperate in weather and home to many people who pledged allegiance to neither Lastrad nor Trencit, but was friend of both. They were tied to their homeland, and Forlern knew that it would take nothing less than a full-scale invasion for them to leave. Similar to the tough folk in the western provinces, they preferred only to stay focused on their own affairs and leave the troubles of war and politics to the greater cities and kingdom of Trencit. Forlern didn't blame them, but in the harsh reality of these times, it wasn't always very practical. Without someone to defend their territory they would all be lost, or driven into the deeper mountains and hills. The taxes levied on trade went towards many things, none less than the payment of fighters under the command of Lastrad, something which Forlern related to and completely understood the necessity for. Admittedly, he enjoyed the challenge and excitement of his calling, but he was not so fanatical that he would give up his life so others could honor his fallen name. No, survival must always be foremost. Homeguard were trained in all aspects of weaponry and warfare, but also in the skills of concealment and escape, and in recent weeks, these had certainly come to play.

But even Homeguard were not prepared to deal with the predators of Grammore and the minions of the Dark Mage. Talent and good fortune were just as important as any skill at arms he had ever been taught, and he was lucky these things had been on his side, at least up to this point in time...

He turned his thoughts towards the presence of Devlent hunting parties this close to Lastrad. The eastern frontier was large in scale, with the great mountain range of the Krale in the north, which completely surrounded Daregil Keep on all sides, broken only by smaller hills to its south through which ran the Grip, the only accessible entrance to the valley which held the Lords of Trencit. They might be considered hills, but they were sheer and rocky, though not nearly as tall as the large mountains of the Krale. The range deepened as it ran east, forming a natural and formidable barrier with its snowcrested peaks and treacherous valleys. The terrain, inhospitable weather patterns, and frequent avalanches prevented the advance of any would-be invading army. Even if all these things were braved, there was said to be other things dwelling in the deep shadows of the Krale which would thwart any daring its secrets. Legends and tales abounded as to the terrors and mystery which dwelt in the shrouded peaks, and only a fool would shrug them off as mere legend. Forlern had never ventured too far off the immediate trails leading into the mountains, although he had often wondered about what lay hidden inside.

Northwatch was an intimidating fortress guarding the east edge of the Krale, housing a strong garrison of fighters. Stocked with plentiful provisions, it could hold out for a long time under siege if necessary. On the southeast tip of the Krale was Druhil, one of Trencit's largest cities, and in the forefront of any possible attack from the Devlents. Druhil's fighting force worked in close conjunction with the Royal Legions which patrolled the gap separating the Krale from the much smaller mountain range which sat directly east of Lastrad, eventually butting up against Clairfeld, another large city. The armies of Trencit which guarded the eastern gap consisted almost entirely of cavalry, the swiftest and most competent horsemen to be found in the kingdom. Here, speed and maneuverability were the key resources in protecting this hugely important region, for if the gap was compromised, the Devlents could plunge into the heart of Trencit and divide it in two, free to maraud the villages which made up the breadbasket of the powerful kingdom. Along the eastern perimeter of the smaller range lay Southwatch, another large fortress, and one which had been the site of many battles and sieges. Both Northwatch and Southwatch were vulnerable due to their distance, and the only thing which kept them from being overrun was the largest standing army of Trencit, which was permanently camped immediately west of the ruined city of Valedoom, an ancient stronghold which served as a no-mans land between the Royal Armies and the unforgiving Devlents, both sides constantly battling to seize the upper hand in gaining territory beneath its crumbling walls and towers. Forlern had served there, taking part in some of the countless skirmishes and raids, many which took place under cover of night and mist, the area blanketed with a carpet of fog and moisture from the surrounding lowlands and small foothills. Further east lay the ancestral homeland of the Devlents themselves, a large and rough territory which was little more than just a name on a map.

Since gaining his promotion, Forlern had been given information concerning the overall strategy and implementation of Trencit's armies, and with the added insight and additional knowledge, he now thought of events with a much more critical eye than ever before. He knew the full rotation schedule, the random patrols, and even some of the covert missions which were not privy to anyone except for high ranking commanders in the field. Interesting and important, he still considered himself very much lacking in the greater scope of warfare, more content in the hand-to-hand fighting for which he had been trained. He certainly had no aspirations of being a field commander, although Homeguard captains made up the brunt of army leadership. He still was uncomfortable in his new position, and not for the first time regretted his quick promotion. Shaking his head and wincing at the pain from his injury, he envied the Foresters of Nighton and the men of the Western Watch. The west frontier was filled with plenty of challenges and adventure, without all the political intrigue. If there were any means to enter their ranks at some point in time, he was determined to find a way, but looking at the demands of his current situation, it appeared highly unlikely. If King Gregor and his own leaders from Daregil Keep felt he was an asset while working directly beneath them, it seemed impossible that he would ever be given the option to serve elsewhere.

Shrugging aside the gloomy thought, he wondered as to the problems immediately facing him. He must find news from Southwatch and elsewhere to see if the Devlent hunting parties were an isolated command, or part of a greater advance, and the only way to do this was to return swiftly to Lastrad and press the couriers. Communication was vital throughout such a large kingdom as Trencit, especially with its isolated outer fortresses and patrols.

The morning grew longer and the road swelled in numbers, as the merchant force getting larger as he closed on the free city. Peddlers wielding carts and on horseback trudged along, entering from other paths as they joined the growing ranks of travelers. In the distance Forlern caught a glimpse of the great Lastrad wall, and knew he would soon be in the city once more. Ahead he heard the pounding of hooves and spotted a company of Lastradian fighters thundering along the roadway, coming towards him. They were at least a score of fighters, and Forlern stopped his mount, hailing them with one hand in the signal of a Daregil Keep envoy. The men approached, the foremost rider halting a few yards before him, peddlers and other travelers giving them a wide berth to either side.

"Hail, traveler from Daregil Keep. Speak your business quickly, our need is great." The man reined his animal close, trying to keep their conversation between them.

"I'm Forlern. I was with Captain Questron hunting for the beast and am only returning now after being forced into the countryside. It's been a long night."

The man's eyes widened beneath his helm. "Captain Forlern," he exclaimed. What news have you to bring? Ill tidings have returned into the city. Are you alone?"

"Yes. Has Questron returned yet?"

The fighter shook his head. "No word from Captain Questron. What can you tell me? What happened to the hunting party?"

"We tracked the creature and came across dead fighters. After we left the woods, we found the first party locked in a fierce battle with marauding Devlents. After defeating these, a greater party assailed us from the forest and we fought an intense battle against larger numbers. I would have fallen myself if I hadn't escaped with another fighter. In the heat of battle, I lost sight of Questron and rode across the fields. The following company never reached us in time. I have no knowledge of what happened after that. You heard nothing?"

"Only scraps of information. It is as I feared then. Several men returned with claims of marauders in the forest, and some of our scouts never came back. The news has been scarce until now."

"Shades…" Forlern rubbed his brow. "I have to speak with the commanders inside to hear news of the raiders and Questron's men." He whispered now, bending closer to the man. "And the fate of Questron himself."

"I have my orders, but I'll send one of my men with you. He can get you where you need to be quicker than on your own."

Whistling sharply, he turned and pointed to one of his fighters, the man immediately coming forward. "Sherit, you'll escort Captain Forlern back into the city and wherever he wishes to go with the utmost speed. Be off now."

Nodding to Forlern, the man urged his horse away, signaling his company to ride. Forlern gestured in thanks, following Sherit and galloping away in the opposite direction. They plunged ahead, moving through the growing throngs of people making their way into the large city. Forlern spotted additional patrols as word was surely spreading about the alarming turn of events. Ignoring the merchants and fighters alike, Forlern continued following Sherit as they entered the tightly guarded field that fronted the great gates, which served as an outer market area for those not wishing to enter the city. At times the Lastradian leadership would levy a small fee to merchants wishing to sell or trade their wares in the sprawling Vanyair market, and those with less money to spare (or a general unwillingness to spend) would find a spot outside among the hundreds of makeshift tents. It took them long minutes to move through this area and eventually they reached the gates and went inside, just another speck of traffic pushing onwards. Guards would pull aside people randomly if they felt so inclined to do so, but by and large, access to Lastrad was open and unhindered. Even with the recent attacks by the creature, the daytime was considered safe. It was under cover of dark when the killings had taken place.

They passed the garrisons which held the Lastrad guard; long, squat buildings which were prohibited for any not serving in the standing army. Large as the city was, there existed a careful attention to organization and protocol, although this practice was kept normally out of the way, designed as it was to make the flow of commerce smoother. Skirting the thoroughway which led to the greater trading holds and eventually the Vanyair market itself, they moved along roads which took them in between the hundreds of taverns, craft stores, and food eateries which dotted the city in the business district. After a while, these dropped off as well, and they entered the residential area, stone buildings rearing up in every direction and of varying sizes. Here there existed no separation between rankings. A merchant could live next to a military commander, or even a blacksmith. If Lastrad represented one thing, surely it was opportunity, both good and bad.

Sherit continued to lead Forlern, but it was little more than a courtesy. Forlern knew his way around, and on his cloak sat a broach designating his office as an envoy from Daregil Keep, and although he had kept it hidden throughout much of his stay in the city, now it could serve him well and expedite his trip. The inner walls of Lastrad finally loomed before them, and here lay the greatest sign of the city's wealth. Huge homes reared their balconied heads before them, structures built by Lastrad's upper class, and the most successful of its citizens. They halted before the massive gate which was flung wide, but heavily guarded. Sherit hailed the pair of guards who quickly approached them, speaking confidently and pointing to Forlern. The guards conferred for a moment, and then motioned Forlern forward. Sherit inclined his head to the fighter.

"May good fortune follow you, master Forlern. I return to my unit. You've been granted a speedy access. They'll lead you now. Farewell."

The man turned his horse, and Forlern replied. "Thank you, Sherit. Good luck yourself."

A pair of guards now led him through the gates and

beyond, but Forlern ignored his surroundings, his wound aching and his stomach growling. It had been a long night, with several terrible battles, and he knew that fortune had indeed been on his side. The early morning sun hid behind a swelling cluster of clouds which were moving in from the west on a brisk wind, and the air felt humid, threatening rain. Lastrad lay in a temperament region, sheltered somewhat on three sides, but the open plains and lands of southern Trencit were directly west, and the openness could lead to strong storms at times.

On they rode, passing parks filled with green, healthy grass, and a multitude of flowering plants. Ornate gates divided property boundaries, and within the individual grounds could be seen statues and other carvings, created for the owner's pleasure. Meticulous detail was paid attention to in the landscaping and trimming of shrubbery, and sumptuous gardens filled with a dazzling array of flowers and bushes were everywhere. Gentle ponds and even streams dissected this part of the city, and if Forlern had been here in less troubling times, he might have enjoyed the texture and scents of inner Lastrad, but another part of him disliked the clear separation between the very wealthy and the average citizen, and he knew that not all of the power and fortune was nobly created. There was nothing to be gained by such thoughts, and it caused Forlern to look at himself with a more discriminating eye, for he himself was now considered one of Trencit's elites after his promotion. As a captain of the Homeguard, and more importantly personal counselor to King Gregor, there were luxuries which had been bestowed on him while he was still at Daregil Keep. He had to admit that excellent food and some of the finest vintages were nothing to overlook, but he was a fighter foremost, and would never stray from that singular focus. A life of pleasure might appeal to many soldiers, but he didn't want any of that. He was at home while in the sparring barracks, out in the field, or on the hunt, and to give himself up for any indulgences would certainly take the edge off his fighting ability, and that was something he would never allow to happen…

The minutes passed and they traveled along the main artery which eventually led to the palace of the Gran Barshara. By now, Forlern was familiar with the area, moving daily on errands with both his men and Questron's, although the city was so large that he could still get lost in the greater districts. A large building loomed before them, and at last they had arrived at the central command center for the Lastradian army and his own temporary quarters. The guards led him up the gated entrance, more a courtesy than anything else at this point, and his horse was taken away by attendants and he bustled inside, heading for the meeting room and eager for communication. Several officers milled about, and the place had the look of an armed camp ready to move on a second's notice. Looks of recognition came his way, and Forlern scanned the large corridors for someone of high ranking. Within moments he entered the large chamber where strategies were laid out and military discussions were held and a number of officers were present, Forlern finally recognizing the telltale red beard and fiery hair of Skelwold, who was second in command only to Questron himself.

The bearish man raised himself from his chair, storming over to him.

"Forlern! What word have you from the hunting party? Captain Questron has not yet returned."

Frowning, Forlern shook his head, slumping into a chair and holding his arm. "Nothing back from him then?" He lowered his voice. "That is ill news. I'll tell you of our hunt, and the enemy's treachery, although I've some need of aid myself."

"You've been wounded?" He snapped to one of the waiting attendants. "Bring a healer, and some food and wine."

Skelwold leaned over him, a pair of other officers hovering nearby. "Now what has happened?"

"We hunted the beast into the southern woods for several miles, coming across slain members of the first party. We continued on, eventually breaking from the forest and hearing a clamor in the fields. Urging our mounts onward, we clearly heard the sounds of battle, and hurried to aid the men, who we thought had finally caught up to the beast, hoping to finish it off."

Skelwold's eyes were hard, his face expressionless.

Forlern continued. "We were wrong though. We found the first party in heated battle against a company of marauding Devlents."

"Devlents? This far from their homeland?" Skelwold cursed, the other men appearing surprised. There was no question that this was the first they were hearing of the news, and that fact left Forlern with a cold feeling in the pit of his empty stomach.

"Yes. We fought a vicious battle, but our greater numbers turned the tide of fighting and we killed them to the last one."

"And the creature," Skelwold pressed?

"There was still no sign of it, and we barely had time to ask questions before one of the rear guards alerted Questron that another party of Devlents was approaching from the forest, larger than the other."

"A second band of Devlents? Shades..." Skelwold gripped the pommel of his weapon in reflex.

"It was Questron's decision to face this new threat, hoping for relief from supporting fighters which should have been quickly following our own company." Forlern gave him a quizzical look.

"There were two hundred men who were immediately dispatched. It took a while to get them mobilized and out of Lastrad, but they were on your trail," answered Skelwold.

"We never saw them," said Forlern. "Whether they arrived after the fighting started, or were waylaid themselves, I don't know. Against greater odds, we were losing the fight. I barely escaped myself, unhorsed in the midst of some terrible fighting. One of your men was nearby; a member of Questron's personal guard, and I rode off with him. If we would have stayed and continued the fighting, we would've been either killed, or taken captive."

"And Captain Questron?"

Forlern shook his head. "I lost sight of him in the heat of the fighting. It was a terrible struggle. One of the fiercest I've seen, and the tide was moving strongly against us. Their numbers were too great. They were not all on horseback, but a mixed company, as is usual for them. Fortunately we were not pursued, but looking back as we rode across the fields, all I saw were Devlents. I was hoping to find Questron back here in Lastrad, but it seems I've arrived before him or the rest of his men, if any were even left…"

His voice trailed off and a young man approached, one of the Lastrad healers. Two other men came near, holding platters of food and goblets of wine and water, which Forlern eagerly accepted.

"And what about the beast?"

"It's dead."

"You killed it?" Skelwold asked.

Forlern shook his head, pausing momentarily as he drank deeply from a goblet. "No. I found a trail of blood leading into a small building. It was already dead when I found it. The creature will trouble Lastrad no longer."

Forlern deliberately left out the part about Klellan, unwilling to let that piece of news go further until he had time to talk with either the Gran Barshara or Questron, so what he said was true enough.

Skelwold backed off, obviously hearing enough of the tale for him to take further action, giving Forlern some time to rest and eat. The other officers followed him, moving to the end of the long table and already in a heated discussion. Forlern had no wish to discuss anything more at the moment, tired and sore as he was. Even if only for a short while, he needed time to get bandaged up and think things through. The young man introduced himself as Haleck, and looked to be hardly more than a boy. He asked Forlern about the injury, probing the area with concern in his eyes.

"I field dressed it, but it's not too serious."

Haleck was silent, pulling out items from a pouch at his side. Seconds later he pulled apart the loose wrap that Forlern had used, swabbing the area down with a moist towel, causing the fighter to wince. Concentrating on eating his meal, Forlern let the man go about his work. Young or not, if he was the main healer in the command headquarters, then he must know what he was doing, Forlern knew. Several minutes passed and Haleck was finished, informing him about the ointment he used, and that Forlern needed to rest his injury and his body.

Forlern smiled to him. "If these soldiers let me rest, then I will. I have a feeling I won't be able to do much on my own anytime soon."

"If you need anything, please summon me and I'll come to see you." Bowing slightly, the man moved away, carrying his pouch. Forlern wondered again about the young healer, but from the corner of his eye he saw Skelwold approaching, the officers seemingly come to some type of decision.

"I hope you've found some remedy to your wound and appetite. A fighter of your rank is obviously not kept down by such inconveniences."

Forlern shrugged, knowing that Skelwold required his services, or at least his attention.

"The arrival of the Devlents is of great concern, as you certainly understand. We cannot afford to have roaming bands anywhere near our city. I've ordered large hunting parties to leave within the hour to scour the countryside in all directions. I've also given the order to mobilize several larger groups of fighters to patrol the regions immediately south of the surrounding foothills and mountains that border our city. We need to hear word from Southwatch, and question how such bands of Devlents were left to roam within the shadow of Lastrad."

"They weren't given permission, I assure you," Forlern replied, just as quickly regretting his choice of words.

"Of course not," Skelwod replied gruffly. "But the Royal Legions are either too thin with their own patrols, or something has occurred. I've sent couriers to both there and Clairfeld to alert them. And what of yourself, may I ask? Will you be leaving for Daregil Keep?"

It might have been a harmless question, or maybe not…

Forlern answered. "I'll wait until Captain Questron returns. We need to coordinate all efforts until we hear otherwise, but I have to send word."

"I'll have a courier come over to you soon with parchment. He'll leave for Trencit as soon as you're done with your message."

It was fairly given and a procedural routine, but Forlern wondered if the man was eager to see him go. With Questron missing, perhaps Skelwod felt nervous with Forlern still lingering in Lastrad. After all, Lastrad was a free city, and not under the sovereignty of Trencit and Daregil Keep. It was not a normal occurrence for both cities to be in close contact concerning military strategies. Of course, with the threat from the Devlents and the Dark Mage, times were troubled, and the uncommon was quickly becoming the norm…

Several minutes passed and a courier came over to Forlern, who was now so weary he could hardly keep his eyes open. He needed rest, despite whatever else was happening outside the city walls. The night had been terribly long, the fighting intense, and he would be of no use to anyone while dead asleep on his feet. After finishing his message to Daregil Keep, he saw the courier off, knowing the man would be back at the capital within a few short days. For himself, he pulled aside one of the nearest officers, informing him that he was returning to his own quarters and wanted to be roused once word from Questron arrived. The minutes dragged by as he returned to his room, the halls empty save for an occassional guard at main junctions. He opened the door to his chambers, finding more food and wine on the table, along with some clean garments. Wincing from his wound, he drank deeply, admiring the vintage, one of Lastrad's finest. A bath had been drawn for him and he quickly washed, drying off and tiring more by the minute. The bed was too inviting and he took off his shirt and light mail underneath, collapsing on the blankets and falling asleep almost immediately.

The next few days passed uneventfully for Sarion's company, and although they rode at a good pace, they all welcomed the reprieve. Sarion spent time questioning Wharla, but failed to learn anything more useful than what she had already told him. She was difficult to read, and gave away no indication that she was either lying or telling the truth. He also had Chertron question her at times to see if he could learn anything new or different, but to no avail.

Sarion was not yet willing to concede his trust in her. With all the treachery from the Dark Mage and his minions, there was no room for carelessness. Chensel's life had been attempted, Mugil had led them into a trap at

The Summoning

Sprechyd Wood, and marauding creatures had been harassing them for weeks. To become complacent or lax now would only result in more deaths, and there had been enough of that as of late.

Traveling in a northeasterly direction, Sarion was leading them to the city of Sharield, where they would find safety under the protection of Lord Berillon, an honorable and respected leader whose family were the ancestral heirs of Trencit's most isolated domain. Little news and even less trade ever issued forth from Sharield. The Western Watch and Sharield's modest fighting force kept no open lines of communication. Once someone passed the areas of Gristor and Sarion's own lands, there could be no protection from Nighton's fighters. Patrols wandered past these areas only by command and extenuating circumstances. There simply was not enough manpower to offer anything beyond a rescue mission if people were in trouble, and in these regions, that usually spelled death. The facts were grim, but true. Once someone traveled too far into the wild, the longer they went overdue and missing, the slimmer the chance that they were ever heard from again.

The weather remained fair and warm as the company urged their mounts ahead, the landscape a restless picture of vast forests, small hills, an occasional swamp, and shallow depressions. Wildlife was in abundance, and birds nested in the overhanging branches from the variety of trees. Sarion looked over Ereck's map at times, but it offered little. On the parchment there were a few towns listed by name in the deeper south that Sarion had never heard of before, but the single most important fact of the westland was the wilderness which dominated nearly everything. Settlements and small towns existed, but the further away from Trencit and Nighton one traveled, the more infrequent they became, until they basically ceased to exist.

Evening was upon them and a gap opened ahead

through the forest canopy. Bright birds fluttered at their intrusion, and several stags pranced away, as Sarion caught a glimpse of higher terrain ahead; the foothills and mountains which gave home to Sharield. They were approaching its outer territory, although they had yet to come across a single traveler or hunter, but Sarion knew that the people of Sharield lived primarily within a short distance of the city. Being isolated from greater Trencit and its larger population, the people in these regions lived in fear of the western wilderness and the predators from the Ridgeline and Grammore. Tales of monsters and terrible beasts were not legends in these parts, but a fact of reality. They both respected and dreaded what lurked to the west, and were much more comfortable keeping their distance from the unknown, huddled against the mountains and placing distance between themselves and the shadow of the unpredictable and dangerous western frontier.

Sarion believed they would reach the city by the following day, probably in the evening. The view gave him a vague idea of where the gap was located which gave home to Sharield, and he thought it would be enough to guide them the rest of the way. This assumption, and the probability of meeting travelers as well.

They rode on for another hour until daylight had faded, and they picked a suitable campsite of the night; a small clearing which gave them enough space to see into the forest in every direction. He wondered about Chardoom and what his plans would be, but still doubted there was any chance of them catching up with the company until they were safely within Sharield. Although it certainly bothered him knowing that one of the Dark Mage's powerful servants was roaming the westland, there was nothing he could do about the matter. They really had no idea of what Chardoom's immediate orders were, despite having Wharla in their control. She claimed that Chardoom was planning to go east at some point in time, and that was all. She claimed that her father had never indulged his relationship and commands from the Dark Mage, although she had challenged him about his allegiance, urging him to leave his control. Thinking about Wharla's explanation, Sarion concluded that east meant either Sharield or Nighton. There was nothing else of importance to be found until one reached Trencit's western borders, so it was not a great leap in figuring any of this out. The Dark Mage's purpose was quite clear.

The fighters went about preparing the camp, which was always a temporary routine as the men were braced for a quick departure. Sarion permitted a small fire to be lighted, and Geld Rinn took the first watch. Sarion took a small helping of dried beef from his pouch, then walked over towards Wharla, the ever-vigilant Lassel only a few paces away. Sarion inclined his head for privacy, moving to Wharla's side.

"You don't seem to mind these long rides."

She shrugged. "As I told you, I was brought up with horses in the days of my youth. Traveling with my father, I learned a lot of things about living in the wild and surviving."

"So your father wasn't always blinded by his ambition," Sarion said.

"No, he wasn't. But he did have a thirst for power that led him to where he is now. I miss the way he used to be..."

She was silent, and Sarion respected her mood for a moment. Wharla had spoken similarly in their previous conversations, and he could find no inconsistencies in her remarks. Whether she was being honest or careful, he couldn't tell. And if it *was* the latter, then the only possibility was that she had things to hide.

"Do you have any additional information as to Chardoom's next move? Something you might have overlooked before?"

Wharla shook her head. "I wish I could help you more. I still think he will try to pursue us."

"How often would messengers come from the Dark Mage?"

"Very few. I don't know if he was waiting on orders, or if something had already been decided."

Sarion considered, but said nothing.

Wharla stared at him, the smoky gray eyes boring into his own. "I still believe he will do everything in his power to get me back," she insisted.

"For a man aligned with someone as evil as the Dark Mage, he has a strange affection for another person, even his own daughter. Are you saying he loves you, that family matters to him after all this?" Sarion asked.

Wharla appeared hurt by the question; Sarion could read this in her eyes, although he knew she was doing her best not to look vulnerable. He felt bad for her, enigma or not...

She shook her head. "It's not love that drives Chardoom, not even for his own flesh and blood."

"Then what is it?" Sarion asked.

"Pride..."

She bowed her head, seating herself on the ground, her back to a large stone. Sarion watched her for a moment, considering the brief conversation while still trying to understand if Wharla was a friend or foe...

The company departed early the next morning, well-rested and spirits high, as they knew that soon they would be within the protective confines of Sharield. Many days had passed while they searched the westland for Gar-kiln, ultimately finding it with the help of Ereck, but their mission had ended in near disaster at the hands of Chardoom and the terrible guardians of the Dark Mage. Much of the horror had gradually bled away while they fled through the wilderness, but not entirely so. There were seasoned fighters among the group, but most of them had never witnessed such creatures of violence. As Sarion glanced among them now, his gaze skimmed over Lassel's lean form. Of all the group, she seemed unaffected by the nightmares they had faced. While dozens of fighters had fallen beneath the Killworm's rampage, she had gone on the attack, fearless and deadly in her own right. Throughout their journey, her attitude had been one of relentless vigilance and a readiness for battle at any given time, Sarion could not see any cracks in her confidence.

In fact, Sarion saw much of himself in the young woman...

This realization dawned on him for the first time. Even comparing her to the capable Geld Rinn, Sarion had to admit that she was at a level of her own, above any other Nighton fighters that he could think of, including veterans like Valadire, Piril, and Bertilik. He may have doubted her back at Nighton, but only because she was a woman, and he had been very wrong in his assumptions...

They made good time through the morning, the hours melting away beneath the eaves of the great westland forest. The sky became cloudy overhead, but these were not rain clouds, the air remaining pleasantly warm. The trees grew thinner as they rode along, and they noticed the ground angling upwards as the elevation increased. They came across a growing number of rocks and small boulders, the forest melding into the foothills surrounding Sharield. They still had failed to encounter any other travelers, but Sarion wasn't too concerned, knowing the habits of the people who lived in this territory. The morning was all but past them when they entered a narrow valley, wooded and climbing higher into the terrain ahead. It appeared to be a natural pathway towards their destination, and Sarion saw no reason to change course. None of the group had ever been to Sharield, so the exact location of the city was still uncertain. Still, it couldn't be that difficult to find. General knowledge was that within the gap of these mountains was where they would find the city. If they needed some assistance, surely there would be at least a few travelers in the area.

They plunged ahead, Sarion keeping them at a steady pace, but not taxing the horses. They covered several miles, making their way deeper into the valley, the path becoming more difficult as the ground grew uneven and pitted with small holes, gravel and rock scattered everywhere. Calling for a short halt Sarion dismounted, the fighters falling into routine with Piril taking watch.

Chertron came over to him offering food from his pouch, which Sarion accepted.

"Sharield sits upon a lake, and a river spills out from its depths. Once we come across that waterway, it should be an easy task to find the city itself. I'm still uncertain as to how close we are. These foothills and mountain ranges grow deep, and appear formidable if you chance its depths." Sarion shrugged.

"You're unfamiliar with this area then as well," said Chertron.

"I'm afraid so. For all my wanderings in the westland, we never sent patrols anywhere close to Sharield. To the north, we would skirt the edges of Lord Pralicon's domains, not much further than Dwellyn. To the east, we rode to to the hills surrounding Sprechyd Wood, and to the west, at times we dared the base of the Ridgeline. But to the south, our foremost patrols would be days away from Sharield. There is simply too much wilderness separating the villages of the westland and the deeper south."

"Aye." Chertron nodded. "Trencit rarely if ever corresponds with Sharield, from my own knowledge. No trade, no envoys, and nothing in the way of news. I'm surprised it even falls under Trencit rule."

"In truth, perhaps it doesn't. Time has changed the face of Trencit, and as the threat from the east has grown, its power and influence to the west has waned. The Western Watch stands on its own. Even though we ask for aid now, I fear that little, if any, is forthcoming. And if Daregil Keep cannot give any, then the people of the westland will think less of future loyalty."

Sarion knew he was assuming much here, but was he really that far off in his thinking? If King Gregor was unwilling – or unable – to send aid, then how would that ultimately affect their loyalty to Trencit and its monarchs? It was an interesting question he posed, but one with little meaning for their present situation. They needed to find Sharield soon, and at the very least warn its citizens of the dangers coming from Grammore and the Dark Mage. Of all Trencit's cities, Sharield was not only the most isolated, but the smallest and most vulnerable. Even though most people had never been there, these things were accepted as fact from everything Sarion had been told before, and he had no reason to disbelieve it. Jerol had been to Sharield himself years ago, and had spoken thus to Sarion.

He looked back the way they had come, admiring the beauty of their surroundings; the climbing heights of the valley to either side, the clean sky overhead with fluffs of clouds pushing along in the breeze, and in the distance, the endless forests of the great westland. As his keen eyes glazed over the lower elevations, he spotted one of the larger clearings they had traveled through, and his eyes fixed on the spot as he saw movement.

Something large and black was making its way across the ground, and heading directly for them...

Still a fair distance off, he was certain of it, as the shape, which was not much more than a blur, disappeared into the brush.

"Chertron, something follows." Sarion pointed, tugging his friend's shirt sleeve, but it was already too late. Whatever it was had vanished into the forest.

"I don't see anything. Are you sure?"

Sarion nodded, a chill going down his spine.

"An animal? A bear, perhaps?"

"Maybe, but it's impossible to say from here." Even after uttering those words, Sarion instinctively knew that something was tracking them, something dangerous...

He turned about, giving Chertron a hard look. "We need to leave. I think we're being hunted."

"Shades..." Chertron muttered, shaking his head. He moved over to the others, several quizzical looks coming his way. Sarion remained where he was, staring down the valley for a few moments before turning away. The Nighton fighters were gathering their belongings, barely off their horses for a few minutes, but none of them complained or challenged the order. Discipline was a thing of pride among the hunters of Nighton, and they held a high degree of respect for all the Foresters.

Sarion approached them, Geld Rinn already back in the lead and awaiting the order to move ahead. Sarion felt a growing sense of dread that something deadly was stalking them, but he needed to alert the fighters first. Valadire moved towards him but Sarion waved him off.

"Listen." He kept his voice low, the wind beginning to stir and gaining strength as they advanced to higher country. "Something follows behind. In one of the clearings we passed through, I spotted something large and dark moving directly along the trail we left. It was too far away for me to identify what it might be, but my heart tells me that it hunts us."

Wharla spoke. "It is as I feared. Chardoom will not remain in Gar-kiln after letting us escape."

"Do you have any idea of what it might be?" Sarion asked. "It was not the Ravenor, and I don't think it was an ogre. I don't believe either one could have stayed so close with us these past few days."

"I think you're right," she answered. "The Ravenor is huge and powerful, but not very swift, especially moving through such thick country. I've never seen it out on the hunt, but still…"

"Then what do you think it might be? Time presses on us, and we need to flee this place." Valadire entered the conversation, looking anxiously down the valley.

Wharla stared at him for a moment, breathing deeply before answering, her face looking grim. "I think Chardoom has sent the Crage to track us. He uses the creature as a messenger of sorts, meeting with other servants of the black one."

The Crage, Sarion thought dismally…The same creature that had taken four of the men in Valadire's group. "What else can you tell us? Anything that can help us defeat or elude it?"

"It's deadly and quick," she answered. "Your men were unfortunate to have encountered it. The Crage will kill on instinct. It moves quietly and with cunning, and if it tracked us this far, surely it will not give up. Even against greater numbers, I fear your fighters are no match for it."

Sarion frowned. It was the last thing he wanted to hear, and although he had no true measure of the creature than her uncomforting description, he was not about to conceded anything. "Does it possess magic of some type?"

"Magic? None that I'm aware of, but I know only a little, and I've only seen it a few times. I have no wish to see these foul monsters my father surrounds himself with…From the little that Chardoom has told me, the Crage meets with other messengers. How it communicates I don't know. Chardoom holds the staff which enables him to control these creatures, and he bears the mark of his evil master on his arm."

"The mark of the master…" Sarion started to

respond, then he understood. "The metal band."

"Yes," said Wharla.

"All right. Let's be off quickly, and stop for nothing. I'm still unsure exactly where Sharield is, and unless I'm mistaken, none of you has been there before." He looked at them hopefully, thinking someone had knowledge to share, but they were all silent.

Wharla put one hand on Sarion's arm. "Listen, your best hope is to avoid it..." She hesitated, "...but it would be more prudent to leave me behind. Maybe once my father has me again in his possession he'll let you go. I don't wish to see you or any others come to harm, Sarion."

Sarion shook his head. "It's not an option. And if you *are* telling me the entire truth, surely you deserve to live your life free, and out of his control. I wouldn't leave anyone to that fate."

"But..." Wharla continued, but Sarion cut off her remark with a wave of his hand.

"Cherton and Lassel take the rear guard. I need your keen eyes and ears where they are most needed. Let's go."

With that, the company was again in motion, the sturdy war horses moving carefully through the terrain, now hampered by rock and scrub brush, unable to gain their faster gait. The traveled along, the valley plunging steadily upwards, and Sarion felt increasingly worried about the higher reaches ahead. If the creature behind them was indeed the Crage, it would not be slowed down as much as the horses, and would steadily gain on them. If the going became too difficult further ahead, they might even lose the advantage of being on horseback altogether, and that would place them in a perilous situation of having to turn and fight at some point; something that he wanted to avoid at all costs. Every encounter he'd experienced with the Grammore predators had ended in disaster, with men dying. Their numbers were now reduced, and they were in unfamiliar territory. The lowlands creature might be far from its own homeland, but if it was like any of its other kindred it was a natural predator, well-adapted to the wild no matter its surroundings. Sarion fervently hoped he was wrong about the whole thing, but his instincts told him otherwise...

The minutes dragged by slowly, at times several of the fighters peering over their shoulders at what might be following, unseen. Sarion could feel the mood of the company change, anxiety worming its way into their thoughts. If whatever he had seen was indeed trailing them, it would catch up with them during another rest, so he continued to push them forward, hoping that they would reach the perimeters of Sharield before the day's end, although he was still unconvinced if they were even that close. As early afternoon turned into late, the company finally breached the upper end of the valley, but found no relief in the landscape. Sarion's worst fears were quickly becoming apparent as the way ahead grew even more dense and harder to navigate. The horses struggled, and their progress slowed further. A stream appeared before them as they broke through a section of pine trees, and Sarion gave a short whistle, signaling for a halt. They needed something to gain them time, a chance to shake off any possible pursuit. He motioned for Geld Rinn to lead them upstream through the water, which was maybe a dozen yards wide but only a few inches deep, no problem for the animals to negotiate. The water would confuse their trail, and it seemed the best plan at the moment. The company urged their mounts into the cold water, moving to the right and southward. Sarion didn't know how long they could travel within the stream, but maybe it would give them enough breathing room to place more distance between themselves and their unseen pursuer. The ground continued angling higher, and soon the way became much more difficult, the stream narrowing and the rocks growing larger. When they could go no further, Geld Rinn led them up a shallow embankment, the sturdy war horses gaining the top effortlessly. Fortune was on their side as the forest ahead was steeper now, but less rocky and dense. It gave them the clearance they needed, and they now pushed the animals ahead with a swifter gait, but not quite a full run. Birds of prey cried from overhead, looking for small woodland creatures to catch, but the fighters had too much on their mind except to make as great speed as possible.

They went on through the forest for well over an hour, feeling more confident, with the sky clouding over, the afternoon waning fast. The air had also grown a bit sharper, and they had long ago emerged from the flatter wilderness which made up the huge expanse of the westland. As they galloped along, the forest thinned out considerably and Sarion paused for a moment, peering back the way they had come. All he saw was the valley behind them, filled with nothing but an endless wall of trees, the sides of the gorge plunging high to either side. The entire company suddenly stopped, as Geld Rinn now reined them in. Sarion looked ahead curiously, immediately spotting the reason for the pause. A narrow but clear trail sat before them, following in the direction they were taking. There was no mistaking it as they all moved forward. It wasn't very wide, but it had all the marks of a well-trodden path.

"At last..." Valadire spoke at his side. "This might be what we've been looking for."

"I think you're right. With any luck it will lead us to Sharield, or at least an outpost. By the looks of the rough country we've come through, it's little wonder we haven't come across a single traveler yet. Hurry now!"

They moved in quick formation, not a single rider out of place. The footing was sure and the horses galloped confidently ahead. Sarion kept them at a good pace, but one that would not overtax the animals in case greater speed was needed later. As of yet there had been no further sign of pursuit, but that did little to ease his worry. He was not about to trust in luck, and to let down their guard now with a false sense of security could prove fatal.

Light was fading around them as a premature dusk settled over the westland, the sun hidden behind thickening clouds. The horses hurtled along relentlessly, their superior breeding giving them lasting endurance with plenty in their reserves. Their formation remained the same since earlier, but Sarion paused for a moment, signaling the others to proceed. He stopped alongside of Chertron and Lassel to speak with the pair, telling them to backtrack to see if anything pursued them, and to rendezvous ahead later. Chertron nodded, agreeing with the plan, but Lassel said nothing, her demeanor unchanged. The girl was focused on the task at hand, and would let nothing distract her. Sarion wondered again about her background which had hardened her into such a tough survivor. Earlier he had talked with Piril, and the fighter was now in charge of keeping an eye on Wharla. At this point in time, Sarion tended to believe her story, but nevertheless, he was not going to keep her in complete confidence anytime soon. He needed either additional time to try and flush out her secrets, or something else from her which would put his distrust finally to rest. As for that, he had no idea what it would take...

The company rumbled ahead, now reduced in numbers temporarily until the pair would reunite with them once again. Sarion slowed their pace, not wanting to place too much distance between both groups.

Nightfall arrived, shadows enveloping the woods and hills around them, and the riders pulled out their torches, all of the fighters realizing that it would be a long stretch before them, facing the probability of little rest and no sleep. Sarion knew they were weary, but weighed against the odds of fighting a potential unknown adversary following somewhere behind, it was an easy decision.

With Valadire directly in front of him, and Bertilik

following close behind, Sarion pushed them onwards, keeping alert for movement in the woods to either side. The landscape remained virtually unchanged, and without the path, they would have wandered aimlessly among the gorges and hills. He had always known Sharield was isolated and little more than a name on a map, but not to this extent...

The path grew wider, and Geld Rinn pulled them up short, turning around. He was little more than a shadow himself in the gloom, his cloak pulled tight around his lean form. Sarion looked beyond him and saw a small building sitting off to the side. The single window was dark and the place looked lifeless.

"An outpost of Sharield. I'm certain of it." Valadire spoke.

Sarion nodded in agreement. "But it seems no one is on guard. Whether by design or event, we don't know." He motioned for Bertilik and Geld Rinn to approach, and he didn't need to advise caution to the fighters. The others fanned out to a small perimeter about it, all of them staying on the path. Geld Rinn entered first, Bertilik at his heels. They disappeared inside for long moments, as Sarion grew increasingly uneasy. Patience, he told himself. Although he was ready for a trap behind every door and wall, he knew that it was not always true. Shortly, Geld's head reappeared, and then the rest of him.

"Empty inside. There are food stocks inside the back room, and a small loft upstairs with padding, but little else. Hay and a few bottles of wine."

"Let's take what we can." Valadire nodded. "Should we rest here for a while?"

Sarion replied. "Yes. I want to give Chertron and Lassel time to catch up with us as well. They should be arriving soon enough."

Geld Rinn went back inside the building with Valadire, Wharla, and Piril, while Sarion remained outside with Bertilik and Jurit. He spoke little with the men, making sure they all took a bite to eat and drank some ale at the very least, which they did shortly after. Geld Rinn tended to the horses, eventually sitting down himself, back leaning against a tree. There was little talk amongst themselves, all of them wondering the same unspoken thought. Where were Chertron and Lassel, and what news would they be returning with?

Sarion made the decision to stay there until the two fighters came back, even if it took all night. He trusted them completely, and even faced with the possibility of encountering an unknown predator which tracked them, he knew they would escape. An even more distasteful thought was that at least *one* of them would escape, and try that he would, this last morbid thought was impossible to entirely banish from his mind. He knew it was the necessity of their mission and service as hunters of Nighton which made him think such grim things, but Sarion had commanded men in his previous service, and never acted in denial of the fact that he would have to again place men in danger, and at times they would die. As much as he tried to take things on himself by putting his own life at terrible risk, he was loathe to bestow the same risk to others.

Yet he must…

He closed his eyes then, feeling guilty that he was able to do so while Lassel and Chertron scouted behind. Several minutes passed, his eyelids fluttering, when Geld Rinn and Valadire shouted, Sarion hearing the same noise and immediately springing to his feet, weapon in hand. The sounds of horses was swiftly approaching, but not from behind them. Someone was riding towards them from the south!

The members of the company were all alert and ready, although Sarion's heart lifted at the sound. He was certain the riders were from Sharield, and they could bring them the news they were desperately seeking. Materializing from the dark were tiny pinpricks of light; horsemen bearing torches, and from the looks of it, there were well over a dozen. As figures finally appeared on the path ahead, Geld Rinn waved his lantern in greeting, Sarion coming forward.

"Hail, riders from Sharield! We are seeking aid from the worthy fighters of Lord Berillon!"

The company reined their steeds in sharply, hoods lifted from cowled faces. The party numbered well over a dozen, and Sarion nodded in relief.

A deep voice echoed forth, and a tall form dismounted from a huge warhorse.

"Who wanders here in the night? Speak your names."

Sarion stepped forwards. "I am Sarion, Second Forester of Nighton." He held his fist high in the westland greeting, the man hesitating for a moment, then returning the gesture.

"Sarion, your name is indeed familiar, even in our fair city of Sharield. Second Forester? What brings such a high ranking officer this far south?"

"It's a long story, and one we have little time for at the moment, I'm afraid. Your aid would be well-received, though."

"Of that you have no fear, then, comrade from Nighton." He grasped Sarion's outstretched hand, squeezing tightly. "My name is Mielkon, Third Captain of Sharield's north guard. Word arrived in Nighton recently that marauders were scavenging the westland, and we should be alert. The warning was well-taken, and goes in hand with the rumors circulating our own territory. If it's true that Nighton itself has been assaulted, then the entire westland is at risk."

"True indeed. We were there when the attack occurred."

Mielkon frowned, his face lightly bearded and his

deep eyebrows furrowing. "What aid can we give you? I'm sure you're not here by chance. Hopefully you've entertained yourself with the provisions inside by now?"

"We have, although we've been riding without rest since daybreak. Two of our fighters are scouting behind, and we await them."

"Scouting behind? Is there some danger nearby?" Mielkon asked.

"I fear we are being followed."

"By what?" Mielkon looked at the company, then past them, further down the trail.

"Possibly a predator from Grammore."

"From Grammore? How certain are you of this?" Mielkon questioned.

"I'm not, but I spotted something in a clearing earlier in the day, although it was some distance off."

"Could it have been an animal, or were you mistaken?"

"It's possible, but due to the nature of our mission, we have reason to believe otherwise. We've battled such creatures before, and fled from the village of Gar-kiln. Have you heard of this place?"

Mielkon rubbed his beard absently. "I've heard the name mentioned before, but it's been years. What happened there?"

"We had information from a prisoner about a servant of the Dark Mage taking shelter there. Have you been told of this enemy from the Lowlands?"

Mielkon nodded. "We took counsel after couriers of Nighton arrived. It was only a few days ago, and we haven't yet had time to fully digest the news or decide on a course of action."

Valadire stepped forward. "You need to do so immediately. The danger is real, and the enemy powerful. The westland has never seen the likes of the evil one and his foul emissaries. We have lost many good fighters from

Nighton."

Mielkon seemed to measure him for a moment, and then held up his hands. "I have no reason to disbelieve any of this, you must know. Your presence here alone confirms that something important is afoot. But I also have a rendezvous scheduled here at the outpost with a patrol."

Sarion felt chills at Mielkon's words. "When?" he asked.

"This very night. When we saw your flames, we thought you were them."

Sarion looked over at Valadire. "It seems we all are waiting on our comrades then…" He addressed the Sharield officer again. "Why don't we go inside? There's much to discuss. I want to send someone back down the path. We need to find out what happened with the rest of our company, and your men as well."

Mielkon nodded, then returned to his company. Moments later a pair of riders moved forward, heading along the trail. Sarion stared at them for a moment, then nodded. He debated whether sending someone else from his own party along with them, deciding that they needed rest instead, trusting in Mielkon's warriors. Shortly, the Sharield fighters set up watch, while Sarion and Mielkon went inside to discuss the situation. Sitting down at the small table, Sarion immediately asked the questions he needed to have answered.

"How far away is the city?"

"We're only several hours ride. This path eventually leads straight to Sharield."

Sarion nodded. "That is good news at least. We've ridden hard the past several days through the wilderness, and have yet to come across a single traveler."

"Nothing unusual there," Mielkon said. "Besides Sharield, there are only a few outlying villages. Less people than ever before live outside the city proper. Once in a while, someone travels north, trying their fortune either in

Nighton or Trencit, and fewer yet go into the deep south where several towns remain."

"How fared the couriers from Nighton?" asked Sarion. He looked around the small building, lanterns on the table casting eerie shadows on the wall. Picking up a piece of dried meat, he realized how hungry he was. It had been long since he had been able to draw a warm bath and sleep in a bed, and he wondered how Edward was doing. Much safer in Nighton than where he had been, surely...

"The messengers were well. At least before leaving our city. From what you've been saying, I hope they remain so. They also brought word that General Charadan has fallen. Even in such isolated regions as our own, we know of his standing. So this is true then?"

"Unfortunately it is. I was on a mission with him. He actually came looking for me to guide him along the Ridgeline."

"For what purpose? Mielkon asked.

"Tracking marauders. We came across an ogre and fought it in a terrible battle. Charadan decided to pursue the creature, thinking it had something to do with the rumors of unrest in the westland. In the end, we found out all too much, I'm afraid."

"Where did Charadan fall?"

"In Grammore. We trailed the beast for days, eventually catching up with it in an abandoned fortress. The ogre killed him, and in the end, I slew the monster. Only three of us returned from the company."

Mielkon stared at him for a moment in amazement, then responded. "If one goes into that cursed land, there can be no expectation of anything except misfortune and death. I've been to the Ridgeline once, and that was enough. And from what I've heard, you led an expedition there against the Glefins."

"I did," Sarion replied. "We actually captured one inside Grammore."

"You did? Then they still survive?"

"I don't know that answer. It claimed to have been the last of its kind. It betrayed us in the end and escaped."

"Not surprising, coming from one of those foul creatures."

Sarion took the opportunity again to ask about Sharield. "Has anything happened within your territory? Raids or tales of marauders?"

"There are stories, but nothing substantial. There are some folk who venture further out from the city and its protection. Mostly trappers and hunters. Who can say what they have seen? Besides a few farms and the handful of villages I mentioned, there are no larger towns in this area. Only Sharield."

Sarion nodded, realizing that Sharield was a bastion of its own here in the deeper south. There could be no help from these people for the plight of the westland, for either Trencit or Nighton. They numbered too few, and the distance alone prevented strong lines of communication or coordinated patrols. At that moment, Sarion keenly felt the fragile situation of the entire westland. If there had been no war ongoing in the east, then perhaps the mighty armies of Trencit could have come into play, guarding large regions of the borderlands, but as it was, Sarion believed King Gregor would send little, if any help, and he knew with a sinking sense of foreboding that Nighton really was on its own. To the north, Gwerath would protect its own lands, and the proud Lord Pralicon had already refused to send men to fight against the Devlents. As he pondered the greater scheme of events, he wondered if Trencit was slowly unbinding, the outer provinces breaking away on their own. If Pralicon declared his territory completely free of any loyalty to Daregil Keep, what would the king do? What *could* he do? At this point in time, it was most likely a loose alignment, and with the prolonged war in the east, perhaps Pralicon was flexing his own wings to an even greater extent. Maybe that was exactly his plan, and what better time to attempt such a bold move than when the very kingdom of Trencit was threatened on both sides? If true, it couldn't have come at a worse moment, when the Houses needed to work together against the evil that was building against them…

"Sarion?" Mielkon leaned towards him from across the table.

"Yes?"

"You seemed lost in thought there. You and your men need rest; that is plain to see."

"You're right, on both accounts. I have much on my mind. Since Charadan came to my farm weeks ago, my life has been in turmoil." Sarion's statement was frank and spontaneous, and Mielkon looked at him with a sincere expression.

"I understand. Often I'm away from my wife and family for extended periods of time. You hold the second highest position in Nighton now, which is no small thing. Chensel is well-respected throughout the westland, as was Jerol. You bear much responsibility upon your shoulders. These are tough times for the Western Watch, and yourself."

Sarion managed a small smile, appreciating the man's understanding. "And right now I'm worried about my fighters, as are you. Hopefully we'll see them soon. The night grows long."

With that, both men lifted their mugs to drink, the room falling silent.

"I think we've come back far enough."

The Summoning

Chertron stared down the forest trail, listening to the sounds of the woods as the night creatures stirred on their nocturnal forage for food. Several bats flapped over their heads, and in the distance a bird of prey cried out, seeking an evening meal. Lassel paused at his side, the girl's face unreadable. Chertron felt strangely confident in her presence. She had proven herself invaluable on the battlefield, and Chertron was not alone among those who had been impressed. He still would rather have Sarion or the shorttempered Forlern as company, but Lassel's presence had a calming effect on the seasoned fighter. She exuded a strong sense of capability, and he liked having that while in the field.

They both had their lanterns out, although they had muffled the light to some extent. Although it would give them away to nearby eyes, without it they would be riding essentially blind beneath the forest eaves. The sky was clouded overhead, and they could not hope for either moonlight or starlight even if they were in a clearing.

So they waited there, both of them probing outward with their senses, trying to discover any secrets which the darkness might hold. There was nothing out there that they could determine, only the normal sounds of the forest. Chertron wanted to wait it out longer. Despite the prospect and certainty that something might well be tracking them, he would rather know this fact for sure, than find out unexpectedly and at some later point. They were also unsure of how far away they were from the city of Sharield; a discomforting thought.

Chertron reached for his pouch, taking the opportunity to quench his thirst. Something fluttered in the branches above his head, most likely a bird, and he ignored the noise, Lassel never even bothering to look. This was not the time or place for discussion, so they both remained silent, focusing on the shadows and the mood of the forest. Without warning, they both stiffened in their saddles, hearing something far off.

It was coming from further down the trail in the direction of where they had traveled earlier. Cherton listened intently, and then he recognized the noise. It was the sound of horse's hooves, galloping along the path, but heading towards them. The lean fighter breathed a sigh of relief.

"Seems like we'll be encountering our first travelers from Sharield. I can't imagine it being anything else."

Lassel nodded, her face lightening. "It will be good to find someone else finally."

"What? Am I not companion enough?" A huge grin broke his face, and Lassel smirked at his attempt at humor.

"Yes, but you're in need of a good bath, fighter."

Cherton's mouth opened in surprise, and then he barely concealed a laugh. The girl had some spark in her; that was for sure. He was about ready to say so when a new noise reached their ears -- one that sent chills down to their very bones...

Screaming. Men screaming in pain and surprise.

"Shades..." Chertron muttered beneath his breath. "That company is being attacked!"

Lassel was quiet now, their lighthearted banter extinguished like a moth into flame. "They need our aid, Chertron!"

The fighter leaned forward in his saddle, torn by indecision. Men were fighting, and probably dying down there, and he had a strong suspicion that whatever had been pursuing them was responsible. If so, then a deadly predator from Grammore was dangerously close, and had been following them after all, possibly the beast known as the Crage. It seemed more likely than a random encounter with something from the lowlands this far east, or bandits waylaying travelers. No, too much of a coincidence...

All these things passed through his mind in a fraction of a second, and he had to decide quickly. The rest of the company needed to be warned. Their mission was the priority, and as a veteran fighter he understood the importance of such, and the sacrifices which came with it as well.

"Lassel, return to Sarion. He has to be warned. I'll go down the path and either help or see what has taken place."

"That's madness. Either we both go or neither of us. Alone, you won't stand a chance against one of those monsters."

They heard the clash of steel and more cries as the fighting intensified. Muttering beneath his breath, Cherton knew that there was no time to waste, so he charged his horse down the trail. It only took Lassel a fraction of a second and she was right behind him, no hesitation in her own decision. The pair raced down the path, catching snatches of sound from the skirmish taking place somewhere close ahead.

Cherton knew they would be upon the scene in moments, and he needed to have a care that they didn't fall victim themselves. Whatever was down there had the advantage of secrecy, while they knew what was going on. He tried to convince himself that it would make all the difference, but he wasn't completely sure...

To his surprise, Lassel now overtook him and was in the lead, her superior horsemanship surpassing his own. Cursing, he now found himself trailing the Nighton fighter, both admiring her skill and resenting her boldness. They continued racing ahead for long moments, then she eased her own horse. They had to be very close, and the woods had fallen silent around them. Chertron spotted a few flickers of light on the ground in the distance, and knew it to be from lanterns fallen from their riders. The entire forest was hunkered down, and the absence of sound was far worse than the earlier screams of men.

Chertron instinctively knew that the members of the

company which had been traveling the path were all dead…

The other harsh reality of the situation was not lost on him as well, that whatever had caused the carnage might very well be coming towards them now.

Both of them stopped in their tracks, scanning the scene ahead. Through the gloom, Cherton saw the crumpled forms of men lying on the ground, and not just men, but their horses as well. He couldn't tell how many were there, but it had to be over a dozen.

In that short amount of time, they had all been killed. He swallowed heavily, feeling a sense of dread which threatened to consume him. Seasoned as a fighter and survivor of terrible ordeals, Chertron felt the clammy hands of fear tugging at him, trying to leave him vulnerable to its clutches.

Even when the attack finally came, it was only through Lassel's skill that both their lives were saved. A huge form erupted from the trees to their left and Lassel grabbed him by the arm and unseated him, pivoting her horse at the same time. Stunned, Chertron held onto her for his life, her steed galloping back up the path as something quick and deadly knocked his horse to the ground, immediately following after them. Fearful that he might slip and be lost, the girl adjusted herself so that he could get a more secure hold, and pulled him upright behind her now. Arms about the slender girl's body, it was all Chertron could do to whisper into her ear, his breath coming in ragged gasps.

"Thank you…"

The Summoning

Sarion and Mielkon discussed strategies between Nighton and Sharield, both admitting there was little either one could actually do for the other. Valadire entered the building as well, at times voicing his opinion, but leaving most of the conversation to the other two.

The discussion touched on several important facts, notably that Nigthon's forces had been diminished the past ten years, especially after the threat from the Glefins had been eradicated. Daregil Keep had requested fighting men for Trencit, and some had gone, while others like Sarion had left the Western Watch for their own affairs. And recently, the Nighton hunters had lost scores of men at the hands of Grammore predators, further reducing their ability to act. Sarion went over the list of patrols in his head, rounding out numbers, succeeding only in dampening his spirits. He told Mielkon what was on his mind, the man nodding and shaking his head.

"As you say. Too few in these dark times. We are fortunate to be isolated, in this case. I hardly think this Dark Mage will openly strike at our city."

Sarion said nothing, but didn't share his confidence. Their enemy always seemed to be a step ahead of them, and the only thing predictable about him *was* his unpredictability. He felt himself trapped in the vortex of events which had swept him up several weeks ago and thrown him about, taking him from the westland and into the dread Grammore Lowlands, forcing him to use all his skill in a veritable daily fight for his life, and now the protection of many others.

"Well, once I meet with the patrol, I'll escort you back to Sharield. But may I ask, what then of your plans? Besides rest and fresh supplies, I'm afraid our city can give you little else in the larger fight against this enemy. Lord Berillon will not send his men much further than the immediate territory around the foothills here, as I'm sure you realize."

"I understand," Sarion replied. "Rest is probably the best thing for us right now. I need to think things through and determine our next move. I thought our venture to Gar-kiln would somehow yield more clarity to our overall war plan, but I find myself with even more questions and too few answers."

Valadire spoke. "Sarion, I fear that even Chensel doesn't know the next step. Originally I was supposed to head up a patrol which would act as a strike force against threats to areas around Nighton, and there's nothing wrong with that idea. But what is the endgame? Our mission was a proactive decision to discover answers, try to unwrap some of these mysteries. As you stated, we haven't uncovered knowledge which can help us to any great degree. If anything, we've only seen more of the Dark Mage's power and the strength of his servants, which is substantial. And disheartening, I might add."

Both men listened, offering nothing.

"I've also heard your earlier notion, which to everyone else sounds desperate. I'm not so sure anymore."

"No?" Sarion asked. "Even though I spoke truly, I second-guess myself now more than before. Meeting Ereck was unexpected, but his knowledge and the map he gave me offered little that we didn't already know. Gar-kiln kept its secrets too closely for us to penetrate. I had hopes that Wharla might reveal some important information, but I'm less certain of that as well. I haven't determined what she is yet. Friend or foe."

"We would be fools to make that assumption. She may yet act in a role for good or bad, but fate will be the one to play that hand." Valadire shrugged. "Going back to your other idea..." He looked over at Mielkon, who had gone over to the shelves now, rummaging around for something. Valadire clearly didn't want to reveal all their plans in front of the Sharield officer, and Sarion agreed. They had to trust their allies with as much as possible, but not everything…

Mielkon returned, grumbling about a lack of dried meat. "Either of you in need of anything else at the moment?"

Sarion and Valadire both shook their heads. "I'll go out and attend to the others for now." Nodding, he left, closing the door behind them.

"I still feel in my heart that this battle will never end in either the westland or Trencit, but in the Grammore Lowlands. As to how or when, I can't say. Something needs to happen first. Some piece of vital information, perhaps. I just don't know…" Sarion held up his hands in frustration.

Valadire sighed. "I understand, my friend. It may well come to that, but now is not the time for such an action. Shades. I hope *never*, in all honesty. I don't know how you managed to survive in that land, after seeing these creatures emerging from that black place into our own lands."

"Valadire, you learn how to survive. Use all your training, but mostly rely on the strength and reliability of your companions." He paused. "Like yourself." Sarion smiled at him. "With such, all things are possible."

Valadire laughed. "Easily spoken, I would say, but I thank you for the compliment. I will not negate such a fair statement, and best to leave it at that."

Sarion stretched, tired but restless. Concerned about the others, he knew there was no way for him to relax until they returned. In the same moment as he sat there thinking about the missing pair, a shout caused them both to leap to their feet. Someone yelled "riders approach" from outside, and the men rushed to the entrance, eager to see what was happening. The entire company was on their feet, fighters from Sharield and his own men. Sarion spotted a silhouette in the distance, coming from towards the valley. He heard the horses' hooves pounding into the ground, and he could see a single rider draw near.

Only one, he thought? His heart sunk, but then he saw that there were two people on one horse. Running towards them, the riders stopped, and with relief he saw both Lassel and Chertron dismount. Several fighters called in recognition, but Sarion moved through the commotion, waving his hand for attention.

"Hail, let's hear them out!" His shout brought order once more, and Mielkon stood at his side, looking the newcomers over.

"From your company, I assume?"

"Sarion, it's good to see you and the others again. Shades…" Chertron came forward, clasping him on the arm. Lassel said nothing, one of Mielkon's men offering her a drink which she quickly grabbed.

"Your horse looks to have run hard. What news do you bear?" Mielkon stood before Chertron, who looked him over curiously.

"This is Mielkon from Sharield, Third Captain of their North Guard. We came across them not too long ago. The city is only a few hours away."

"Hours away yet? We might not have the time," Chertron muttered.

Sarion knew already that something unforeseen had happened to unhorse Chertron, but he had an ominous feeling about what the lean fighter would say next…

"We scouted along the path as was our plan, hoping to find out if we were being tracked."

Sarion nodded. "And?"

Mielkon interrupted. "Did you come across any of my men? We have a rendezvous set up at the outpost, and they are due here soon."

A pained look came over Chertron's face as he glanced at the Sharield fighter, but he turned back to Sarion.

"We were being hunted." Lassel spoke now.

The Summoning

The men were silent around them, Sarion holding his breath in anticipation.

"We need to leave immediately," she continued.

"Not without my men," said Mielkon.

Now Chertron spoke. "We heard cries coming from further down the path, to the north of us. We decided to ride there and give what aid we could, but when we arrived shortly after, it was already too late. The company was ambushed; killed to the last man, including their horses."

Sarion bit his teeth, his fist clenching in reaction.

"All my men are dead? Are you certain?" Mielkon's face was drawn in the gloom of the torchlight, and Sarion saw both anger and shock deeply etched into his features.

"It was a predator from Grammore. I'm certain of it. Something large and quick came out of the brush, and if it wasn't for Lassel's reaction and horsemanship, it would have had me as well. My friend, it was *close*."

Sarion saw the intensity in Chertron's eyes, and realized the truth of his words. His friend had been very near to being caught himself, and was still shaken from the experience.

"Shades..." Sarion muttered to himself. "Mielkon, we must leave now." Sarion gave the signal for his company to be off, making for his own steed. The Sharield fighter seemed indecisive for a moment, and then quickly followed suit, gesturing for his men to pull their ranks. Already a pair had thundered off, and another two took up a temporary position of defense as rear guard.

"Whatever manner of beast it must be, it won't take us by surprise. All my men?" He shook his head. "Over a dozen of Sharield's fighters, gone in one attack..."

"I'm sorry about your men, Mielkon. We will have a chance for revenge at some point, but not now. You don't know these monsters from Grammore. They are terrible."

Wharla was on her horse and came up to them. "I fear that Chardoom has sent the Crage after us. It can move quickly and silently through the wild, and is capable of such violence. I'm sorry about the men."

Sarion merely nodded, knowing there was nothing else to say. Wharla had warned them before about the possibility of the Crage hunting them down. He had seen something himself earlier in the day, and he was fairly certain it was after them now, closing in for the kill. They had no time to waste. Within moments, the combined companies were off, the horses galloping along the path, the dawn still several hours away. But would they reach Sharield before the beast could track them down, and how fast could the Crage travel, if it were indeed close on their trail? Surely it would never match the speed of the horses. Did Wharla really know that much about this creature? If her story were true, then Chardoom kept nearly everything from her knowledge, and they had no idea of the monster's full capabilities. The thing had been powerful enough to take down a dozen mounted fighters though...It had been a terrible quirk of misfortune that had placed them in its path, just like the other Nighton fighters in Gar-kiln. Sarion felt the blame for all these losses on his shoulders, but he shook the feeling off, knowing it was misplaced. Men had died under his command before, and more would die in the future. It was a simple but harsh reality, and one that couldn't be changed. The only thing he could do was try his best to keep them out of harm's way unless there were no other options but to stand and fight.

The combined companies traveled swiftly and time passed, the night deepening, with little change around them. The woods remained thick, the ground growing steadily higher and rockier, the sky clearing above them. There was no one else along the path, and they didn't come across any additional cabins or settlements. There was no questioning the isolation of the region, and Sarion again felt the improbability of coordinating activities between Nighton and Sharield. The best they could do was to warn the people and convey news, although by the time such information reached one or the other, there was little that could be done.

They traveled like this for several hours when the lead riders slowed their pace on Mielkon's orders, with Sarion approving.

"How much further?" Sarion spoke to the Sharield fighter, who rode alongside him, the path comfortably allowing the passage of multiple horses simultaneously.

"Maybe two more hours to the city," he answered. "Up ahead is our largest outpost to the north. I'm confident that we'll be safe once we arrive there."

Sarion considered the man's words a moment before replying. "The shelter will offer protection, but we still need to gain the city. Miles separate both."

"Do you think this beast will yet track us after we reach the outpost?" Mielkon appeared surprised by Sarion's response.

"I don't know, but one thing I've learned is to not underestimate these predators from Grammore. Their abilities are exceptional, at both hunting and tracking. Worse yet, some are magical in nature, like the Killworm we battled."

"And yet you defeated it," Mielkon answered. "According to every legend I've heard, the monster could not be harmed by steel or fire. So perhaps that is one tale that didn't hold true. I lack your knowledge of these creatures, Sarion, so I will respect your advice. It grieves me to lose good men, and I would like to kill this monster if we can. These are my lands and my people. To leave such a creature roaming at will is not something myself or Lord Berillon can permit."

"I understand," Sarion said, trying to think of the best approach for their situation. The safest option would be to bring people inside the city where the walls and their fighting force could best protect them, but Sarion didn't think that Lord Berillon would follow through with this idea. Sarion was fairly sure that many of the folk would stay at their homes, like most others in the westland. He didn't blame them, and it would be impossible to go out and make an appeal. Unless someone encountered one of these creatures in the flesh, there would always remain doubt as to their ferocity, or even their very existence. So the question remained; what should they do next?

"How many fighters are in the outpost?" Sarion questioned.

"There should be around fifty now. Patrols were recently sent off in several directions, and sometimes they are out in the field for longer. I just sent out another to the west, and they won't return for several days. You must have similar routines at Nighton."

Sarion nodded, noticing that the sky was gaining a bit of color, dawn starting to push back at the darkness.

"What if we try and flush the beast out?" Mielkon glanced over at him. "Lay a snare for it, perhaps? And Sarion, I must tell you that with this creature roaming our forests, I must stay behind and deal with it. I can offer you a small escort to get you to Sharield by the proper path, but my responsibility is to guard this area. If there is indeed something trailing us, then I need to put an end to it."

Mielkon was speaking the truth, and Sarion wasn't about to question either the validity of his statement or his intentions. Spoken truly by an officer in the protocol of enforcing his position and its calling…He understood this all too well, but knowing any of this did nothing to solve his own dilemma about how best he could help. He certainly didn't like the idea of leaving these men behind to face a possible attack, but would they still be in danger if his company left for the city? Might that not be the key in avoiding an attack on the outpost, having them break off and reach Sharield? Exactly how far would the Crage go in hunting them down? If Wharla were right, then the creature had been sent by its master Chardoom to track them. It had already followed them several days across the wilderness of the westland. Would it really stop now, or might the creature try and find some means of fulfilling its dreadful mission?

Torn by indecision, Sarion remained silent, debating the wisest course of action here. His own mission was uncertain. They had reached Gar-kiln, discovered useful information, and had also made contact with Sharield's command, giving them fair warning of the threat from the Dark Mage. It was not his place to construct their response, nor did he have the authority to do so. Despite these facts, he *was* entrusted in defending all the people in the westland to the best of his abilities, and that included Sharield...to an extent. When they had left Nighton, Chensel spoke to him about lending aid where he could once they found Gar-kiln. If he chanced a return to Nighton, then couriers from King Gregor would surely be waiting there to escort him to Daregil Keep, the one place he did not want to be. He'd thought about his next move for the past few days, but had not thought much farther than reaching Sharield. He did have a rough plan worked out, and would need to act on it very soon. Sarion had decided to send a message back to Chensel, further breaking up his company, which was now diminished, but besides his keeping the rod out of Trencit, the greater plan was lacking. Once they reached Sharield and had time to rest and recover, things might become clearer. At the very least they would finally have the chance for a deeper discussion…

The company rode on and before them the forest opened up, the trees spreading wider to either side, a pair of buildings looming ahead of them in the dim light. The first structure was much larger than the outpost they had left behind, and armed men held positions in every direction. The second building sat behind the larger one, and appeared to be a holding stable for horses. Beyond both of them the path continued, the woods again closing inwards several dozen yards in the distance. Chertron now rode beside Sarion as the company slowed, the leaders already dismounting.

Chertron pointed. "I like not the look of where that path goes. Higher into the hills, with the forest crowding it on both sides. It would be much too easy for an ambush to take place. I fear we cannot linger here too long with what follows."

Sarion agreed completely, and it was the first thing he noticed as well. Whatever his decision was to be, it had to be made quickly...

Mielkon jumped off his horse, speaking to the pair of guards who came forward. The front gate was open and more men came out, some of them taking the reins from Mielkon's company and leading the horses away. Sarion left his own mount, tying him quickly to one of the bars, his mind racing as he tried to figure out his next move. Uneasy, he knew that the creature would be coming up the trail, relentlessly stalking them. All his instincts told him so, and he felt time pressing against them. Should they leave immediately and make for Sharield, hoping that Mielkon's men would be safe from attack? Or should they stay here instead, hoping to snare the creature somehow and put an end to it with their superior numbers? His heart urged him to follow this thought, but another part of him argued otherwise. If the thing hunting them was indeed the Crage, as Wharla believed, then it was cunning as well as deadly. He doubted that the creature would attack a fortress armed with men, as it would surely lose its natural advantage. And if they did wait here with Mielkon, there was no way of knowing how long their pursuer would wait *them* out. Sarion was convinced that if they tried to capture it while it hid in the woods, it would prove disastrous, and men would be killed. No, the best chance any of them had would be to fight it in the open, where they could at least be able to gauge its abilities, and both defend against it while attacking in turn. He recalled the battle they had fought against the ogre, where Charadan's men and himself had forced it to a stalemate, chasing it off, but with losses on their side. Sarion might be more knowledgeable concerning how ogres fought, but this unknown predator was a mystery.

"You're thinking the same thing as I am, my friend." Chertron came closer. "Will they be in danger if we leave, or will the creature continue to follow us? My heart tells me it won't stop here, but will avoid this place if it can determine we've left."

"And what if it lacks the ability to know if we did leave? They might become trapped here."

"Then we need to urge Mielkon to be vigilant, and utilize their numbers if this thing attacks. They are capable men, and this creature must have its limits."

"We hope so…" Valadire joined them, listening to their discussion. "It's a difficult decision either way." He shrugged.

"What's your counsel then?" Sarion asked. "Whatever we should do, we need to decide quickly. The longer we remain here, indecisive, the swifter our pursuer gains on us."

"I know." Valadire looked behind them. "I'm encouraged by the new day, but we won't truly be safe until we reach Sharield."

Nodding, Sarion clapped them both on the shoulder, his mind made up. "Let me speak to Mielkon, and we'll be off. Get everyone on horseback again, Valadire." Several of them had dismounted, thinking they were going to stay. Wharla stared at him as if she could read his mind. Maybe she could…

Sarion walked ahead to where Mielkon was still conversing with his men. He turned as Sarion approached. "I can spare two fighters to guide you safely to the city.

221

Based on what happened to the patrol, I can't risk sending a stronger force, so I hope you understand."

"I do," Sarion answered. "I appreciate your help."

"I also have the feeling that your company is quite capable. I have heard of your own skill, and I'm certain that your hunters have been hand-picked from among the best that Chensel has."

Sarion nodded, replying. "I must urge you to use extreme caution. We don't know what pursues us, but I would not send small groups of men into the woods. Give us time to leave this place before doing anything. Once we have left the outpost, it is my belief that whatever hunts us will avoid you and your men as it continues to track us."

Mielkon nodded, but Sarion saw that he had his own thoughts on the matter. "We'll be very careful, but I can't stay holed up here. Word must be spread about this thing's presence, and I also must go back to look upon what has happened to my men. Perhaps someone survived the attack."

"I can say with certainty that none did." Chertron spoke. "I'm sorry about your men."

"Regardless, it must be done." Mielkon said nothing more on the matter. "Now, is there anything else I can do for you, Sarion?"

"I'm afraid not. I'll speak with Lord Berillon when we arrive at Sharield. Thank you for your assistance, and take heed of my warning."

Mielkon held his hand out and they clasped, Chertron doing the same. Valadire approached, the company from Nighton awaiting their orders to ride again. Sarion glanced over his fighters for a moment, knowing how weary they were. Unfortunately, they were yet unable to get the full rest they needed, but it wasn't that far off. Geld Rinn was already speaking to two men who had been assigned as their escort to Sharield, and others were going back and forth to the stables. It would be a few more minutes and Sarion knew they would be leaving. He looked over the landscape, spotting the sentries. There was a man on guard in all four directions, surrounding the outpost and the stable, but Sarion felt the inadequacy of their defense. It appeared that the structure was accessible only from the front gate, with no windows on the lower level. Several were on the second floor, and he noticed the enclosures that would allow shafts to be sent while offering the archers some measure of protection. Overall, the outpost was similar to others in the westland. Not very complex in its creation but practical in its defense, unless the occupants faced overwhelming odds. Sarion figured that there had never been an actual assault on this one in recent times. Without the roaming bands of Glefins threatening the westland anymore, the only other possible dangers would be bandits, and he doubted there would be any bold or strong enough to assail an outpost under the control of Sharield, or any other large city. Of course, in any given time, there would always be the possibility of some wild creature that had traveled from the west, but being this far away from the Ridgeline it was highly unlikely, the threat virtually nonexistent.

Of course, things had now changed...

The lifestyle of anyone dwelling in the westland had undergone an unpleasant transformation, and wouldn't be going back to any semblance of normalcy in the near future. The most frightening thing about this fact was that most of the people living in the borderlands were probably unaware of how serious things had become. He hoped to make a difference through his efforts and those of Chensel's, and that it would result in saving lives.

Sarion looked over the structure again, trying to see if there was anything he could suggest before they left, and like everyone else he was taken by complete surprise as the unexpected happened...

A shout rang out from beyond the building, coming

from the direction of the stables. Everyone stopped in their tracks, confusion taking hold, the leaders trying to discover the source of commotion. A scream echoed from somewhere unseen, followed by another, and Sarion knew that their unknown pursuer had finally caught up with them...

His company was already on horseback, and he jumped astride his own horse within the span of a few seconds, Mielkon's men rushing toward the back of the building.

"The beast is here!" Sarion signaled for the fighters to back away, fan out enough to give themselves space. They had no option now but to hold their ground and fight, but he couldn't leave Mielkon and his men to fend for themselves. The predator had to be dealt with by all of them.

Now...

A bell sounded from above, giving the alarm that an attack was underway, Men swarmed from the outpost, some with swords in hand, others with a variety of weapons as the cries of anguish had not gone unnoticed. Sarion motioned for Geld Rinn and Jurit to start circling around, keeping to the outside while Mielkon's men flanked the outpost to both sides. Piril and Bertilik went immediately to his front and back, while Chertron, Valadire, and Lassel followed, Wharla staying close. A thundering erupted from somewhere in the distance, and horses burst from the stables, running in a frenzy. Whether they were terrified by the creature's presence, or driven out by it directly, there was no way of knowing. Mielkon shouted from ahead, and Sarion watched as the leader and perhaps two dozen of his men made their way toward the stables, some on foot, a few still on horseback. Chaos ensued for long moments as the horses ran loose, most of them running south on the trail in a reckless herd.

Sarion gritted his teeth, his bow in hand now as he

searched for a target, but there was no sign of their unknown assailant. He stopped short as he heard shouts from the far side of the outpost. The creature was attacking from over there, and he motioned for his companions to go, all of them urging the mighty horses onward. Within moments they breached the front left corner of the building, hearing new cries of anguish as more men fell victim to the relentless predator.

"Beware! It must be the Crage!" He heard Wharla's warning shout, but ignored it. He didn't need to know the identity of their attacker or how dangerous the creature was, only how to kill it...

As he rounded the building, his breath caught as he spied a glimpse of the carnage happening further ahead, and then he finally saw the thing; this creature which had been pursuing them across the endless miles of the westland, and could only be the deadly predator known as the Crage.

Sarion was daunted. Men lay dying or dead on the ground surrounding it, and the beast whipped its claws at another pair of fighters, bringing them both to a grisly end. It was tall, perhaps eight or nine feet in length, and powerfully built, muscles rippling along a hairy frame, its head wolf-like with a pair of long pointed ears, terrible yellow eyes matching Sarion's own for one brief second.

The creature never stopped moving, unwilling to give anyone a sitting target, as Geld Rinn and Jurit let fly several arrows, the creature dodging them effortlessly. Sarion notched his own bow, his shaft striking the ground where the Crage had been only a moment before. The creature stared the fighters down, three of Mielkon's men backing off in distress at the monster's ferocity and looking to form a better plan than the failed one used by their fallen comrades.

Sarion measured the beast, and he knew that the Crage was doing the same, certainly knowing that his quarry was now in front of him. Behind the barn, several new fighters now appeared, bows singing in the fresh morning. The Crage was surrounded on three sides, and Sarion was concerned about Geld Rinn and Jurit, both of them dangerously close to the beast. Even before he could warn them, guessing where the creature would go, the monster charged the two fighters, Jurit going down in a flurry of limbs as he flailed desperately at the beast and Geld Rinn's horse rearing up in terror, the Crage slicing long talons across the unfortunate animal's throat. Geld Rinn dove from his mount, Piril and Valadire the closest, swords held before them as they tried to engage the monster and keep it from reaching the young fighter, but the Crage had something else in mind, moving unexpectedly. Instead of fleeing into the woods, it lurched in the other direction, straight toward the stable, reaching the side and leaping upwards in a tremendous show of strength and agility, gaining the rooftop effortlessly and disappearing down the other side.

"By the Seven!" Chertron cursed, several men yelling warnings to their companions on the other side, who were unaware of the danger. Within moments the first scream erupted as the Crage surprised the fighters on the other side.

"Keep your bows ready!" Sarion yelled. "We can't hope to outride it!"

If they all rushed over, as Mielkon's men were already doing, it could escape more easily on this side, but Sarion had a sinking feeling that this wasn't the creature's intention at all. It could have gone past Geld Rinn and into the forest, but instead had leaped onto the roof, savagely renewing its attack on the others. Their only hope was to pin it to the top of the building and surround it when it came back to the ground. Its speed and agility was frightening to see, and Sarion now understood how the creature could have them tracked them so far, and with such quickness through the wild.

Chardoom's messenger, Wharla had said.

The Crage was a ferocious predator from the Grammore Lowlands, and it was easy to see why the Dark Mage had given it to Chardoom for his own use…

The sounds of fighting continued from the other side, and Sarion heard Mielkon shouting orders. He disliked being out of the fray, and needed to see what was going on in order to be of any help.

"Piril! Follow me! Everyone else stay here and be ready if the creature returns!" He didn't pause to gauge anyone's reactions, and didn't have the time to do so. Urging his horse forward, he thundered around the back of the stable, Piril right on his heel. Never taking his eyes off the rooftop, he quickly rounded the building, catching glimpses of armed men in every direction. It seemed that everyone from the outpost was now outside and trying to engage the creature in combat. Arrows flew through the air, and Sarion saw the monster several dozen yards away yet, on the edge of the forest to their west, some of the men finding a mark at last on the elusive creature. With a quick move, it now went down on all fours, loping into the brush at great speed and disappearing as numerous arrows followed after, at least one more burying itself into its back.

Then it was gone…

Mielkon signaled for some of his men to pursue it, glancing over in Sarion's direction as he approached.

"Sarion, we need to buy you time to reach Sharield. I didn't doubt the validity of your tale, but now I've seen what we're up against in the flesh. What a beast! And it has traveled this far east? Into the heart of our own territory?"

"How far will they give chase? I think it's too dangerous to track in the wild." Sarion watched as at least twenty men were in pursuit; close together, but Sarion knew they would be vulnerable if the monster waited to trap them.

"Not very far at all. I think the monster will leave us alone and try to pick up your trail. If it's come this far, it won't stop now. Once inside Sharield you'll be safe. Good fortune."

Sarion agreed, but didn't have time for further discussion. Too many men lay dead or dying on the ground, and there was nothing else to gain by staying at the outpost. With a quick nod he was off, Piril staying close. They rounded the edge of the stable again until they were within sight of the others. With a wave of his hand, he brought them all forward, starting down the path himself, knowing that they would leave behind yet another worthy fighter. Jurit never had a chance against the creature's attack, and Geld Rinn was fortunate to be alive.

They all were...

A single rider angled towards them, and Sarion paused for a moment.

"Forester Sarion! My name is Ramile, and I'll guide your company to Sharield."

"All right then. Lead on with Geld Rinn."

The others now reached them and Sarion never hesitated, sending his company riding at nearly a full run. The time for speed was on them, as they needed to gain the lead on the Crage, but he had a sinking feeling that the beast would soon be able to elude Mielkon's men and take up the chase once more. It was wounded, and that was hopeful, but strong as the creature looked, Sarion believed the injuries were not going to hamper it substantially. He hoped the injuries would be enough to see them safely away and give them the edge to reach Sharield.

Ahead of them the path opened wider and they made good speed, the day growing brighter around them, and it appeared as the weather would be favorable for riding at a quick pace. The fighters were all tired, each one of them anxious and excited from the recent skirmish. Sarion looked around, trying to gauge their strength, knowing what was needed from them. The horses were also weary, but he believed they would be up to the task.

They *had* to be...

Their only other option would be to stop and face the deadly Crage, something in which the outcome was uncertain. Sarion had seen enough of the Lowland predators not to underestimate them, but what good was this foreknowledge? If they were outmatched while fighting them, all the caution in the world would do nothing to turn the tide of battle. Like Wharla, he didn't think the creature was magical, and this might be favorable to them, but the Crage didn't *need* magic to be effective. Having seen it in battle for the first time and getting a good measure of its abilities, Sarion quickly understood what they were up against. What the Dark Mage lacked for in sheer numbers, he made up for it by controlling a host of terrible creatures which carried out his bidding; ferocious beasts of varying sizes and strength, and all of them incredibly dangerous. He wondered what exactly it was that gave him such power. By what means was he able to exert this control? They already knew it was magical in nature, but what was the source? Perhaps a talisman like the rod he himself carried? It was probably something similar...The likely conclusion was that the Dark Mage had found a way to tap into a very powerful and possibly ancient object of power, enhancing his own abilities to a degree large enough to threaten a kingdom as mighty as Trencit.

The implications were staggering, but unarguable. This notion had been in the back of his mind for a while, and certainly his companions as well. But if they could discover the source, and find a way to destroy it...

Sarion didn't need to play around with this line of thought. It clearly led to one eventuality, that at some point in time they must strike directly at the Dark Mage, and seek him out in the Grammore Lowlands. He had told Chertron and Valadire this already, and Chensel had warned him not to go down that path after their victory over the Killworm at Nighton. But in Sarion's mind, there was no other way for them to defeat their enemy. He *knew* this would happen. Sarion felt the truth in his heart, in his very core. His earlier words would come to pass. Maybe not right now, but in the future…

Collecting his thoughts, he dared not dwell too much on such things. Danger was nearby, and he had responsibilities that could not be ignored.

They rode on for a while and Sarion noticed that Wharla was urging her mount closer to him, Lassel catching his eye for a moment, the fighter clearly wondering what she was about. Sarion let her close on him, Piril giving her room, but ever vigilant.

"Sarion!" She shouted over. "I wish to leave your company. The Crage wants *me*. I'm the one bringing peril to your people."

He stared over at her without replying. Did she think he would just let her go off on her own? There was no chance of him agreeing to that. There was no guarantee she would be safe even if she did leave. Could Wharla really trust someone as evil as Chardoom, father or not? He didn't have the answer to that one, and there was another reason for him to refuse. If she *had* been lying to them the whole time, this might be the perfect opportunity for her to escape, and take information back to Chardoom about themselves. No, plead as she might, he would not concede to her wishes.

"No, get back to your place." He shook his head for emphasis, her features tightening in anger.

"Foolish choice!" She snapped. "You place yourself in grave danger. You should have left me in Gar-kiln. You can't defeat Chardoom or the Crage. Why won't you listen to me?"

Sarion turned his head away, ignoring her stare. After several long moments she gave up, easing her horse back and regaining her earlier spot in the company. Sarion was content for the moment, having no fear that Wharla would attempt something, as Lassel was more than capable of putting a stop to anything she might try. His mind firm, Sarion tried to put the matter aside, knowing that Wharla was not going to be released anytime soon…He felt she had a part to play in coming events, although he didn't know on which side of the battle her loyalties would land. Wharla was just one more piece of the massive puzzle which buffeted them mercilessly in several haphazard directions; all of them uncertain, and most of them deadly.

Through thick forests and the ground swelling at their feet, the company thundered ahead on the last leg of their journey to gain Sharield, the most isolated province of Trencit. The sky was blue and bright overhead, the air growing cooler and fresher, the aroma of moss and forest greens giving way to something which spoke of tall mountains and hidden valleys, the high country which lifted and paired itself away from the great woodlands of the west. At times they passed small cabins to either side, most likely the temporary lodging for hunters and trappers. Trails appeared at times, weaving off into the woods and vanishing quickly, but they met no one else on the road, which neither widened nor grew tighter, instead maintaining the same width. A large tree loomed before them, its great bulk heaving itself across the path, and Ramile quickly guided them around it, the company watching the forest for signs of movement. Sarion felt certain that the Crage would not be able to catch up with them at this pace. Although it moved on both its hind legs and all fours, its sheer size would prevent it from keeping up with the war horses. Sarion knew of no other creature which compared to their speed and endurance. The steeds from the borderlands were as fine as any to be found in greater Trencit, and with a sure path at their feet could run swiftly for miles on end.

There were time when they had ridden them hard through the westland, but not long or hard enough to overly task them. Sarion had faith in their ability, and he could sense the walls of Sharield somewhere ahead, getting closer by the minute. Shortly they were around the tree and back on the path, no worse for the wear. He asked Ramile how much longer, the man replying a few miles, and with that they galloped off again.

The next several minutes were uneventful, the path finally changing, growing broader, and homes began appearing with some frequency, small settlements breaking through the landscape in flatter areas. But these were small, and numbered only a few dozen at most. A group of riders broke through the woods to their right, coming up from a path which turned down into a valley, and Sarion called for Ramile, pointing over. The fighter didn't need to ask, and he headed over to them, hailing their leader by name. Sarion pulled the reins on his horse, finally giving the animal a chance for rest along with the others. Chertron remained as rear guard, his keen eyes gazing over the trail behind them, Piril and Bertilik positioning themselves to either side of the company for protection. Sarion waited as Ramile warned the patrol of the danger, the leader of the company clearly looking alarmed. Another minute passed, with Sarion's uneasiness growing, but then Ramile turned his mount, coming towards them.

"The people will be warned. Riders will be going to each village and settlement, bringing news of the creature. They each have their own company of fighters, but some men will be away. All will be given sanctuary in Sharield if they so desire. The city gates are always open for its people."

"Good enough. They're probably in more danger the longer we linger."

"The question is, what will the Crage do once we enter Sharield?" Valadire arched an eyebrow, and Sarion shrugged.

"That is something which I don't have an answer for…" He looked questioningly at Wharla, her eyes smoldering.

"I've warned you to let me go. The Crage has been sent for *me*. Chardoom will not stop."

"Even if his black master has no knowledge of what has taken place?" Sarion replied. "How much do you really know of your father's plans?"

She matched his gaze, never wavering. "You still think to test me, or that I can't be trusted. I know this, Sarion."

He shrugged.

"I told you back in Gar-kiln to leave me there, yet you refused. You thought I was a prisoner at first, and that much was true. But I still argued against your taking me away."

"I have no choice but *not* to trust. I feel you still withhold information from me." Sarion didn't hold back in his response, but he was certain she already knew his mind.

"Information? No. The only thing I hide is the pain of my life, the fear of terrible creatures which came from nightmares, and the reality that the worse monster of all is my own flesh and blood. You can never know what I know. The pain, the fear. The shame…"

The company was silent around her, Sarion measuring Wharla for any indication of deception, but the woman was impossible to read.

"Sarion, let us leave now while we still can. Time grows short." Valadire spoke, and Sarion nodded, all of them guiding their mounts into formation once more, the proud horses gathering speed.

The last part of their trek was now upon them, and Sarion commanded the company to ride swiftly, the roads becoming broader and well-traveled, their footing more certain. The horses galloped ahead confidently, their proud manes waving in the cool mountain air. The trail began angling due east, sloping ever upwards as they cut their way deeper into the higher elevations of the range which bolstered the westland on this side. At one point Sarion heard a roaring in the distance which steadily grew louder, a gushing of water gaining volume over the constant thumping of the horses' hooves, and soon the forest opened wider as a river came into view flowing alongside the road. The bank was steep to their right, a strong current sending the water plunging recklessly over boulders and small waterfalls until it again disappeared into the woods.

Ramile and Geld Rinn paused in front of them, the Sharield fighter approaching. "This is the Brightening which flows from Gushing Lake, a dam built at the same time as Sharield, molding the natural landscape into a beautiful but formidable protection for the city against assault. To the north the mountains shelter Sharield from the stronger winds and storms, and are treacherous to cross, preventing access by an enemy army. Higher up and to the eastern backing of the city, the area becomes rougher and more inhospitable, soon reaching elevations which are unfit for habitation. You can find a few shepherds tending their flocks and a number of hunters, but little else."

"Are there any paths that lead deeper and through these mountains?" Sarion asked.

Ramile shrugged. "If there are any, then they're not common knowledge. I've wandered into the lower heights, and the terrain is rugged, the footing uncertain. Avalanches, high winds, and quick forming snowstorms are enough to prevent a wise man from tempting fate."

Sarion nodded. On the other side of the range lay a no-man's land which was beyond the borders of Trencit, even further south than the free city of Lastrad. People lived there from what he knew, but there was no regional structure and lawlessness was the rule of the day. He thought there might be villages yet, but with the threat of

marauding Devlents and bandits, their existence was
uncertain. He knew very little about the area, and assumed
it was similar to the deeper southlands which lay miles
away from even Gar-kiln; home to a scattering of
settlements and people, most of them in a daily fight for
survival.

Whatever the real truth of the matter, he didn't
know...

"How soon until we reach the gates of the city?"
Sarion asked.

"A few short miles. That's it." Ramile replied.

"Patrols?"

"One or two, and these stay near the entrance."

Satisfied, Sarion turned around, gazing across the
area they had traveled, half-expecting to see the Crage
breaking through the brush in a last attempt to catch them
before they passed beyond its reach.

"All right. Let's be off, and no stopping until we're
safely inside the gates of the city." Sarion pointed ahead,
and Ramile returned to the lead spot with Geld Rinn.

The company charged ahead, and Sarion was
convinced there was no way the Crage would reach them
now. He had seen the creature in action as it made its
escape, and it certainly had shown great movement and
agility, but it simply could not match a horse's gait on the
run. For the first time in a while he felt a sense of relief,
that his company would finally have some measure of
security surrounding them, taking refuge again in one of
Trencit's cities. Sharield might be the smallest of them, but
it was still a fortress guarded by a standing army of capable
men.

The minutes dragged on, all of them eager to see
this leg of the journey finished. Clouds overtook the sun,
the day moving into afternoon. The ascent the past two
days had been steady, they were well above the floors of
the greater westland forests, the air around them crisp and

clean. It was invigorating, even to his own weary bones. The mountain range was large in its own respect, deeper and higher than the Ridgeline, which was formidable in itself but much longer and shallower of depth, offering easier access in many spots. The greatest and highest range of known mountains were the Krale, which surrounded the plateau housing Daregil Keep. Permanently snowcapped, the region was steeped in legend and mystery. Sarion was not native to that area, but even in the deepest reaches of the westland whispers were told about the treacherous mountains and the dangers which lay hidden, both natural and unnatural. Despite sitting on the very threshold of Trencit, it was not unlike the Grammore Lowlands and Sprechyd Wood in many ways, wrapped in folklore and shadows. These were all places of danger, and Sarion had come to understand firsthand that a hazy line existed between reality and fantasy, where nightmares could at times emerge from lost tales and into the waking lives of men, with terrible and unpredictable results…

Staring ahead at the landscape, the road wound back and forth, following the line of the Brightening as it plunged down the valley, soaking the rock and grass which edged it on both sides in a raging torrent of white spray. The woods grew thick to their right and they rounded a wide curve, the horses running ahead for several minutes until the forest opened before them, revealing a huge wall of stone, the Brightening erupting from several openings. It was a dam, and they had reached Sharield at last. The wall continued onward to their left, and Sarion spotted a patrol on horseback, the men looking in their direction from several dozen yards distance. Behind them loomed a large postern gate, fully opened, and small towers and battlements hovered above the stone, figures moving about. The wall continued northwards, curving backwards on itself until disappearing from sight. It had the look of a formidable fortress, and the guards were vigilant, the patrol moving forward to greet them.

Ramile met with their leader, speaking for several long moments, until he finally returned to Sarion.

"My apologies for the delay, but word must be spread to the masters of the Sharield Guard and Lord Berillon. News of your coming and the attack at our outpost will not be taken lightly. I can't remember such a loss of men in all my time of service, or before. Let's go. I can see you into our city where you'll be safe at last."

They quickly followed after him, the company galloping past the patrol, which was already in motion. Sarion thought the walls of Sharield would not be easy to overcome, but there was a lot of undergrowth from where they had traveled, with thick forest everywhere. Although an enemy might stop short of the walls protecting Sharield, Sarion had the uneasy feeling that they could get uncomfortable close, especially a creature as cunning as the Crage. He would make a point of it for all entrances of the city to remain heavily guarded. There was no way the beast could climb these walls, and it would be seen as soon as it breached the nearby cover. Still...

Soon they were through the gate and at last into the city of Sharield, a place which had not necessarily been a focus in the past few weeks, but circumstances had now dictated otherwise. Sarion knew that it was a welcome relief after being hunted by the deadly Crage, and his company needed rest more than anything. Their harrowing flight from Gar-kiln had taken its toll on the fighters. They were all physically and mentally drained, having fought against both the servants of the Dark Mage, and an unfortunate encounter with a roaming predator from Grammore. Good men had been lost, and they were all lucky to have survived. If they had been forced to fight directly against the Crage on their own, the outcome would be uncertain at best.

An escort came over to them and they dismounted,

the Sharield handlers leading their horses away for a respite of their own, the animals having served admirably in the trek through the wilderness and flight from pursuit. Sarion watched them leave, knowing that their speed and reliability would be tapped again, although he hoped it would not be anytime soon.

A smiling man came up to them, dressed in a robe of gray, his hands held up in the westland sign of greeting. He was heavy, his face red as if he had just hurried from somewhere, although it was clear to see he was no fighter.

"Hail warriors of Nighton. It is rare indeed to see a company from our brethren city. On behalf of Lord Berillon, I welcome you all to the fair city of Sharield. My name is Barthaniel, Ward of Sharield. All of your needs will be fulfilled; you need only ask."

Sarion came forward, grasping his hand. "Our thanks for the kind welcome, Master Barthaniel. I am Sarion, Second Forester of Nighton, but our needs are not overbearing. We simply would enjoy a warm bed and bath, and whatever food and wine you have to spare. As fighters we're not used to any special priviledges, and would not ask for any regardless."

Barthaniel laughed, a deep, throaty chuckle filled with good humor, then bowed with one hand held over his heart. "Spoken like a true warrior indeed! The Western Watch is honored throughout the westland, but it would never be said that our traveling kindred to the north would sleep on hay and inside a barn while visiting Sharield."

He burst into laughter, and Sarion saw Valadire give him an odd look, but Sarion smiled in response.

"It's good to hear laughter after many hard days, and the sound is quite welcome. We will request a counsel with Lord Berillon as soon as it's convenient for him. I don't want to be impolite since we've only just arrived, but the need is pressing."

Barthaniel nodded. "Word of your coming has

already been sent. Ramile spoke to the guard, and I see that he's leaving us already."

They all turned to look, watching as Ramile was on horseback once again and galloping through the gate.

"He is a loyal fighter, true to Sharield." Sarion said. "Men have been lost, and he returns swiftly to danger."

"That is ill news, Captain Sarion." Barthaniel's face clouded. "Come, I'll lead you into the city where you can find comfort. We'll speak as we go."

Barthaniel led them away, passing the barracks which surrounded the entrance on both sides. Squat, long buildings, they were similar to others which could be found in the westland and beyond. Some distance to their right, Sarion spotted a stone walkway which edged Gushing Lake. Where the walkway and the outer wall intersected, a fortress tower had been constructed, protecting that corner of the city from attack. Sarion saw the glint of steel, and felt confident it was amply guarded. Barthaniel led them closer to the water, angling deeper into the city and lake.

"There is a causeway along the water's edge which is used for matters of importance. Horses are not allowed in the city proper, and this path is the quickest avenue to access the interior grounds surrounding the castle."

Walking along, they passed a variety of buildings, all of them appearing to be either a craft shop of some type, or a place for food. Smoke poured from chimneys and hearth alike, and they caught snatches of metal being pounded from smithies nearby. The air remained cool as the afternoon grew long, and all about them were the sounds of a small but thriving city. The streets were clean and the people seemed content enough, going about their individual business, nearly everyone greeting Barthaniel, the Ward beaming with pleasure in response. Sarion felt an immediate liking to the man, who had a natural way of putting someone at ease. It was obvious that he had been chosen for his position for this very reason, and Sarion wondered about what type of man Lord Berillon was…

His city might be the most isolated and smallest in comparison to the inner holds, but neither of these facts meant anything. It was his province, and his family had been in power for long years. He was a virtual king in his own domain, at least if he chose to be so.

Barthaniel led them up a staircase, and they found themselves on a stone walkway overlooking the lake. Docks were scattered about, and nestled between the piers were small structures which Sarion assumed were fishing stations. Several boats were out on the lake; some nearby, others further out. The lake stretched forth until it reached a steep bank on the other side of the dam. Barthaniel followed his gaze, pointing.

"Gushing Lake runs yonder to the far shore, a mile in width. The dam is higher on that side and cannot be scaled, and small watch is always on guard. Is this not one of the most beautiful sights you've seen?"

Sarion agreed.

Smiling broadly, Barthaniel spread his arms wide for a moment, emphasizing the view, then he led them up a short flight of stairs, the greater part of the city now exposed. The mountains ringed Sharield about on all sides, the fading rays of the sun glistening off the icy blue of the lake's waters, a persistent breeze rippling the surface at spots as it lapped against both wood from the docks and support stones which edged Gushing Lake along the entire side. It was a tranquil sight, and Sarion felt a certain touch of magic in the natural beauty of Sharield, tucked between mountains and water, the entire area radiating a subtle but powerful sense of peace and solitude. He immediately felt uneasy, knowing that his arrival might have been the catalyst for bringing pain and terror to this otherwise quite part of the westland. The shadow of the Dark Mage had been growing outwards, spreading forth from somewhere deep within the Grammore Lowlands, past the Ridgeline, and into the greater westland, and as of yet had not touched upon Sharield and its people. Now, because of their venture into Gar-kiln, they had disturbed the evil which had waited there, and had been pursued for several days by the Crage. Sharield fighters lay dead in the valleys below, and Sarion had unwittingly brought danger into this region. He knew it was unfair on himself to feel guilty, but circumstances had made it into a harsh reality. The Dark Mage was attempting to bring the westland under his power, and surely Sharield would have been a target at some point in time, although this notion did little to ease Sarion's conscience. He had known it before and it seemed to be a terrible pattern; wherever he traveled, evil soon followed.

"Let us be off, friends. There are many spots with such views throughout our fair city." Barthaniel smiled, continuing onwards. They walked along the path, heading deeper into Sharield, the company silent. Sarion was lost in his own thoughts, and looked forward to finally having time to think through the vortex of problems facing him. He was comforted by both his surroundings and his companions, but as he looked into the waters of Gushing Lake, he knew there would be no easy answers to find.

Time passed, the afternoon quickly fading, and the company found themselves facing an area where the buildings grew fewer, and the city fell away. Sarion knew they were near the home of Lord Berillon, and he stared down a short flight of steps which was guarded by several men in full armor, their helms flaring with a blue plume, their shields emblazoned with a streak of blue lightning, the arms of House Berillon.

Barthaniel bowed to the guards, who nodded in return.

"Fine men. Some of our best, who keep Lord Berillon and his household safe from harm. We will go down these steps and enter the grounds surrounding the mansion, a place where every citizen of Sharield is welcome. But first, I must ask you all to hand over your armaments and put them on the holding table. No weapon is allowed in House Berillon, unless it belongs to one of the House Guards."

Sarion paused for a moment, both Valadire and Chertron frowning. He looked over at the Ward. "We do not wish to offend anyone, Barthaniel, and would like to follow all the rules of Sharield."

Barthaniel bowed, his face unreadable.

"However, is there some other way around this?"

The Ward was silent, listening to his words.

Sarion felt a moment of awkwardness. He respected the law of Sharield, as in all other of Trencit's cities. Rules were put in place by their individual governances, and held sway. But at the same time, he felt extremely uncomfortable at the idea of giving up their weapons, even under the protection of Sharield.

Valadire spoke for him. "We are fighters of Nighton, and are not used to being weaponless, even within our own walls of the Western Watch. It is our life to be ready for anything."

"Even within the protection of Sharield? Lord Berillon allows no breaking of his laws. You have no worries for your safety while staying here, I can assure you."

Sarion came forward a step, moving closer to the Ward, watching the nearby guards who stood attentive, and who were well within hearing. Another pair of guards blocked the stairs, and had not moved since their approach.

"Barthaniel, please understand. We would not question your vigilance or laws."

Barthaniel smiled, bowing again. "Indeed, I never thought otherwise, Captain Sarion."

Sarion continued. "But there have been events taking place in the westland which have given us reason for greater caution, the news of which has yet to reach

Sharield."

The man nodded.

"Chensel, First Forester of Nighton, barely escaped with his life. Our enemy tried to assassinate him."

Barthaniel frowned, his face tightening. "That is ill news."

"Worse yet, the attempt was done within his own sleeping chambers."

"Are you saying that one of his own men tried taking his life?" Barthaniel's eyes narrowed, the heavy brows furrowing.

"No, it wasn't one of Nighton's men," Sarion answered. "A creature from Grammore killed two of his personal guard, and nearly had *him*."

"How is this possible? Nighton is a powerful and well-protected fortress. How could something infiltrate Nighton itself?"

"It was a winged creature. It flew in at night, unseen. Chensel slew it himself. He spotted the slain men and confronted the beast. All the officers in Nighton saw the body before it was burned, so they could understand the true nature of what we are fighting. Without this knowledge, it can be difficult to gain such comprehension..."

Barthaniel stared at him, and Sarion saw that the man knew exactly what his point was, and how he was attempting to get it across.

"...to fully appreciate the steps needed in being vigilant. Our enemy has great resources at his disposal." He finished his sentence.

"Hmm. So you're saying that even in Sharield, under the watchful eyes of our guard, that another such creature could penetrate our defenses?"

"That's exactly what I'm saying." Sarion matched his gaze, his eyes unflinching. "I don't know of a single place in the westland that I can truly feel protected. And it's not the lack of faith in men that concerns me, but the unknown strength of our enemy, and *that* is a fact of which I will never underestimate again."

The company waited in a small anteroom near the steps, some of them in chairs, others dozing off. Their trek had been long and dangerous, all of them needing rest. Sarion was no different, but he refused to shut his eyes, even for a moment. Valadire sat next to him, looking as ready as ever.

"So you think this move of yours will give Lord Berillon pause for thought? We could have just handed over our weapons, after all. It would have been much easier."

"I could certainly use a bath and a warm bed." Chertron said, gripping a goblet and downing a large mouthful of wine.

"Keep drinking *that*, and Berillon will think that the fighters of Trencit have all become soft and drunken louts by the time we get to see him," Valadire said.

Sarion laughed, shaking his head, while Chertron scowled.

Night had fallen, and Barthaniel ordered food, drink, and clean blankets for all of them as they waited. He had appeared uncomfortable by their refusal to enter the grounds without their weapons, but playing the perfect and polite host that he was, had made sure that all of their needs were taken care of before he left to personally speak with the household guard, and perhaps Lord Berillon himself. Sarion had not asked where the Lord was, and his whereabouts had not been spoken of either. They had waited there for a while now, the evening claiming the mountain city, the air growing much cooler. The fire crackling in the corner was welcome to all, and he looked over at his companions, each of them trying to make the best of it. Piril alone was on his feet, either himself or Bertilik always guarding him. Lassel sat on the floor near the hearth, Wharla lying on a wool blanket. Geld Rinn looked asleep in one corner, his cloak wrapped tightly about his shoulders. Jurit and Bertilik both sat in chairs, heads bowed. Sarion certainly could not begrudge rest to any of them, feeling the need himself. The three of them had sat at the table for a while now, talking in snatches, none of them willing to speak too freely while Berillon's men stood right outside the door.

"Shades, I'm tired." Valadire said.

"Go ahead and get some rest," Sarion replied. "You deserve it as much as any of us."

"Yourself included," Chertron added.

"My body is weary, believe me. But my mind is fully awake…There's too much to sort out. My hope was to find a brief reprieve here, and to think things through; something we really haven't had the time for lately."

"Aye, you won't hear me disagree." Chertron rubbed his eyes. "I wonder what's taking them so long."

Sarion gave him a warning glance, nodding to the door, but Chertron merely grumbled in response. "Let them hear. I care not, at this point."

Frowning, Valadire spoke. "Similar rules apply in Daregil Keep, do they not?"

Chertron raised a hand. "Generally, but it depends. Men are not required to give up their arms. The fortress is filled with nothing but fighters and guards, for the most part. Gregor has much trust in the men who serve him."

"Enough." Sarion lowered his voice. "You can't expect swift changes to any longstanding traditions." He bent his head, whispering. "And I'm trying to make a point. I want Lord Berillon to understand the seriousness of our plight. The entire westland is threatened. Isolated or not, the Dark Mage has plans for us all, and none of them are good."

His words were chilling, and neither of his companions contradicted him.

"Ah well, I'm off to find a warm corner somewhere." Chertron stood, refilling his goblet.

"You'll sleep soundly enough once your wits are thoroughly drowned in that Sharield vintage. It has quite the bite to it." Valadire took a swig from his own goblet.

"It *is* rather good," said Sarion.

Chertron left, finding an empty chair and making good on his promise. Valadire grinned, but Sarion only shook his head slowly in reply. They sat there in silence for long minutes, the night deepening. After a while, Valadire muttered about the late hour and moved off as well, leaving Sarion alone at the table, Piril outside the door but still vigilant. Sarion heard him talking lightly to one of the guards, and the conversation sounded friendly enough.

The minutes passed and he closed his eyes, feeling the need for sleep growing stronger, his eyelids fluttering. Soon he would have no choice but to rest. He was about to stand, when Piril stuck his head through the doorway, nodding his head and gesturing for him to come out. Sarion looked around the room, and it seemed that all of the companions were now asleep. Quietly, he left the room and went outside, feeling the brisk mountain air over his face. The guards had never left their positions, but Sarion noticed someone who had not been there before. Tall and dressed in light armor, Sarion immediately knew that he was an officer of the city, and the man came forward to meet him, one hand extended in welcome.

"Greetings, Forester of Nighton. It is rare indeed to have someone of your rank in Sharield, or any other fighters of the Western Watch."

Sarion accepted the hand, the man's grip tight and

confident.

"My name is Glorafin, Captain of the Sharield Guard and Defender of the city. You and your company are welcome here, and I apologize for the delay."

"No worries, Captain. Our request is unusual, and I didn't wish to offend anyone. It's just that you haven't had the experiences we've gone through the past several weeks, and danger stalks the entire westland, in many guises and forms. You've heard then of the attempt on Chensel's life and the manner of it?"

"I've been told of all matters. We are shocked to hear such a thing. Most disturbing is the news of our men being killed by this unknown predator which hunted your company."

"Has there been additional news?" Sarion asked.

Glorafin shook his head. "No. Our hunting parties are scouring the countryside and warning our people. The outpost where you were attacked has been reinforced, along with other outposts."

"No sign of the creature?"

"Nothing. It must have fled from our hunters."

Sarion was silent in reply, keeping his thoughts to himself. He didn't know where the Crage was, but the beast would not easily give up. Reaching Sharield was certainly in their favor, and their new position would stop the monster from reaching them, but that didn't mean it would just return to Gar-kiln. Sarion knew enough of these Grammore predators not to underestimate them...

"I'm here to take you to the mansion. Lord Berillon wishes to greet his guests. You are also allowed to carry your weapons."

"My thanks."

"But Lord Berillon will meet only with you. Your companions must stay behind. I will escort you personally."

Only himself? Sarion wasn't about to refuse the summons, but it was an unexpected demand. The others would have to stay here, and a few of them would certainly not like that.

Sarion turned to Piril, who was waiting nearby. "Captain Glorafin, Piril is one of my personal guards. I'll have him tell the others of your Lord's wishes when they awaken, and he will remain behind."

"I will have better quarters for them to lodge in while you stay at the mansion. Their needs will be met, most especially in warm baths and bed. Barthaniel will be returning soon."

Sarion spoke. "I have a modest request. Can you let them rest undisturbed until dawn, at the least? They are all very weary from our flight and the attack."

"Certainly. Are you ready?" He held up one hand, pointing towards the steps. Sarion nodded, and they left. The guards parted to let them pass, bowing slightly in deference. The staircase was short, and at the bottom was a path carved of round stone which soon bent around a curve. Trees edged the path on both sides, well-manicured grass carpeting the grounds. Torches were placed at regular intervals, and to their right, the shadows soon swallowed everything. Sarion knew that the outward path and wall continued along the breadth of the lake, but he was struck by the solitude surrounding them as they walked along. They kept onwards for a while without seeing a solitary guard, which bothered Sarion. Maybe they were scattered about, well hidden. If true, it would make him less uneasy, but not much so…He thought about asking Glorafin, then decided against it, choosing to follow the man's lead. They soon crossed over a wooden bridge with a small brook dancing beneath it. Torches lighted the walkway, and a pair of guards stood silently at the far end. They stepped over it, Sarion glancing down into the water below. Once on the other side, Glorafin turned to him.

"We have now entered the personal grounds of House Berillon and his holdings. The other side of the bridge is common ground for all of Sharield's citizens, similar to other Trencit cities. On this side, one can only enter on official business of Lord Berillon and his councilors."

They walked around a small pond, the air before them brightening as dozens of torches came into view. A large building sat before them, and Sarion knew they had arrived at Lord Berillon's mansion at last. It was not a huge or sumptuous structure, but stood several stories high, sprawling out to either side. It was large enough to house many people, if necessary, and Sarion wondered who else besides Lord Berillon made this place their home.

Well, he would soon find out...

A small set of stairs led towards the front gate, which was guarded by a pair of armed men. Roughly twice the size of a normal door, it was not made to withstand a heavy attack, although it appeared sturdy enough. Sarion looked to both sides, and he spotted several other guards along the mansion, which made him feel more at ease. The attack on Chensel's life in the very heart of Nighton had sent a powerful signal that the Dark Mage's emissaries could penetrate even the most secure stronghold, and he wasn't about to forget this fact. The men parted as Glorafin walked ahead, Sarion in tow, the small gate opening from within. Seconds later they were through, more guards standing ready. The gate closed behind them and Sarion found himself in a well-lit hall with pictures and tapestries hanging on the walls. A huge fireplace crackled on the far side of the room, and several hunting dogs eyed him warily. Chairs were placed around the hearth and in one of them sat a man, only the top of his bald head visible as he faced the blaze. Glorafin walked towards him, motioning for Sarion to follow.

Was this...

But immediately the idea was squashed as Glorafin rudely kicked the bottom of the chair, causing the man to start.

"I knew you would be asleep as soon as I left."

"Nonsense. I was only collecting my thoughts."

"Your thoughts, eh? More like drowning them in that valley wine. Here now, our guest has arrived. This is Captain Sarion, Second Forester of Nighton."

The man stood, scowling at Glorafin, then gave Sarion a puzzled look. "Ah, from Nighton. A rare visit indeed. Who will be next? The King of Trencit?"

Sarion was silent, unable to figure out the man's demeanor.

"A poor welcome." Glorafin sighed. "I'll do the honors myself then. Sarion, this is Rusteg, Chief Councilor to Lord Berillon, and master of his mansion. I leave our good Forester in your hands, Rusteg, since pressing matters demand my attention."

With that, he nodded to Sarion and walked away.

"Don't mind him." Rusteg slapped at the air. "He doesn't know one wit about what it means to sit down and relax, even if only for a moment."

Sarion said nothing, but he could certainly sympathize with Glorafin...

Rusteg put his hand before him, Sarion matching the grip, which was far weaker than he expected. "Please be welcome in our fair city. Barthaniel has seen to the needs of you and your fighters?"

"He has."

"Very well. The hour is late, and I know you have traveled far. Word of the attack has caused quite the stir in the mansion."

"Is Lord Berillon here?"

Rusteg shook his head. "No, I'm afraid not. He will speak to you tomorrow." He waved a hand, motioning forth a young man from a passageway entrance to their right.

"Lead Captain Sarion to his chambers. A warm bath has already been drawn, and you'll find enough food and wine to satisfy your cravings. We'll talk more in the morning. Rest well."

Sarion felt uneasy with a welcome that felt rushed, but he was too tired to argue. He was certain it would get him nowhere. Equally troublesome was the delay in meeting Lord Berillon, but again, he was a guest in the Lord's house and there was nothing to be done about it. Following the servant, he walked along the corridors of the mansion's right wing, passing closed doors and staircases which led both higher and lower. They passed other servants going about their business, despite the late hour. It was only a short walk before the servant halted, leading Sarion into a well-furnished bedroom with a large wooden table in the center which was filled with enough food and drink for several men. A small but cheerful fire sparked in the far corner, and the servant bowed, handing him a bell.

"Please ring this for anything you need. Myself or another will be outside your door at all hours. Rest well, Captain Sarion."

And with that he left, closing the door behind him and leaving Sarion alone.

He moved over to the table, slumping into a chair and feeling weary to the bone. It was odd, being alone in the mansion, and he missed the companionship of the others already. He knew that word of his sequestering would not be well-received by Chertron and Valadire, but there was nothing to be done. He grabbed a hunk of bread, pouring himself a goblet of wine at the same time. Despite eating earlier, he was still hungry and the food was good, the vintage one of the finest he'd ever had. The last few weeks had been so tumultuous that he was not about to feel guilty for his indulgence. His high ranking had other benefits, and he was going to take advantage of the situation for the moment.

Sarion sat there for a few minutes, trying to relax and enjoy his meal. There was so much to think about, and perhaps this respite would give him the opportunity for some clear thought. There simply had not been enough time lately. Shades…

He moved toward the bed, holding his goblet in one hand, but hesitated. He was in need of a good bath, and he eyed the adjoining room. Tired as he was, the temptation was too great, so he entered the bath area, finding the promised tub filled with warm water. Disrobing, he lay down in the water, letting the heat radiate throughout his body. His eyelids fluttered, and he immersed himself in the liquid, a rare sense of calmness coming upon him. He knew it was due to his weariness (and the wine), but he let the feeling embrace his aching body, knowing that such relief would not always be available. Resting in the water, he replayed the events which had now brought him to Sharield and the home of Lord Berillon. The perilous expedition to Gar-kiln, the chance meeting with Ereck, his seizing of Wharla after their sighting of the dread Ravenor and its master Chardoom, the disastrous flight from the cursed village and eventual arrival at Sharield, ignorant of the fact that the Crage had been sent to track and hunt them down. All this.

But right now it was time to think of the future.

His next move.

Regardless of their dangerous situation, Sarion *had* thought about what to do next, and he had come up with a plan.

Opening his eyes, it was time to leave the bath. He had no desire to be found in the room the next morning after drowning in the tub. What kind of an ending would that be for him after surviving all of the other horrors?

Grinning at the ridiculous notion he toweled off, stepping back into the main room and grabbing a handful of black grapes. The bed and sleep were calling him, stronger than before, and he finally succumbed, dropping onto the bed and wrapping himself in the blankets.

The Summoning

He would not linger in Sharield very long. A day or two at most. He wanted to speak with Lord Berillon, convince him of the danger, and at the very least try to keep the lines of communication open between Nighton and Sharield. Geography and the lack of manpower would prevent much else, but it was important for them to protect against further isolation. He shook his head, doubting that patrols could rendezvous. Now that he had finally reached Sharield, the westland seemed even vaster than before, especially with marauders from Grammore roaming at will. There were just too few men...

So where would *he* go?

The short term answer was clear. He was needed closer to Nighton where he could be most effective. He still had no desire to travel into Trencit and Daregil Keep, but he had a duty to the Western Watch, and was not about to cast aside his obligations. He actually liked the idea which Chensel had first proposed for Valadire, sending the new Forester out to be used as a strike force, moving quickly into regions of trouble. Sarion's own plan would be to keep both Valadire and Chertron with him as they tried to flush out more of the Dark Mage's servants, attacking them when they appeared. He had the magical protection of the rod, and that was not a small thing. Would he use it as a tool? Never... He had felt its allure once, and that had been enough. But the talisman offered a defense against creatures of magic, and this was exactly the weapon they needed in case the Dark Mage sent out his most powerful emissaries.

And Sarion would be there waiting for them...

They already knew the greater plan behind the Dark Mage's motivation; to overcome the westland and its leadership, disband its fighting force, and eventually seize Nighton. If he were able to accomplish these things, then Trencit would be the ultimate prize. Still, it was hard to imagine such an outcome, as Trencit and its cities were powerful, the standing army well-trained and large, its defenses virtually unassailable. But Sarion was not going to underestimate the enemy. No. He would remain constantly vigilant, and ready for anything. It sounded simple enough, but nothing could be further from the truth. He was not about to fool himself.

The last thing which passed through his mind were the words he had spoken to his companions about confronting the enemy in his own homeland. They could defeat his enemies, but if they ever hoped to destroy the Dark Mage for good, they would have to enter the Grammore Lowlands and seek out his fortress hidden deep inside the vast wilderland. The idea seemed like a child's fantasy as Grammore was unexplored and perilous. No text or legend had ever revealed the boundaries of that terrible country, or touched upon its darkest secrets. Uncharted and avoided at all costs, it was a huge expanse of blackness on any map he'd ever seen. Even Erech's map had merely outlined some of its easternmost edges, and for anyone daring enough to breach the Ridegline, that fact was easily evident, as one stared down into that hungry maw of jungle and swampland which defied the most brave – or foolish – adventurer to enter.

And yet he had done so. Twice now. The first time skirting its frontier while hunting down the last of the Glefins, the second time with Charadan and the company of fighters from Trencit. Both expeditions had ended in disaster, with most of the men being killed by lowland predators. But Sarion had emerged, able to fight another day. He knew that Grammore *could* be challenged, and one could tempt its dangers by keeping vigilant to every possible hazard of both flora and fauna. With a high degree of skill and caution -- combined with no small amount of good fortune -- Grammore *could* be entered with some hope of leaving again.

Despite his own assurances of such, Sarion knew

that if one dared to delve into Grammore too deeply, or stayed too long, the odds were severely stacked, and either the hidden dangers would finally snare you, or the greater predators would come across your trail and hunt you down. And lastly, the Dark Mage's fortress would certainly not be easy to find.

Sighing, his mind gradually went blank, the night-wings of sleep soon swooping invisibly down and claiming him as victim.

Sarion slept soundly that night, his body bathing in the much-needed rest, and when his eyes eventually opened, he knew the morning had come and gone. Peering from beneath the blankets, he saw that the fire was well-tended, and fresh plates of food and pitchers of wine and water were on the table. The attendants had entered at some point, not disturbing their guest, bringing breakfast to him before he awoke.

Not wanting to leave the comforts of soft pillows and plush blankets, he lay there a while, yawning heavily, closing his eyes several times. The sleep had done him a world of good and he felt refreshed, able to take on the new day and whatever it might bring, although he fervently wished it would prove uneventful. He finally brought himself to get up, so he pushed away from the bed at last, quickly dressing and pulling on his boots. Even while asleep he had kept a knife handy. It was an act of instinctive survival, and he would never put aside his caution. The day he let down his guard would prove to be the day when even his considerable luck would be unable to protect him…

The room had one window and he looked outside. Iron bars were fastened across the glass, and it showed that the Lords of Sharield were perhaps not as lax as he thought. The mansion was old, and most likely certain protections had always been in place. The day was moving along, and he believed it to be approaching noon, the sun hidden by clouds. He saw guards holding position at several spots, and he wondered if more had been added overnight. With news of the attack on the outpost, normal routine would be shaken, the people of Sharield put on notice. From what he'd learned from the Sharield fighters, the province had not been assaulted for years, and even when the Glefins had been terrorizing the westland, Sharield was too far away from their own homeland to attack in force. Their touch had certainly been felt throughout the borderlands, but the treacherous creatures had simply not possessed the numbers to challenge a guarded city. Despite this fact, the Glefins had done enough damage in other ways. It was an unpleasant chain of thought, and Sarion shook it off, unwilling to dredge up grim memories.

Turning away, he focused his attention on the table filled with food and drink, sitting down for long minutes and basking in the simple task of satisfying his appetite and quenching his thirst. Although he had feasted pleasantly the previous night, he had slept late, and his cravings had grown with the new day. Nearly full, he palmed an apple, admiring the deep red and smooth texture. He put it in his pocket, expecting to snack on it later. Grabbing another, he bit deeply, deciding that it would make the perfect finish to his meal. He was about to take another bite when someone knocked on the door.

At least I had the chance to eat, he thought. Taking a swig of wine from his goblet, he stood. "Come in."

The door opened and one of the attendants entered, bowing. "Captain Sarion, your presence is required in the meeting hall. Lord Berillon will speak with you now."

Sarion nodded, eager to finally meet with the Lord of Sharield. Fully dressed, there was nothing else he needed from the room, so he beckoned the man to lead on, following on his heels. They went back towards the main entrance, passing other attendants and several armed men, none of them doing more than politely nodding and going their own way. Boots echoing across the stone floors, Sarion now had the opportunity to take in more of his surroundings. Few windows broke the monotony of flagstone and torch holders, and when they passed these, Sarion saw that they were all barred as well. Soon they went down a flight of steps, entering a wider hallway to their right. A set of wooden doors was open, and after that sat more steps. They moved downward, passing closed doors to both sides, and then a larger door reared up before them, this one guarded by a pair of men in full armor. Sarion knew they were closing on the heart of the mansion, probably near Lord Berillon's personal quarters. The guards let them pass without speaking, opening the door and ushering them inside. Sarion found himself in a wide room split down the middle by an oval-shaped table filled with chairs, the furthest one adorned with carvings, the seat covered with a plush cushion. Undoubtedly it was for Lord Berillon himself, and the attendant led Sarion to a chair on the left side of the table.

"The council will be here soon. I'll remain outside to take you back. My name is Raphiel, and I will serve you after you have finished here."

Sarion nodded and the man left, leaving him alone. Another pair of doors sat at the end of the room, and these were closed. A fire blazed merrily on the side opposite of him, and tapestries hung along the walls, depicting warriors in various forms of activity. The material looked aged, and he figured they had been in the mansion for generations. Several minutes passed but no one else entered. He fidgeted with one of his boots, one hand tapping absently at the table, when he heard voices from the inner door. The conversation was muffled, and he failed to catch any words. The door slowly opened, and several men now walked inside, moving forward until all had found a seat. They numbered six in all, and they nodded at Sarion, their faces neutral. He knew that his coming would have mixed reaction as word of the assault spread through the city, yet Nighton and Sharield had always shared a common bond as strong fortresses protecting Trencit's western borders. Even though Sharield had become an isolated province at best, it still represented the power of Trencit, long miles from Daregil Keep.

The other door now opened, Rusteg's face peering into the meeting room. He spoke with the guards for a moment, and then he came inside, walking towards Sarion, his hand held out in greeting.

"Captain Sarion, I hope your rest was deep and the food adequate?"

Rising, Sarion matched the grip. "Yes on both accounts. It was well-needed, and you have my thanks."

Rusteg made a slight bow. "Your men have been taken care of, although I heard there was some grumbling about the arrangements." He raised an eyebrow.

"My apology for their behavior. They're not used to being separated from me. We've spent many days in the field under constant threat."

Rusteg nodded but said nothing. He looked around at the other men, most of them in conversation with each other.

Sarion followed his gaze, trying to gauge their measure. All of them wore robes of deep gray, and were either well into middle-age or beyond. None of them appeared to be in condition as fighters or officers, and he assumed they were either merchants who had gained power and influence over the years, or were directly related to Lord Berillon.

Rusteg cleared his throat, gaining their attention. "Council Lords, as you already know this is Captain

Sarion, Second Forester of Nighton. He brings knowledge concerning the assault on our northern outpost. Please wait until Lord Berillon arrives to question him."

Sarion's face was impassive, and he wondered how they would react. The news had obviously taken them by complete surprise, and they would be looking to him for explanations...

The inner door opened again and Glorafin entered, Barthaniel right behind him. The Captain nodded in his direction and took a seat among the Councilors. Barthaniel came towards him, bowing deeply in greeting. Sarion gripped his hand.

"I hope you are well, Captain Sarion. Your companions are in comfort, although understandably anxious. You command a strong sense of loyalty among your fighters, I see."

"They are good men – and women," he added, remembering Lassel.

"They'll have the opportunity to visit our sparring grounds to keep them active. Several of them requested it."

"That's no surprise..."

Suddenly the inner door burst open, a pair of guards thrusting themselves inside. "Lord Berillon has arrived," one of them said.

Everyone in the room stood, and a large man now entered, dressed in a sweeping robe of black, a small golden circlet on his head. He reminded Sarion of Rusteg, but even larger and older.

"My Lord." Sarion approached, and Lord Berillon waved a hand.

"Welcome to Sharield, Captain Sarion. It is indeed rare to have one of Nighton's ranking Foresters among our ranks. Please be seated, and find yourself to be here with your brethren."

"Thank you for your welcome and hospitality." Sarion bowed, moving back a pace, as Lord Berillon eased down into his chair, the rest of the room following suit after he was seated.

"I'll start this meeting off directly to the point." He looked across the men in the room, his brow sinking into his weathered face. "There has been an attack on our outpost, the likes of which has never been seen before in our lands. A creature from unknown parts and origin has slain one of our patrols to the last man, and dared to attack an armed fortress."

The councilors murmured amongst themselves, but no one interrupted.

Lord Berillon looked over at Glorafin. "Speak, Captain."

Glorafin rose.

"Hunting parties have been sent out with doubled numbers at my command. Homesteads have been warned and the outpost has been reinforced. I've had our entire fighting force mobilized in an effort to track down and kill the marauding creature."

"What do we know of this monster?" A man seated closest to Sarion spoke.

"We have no knowledge of it. I'm hoping Captain Sarion can answer this question."

All eyes rested on him now, and Sarion felt the anxiety and fear rippling throughout the chamber in unseen currents. He had to speak confidently and forcefully in order to gain their trust.

"My Lords. I do have some understanding of the creature's nature." He paused a moment. "My company set out from Nighton after a deadly assault on our western wall, as our couriers have relayed."

"Yes." Lord Berillon answered, but said nothing else.

"We captured a man who directed the attack against us."

"Is it true that you were attacked by a Killworm?"

Another councilor asked the question, the man seated at Lord Berillon's right side.

"Yes, it's true."

Several of the councilors gasped, shock registering on more than one face.

Sarion continued. "We were able to defeat the monster and capture its master, although the cost in blood was high."

"How could you have killed such a creature?" Rusteg asked. "Are you even sure it was a Killworm? Legend says they are magical and can only be killed by such."

"Magical or not, we slew the beast." Sarion left it at that. "I was in the middle of the fight. There can be no doubt as to the nature of the creature *or* the final outcome."

None of them challenged his statement.

"This is ill news to hear of Nighton's plight, and now *we* have been assaulted as well." Lord Berillon spoke, his eyes dark. "We will do everything to protect ourselves from such creatures, even if it means bringing all the outlying homesteads inside Sharield where they will be safe."

Safe, wondered Sarion. Was there anywhere secure to be found in the entire westland?

"So tell us more about what happened after the battle." Lord Berillon continued, and Sarion felt the intensity of the leader's gaze on him. As of yet, he had no real measure of the man.

"As you wish." Sarion inclined his head. He spent the next few minutes describing their journey south and the dangers they faced. When he mentioned Gar-kiln, there was some recognition as to its existence, but little was said. He told them how they entered the cursed village, and what had been done to its people. Sarion told the council about the ogres, Chardoom, and the monstrous Ravenor, and the room grew silent. Detailed as he was, he realized that there would be both shock and skepticism about his story, and it remained to be seen what impact it would bring. He moved his tale along until he brought them full circle about his arrival in their own lands and the relentless hunter which stalked them.

"So…" Rusteg interrupted. "This creature sought you out across many miles and dangerous country to reclaim this woman Wharla?"

"She seems to believe so. In truth, there's no way of knowing. Chardoom would certainly have been enraged upon learning about her capture and our arrival in the village," Sarion answered.

Glorafin spoke. "She might yet prove to be of some value. Perhaps she still holds secrets about this Dark Mage."

"My Lord." Rusteg turned to Berillon, who had been quietly listening for the past few minutes while others spoke. "It is my strong suggestion that we stay out of this fight."

Sarion frowned, feeling uneasy at the man's words. "How can you stay out of something from which you will be dragged into?" Sarion replied. "Already the enemy is at your doorstep. The plans of the Dark Mage are obvious."

"I'm not convinced of anything yet." Lord Berillon finally entered the conversation. "The creature followed you here, and would not have come otherwise."

"There's no way of knowing that." Sarion answered. "The Dark Mage's plan is not difficult to understand. He wants to conquer the westland and move into Trencit. His marauders have come as far as Sprechyd Wood. He's attacked both Nighton and its leaders directly. Jerol is now dead, and Lord Chensel barely escaped with his own life. These are acts of war and he seeks to overrun us all."

"We have not had any problems until now," said Rusteg. "The Dark Mage might have left us alone for all we know."

Sarion felt anger building inside, and he knew that he must restrain himself and tread very carefully here. "Both Nighton and Sharield are provinces of Trencit. An assault against one is an assault against all."

"Maybe in years long past," said Rusteg. "But we have little if any correspondence with Daregil Keep these days. Distance and time have separated most of these ties."

"We are brethren, but nothing else. Sharield stands on its own, neither asking for nor offering aid to Trencit and its problems." Lord Berillon spoke softly, but behind his words was an undeniable confidence.

The other council members acknowledged his statement to the last man, nodding in deference, the only one seemingly neutral being Glorafin, who might be the one person Sarion thought he could convince otherwise. And there it was...Sarion had suspected as much. Sharield now considered itself to be an independent province, fully autonomous. They might talk about their kinship with Trencit and Daregil Keep, but its power had not reached into these lands for a long time, and clearly the council and Lord Berillon were quite content with the arrangement.

Sarion tried again. "Nighton and Sharield have always had a strong relationship with each other."

"And we still do," added Lord Berillon. "That will never change. However, we don't have the strength to send fighters off to defend the walls of Nighton. Or the opposite, from what it sounds. In the past, perhaps, but our numbers have dwindled over the years. It is enough that we can adequately protect our own citizens. We may fear no assault against our walls, but that doesn't mean we can attack an enemy across great distances. No, Sharield must remain true to its people and show all potential adversaries that we will not be intimidated. We can offer sanctuary for travelers from Nighton like yourselves, but our power must stay in Sharield."

The Summoning

Sarion heard the finality of the leader's words. Lord Berillon believed that the Dark Mage would overlook Sharield and be daunted by its guarded walls and lake, but he knew differently. They did not realize the depth of the threat. The Dark Mage was hungry for domination, and that included everything not already under his own power. Eventually, Sharield would be a target as well. Sooner or later...

Rusteg spoke again. "What of the northern provinces? Lord Pralicon's holdings are much larger than ours, and he has a standing army which ranks among the finest in all of Trencit. Surely he can supply Nighton with all the help it needs?"

Sarion listened to the man's words, which only succeeded to convince him moreso where Sharield stood. They did not fully appreciate or understand the resources of their enemy. But could he really fault them? They had been isolated for so long without major trouble that it seemed the norm for their province. At best, they could probably offer a few hundred men to assist Nighton, and that would be gladly received at this point. This was the most likely scenario that Sarion had hoped for; at least a showing of mutual support, and maybe targeted hunting parties, but it now seemed certain that this would not come about. Lord Berillon and his councilors would never accede to this idea, and Sarion knew that if he pressed them it would only serve to rile them further, perhaps even antagonize them, and he didn't want that to happen. As a high-ranking envoy from Nighton, he needed to be both reasonable and political. Time and geography had both played a part in separating Sharield from the rest of the westland, and if what he had just heard was true about their decreasing population, then it was hard to argue against the fact. In the end, Nighton and Sharield would both stand – or fall – on their own.

Sarion replied. "We've been in discussion with Lord Pralicon, and he has sent out additional hunting parties. From what I last heard, he had not suffered the same excursion from marauders as the central part of the westland. That's not to diminish the level of threat we face, however, as predators have been sighted as far east as Sprechyd Wood. But Nighton and the outlying villages have suffered the brunt of the attack. It's clear that if Nighton falls, it will further isolate both Sharield and Lord Pralicon's holdings, along with opening up Trencit to an attack from the west."

Another councilor spoke up. "How can you be certain that Sprechyd Wood itself is not the origin of such creatures?" Several of the others nodded in agreement.

Sarion was unwilling to speak openly of his experience with the Keeper of Sprechyd Wood, and seriously doubted that he would be believed even if he did talk about it…no, better to keep that out of the discussion.

He spoke. "From knowledge of our expedition into Grammore, and those we have encountered along the way, all these things lend support to the existence of the Dark Mage. I have no reason to think the man we captured was being untruthful. What would he have to gain at that point? And where would someone acquire such power to control these creatures?"

"Regardless, one explanation is as good as the other." Rusteg spoke, shrugging his shoulders.

Sarion inwardly winced. *They debate things which they have no purpose in arguing,* he thought. *It seems they would rather downplay the events than to face them head on, even after their own outpost has been attacked.*

The councilors murmured among themselves, and Lord Berillon seemed content to let them have their own discourse rumbling beneath the main conversation. Sarion figured this was their normal method of debate, and there was little he could say or do that would thrust them into an entirely different mindset. Throughout most of the discussion, Glorafin had remained silent. Sarion caught the man staring at him several times, his face expressionless. What was he thinking? Sarion doubted the officer was of similar persuasion as the councilors. Maybe it was normal for Glorafin to stay neutral in such matters. It seemed that the less controversy that surfaced in Sharield, the better. Lord Berillon and his councilors were unquestionably set on keeping it this way, and there was little doubt that the citizens were in agreement. That way, everyone was kept happy.

Voices raised and lowered over the next few minutes, and it appeared that Sarion was no longer the focal point. A consensus had been decided. The city was going to remain vigilant against the Crage and any other marauding creatures, which would be tracked and killed, if possible. The outlying villages and homesteads were already being alerted, with the offer of haven within the walls of Sharield. There was ample room, and it was a good sized city with many resources of its own, independent and steeped in its own traditions. Sarion was now a spectator himself, listening to the councilors, some of them speaking up at times and holding the rest of them to attention, before someone else took the reins and offered new input. The meeting was really going nowhere, and Sarion found himself blocking out the voices and considering his own options. Whatever he decided on next, Sharield would not play any role. The city would remain on the edge of the westland in terms of both scope and importance. The people thought that they could fend for themselves and remain isolated, so there was nothing else to be done here.

He had fulfilled his own obligation in warning them of the danger, and if a marauding creature from Grammore within their own boundaries failed to convince them, then nothing else would. And if they *had* never arrived here, there would probably not have been any immediate assault. Sarion felt a pang of guilt, realizing that their arrival had caused the deaths of Sharield fighters. But it seemed that wherever he was fated to go, death always followed. He shook his head, chiding himself. Sarion and his companions risked their lives every single day in protecting the entire westland, so he simply wasn't being fair to himself by thinking this way. But maybe the councilors had been partly right, that the Dark Mage would not have any short-term intentions of moving towards the mountain city.

Or would he? Wharla had spoken about Chardoom's orders, which were to eventually go east, or something to that end, hadn't she? Yes, he remembered her saying something similar. That probably meant Nighton and Trencit, but it also could have meant Sharield.

He gazed around the table, the conversation moving one way and then another. Lord Berillon seemed to be half-asleep, his head nodding, his eyes partially closed. This was pointless, and Sarion felt the urgency to move once again; to leave Sharield and the terror of Gar-kiln behind. He longed for his own lands and household, and most of all his nephew Edward, who was now safe at Nighton. Yes. He had spent long days in the wilderness searching for the cursed city. His task now completed, it was time to be on the move once more. The servants of the Dark Mage would not be idly sitting around. There was no way of knowing where they would strike next, but he had to be ready.

Sharield felt so far away from Nighton, Trencit, and the greater part of the westland. He couldn't blame the people for wanting to remain isolated and keep to themselves. Isn't that exactly what he had done himself after leaving the Western Watch? True, the threat from the Glefins had been destroyed, the wicked creatures hunted into Grammore by a company of fighters under his command. The Foresters had wanted him to stay on at Nighton as a candidate for further promotion, but Sarion was finished at that point, and only wanted to find some peace for himself. His own kin slain by the Glefins, he had enacted revenge upon the marauders, but there was no satisfaction from the result. No, all he wanted was to return to his own lands and be left alone.

There was no misunderstanding here as the council was convinced of its decision, and Sarion decided to leave it that way. Depart the city under the cloak of friendship and vows of mutual loyalty, but little else. It was time to go...

Sarion took the measure of the room, and things were quieting down. Lord Berillon still seemed half-drowsy, while Rusteg carried the conversation on his own. Even Glorafin appeared disinterested, and Sarion believed the man to be a typical fighter; more comfortable in the field and with his men, and not bickering among the political leadership, especially under trying times like these.

The entrance door suddenly opened and Sarion heard footsteps enter, although he took little notice. He was mentally preparing himself for a few last words of caution and greatfulness, but then his attention changed as all heads turned to the door as a herald spoke out.

"Lord Berillon and good councilors of Sharield. We are honored to have additional guests who demand immediate attention among our leadership."

More guests, Sarion thought? Who else could have arrived here? Glancing about the room, it seemed the council members were surprised as well as they murmured to each other. He looked at Lord Berillon, whose eyes were fully alert now, although he didn't seem to be phased at all by the interruption.

Looking towards the entrance with everyone else, Sarion watched in amazement as the herald came forward, clearly dressed in the markings of a Trencit Royal envoy.

"My Lords, it is my honor to announce the presence of Prince Thustan from Daregil Keep, accompanied by Barimon, Chief Mage and advisor to King Gregor. Please rise to greet them."

Sarion barely contained a gasp of shock as his heart sank. Thustan was *here*? How could they be in Sharield? Even *he* had not known his eventual destination.

Two men entered, the first one in riding garb. Sarion had never seen either of them before, but there was no mistaking the way Thustan carried himself, or the mage Barimon, who was dressed in a black, sweeping robe, his hands gripping a gnarled staff.

Lord Berillon stood as well, looking genuinely surprised for the first time since the meeting began. He rose, speaking words of greeting which Sarion scarcely recognized. How had they managed to even find him after all these long days? And what would the future hold for him now, his plans dashed, as Thustan would undoubtedly take him to Daregil Keep where he would finally stand before King Gregor? Sarion's mind scrambled for purchase, desperately trying to figure a pathway out from his predicament. Surely he couldn't flee, as that would be considered an act bordering on treason itself, and he was too loyal to even consider it as an option. Could he slip out? Perhaps they didn't know he was even here yet. But how could he possibly leave now? Such a move would draw the attention of the entire room, and certainly Lord Berillon would announce his presence, which was rare in itself, although not to the extent of Thustan's visit...

Thustan and Barimon stood before Lord Berillon, exchanging additional words of greeting. The councilors listened attentively, all of them on their feet now, some of them shaking their heads in astonishment. Glorafin stared at their backs, and Sarion couldn't tell if the man had known of their arrival or not. He assumed Lord Berillon had perhaps not been made aware himself.

The master of Sharield was speaking deeply with the two men, who were focused on his words at the moment, and Sarion knew that he was trapped. Even if he managed to somehow slip away, it would be considered a deliberate act of avoidance. There was nothing for him to do now but await the inevitable, which seemed to be happening sooner rather than later…

Thustan and Barimon pivoted together, surprise clearly evident on both their faces as Lord Berillon announced his other guest.

"Sarion, Second Forester of Nighton, has come to our city as well, a rare visit from one of Nighton's Captains."

Thustan hurried forward, Barimon on his heel.

"Sarion! By a stroke of luck we've managed to find you at last!" Thustan stared deeply into his eyes, Sarion matching the gaze without flinching.

"Maybe, or not." Barimon spoke, his voice low, Sarion uneasy at his words.

"Good fortune or by purpose, you're the reason we've come this far." Thustan nodded. "I'm glad to finally have the chance to meet with you, Sarion. Very glad."

The man seemed genuine enough, and Sarion had heard nothing but good things about the man's character. But it still didn't change the facts of his circumstances…

"Let's speak with Berillon quickly and move somewhere with Sarion." Barimon lifted a finger, the long nail pointing directly at him." We've wasted enough time finding you…"

'

❋ ❋

Forlern slept like the dead for the rest of the day and into the early evening.

His repose tormented by vivid nightmares, at times he thrashed about, moaning in his sleep, fighting a legion of terrible creatures without faces, all teeth and claws. At some point in the night he rested more soundly, his weariness overtaking him and giving him several hours of uninterrupted peace at last. More than once he awoke, wondering where he was at first, but quickly relaxing and letting his mind and body take comfort in his surroundings. During these moments of brief consciousness, he lost track of time, his room illuminated by a pair of candles, the beeswax fat and dripping down the sides. The chamber had no windows, so no touch of daylight broke through to disturb him. At long last he came to, tossing about restlessly, eventually just lying there in the bed, his eyes yet closed but his mind swiftly awakening. Hunger grabbed his stomach, eager to quench its need, and Forlern rousted himself fully from the bed, stretching his arms and quickly drawing back, wincing from his injury. Cursing aloud, he lifted himself up and shambled over to the table, examining its wares. Servants had come inside the room to check on him, he knew, as there were fresh offerings to be found, which he greedily attacked. For the next few minutes he thought of nothing but food and drink, and how much he had needed rest. Finishing up a last piece of salted meat and admiring the flavor, he dressed himself, snatching some fresh clothing which had been placed in the bathing area. It took him another pair of minutes until he was fully clothed, weapons back in place and all. Nodding to himself, he wondered as to what had been going on while he slept. Certainly the city's leaders had not waited idly, with Questron missing and battles raging outside its walls.

Forlern glanced around the room once more, as if sizing it up. He grabbed a generous portion of salted meat, stuffing it in his tunic. He also gulped at some more wine, debating whether to take the rest of the bottle along with him, then decided against it.

"They'll think me a drunkard," he said to himself. "Ah, there's no shortage around here."

He opened the door, finding a servant waiting in attendance. "Captain Forlern, I hope you slept well?"

He nodded.

"Is there anything you are in need of?"

"Not that I can think of," he replied. He felt like asking the man for any news, but thought better of it. The servant would not be in a position to offer what he needed, so there was no reason to question him, curious or not. "I would speak with the commanders in the meeting room. I needed the rest, but the day has grown long."

"It has indeed, Captain Forlern. I've been instructed not to bother you, but upon awakening, you are requested at the meeting hall immediately. If I may lead you there?" He inclined his head, and Forlern signaled for them to be off. They passed down familiar hallways, the building seemingly empty. The only sound was their boots clicking against the hard stone, the echoes quickly dying away. Corridors and closed doors passed them by to either side, and soon they were at the meeting room. Guards nodded as he approached, opening the wooden panel to the large chamber beyond. The servant left and Forlern entered, his eyes opening in surprise as Questron nearly collided with him.

"You're back!" Forlern exclaimed.

"Indeed I am. It seems we've both been fortunate. I hope you've been attended to?"

"Yes, but we need to talk."

"Aye. Let's return to my quarters. My business is done here for now."

Keeping his questions at bay, Forlern followed the man, who looked none the worse for wear considering the terrible battle they both had been through.

And survived…

Questron hurried through the halls, Forlern on his heels. He figured the man was as eager to speak with him as he also felt. Questron approached a broad stair, a pair of fighters guarding the bottom, both men moving aside. The Captain of Lastrad bounded up the staircase, reaching the top after a few dozen steps, and then turned to the right.

A solitary door was closed before them, a single fighter in attendance.

"Captain." He bowed, opening the door, and Forlern found himself in a sizable chamber which clearly exhibited the man's ranking. Ornate tapestries hung on the wall, the room furnished with polished oak chairs and tables, scrolls and documents stacked neatly about. Food and drink sat on silver platters, and Questron motioned Forlern forward.

"Be at ease here, Forlern. We have much to discuss. Help yourself to a drink and a bite if you like."

Forlern wasn't about to pass up the offer for more of the fine Lastrad vintage, and he seated himself at one of the smaller tables, Questron a second ahead of him.

"I heard of your arrival upon returning to the front gates. I had some doubts as to your situation." Questron leaned back in his chair, stretching his legs out.

"I can say the same. So what happened?"

"My tale first? Ah, why not. You handled yourself admirably on the battle field. It's the least I can do." Questron's mouth twisted into something that was close to a smirk, but not quite… "The following company never appeared, and the battle seemed to be going against us. I ordered the rest of my men to head east, which I figured was the last direction they would expect us to go. It was not easy breaking through their ranks, those devils. I watched as several more men went down, but we broke through in the end. I looked about, but you were gone. Things were chaotic, and I assumed your position to be neither better nor worse than our own, at that point. Plus I knew you were quite capable to find your way off that field of death."

Forlern took it as a compliment, and nodded. "I couldn't see you either. I lost my horse and was in a fight for my life."

"We all were. We rode on for a while but they didn't pursue us. I was worried about the hunting party that was coming after us, and we angled our way back into the woods after going what we thought was a safe distance. Unfortunately, there were Devlent scouts everywhere, and we had to go much further out of our way. It was a long ride, but we eventually cleared the forest, but without any word or sign of my men. By the time we approached the city, I caught scattered bits of information, enough to piece together the facts on my own. The party was ambushed by more Devlents, and suffered heavy losses. They were unable to come to our aid."

"A carefully laid out trap." Forlern shook his head.

"Indeed. We managed to finally gain the city, and I organized larger patrols to sweep the countryside in every direction. When I came back my men told me that you had already returned, although injured to some degree."

"Sore, but I'll be fine."

Questron accepted his answer with a curt nod. "Since then, I've mobilized the Lastrad army. That's kept me busy enough, along with meeting the Gran Barshara. He is not pleased at the turn of events."

"I couldn't imagine why…"

"And he's disturbed because Klellan is now missing as well." Questron stared intently at him, as if already knowing that Forlern had knowledge of the Ja-Ravel's whereabouts. He wasn't about to disappoint him.

"Klellan is dead."

Questron leaned forward, his brows narrowing, his voice lowering. "What do you speak of?"

"It appears that *he* was the one responsible for the attacks. It was Klellan that controlled the creature."

"What? These are grave accusations. How do you know this, Forlern?"

The young fighter pursed his hands together. "After leaving the battlefield, we rode on for a while until we spotted a small farm building of some kind. I saw movement there, as of someone trying to conceal themselves. We approached carefully, and I'm afraid your man was killed in a surprise attack. I barely missed being skewered myself. I was lucky, and only avoided a serious injury by dismounting at the right time." He shook his head, recalling the close call.

"Go on," Questron pressed him with little patience in his voice.

Forlern shrugged. "I hit the attacker with my knives, and held him at bay, my sword at his throat. It was Klellan."

"And you killed him, that easily?"

A bit put off, Forlern shook his head. "I'm afraid I never had the chance to confront him in open combat. He was already dying."

"Dying?"

"Yes. He was somehow connected to the creature, perhaps in some magical way. He wore a band around his arm which he showed me, still mocking me until his end. He was the creature's master, directing its attacks, and when the beast died, Klellan died as well. He admitted it before his end. Strange indeed, and I can only surmise that he'd been serving the enemy for some period of time. And right beneath the Gran Barshara's very nose."

Questron rubbed his chin, leaning back in his chair. "Well, that is a fascinating turn of events. Wait until the Gran Barshara hears of Klellan's treachery. But it all connects. He had to have been hiding the beast within the city."

Forlern looked at him, and the Lastrad Captain had a sneer on his face. Clearly Questron was pleased that Klellan was now dead, and of course it would make the Gran Barshara's decision to keep the dangerous man as his personal bodyguard look like an extremely poor choice, perhaps enough to undermine the powerful leader's position. The more Forlern gave it thought, the more it made sense. Questron himself had come under much fire lately as the killings went unabated. Now he had fodder to defend himself and his own position, with evidence from Forlern to bolster the facts. It would pivot much of the blame from Questron's shoulders and fall into the lap of the Gran Barshara himself…

The Lastrad Captain matched his gaze for a moment before speaking. "I'll need the location of this building to send men out to bring back the carcass. And shortly I'll also be meeting with the Gran Barshara himself. Of course, I'll need your presence there to recite your tale to him directly."

Forlern considered his words. True, he had been sent to Lastrad to help them find and destroy the predator, and his mission was now finished, so there was no reason not to see it completed. But something tugged at him as he fought to unravel the political intricacies of his situation. There were many moving parts in this grand puzzle, and he felt obligated to understand the larger picture, and Forlern himself would come out looking very good, having succeeded at an impossible task. Questron stared at him as if reading his mind.

"Is there something else you want to talk about?"

Questron was sure to gain leverage over the Gran Barshara now, but he needed Forlern to add full credibility to his story. Or did he? Once Forlern revealed the location of the building his little secret was up, but it wouldn't be that difficult to find since it was near the battlefield. And what was he thinking anyway? Questron had shown him respect from the start of his venture here. The Lastrad Captain was a powerful man, and a dangerous one. He could be a strong ally, for now and into the future. But could Forlern entirely trust him? The Lastrad chain of power was ruthless and cunning, with no quarter asked or given. Only a fool would think otherwise, and Forlern didn't consider himself a fool…

"Forlern, you seem to be a man of much talent for

your age. I see you consider your words first, and have something on your mind. Are you seeking some other gain? Money, or something else? I can assure you, the Gran Barshara will not let your actions go unrewarded. His resources are vast, and I'm also in a position to compensate generously."

"I understand," Forlern replied. "And I also realize that the Gran Barshara will do everything he can from letting the truth be revealed about Klellan."

The Lastrad Captain now hesitated, and Forlern saw the faintest glimmer in the man's eye. "He may." Questron shrugged. "But what of yourself? King Gregor and your leaders will press you for the truth. Even whispers spoken from the highest ramparts can reach the lowest valleys..."

Forlern stood up, stretching for a moment, before sitting down once more. He downed another swig of the wine, enjoying the taste, but felt a chill at Questron's words. Was the man warning him? Could he truly speak his mind to the Lastradian Captain? Ultimately, where did Questron's loyalties lie? He knew he had to be careful here, very careful...On the surface, it seemed his duty in Lastrad was fulfilled, and he could be shortly on his way back to Daregil Keep, and hopefully a reunion with Sarion as well. He also must not forget that he was an ambassador between two powerful provinces, and his superiors would certainly frown upon anything he did to muddy the waters. He was here as a fighter in the Homeguard, not to play politics, which he found distasteful, yet here he was, doing *exactly* that, and with someone who had a much higher degree of skill and experience in the act thereof...

"Are you asking me to keep this a secret?"

"I'm not asking you anything. But I can't speak for the Gran Barshara."

"You think he will demand my silence on the entire truth?" Forlern now felt his anger rising inside. He wouldn't forget his first encounter with the Gran Barshara.

The man had been extremely arrogant, along with his personal bodyguard, the Ja-Ravel assassin Klellan. Like Questron, he would shed no tears at the man's death, but he did feel a grim satisfaction at how circumstances had played out.

"As a captain of the Homeguard, it is my obligation to report back to King Gregor and my leaders."

"Noble of you. I would expect nothing less from someone in your position."

Forlern frowned. "Then what's your suggestion?"

"Perhaps accept a token of the Gran Barshara's forthcoming generosity."

Forlern shook his head. "Whatever it is, the only thing I can accept is his thanks. If he's unwilling to give me just that, then there's nothing I can do. I want to maintain the ties between Trencit and Lastrad, especially with the combined threat of the Devlents and Dark Mage. If I wasn't a member of the Homeguard…well, things might be different."

"Lastrad has much to offer. Do your thoughts turn to a position here?"

"No, no they do not. I fear I would be too constrained within these walls."

"Yet not so back at Daregil Keep, awaiting your next dangerous assignment?"

Forlern knew that Questron was probing him now, feeling him out, but as to what purpose, it was impossible to say. For himself, or for the Gran Barshara's benefit? Or neither? Forlern knew he dared not completely trust the man. True, they had worked admirably together, fought side-by-side against deadly foes and superior numbers, both of them returning unscathed. But he simply could not put all his faith in the man…

"We have former Homeguard here in Lastrad. They came seeking positions, knowing that their compensation is much greater than they would ever have received in

Trencit. I'm not saying this as opinion…" he added, Forlern readying a quick retort. "Hold your tongue for a moment. Your skill in the battlefield surpasses your experience in dealing with the mechanics of a powerful kingdom, or provinces like Lastrad. I only state the truth. I'm not saying they are bad men for seeking profit over honor, and we do have our own sets of code here, much maligned as it sometimes is. A fool will quickly meet his end in this city. However, a wiser, more patient man, possessed of talent, can exceed his wildest dreams. Now hear, what untruth have I spoken thus?"

He held his hands up in appeal, and Forlern considered his reply. He was even more confused now as to where this was going, and felt a sudden need to end the conversation.

"Honestly, your perception seems solid. Men will go where their heart leads them. Sadly, I can only speak for myself."

Questron stood, the tall man appearing even more menacing. "I can offer you a position within my own guard. An officer of Lastrad, with rewards far beyond your imagination, Forlern. I understand the delicacies of where you now stand, but perhaps a future arrangement can be made, agreeable to the three of us? You speak of honesty, but will you also relay the contents of our conversation? Your superiors might frown in great disapproval, and we don't need any distrust to arise in our relationship between Daregil Keep and Lastrad."

Forlern was now convinced. He'd heard enough to make up his mind. Questron was sowing the seeds to draw Forlern into their own fold. Maybe they had seen something which he could offer them, or maybe *he* had become an unwilling accomplice for events beyond his scope of control which threatened to carry him away. He didn't want to cause a rift here, and he also didn't want to place himself in a bad light once he returned. No, his loyalty lay entirely with the Homeguard and Trencit.

Forlern stood, emptying the remainder of his cup, moving towards the door. "Captain Questron, I appreciate the breadth of your candor, but I must return to my quarters for rest. I would like to meet with the Gran Barshara as soon as possible, and discuss some other matters of strategy before I depart for Daregil Keep."

Nodding, he walked past the Lastrad officer, turning his back and moving to the door, feeling no small amount of relief that he had left unchallenged…

Forlern didn't have to wait long, and within the hour he was escorted to the palace and found himself once more in the presence of the Gran Barshara. Questron had arrived ahead of him, so Forlern knew that the tale had already been told.

"Be seated." The Gran Barshara waved a hand, and Forlern dropped into an ornately carved chair, cushioned with what could only be some of the finest silks in the southland. He scanned the room absently, amazed at the wealth that was on display here. This appeared to be a smaller, more secluded meeting room within the large palace. Tapestries adorned the walls, while several tables embedded with large jewels were laden with food and wine.

"Questron saw fit to speak of Klellan's death and the end of the creature. It seems the original judgement I presumed upon our first meeting was made in haste. A man in my position cannot afford errors, you understand."

Forlern shrugged. "I try my best not to underestimate anything these days, My Lord. My travels in Grammore have given me greater knowledge which I have learned from…"

"Wisdom comes upon a man in many ways and at unexpected times. Opportunity is always there for the quick and the cunning to seize upon."

The Gran Barshara's face was impassive, but Forlern knew the game being played here, and didn't like it one bit. Unfortunately, he had little recourse but to see things through to their end. The sooner he left Lastrad, the better.

"My thanks to the role you engaged yourself in by ending this great threat to Lastrad and its people."

Ah, the Gran Barshara shows a rare display of humility.

Forlern stood. "Understood." He made a slight bow. "On behalf of King Gregor and Trencit, I only did my best for what was asked, for the sake of both Lastrad and Daregil Keep."

"Hmm. You also then understand that having Klellan so close to my person might be viewed as a critical mistake."

"We all make mistakes, especially against such cunning adversaries. I do have a question though…were you aware that he was indeed a Ja-Ravel assassin?"

The Gran Barshara nodded. Forlern chanced a quick glance at Questron, but the man remained seated, content to keep himself out of the conversation, his face expressionless.

"And you didn't see the potential danger of hiring him?"

"He never denied it. I look for the best and most talented men for whatever it is I need. He was the one most suited to the task."

"And you weren't concerned for your own safety?" Forlern pressed him, seeing how far he could go.

"Why should I have been concerned? He was paid handsomely. A fortune in your terms. What would he have to gain by harming me?"

"Their legacy is an evil one, filled with mischief. I would never trust them. Are there others in your guard?"

"If there were, why would I tell you such?" It was a rebuke, but lacking the usual sarcasm from the man.

"My pardon, but surely you see the danger now? The forces of the Dark Mage are at work, and move against Lastrad and Trencit."

"Of course I know that." The Gran Barshara frowned. "For your curiosity, I will answer. No, there are no others."

"That you know of…"

The Gran Barshara didn't seem the slightest bit put off. "Matters in my household are well under control now."

Forlern sat down again.

"Now, this leads us back to a more delicate subject. It is in no one's best interest for word of Klellan's treachery to surface. Ever." His eyes were pools of ice, and Forlern knew the man was deadly serious.

"That leaves only King Gregor and us three to know then," Forlern offered. He was on dangerous ground here, exactly as Questron had told him earlier.

"I'm afraid that's not good enough."

"Not good enough? King Gregor sent me here to aid you, and now you ask me to bolster a deception? That borders on treason for myself." Forlern shook his head.

"Treason? A word, Forlern, a word…nothing more."

"Maybe to *yourself*. I'm a member of the Homeguard and advisor to the king, unless you've forgotten." Forlern could barely control his rage at the man's audacity. The Gran Barshara's arrogance knew no bounds. Leader of Lastrad or not, Forlern was tired of playing coy with the man.

"Regardless, the truth must not come out."

Forlern lowered his voice. "Are you threatening

me?"

"We're propositioning you." Now Questron spoke, rising from his chair.

Forlern pivoted to him, responding. "We've had this discussion before."

"So now it's time to make your decision."

"What? Go along, or have my throat slit right here?" Forlern's hand crept ever-so-slightly to the knife at his side, a move that Questron didn't miss.

"That would be foolish."

"No less so than what I'm hearing here."

"You'll never make it out of this room alive, Forlern. There are guards hidden away even from your prying eyes."

Forlern shrugged, casually standing on his feet, balanced and prepared for anything. "I've faced worse odds before…"

He stared at the Gran Barshara, not intimidated in the slightest. He certainly had no enthusiasm to spar with the deadly Lastrad Captain, but he would go down fighting, at least. After all he had been through, it seemed outrageous that it would end here, and like this…

"You have only to gain from this situation, Forlern. Won't you be seated? I offer you a position in my personal guard as an officer of the palace."

"What, just like that? And not return to Daregil Keep?" He shook his head in amazement. "Surely you don't think King Gregor would believe that."

"And why not? A young captain out on his own, and there are no laws binding Trencit and Lastrad to prevent you from staying."

"That's not true. I'm an advisor to King Gregor now. Is this how you treat his personal ambassador? Even if I would accept your offer, what guarantee do you have that I won't tell the king everything? My word alone?"

The Gran Barshara laughed, deep and mirthless.

"How naïve do you think me? I didn't gain my position by playing a fool. So young, and so ignorant." He shook his head, continuing. "We have resources which will give us the peace of mind we seek."

Forlern felt chills at the powerful leader's words.

"You will eventually return to Lastrad. Your position will be of high importance, the rewards beyond your comprehension. Our guarantee is such." He motioned for Questron to move. The Lastrad Captain came forward, hands in the air.

"Forlern, there is a symbol of our own which we bear. The Gran Barshara's personal mark. Maybe you are unfamiliar, but there are those in Daregil Keep who certainly know about it. Please disrobe."

"What? Are you mad?"

"Quite sane. Please. You will not be harmed."

Forlern looked from one to the next. What were they about? Taking his weapons, and expecting him to stand by idly while they slit his throat? Madness...

Forlern heard the sound too late, and felt twin pinpricks as darts pierced his side. The ambush came from somewhere unseen, and he knew that he was finished. He expected Questron to attack, but the man continued to hold his hands in the air.

"Strike me if you want. I swear to you, as a man of honor myself, you will *not* be harmed. I would rather have you complete of senses right now. Soon, the poison will put you to sleep."

Questron came forward, and oddly enough, Forlern believed him. What other choice did he have left?

"Please put down your knife. Trust me."

Trust...

His mind already blurring. Forlern's knife slipped to the floor. Questron came over to him, gently removing his tunic. Forlern heard movement as others appeared, and he smelled something burning.

"I need you to remain standing, but turn around."

Sluggishly, Forlern did as he was told. He felt Questron's callused hands as he lifted his shirt, and lowered the crease of his back pants.

"All right, it will be over in a second. I'm going to hold you tight for one moment. After the deed is done, you will be given a healing ointment, which will act quickly, and then you'll sleep afterwards. Ready?"

Forlern was too tired to object, and he felt Questron's iron grip holding him tight. The man was incredibly strong. A moment later Forlern felt a searing pain in his lower back as something which had to be an iron brand scorched his skin.

"Hold there. It's done."

Gasping in pain, Forlern sensed more than saw the others around him, and he felt something which felt like soothing ice cover his burn. He remembered nothing more…

❊ ❊

Sarion stared at the two men who returned his gaze, still stunned by this new set of circumstances. Sequestered away in a small chamber, Sarion felt as if there was no one else left in the entire world but the three of them here, now.

"Forlern recited the tale from your venture into the lowlands. Unless he left something out, we know everything." Thustan spoke, his face expressionless. "Know this. The King has been gravely marked by the passing of his close friend and most powerful leader. Trencit has been hurt by Charadan's loss."

"From the time I spent with him, I can only say that I understand why. I miss him as well." Sarion replied, careful to remain neutral. He had no idea what they thought of him, although they certainly had read Charadan's letter.

"We realize what you did in leading the company after the ogre. It was Charadan's decision and King Gregor's as well to probe the lowlands. It was a great risk, but necessary."

Sarion nodded.

"There is no need to keep reciting the tale of what we already know." Barimon stepped forward. "Bring out the rod."

Thustan frowned, and Sarion hesitated. Chief advisor to the king, there was little else known about the mage Barimon, who was spoken of as a mysterious figure holding great influence in Daregil Keep. For him to be now demanding that the rod must be revealed was a bad omen. Sarion needed to convince them of the rod's powers, and its dangers as well. Quickly...

"It is a perilous item. One that cannot be used as a weapon." Sarion decided to be as direct as possible, in the hope of dissuading any talk of its use.

Barimon frowned. "Oh? Are you a mage yourself, Sarion? Someone who has knowledge and power of such an ancient magical relic?"

"I don't claim any such thing," he responded. "But I have been the bearer of the rod since Charadan's fall, and I've learned much about it."

"Have you indeed?" Barimon's orbs glittered, and Sarion felt an increasing dislike of the man.

Thustan spoke. "We wish to hear everything you know about it. We're not going to try and use it now, Sarion. Show it to us."

Sarion had no choice in the matter. He certainly couldn't refuse a request from Thustan. Slowly he brought out the rod from within his tunic, holding it in his hands for them to see. Thustan's brow furrowed in concentration, while Barimon's eyes narrowed.

"Yes, a beautiful talisman from an older age, there

can be no doubt. Marvelous how such a thing can remain hidden for so long, only to be found again after long ages. Crafted by the ancient race of giants, it holds secrets, powerful and dark." Barimon's fingers rubbed together, and Sarion knew the man wanted it in his own grasp.

"Tell us what you know of it." Thustan spoke, looking at him now.

"I believe it is an ancient weapon as well. When we slew the Killworm at Nighton, Chensel and I discussed how such a thing could be done. According to all legends, the monster was spawned in black magic, and could only be harmed by magic. It is our belief that the rod negated the magic which made the Killworm invincible."

"An amazing possibility, but one that makes sense. A weapon of magic against other powerful magic." Thustan nodded, rubbing his beard.

"What else do you know, or suspect?" Barimon questioned.

"When the Killworm was inside the wall at the west gate, the tide of battle appeared desperate. The creature seemed to shrug away all attacks. I took the rod out, and focused on channeling its hidden power, attempt to coax it from slumber. At first, nothing happened."

"And then?" Barimon pressed him.

"It awakened." Sarion's voice grew soft as he recalled the exhilarating flood of energy that lay dormant inside the talisman. "I brought it to life. It contains power beyond comprehension."

Both men stared at him in awe. Thustan's mouth hung open, while Barimon's eyes seemed to grow wider.

"It welled up inside of me, and I wanted to use it, *needed* to use it. But I stopped."

"Why?" Barimon snapped.

"It was too much. I felt ready to burst. I knew that the power within the rod is too great for anyone to wield. It was a terrible struggle, and I was afraid that I had gone too far. I managed to stifle the reaction, and the rod's energy died. It was not easy…I don't know what would have happened if I had been unable to shut it off."

"Fascinating." Thustan whispered. "We have texts describing such talismans of old, although they are vague, and little more than references for the most part. It would seem that Charadan – by pure chance alone – came across the rod within the Killworm's lair, hidden among the bones of victims throughout the ages. The ogre might have known about the place, but we can't be certain."

"What do you mean?" asked Barimon.

"Well, it could have stumbled across the rock foundation and recognized it for what it was. The race of ogres are ancient themselves, and well-aware of the history and dangers located with Grammore. Yes, it could have been an accidental discovery, but one that played in its favor to trap its pursuers."

"We never considered that." Sarion shrugged. "We assumed it knew of it, with the hand of the Dark Mage in the background. Both Charadan and myself thought it was a deliberate trap as well; concealing an egg within the lair, but the more I consider your notion, the more I believe it. The Dark Mage can't have predicted our whearabouts thus setting up the entire episode. If so, he would have had several ogres waiting to ambush us."

"The reality is unimportant right now." Barimon spoke, both his voice and face reflecting impatience.

Sarion considered the man again, and based on a lack of reaction from Thustan, he realized that the mage was in very high favor with King Gregor to be so forward in front of Thustan. The prince must also be close with Barimon then…and was fully aware of his temperament.

"I wonder what other treasures wait within that lair," Barimon mused, rubbing the point of his beard.

"If you have the time and inclination, I could lead you to the area again." Sarion spoke with a straight face, but felt no remorse in jabbing at the mage. He smiled inwardly, knowing that Forlern would certainly have appreciated the comment.

The mage was much too shrewd to miss anything, though, and took the bait. "Perhaps you won't be so lucky the second time around, Sarion."

"You're talking with someone who has traveled through Grammore, and come out alive. Twice."

Thustan entered the fray, surprisingly coming to Sarion's support, and quickly. "And he survived where a King's Champion could not."

Sarion looked at him, and he noticed the intensity of his gaze.

Barimon snapped. "Enough of this. We need the rod. Charadan found it, and gave it into your keeping to hand directly to King Gregor."

Sarion stared at Thustan, who nodded. "You have done your part, Sarion. None could ask for more. But it's time to relinquish the rod. I will bear it now until our return to Daregil Keep, where we will decide on its use – or lack of."

Clearly Barimon was hoping to take possession, but Sarion felt a pang of disappointment. The rod was the only weapon they had against the magical creatures of the Dark Mage. Without it, what hope did they have in a fight if another such creature emerged? They already knew that at least one other Killworm was loose in the westland…

He handed the rod to Thustan.

"I understand your hesitation. Fear not. We will consider its use under the guise of your belief in its capability. And I will tell you this; there are other weapons at Daregil Keep which are magical in nature as well."

Surprised, Sarion started to speak, but Thustan waved him off. "When we have time…"

Barimon sank back in one of the chairs, keeping his thoughts to himself for the moment.

The Summoning

Their conversation never had a chance to renew, as a loud knocking came from the door.

"Yes?" Thustan called. "Come in, but I hope it's important. My command was firm."

One of his guards entered, bowing. "My Lords, you are all summoned to the front gates of the city."

Sarion slowly raised himself from his chair, his heart filled with dread.

"An envoy has arrived from Grammore, and wishes to speak with the leaders of Sharield."

The three men stared at the guard in silence, none of them daring to speak.

Sarion stood above the gates of Sharield, staring down at the valley which lay at their feet. The air was crisp and a cool wind ruffled his hair, which was growing long. It had been a scramble for them to get here, and Sarion had requested that his fighters accompany him. Chertron and Valadire now stood at his side, and all gazes were fixed below, hard and unwavering.

Six ogres and one solitary figure of a man slowly approached the gates. The brutes had their shields halfway raised, their weapons lowered. A horn rang out from nearby, and Glorafin was designated spokesman for Sharield. Sarion chanced a glance towards Lord Berillon, who stood over a dozen yards to his right, flanked by his personal bodyguard and councilors. Thustan and Barimon were between Sarion and Berillon, both of them staring intently below. Sarion knew that this was their first encounter with the emissaries of the Dark Mage, and he wondered how it would play out. Even more than that was his curiosity of what the parlay would be…surely nothing good.

The man below moved forward, waving one hand in appeal. There was nothing remarkable about him, and he appeared in casual dress, weaponless and on foot. He stopped a short distance from the gate, the doors locked solidly.

"Lord Berillon and leaders of Sharield, my name is Morlek. I speak on behalf of my Master, and also Chardoom, one of his servants. Please allow me to talk without firing your arms." He lowered his hand.

Glorafin came forward, perched at the edge of the wall. "You have Lord Berillon's word of protection, but by what right do you claim fairness, when your creature slew a number of our fighters, unprovoked?"

"An unfortunate series of events. It is a wild beast, and acts only in self-preservation."

Valadire spat. "Lies, lies…" He spoke, but not loudly.

"And does it still seek to harm our people?" Glorafin asked.

"Chardoom has ordered it to back away."

Sarion didn't believe anything, and he wondered how this group could have reached the gates of the city itself without fighting any of the patrols.

"What do you seek from us? We have no quarrel with your master."

Sarion knew that Glorafin was following a very close script from Berillon, and he was interested to see just how far this conversation would evolve. Could they learn something of value?

"A hunting party from Nighton has entered your city and is within your protection, along with a large patrol from Trencit. These people are our concern."

"Indeed." Sarion heard Thustan reply, but not to the envoy.

Morlek continued. "They slipped into Gar-kiln and

took Chardoom's daughter, Wharla, away. We ask for her return."

Sarion's heart sunk. If this was their demand, Lord Berillon might very well follow through to avoid battle. Right now she was being watched by Jurit in a cottage near the lake. He still wondered about her and if she yet held secrets, but based on the appearance of Chardoom's marauders, it seemed she had been telling the truth all along. It was difficult to discount her claims now.

"We've heard stories of atrocities committed in the village by your creatures against innocent people. What have you to say about this?" Glorafin challenged him.

"You don't know the entire story. You hear what some wish you to believe."

"The arrogance of the man." Valadire fidgeted uneasily, appearing as if he were ready to leap down the wall and assault the man himself.

"Easy, my friend." Sarion held him close. "There's a dangerous game being played here. This envoy will not reveal their true purpose. Not yet, at least."

Sarion stared down at the ogres, the brutes holding rank and appearing very confident and disciplined despite their savage countenance.

Glorafin retreated for a moment, speaking with Lord Berillon. Nodding, he came forward again.

"The Lord of Sharield does not know this woman, and it is not in his standing to hand over anyone to such a company of ill creatures, and a woman no less, most especially beneath the shroud of threat. He responds in kind. Why should he listen further? You test his patience, and must realize that the army of Sharield waits beyond these closed gates. He has no fear of yourself and the ogres. You remain here on borrowed time. Speak swiftly."

Sarion nodded to himself. An appropriate response at last. Perhaps the arrival of the Dark Mage's emissaries had finally struck a nerve with Lord Berillon. He had lost men, and now was being further insulted by these demands. The envoy showed no sign of intimidation or temperament, however, as he looked calmly upwards.

"Ah, if he has no fear, then maybe he should. We have reached this far into his realm unimpeded, and now we stand before the very gates of your fair city. Is this by mere luck? I think you know better."

Sarion overheard one of the councilors. "They can't possibly think to attack us by force of a few ogres? Fearsome or not, they have not the slightest chance."

"Is this all you have come here to say?" asked Glorafin. "Then you have wasted our time, and offered nothing but an empty excuse for the deaths of our men."

The afternoon was growing late, and a premature nightfall weighed down on the landscape as heavy clouds rolled in from the westland, carrying with them the promise of rain. Already guards were lighting watch fires along the wall, moving in sequence from north to south, eventually going across the great lake itself. Sarion waited with everyone else to hear the envoy's reply.

"I have more to say." Morlek's reply was short, and he stood there with arms folded.

Glorafin placed both hands in the air. "We are still listening. And why doesn't your master come and speak for himself? Where is he now?"

"He is close enough, fear not." Morlek grinned, a wicked gesture empty of humor. "I will continue. Your Lord plays host to the group that entered Gar-kiln. They are fighters from Nighton led by a captain."

"We are here." Sarion now stepped forward, surprising them all. He pointed down at the man in accusation. "Your tongue is twisted like a serpent, and your master is a coward. I have no fear of him or any of his minions. I've cut the head off of one ogre already. My blade thirsts for more."

Several of the brutes grumbled among themselves at

Sarion's brash words, staring up at him directly now, and he felt their cold, iron gaze on his skin.

"Well said." It was a whisper, but Sarion imagined the approving grin spreading across Valadire's face.

Thustan grunted, and Sarion feared that he had overstepped himself this time, but no one called him back.

"I'm not afraid of hiding behind any walls. Here I am, so speak, groveler."

The envoy seemed rattled now for the first time. "*You* are the one who crept into the village and took away Chardoom's daughter, a woman who is innocent of the troubling events plaguing both our kingdoms. So we meet at last. All right then, hear the rest of our demands. Listen to me now, wise leaders of Sharield." He almost spat the last part of his sentence, and Sarion knew the moment of revelation was nigh…

"Lord Berillon, you are to hand over Wharla to us. You are also to hand over the fighters from Nighton so that they may receive their *punishment*."

It was outrageous, but Sarion couldn't help feeling chills claim his skin at Morlek's words.

"You will do all of this within the hour, or you will see Sharield destroyed."

"How dare you threaten us!" Glorafin had now lost all semblance of patience. "Justice will find your head staked on a pole at these gates within this very hour, your lying tongue cut out!"

"Within the hour. Time starts now." Morlek replied, looking at the ogres, all of them in ready formation. "And if you are thinking about failing to comply with our demands, then I will give you an additional demonstration about the consequences you will face."

He gestured to one of the ogres, who brought out a curved-shaped horn. The brute placed it to his mouth, sending a long wail which echoed eerily across the valley.

Everyone grew still, most of them wondering as to

what it meant. Most, but not all…Sarion and his companions stood there, rooted in apprehension, because they had heard the same dreadful call before in the wilderness of the westland, and they knew the call for what it was. A summons…

Sarion was silent, telling himself that it wasn't possible, and he felt Chertron grip his arm.

They all waited for long moments.

Waited…

And then the first noise came from below, hidden somewhere in the deep forest. Another sound, followed by a great thud. Another…The sound grew in volume and proximity as something massive made its way towards the gates of Sharield. Time dragged, and the leaders of Sharield huddled together in fear and disbelief.

Thustan approached Sarion. "You know what comes, do you not?"

Sarion nodded.

"The great beast?"

Sarion's eyes never left the valley as a terrible thundering echoed along the rocks and walls, several trunks crashing to the ground in fury as a huge bulk appeared from below, part of it dwarfing some of the surrounding trees.

"Beware, the Ravenor comes…" Sarion said.

Fighters backed away in horror at the sight of the Ravenor, a monster which haunted the darkest nightmares, and could not possibly exist within the fabric of their reality. Thustan and Barimon watched as well; not in fear, but no less surprised and shocked.

"A greater predator from Grammore, emerging this far into the westland." Barimon spoke, the words flat and expressionless.

"Shades, what a terrible beast. It defies belief…" Thustan responded, the emotion evident in his voice.

"It followed us from Gar-kiln. I didn't think it would, or so quickly." Sarion spoke.

"You have been hunted since leaving that cursed village. Chardoom has been on your trail ever since," Thustan replied, his voice measured. "We need to think of a plan."

The Ravenor came close, its head on a level with the wall itself, a fact lost on no one. Its terrible eyeless face weaved back and forth, fixing at last on Sarion and his companions. Without knowing how, Sarion's instincts blazed in warning, telling him the truth. It *knew* who they were...

The Ravenor paused there for a terrible moment, making sure everyone could lay eyes upon its ghastly countenance, and then it lumbered to its right, toward the dam which held back the lake.

"It seeks to destroy the dam! Does it have the might?" One of the councilors yelled and Sarion didn't know who it was, but the man's words were accurate enough. Everyone wondered the same thing. Could it tear down the dam?

Sarion thought it very well could...

"Less than one hour. Use your time well, leaders of Sharield." Morlek called up to them. "Send us Wharla and the Nighton fighters, and we will leave you in peace. If you decide otherwise your doom will fall upon you this very night, and none will be spared from the Master's wrath."

He didn't continue, now moving back into the ranks of the protective ogres, the group of them retreating warily back towards the forest.

The men along the walls were silent, both fighter and city leader alike. None had been unaffected by the sight of the massive predator, now moving off in the distance, more a shadow in the gloom than anything else. A light rain fell, thin layers of mist beginning to seep off the ground and the waters of the lake. Sarion stared below for a moment, then turned his back, heading for the stairs, both

Valadire and Chertron in tow. Thustan and Barimon watched his progress and followed after.

"We have company," Valadire whispered.

"Good. All of them need to see what we face from Grammore. It's easy for them to make decisions based on their own opinions while sequestered many miles away from the danger."

"Their arrival was quite unexpected, more a stroke of luck than anything else." Chertron said. "Ah well, it was bound to happen sooner or later."

They reached the lower platform but Sarion kept going downwards, no real destination in mind. Things had gone from bad to worse, and quickly.

"What will we do now?" Valadire asked.

"We?" Sarion turned to his companions. "Don't you realize that we no longer control our own destiny? They'll try and bring me back to Daregil Keep. If we can elude the Ravenor and ogres, of course...No small matter."

"And if we don't get turned over to Chardoom first, you mean." Valadire grinned. "I can picture us all being led away in shackles, prisoners to the Dark Mage."

"I find little humor in that statement," Chertron snapped.

"It's not my decision anymore," Sarion said. "Others can decide the fate of Trencit and the westland."

The caustic remark was intended for the ears of their followers, as both Thustan and Barimon overheard his comments, along with several council members.

"What do you know of this creature?" Barimon demanded.

"Can you see with your own eyes? Sarion snapped. "What more do you need to know than the monster is capable of destroying this city. It must be stopped."

Sarion had attracted a small crowd, and even Lord Berillon hovered nearby.

"Tell us of this monster. We cannot stand against

it." One of the councilors spoke from his right.

But Sarion was far from finished. "Yes. Now that the danger is at the foot of the city, people wish to hear my counsel, when it was ignored earlier." He glared at Berillon and some of the other councilors who stood protectively near him. To Sarion they appeared like frightened animals seeking comfort in the close proximity.

"I'm only one man, and the master of Sharield stands over there. Lord Thustan and Barimon can give wise counsel as well. For myself, I'm tired and hungry. Now that you've seen what kind of creatures we've been battling for the past few weeks perhaps you'll be more sympathetic to my opinion."

He headed off into an opening that appeared to be a galley of some type, smelling food being cooked, Valadire and Chertron on his heel. Barimon grumbled, but Thustan laid an arm on the mystic's shoulder.

"Peace, Barimon. He has gone through and seen much more horror than we can imagine. Right now, we need to take counsel with Berillon. And swiftly."

Lord Berillon came towards them, gesturing for his councilors to attend. "There's a meeting room down the next hallway. We will meet there in five minutes."

Thustan nodded, and the leader of Sharield quickly left, his council following.

Sarion found what he was looking for, quickly grabbing some food and a large pitcher of wine and heading for a small table secluded away in one corner. A few other guards were eating as well, servers walking about in various modes of work.

"A strange way to make your point, my friend,

although quite humorous in the same breath. Remarkable."
Valadire grabbed a goblet of his own, moving towards the
pitcher. "I'm thoroughly impressed."

"If your intention was to anger Thustan, the mage,
and all the leaders of Sharield, I think you've succeeded."
Chertron said.

Sarion shrugged. "I had intentions, but probably not
what you think. We must speak swiftly. I'm sure we'll have
company shortly."

"Thustan and Barimon," said Valadire. "I already
see them entering the hall from yonder."

Sarion didn't need to look... "You don't understand
our plight. The rod has been taken from me."

"What?" Chertron exclaimed.

"Thustan has it now. Barimon was so eager for it, I
thought he might try to wrest it from my grip. I don't trust
that man."

"He holds high favor with King Gregor. He's Chief
Councilor to the King, although he's a mysterious figure in
Daregil Keep." Chertron said.

"The rod gone..." Valadire said.

"And our magical protection." Sarion shook his
head. "They are fools if they think they can use it as a
weapon."

Thustan and Barimon spotted them, hurrying over
now.

"Quickly, what is your plan?" Chertron said.

"A simple one." Sarion replied. "And one that I
don't have time to elaborate on at the moment. It's time to
leave Sharield. I fear Chardoom will not keep his word, and
the city is doomed."

Valadire replied. "I agree, although I think we have
a better fighting chance inside. And what defense do we
have against the Ravenor?"

"We can outrun it, at least. I didn't come this far to
be conveniently given to the Dark Mage and his emissaries.

If Berillon thinks to hand us over weaponless and on foot, then the battle for our lives starts inside *here*..." He trailed off ominously, not wishing to elaborate further on such a terrible possibility.

"You really think..." Cherton started to speak, but was quickly cut off.

"Sarion, that was quite impudent back there," snapped Barimon, coming forward. "You forget your place and position."

They rose as one, giving deference to Thustan, but Sarion pointed a finger in accusation at Barimon.

"Maybe it is yourself that forgets, mage. I'm Second Captain of Nighton, not some squire struggling on the proving grounds at Daregil Keep. I've earned the right to speak my mind!"

It was as bold a statement possible considering their company and ranking... Chertron actually gasped at his friend's demeanor. Barimon stared at Sarion with a look of anger and disbelief, seemingly at a loss of words, but Thustan stepped in, ending it immediately.

"That's enough! We have pressing matters at hand, and we need your counsel, Sarion. Barimon, you must treat Sarion with more respect. These men have gone through unimaginable horrors in protecting Trencit. I think it's not asking too much. And Sarion, you forget the finer points of diplomacy. That was rash."

The mage glared at Sarion, and surely wouldn't be forgetting the confrontation anytime soon by the expression on his face.

Thustan continued. "I know you do not like my decision to take the rod from your possession. We will talk about all this later, though. Your fate is tied into our predicament. I fear the councilors will wish to make a parlay, turning you over to the enemy."

"They wouldn't dare," said Valadire.

Thustan shrugged. "It's possible. Desperature

measures are taken by desperate people. They wish to avoid conflict, and the sight of the beast has shaken them to their very bones. What a monster...come, let us attend the council, Sarion."

"Lord Thustan, I wish to have my companions sit with me. Their input is invaluable. Valadire is a Forester of Nighton, and Chertron a member of the Hybril Legion, handpicked by Charadan himself."

"Very well. But no more talk. The meeting will have started by now."

The five of them hurried off, Sarion remembering to bring the wine with him. He had gone too long living off only the land, and was not about to take any luxury for granted, at least for the moment...He thought he deserved this small part of it. Another minute found them standing before the meeting chamber, all of them hearing the din of rising voices – and temperaments – from within. Thustan waved the guards aside, both of them bowing, knowing who he was. He thrust the doors open, and the clamor lowered as people recognized his face, Barimon standing right beside him.

"My Lords and leaders, we are here to help decide a course of action in defending Sharield. Please understand that you have all my power in this action, of both myself and my men. Five hundred strong of us have made our way to Sharield."

This was the first time Sarion had heard this. Thustan had brought with him a sizable force from Trencit indeed. It might very well play a factor in what was to come.

"You are most welcome in our hour of need." Lord Berillon stood, bowing his head slightly in deference. "Please come sit with us."

A few chairs had been left open, and Sarion motioned for Chertron and Valadire to find seats in one corner. The room was filled with leaders and military officers, and Sarion saw Glorafin near the far door, standing behind Lord Berillon's chair. The Sharield Captain stared at him, his face expressionless.

Berillon spoke. "Sarion, we look to you for knowledge to share of this terrible gathering before us. I understand your reservations, as we pressed you earlier, but this is our normal mode of discourse here. Please take no offense."

Sarion felt like saying something entirely different, but fought the urge off. "I came here to warn and give advice. My status hasn't changed." He left it at that.

"What of this creature, the Ravenor? What do you know of it?" One of the councilors interjected.

"It is a greater predator from the Grammore Lowlands. We only saw it once, briefly, while in Gar-kiln. One of the refugees warned us of its existence. When Chardoom first came to the village, they hunted and captured all the people, taking a few away, and feeding the rest to the beast." He wanted to tell them everything, make their hearts tremble in fear and revulsion. Sarion went on. "The creature swallows and digests its prey over a period of several days, the unfortunate victim still kept alive inside the monster."

The room went deathly quiet, and Sarion could feel the waves of horror coursing through the air like a living thing of flesh and blood. Several people gasped out loud.

Berillon continued. "What of its strength? What is it capable of? The ogres alone cannot hope to successfully assault our walls. But this beast…"

"I don't know the limits of its power. It might be magical in nature. It has no eyes, so it goes by other senses. Hearing, smell? Our only defense was to flee."

"But *we* don't have that option!" One of the councilors snapped, slamming the table.

"You ask me what I know. This is what I know." Sarion replied, his voice even.

Glorafin came forward. "We can make defense to the best of our ability. Most of our entire standing force is housed here now, on full alert. We can bombard the enemy from above, spilling hot oil on the beast if it approaches."

"Did you not see that monster? Its head towers to our very wall!" Another councilor spoke, rising in his chair, and others came to his support. "And what about the dam? It could destroy it, flooding the valley below and opening us to attack."

"Do not underestimate the power of our fighting force. And now we have Prince Thustan's men as well." Glorafin loomed over the table, but the voices of opposition drowned him out. It went on like this for several moments until Lord Berillon held his hands in the air for order. The city leader turned toward Thustan.

"My Lord Prince. Is there anything else you can tell us? Perhaps knowledge of such a beast from Daregil Keep?"

"Nothing, I'm afraid. Sarion is right. It's an unknown monster, something beyond our learnings, both in recorded history or legend. I've never heard the name spoken before."

"Nor I." It was the first time Barimon spoke, the mage adding nothing to the conversation.

"Time moves swiftly," someone off to the right spoke.

The rear door opened, and heads angled in that direction, curious as to the interruption as a guard hurried forward. "Lord Berillon."

The leader nodded.

"I bring word of a new occurrence."

Sarion froze.

"The woman known as Wharla is gone."

"What?" Sarion rose.

"It seems she has been taken."

"Taken?" Thustan questioned.

"I'm sorry to tell you that the man guarding her was found slain. There were signs that something broke in from the window, although how this is possible, I can't say."

"Jurit is dead..." Sarion slumped back into the chair, his stomach turning.

"The Crage took her. It managed to enter the city under cover of darkness." Valadire stood now, speaking.

"He's right." Sarion replied. "I'm certain it was the Crage."

Rusteg now spoke for the first time. "We are in grave danger even behind these walls, my Lord." Berillon focused on him, his chief councilor. "Unless we make the right decision, war and destruction will be set upon us. I think the decision must be made, although it will seem harsh. We must hand over Sarion and his companions to Chardoom."

The room sat in stunned silence for long, terrible moments. Valadire cursed beneath his breath, but loud enough for Sarion to hear. Sarion was dazed, and had hoped for better from these people, that they would show the courage to stand and fight, but it seemed time and apathy had led them down a less noble road, one which gave rise to the ability to consider appeasement, no matter the cost in honor.

Or blood...

He had believed this type of capitulation possible, but it was no less devastating to hear it outloud, now that it had actually come to light.

If Lord Berillon agreed, these people were truly lost.

"Do you jest?" Valadire stood, coming forward. "You would hand over your kin and allies to these monsters? Forsake all our past history together?"

"It is not an easy decision to make, but we weigh the scale against the loss of hundreds, possibly thousands, of other lives. The lives of our citizens, innocent in this matter." Rusteg answered.

"And what of the innocent people of the westland? Gar-kiln? What crime did they commit to deserve such foul justice?" Valadire raged.

"Did I say they were guilty of such?" Rusteg replied. "Fate and ill fortune are to blame. And *you* are also to blame, in part, for leading this foul company to Sharield."

And there it is, Sarion thought. The path to justification...

"We are out protecting the people of the westland from danger. *All* people. You hide behind these walls for now, but there's a price for your safety. How *dare* you stand there and offer us like lambs to the slaughter!" Valadire was furious.

Rusteg stood, answering. "If you knew the danger, then maybe you shouldn't have come here."

"*Truly* I regret so now. Never would I have thought to hear such cowardice in the entire westland."

The room rumbled in discontent, but Valadire wasn't finished.

"And what makes you think the enemy will not disregard its part of the bargain? What guarantee do you have then?" Valadire snapped at him.

Rusteg answered. "Your company is small. What difference could you make in a battle against these creatures? There is no sense in that."

"No difference? Shades..." Valadire pivoted away in disbelief. "And I saw fit to call you brethren. Why..."

"Hold, Valadire." Sarion stood, cutting him off quickly, knowing what was coming next. "I understand their position. It's not an easy one to make, nor would I choose it myself if roles were reversed. But they're not. We must abide by Lord Berillon's decision in this matter, distasteful as it sounds."

"I for one will not go away willingly. I'll fight

against the enemy until my last breath! Unlike these shameful cowards…" Valadire was not to be talked down.

The room erupted in shouting, many of the councilors storming to their feet at the insult levied at them by Valadire. Even Berillon couldn't quiet them now, and tempers were increasing, Valadire livid with anger. Thustan stood, holding his hands for peace, his face twisted in a look of dismay. Barimon remained seated, the mage staring at Sarion as if probing his mind.

Go ahead, mage. Try to unlock my thoughts.

Sarion matched his gaze unflinchingly, refusing to be intimidated. Despite the betrayal of the council, Sarion felt only sadness for the people of Sharield, unable to share Valadire's wrath. They had sunk to a terrible low, terrified to fight for what should have come natural for them. Complacency and apathy had taken hold, and he doubted that they would be able to come back from the brink of their own shortcomings.

Things in the chamber were out of hand, and it was several minutes before order was again restored. At last, Lord Berillon stood, holding his staff high, demanding silence.

"The time has come for a decision! We cannot wait any longer. Lord Thustan, do you have any more counsel to give?"

Thustan moved forward. "Yes I do. I surely hope you are not considering giving in to this black bargain? We are all honorable men here, fighting for the same cause against a foe who will show no mercy."

Lord Berillon slowly shook his head. "I've been placed into an impossible dilemma here, and I'm afraid I must consider the offer, bitter as it tastes. I have to protect my people first."

Thustan now showed signs of real anger himself. "Nighton is under the direct command of Daregil Keep and King Gregor. Sarion is an officer of Trencit. I will not *permit* such an action to take place." His eyes smoldered, and Sarion was taken aback by the power of the man's intensity, now fully awakened.

"I fear you have no say in this matter." Lord Berillon replied. "I am leader of Sharield, not you or your father. We are an independent province. Trencit commands us no longer, and hasn't for quite a long time."

Sarion nodded to himself. There it finally was, at long last. Berillon had taken the notion to its conclusion, effectively severing the ties which had bound his lands for countless years, and he would not be dissuaded. His pride of rulership would not allow old ties of loyalty to be followed. He was the sovereign of Sharield in name and power, and there could be no going back from such a decision, once made.

"Do you know what you are saying?" Thustan replied, his voice low and dangerous.

Berillon countered. "I know exactly what I am saying. I command here, no other. This is not to say we wish to cast you out of our city, or call you anything other than friends and allies, but the passage of time has changed our situation, and this is a new reality. To be honest, we have not paid tribute to Daregil Keep in many years. We have evolved on our own."

Thustan hesitated for long moments, the room going silent around him, awaiting his reply. His eyes were unfocused for a span of time that seemed to drag forever, and then he turned his gaze back to the councilors before finally settling on the Sharield ruler. He lifted one finger, pointing as he spoke. "Very well. Your decision is made, and you must take sole responsibility for all present and future consequences."

Lord Berillon only shrugged.

Thustan turned to Sarion. "I'm sorry that circumstances have led you here, Sarion. Your loyalty deserves far better than this."

Sarion nodded, knowing that Thustan truly had no choice in the matter. Even if he commanded his men to action, they were far outnumbered and sequestered elsewhere. Bloodshed of this type would only taint the situation further. They didn't need that to happen...

Thustan continued. "But know that you are not alone in this predicament. My men will leave Sharield with you and your companions. You will not face Chardoom alone." There was a fire in his eyes that burned with promise, and Sarion knew that Thustan was a man who could make powerful decisions in his own right.

Sarion grinned in appreciation.

Lord Berillon seemed stunned by this new revelation. "Are you certain you wish to do this? They have only asked for Sarion's group."

Rusteg spoke up. "My Lord, this might further antagonize the enemy and destroy the bargain. Can we even permit them to accompany Sarion?"

Now Barimon stood for the first time, the mysterious and unpredictable mage immediately capturing the full attention of the room, all eyes upon him. "You dare threaten us as to what we will or won't do? If you so much as try and intervene, you'll be facing the Royal Armies at your front gates within the coming days, and I *promise* you there will be no chance of a parlay."

He approached Rusteg and Berillon, stopping a few feet away, his staff held firmly before him, the top of it seeming to glow with an inner fire of its own.

Rusteg held his hands up. "I was not threatening you or anyone else in your party. My pardon."

Lord Berillon ended the confrontation before it grew worse. "It is their decision to make. We can let the emissaries understand this, and will draw our own line of negotiation there. The council is now adjourned. Sarion and his companions will be led to the gates and must leave immediately. Gather all his company."

The Summoning

He turned towards Sarion now. "I am sorry to make such a terrible choice, and I know that nothing I say will ease the bitterness you must feel. Farewell, Sarion. Lord Thustan, I wish you good fortune against the enemy. We must play a neutral part if we are to save ourselves. This is *not* our fight."

"Sarion!"

All eyes turned as Glorafin came forward. "You will have more than just Thustan's company. I will go alongside you."

"What? You can't leave." Rusteg demanded.

"I *can* and I will. You know the laws of Sharield as well as myself. I can resign at any time, for any reason."

Lord Berillon seemed to hesitate, then nodded. "It is our law, and we must follow."

Someone else moved forward, and Sarion noticed Barthaniel's presence for the first time. He must have been secluded off in some corner, he thought.

"I go as well." There were tears in the man's eyes.

Sarion shook his head, touched by the man's emotion. "You must stay behind, my friend. You are no warrior."

"Nevertheless, I go to meet my doom then. I cannot bear to stay behind, knowing that my people have tossed you aside so. We are kindred, and this makes us appear less than human."

Glorafin slapped him on the shoulder. "I hear you, Barthaniel." He looked first at Rusteg, then Berillon. "I feel the same. I am shamed by my peers." He glared at the council members, then turned towards Sarion and Thustan. "Come, we have little time to formulate a plan."

"We'll need one. Shades," muttered Chertron.

Forlern sat awake on his bed, flexing his back. The mark seemed to have healed already, and he felt no pain. His anger was still in place however, although not quite as bitter as it had been. Earlier he had imagined the Gran Barshara's throat within his grip as he pulled tight...

"Shades."

He spat, getting up, pacing back and forth, wondering where he was now being housed. He could see through the windows, and based on his surroundings, he was now in the residential district where some of the wealthier citizens of Lastrad called home. He heard someone at the bedroom door, but couldn't tell if it was more than one person, either a guard or servant. Forlern didn't want to let anyone know he was awake until he figured things through.

Regardless, he had to get out of Lastrad quickly. Forlern had no trust in the arrogant Gran Barshara, and he also didn't trust *himself* not to throttle the man if they met again, which he doubted would happen. Since he was still alive, he also had no reason to *disbelieve* what he'd been told, so he should be free to go soon. They needed to discuss additional strategy between Trencit and Lastrad based on the marauding Devlents, and awaited word from Southwatch and Clairfeld. The latter was less than three days ride to the northeast, but Forlern had already determined he would not wait until he heard news to leave. He really didn't need to talk about plans at all, actually. He was not a captain of the army, but a member of the Homeguard. His mission was not one of war plans, but to kill a predator, which was now dead, although his earlier presumption might have worked against him, thinking it best to assist the leaders of Lastrad in any way he could.

Now, he knew better...

The Summoning

He took out one of his knives and spun, throwing it at a tapestry behind him. It hit squarely in the center, but he took little satisfaction from the act. His wound felt improved, and he was ready for anything now. They had actually branded him with the Gran Barshara's personal mark! He couldn't believe it, and despite their assurances, he knew it meant nothing. The Gran Barshara had gotten the best of him, and this fact bothered Forlern more than anything. He bristled in anger, the rage returning.

Suddenly he heard movement outside, and he turned to face the door. Someone knocked.

"Who is it?" He demanded.

"Captain Questron has come to see you. May I let him in?"

"Questron..." Forlern said to himself, debating about whether to challenge the man here and now, but thought better of it. "Like I could prevent it?" Forlern scoffed in return. When there was no reply, he responded. "Let him in."

Shaking his head, Forlern sat down in a chair facing the door as Questron's broad frame entered, the Lastrad Captain gazing down at him. "How do you feel?"

Forlern sneered. "If you expect a pleasant response, then you don't know me very well by now."

Questron shrugged. "Exactly what I believed your reply would be..."

"So where am I now, for starters?"

"Actually, it's your home, Forlern."

"What?" Forlern looked at him as if he were mad. "What's the Gran Barshara's next scheme? To try and convince me that I'm someone else now? I'm really tired of these games. Breaking your word so quickly? So much for telling me I was free to go..."

Questron moved about for a moment, sitting down at the main table and pouring himself a goblet of wine.

"No, I speak the truth once more. This is your house

now, and it will remain so, until you choose to stay in Lastrad for good. And you're free to leave at anytime."

Forlern laughed. "Such overconfidence does not fit well with you, Questron."

"I didn't say I believed my statement would come true, but this *is* yours now. The Gran Barshara has made it so."

"Another part of his plan to keep me from revealing the truth." Forlern chuckled in contempt.

"You may choose to not heed my words, but who can know the entire truth? I am not privy to all his thoughts."

"Hmm. If you say so...And I can leave my *new* home?"

"At any time of your choosing. You are free to return to Daregil Keep as soon as you are ready."

"Oh really?" Forlern refused to believe him.

Questron nodded. "Yes."

"With no additional terms?" Forlern pressed him.

"The Gran Barshara is sending several guards along with you, and a token of his gratitude. A small chest of valuables for you to do with as you will."

Forlern immediately grew suspicious, but decided to keep his thoughts to himself. He certainly had no intention of trusting Questron, and if he feigned a change of heart so soon, the man was much too shrewd to believe him. Best to play along until he was safely away from Lastrad.

"Well, then I plan on leaving within the hour."

"Your escort awaits you at the gates already."

"Of course they do..." Forlern added. "Tell me, Questron. What makes you and the Gran Barshara think I still won't say anything? You risk much, despite going through great effort to see otherwise."

"This is little effort on the Gran Barshara's part."

"You might be right there...but still, there's no

guarantee of my silence."

Questron stood, looking out the window. "You're right. There is none."

Forlern waited for more, knowing that Questron had only finished his sentence, not his line of thought.

"Come now, do you expect me to leave it at that?"

"No, I don't. We both hope that you consider the offer of a position here, and the house will be ready for you, whether it's ten days or ten years from now. The Gran Barshara's word is final in Lastrad."

"And?"

Questron turned around to stare at him. "I thought you would have figured out the answer to your question by now."

Forlern raised his hands in appeal.

"All right, maybe you haven't. It shows your lack of political maneuverings once more. The Gran Barshara has ears throughout Trencit, even in its most fortified holds."

Now Forlern knew what he meant…

"If you revealed the truth, it might yet remain a secret between yourself and Trencit's highest leaders. Or…it might fall upon other ears nearby."

"You want me to believe there is a spy in Daregil Keep? In close confidence with King Gregor yet?"

"Please don't put words in my mouth. I never said that. I merely offer a potential reason for you to think deeply before taking action. Daregil Keep is a huge fortress with many officials there. Homeguard are all about as well. Perhaps even a Ja-Ravel assassin has managed to infiltrate your innermost holds. Who can say for sure…"

"I don't believe it. There is no Ja-Ravel within our ranks, I can assure you." Forlern snapped. "I know enough about their ilk. They look for instant gain and profit. Lastrad offered both to Klellan. He would have found no such recourse in Daregil Keep. And our training is long and arduous, the candidates vetted well in advance of acceptance. You'll have to do better than that, Captain Questron."

Questron shrugged, his face impassive. "*Now* who is being overconfident? Money can purchase anything, most especially a man's loyalty. If someone were able to survive the Ja-Ravel training, do you think they would fail at Daregil Keep? And would you be able to sleep at night after revealing the truth of what took place here? You had better watch your back if this is your choice. And realize, we of course will do our best to discredit your tale. Who would dare believe we put that mark on you? It's nothing personal, Forlern, but I am a mercenary, and it is my sworn duty, under fear of persecution and death, to obey the Gran Barshara. In all ways he commands me."

Forlern waited, half-expecting Questron to attack him for his insolence. The Lastrad officer stood there, unmoving. After several tense moments, he shrugged again, reaching for the goblet of wine, but in a fraction of a second, Forlern slipped a knife into one of his hands and threw it before Questron's stunned face, watching as it shattered the goblet, wine spilling on his tunic. He spun on Forlern, furious.

"Fool!"

"Don't try anything rash yourself now, Captain Questron. Your master might be displeased..."

They squared off, Questron's own knife appearing catlike in his hand. Forlern had risen from his seat, but made no additional move.

"We can end this here without a fight, but here's a final word from *me* now. For you and the Gran Barshara," he sneered. "Know this. Don't attempt to predict all my actions. And I *will* discover the nature of your spy in Daregil Keep, if they even exist. I would hesitate to press me further. I'll be ready, take my word on it. I'm not afraid of you or the Gran Barshara. I helped save your city along with both your positions, and in appreciation you have dishonored my acts. I'm leaving *now*. So if you're going to kill me, at least give me a fighting chance and not a dagger to my back." Forlern sheathed his weapon as he found himself again moving past Questron, this time the man in a considerably worse mood. Forlern had already gathered his items, and he picked them up now, heading to the door, never taking his eyes off the Lastradian captain.

He called to the outside man, guard or otherwise. "I'm ready to depart now. I require a horse to take me to the city gates."

Questron stood there quietly, his arms now folded. "Yes, farewell, rash one. You fought admirably in the field, and I only hope your common sense catches up to your battle skills. You'll need both to survive very long. One day, perhaps soon, you'll look around and realize that opportunities are within your grasp, one's that you've never even dreamed about."

"I'm only a fighter, doing what I know best." Forlern shrugged absently as the door opened, a single guard appearing. "Lead on. I'm done here."

As he walked away unhindered with Questron quietly laughing behind him, Forlern realized that he'd just committed the most foolish and dangerous act he could remember...

Surprisingly enough, an hour later Forlern found himself exactly where he wanted to be, standing before the great open gates of Lastrad, a trio of fighters awaiting his arrival. Five horses were at the ready, and they quickly moved away through the crowds, leaving the city behind at last. The men identified themselves by name, claiming to be a personal escort sent by the Gran Barshara himself to protect Forlern until he reached Daregil Keep. They had also brought along a chest strapped to a fifth animal, filled with what Forlern was certain contained the promised valuables.

He never bothered to ask about it, no less open it.

They made decent time, traveling far the next few hours, heading steadily north on one of the main causeways. Forlern was unsure of his escort's purpose, and of course he didn't expect them to reveal anything to him. They were quiet most of the time, little conversation passing among them. Forlern wanted to make his move soon, but not quite yet. Their lower number bothered him more than if there would have been say twenty, which would have been enough odds to overwhelm him, but only three? It made him even more suspicious...Would they have orders to kill him, undoubtedly while he slept? And would the Gran Barshara and Questron think him to be that naïve?

No, there had to be something else...He hated to admit it, but maybe they *were* ordered to do exactly as he was told, to simply escort him back to Daregil Keep. But he couldn't go without sleep for days on end. At some point in time he would falter, and if they were looking for an opening, they would easily have their chance. Questron's tale might be elaborate, but would they really need to go through all of this effort if they could have killed him already? Probably not, but that had been before his outburst. If they were awaiting his reaction, then what better time than on the road to Trencit?

Night was falling and he mentioned to them about finding a suitable camping site. Shortly, they left the road, leading their horses into a small clearing. Setting up a small camp, they lit a fire and one of them acted as guard, the other two preparing food. They ate, talking little, and made plans for the night.

"I'm not very tired, to be honest," Forlern said. "Too much on my mind. I'll take the first watch and awaken one of you at midnight."

The three of them looked at each other, deciding on a response, then one of them named Kagil, spoke. "It is no trouble, but one of us needs to be awake at all time. It is our order to protect you, and I cannot agree to anything else, Captain Forlern. Your pardon."

Forlern shrugged, feigning indifference. "Your decision. Just thought I would offer." He stretched, moving a few steps closer to the horses before sitting. "The blaze is warm." He said nothing else, and the three men positioned themselves, two of them resting on the ground while Kagil remained alert, propping himself alongside a fallen tree.

Then the waiting began...

Forlern was tired, but he forced himself to stay awake, keeping an eye on the three men. After a while, it appeared that two of the men were asleep, their breathing finally relaxing and growing heavier. Kagil, however, showed no signs of succumbing to weariness, his gaze falling across the silver landscape awash in the moon's glittery beams.

Forlern decided it was time, and he now stood, yawning with one hand over his mouth, slowly approaching Kagil.

"Still have no desire to follow my offer?" he whispered.

Kagil eyed him warily, shaking his head.

"How about a swig of wine from your pouch before I retire? I'm afraid mine has a leak in it, and water just won't do."

The guard hesitated, then shrugged, reaching for his own pouch, and Forlern lashed out. With a quick thrust of his elbow he smacked Kagil in the side of the head, knocking him out instantly. Forlern winced at the pain, but his eyes were already on the two sleeping men.

Neither of them flinched.

Nodding to himself, Forlern made his way to the

horses, strapping the chest to one of them before gathering the reins and leading them away from the clearing. On foot there could be no chase, and the men would later awaken, finding him long gone. As good a plan as any, he thought…When he reached the road he paused, waiting for a while and listening to the night. There was no sound behind him, only the forest insects droning and buzzing, and the road appeared to be empty of travelers. It was time for him to make his move. He tied them all together with rope then carefully mounted his own, the others trailing behind as he kept them in check, still holding them in formation. He didn't want to let go yet, as the men would call them when they realized what had happened, and there was a good chance they would not wander far off. He needed to make sure they were stranded here. Forlorn had no wish to confront the guards and shed needless blood. Under such circumstances, they probably had been ordered to do *something*, but he really didn't want to find out what…

Forlern traveled through the night, the hour growing late, until finally he stopped. He kept the chest, but untied the other four horses, sending them ahead of him to the north. He would most likely catch up with them soon, but at least they were going in the right direction. He watched as they galloped ahead, one of them swerving to its left, the other following. They trotted into a field of tall grass, pausing for a moment, probably finding something to their taste.

"Good enough."

He placed the chest before him and mounted once more, wishing to make some time before dawn arrived. He was unwilling to pause, but would rather find shelter during the day for a few hours rest. These lands were technically under the control of Trencit, but little was to be found here except scattered homesteads and small villages. He would find more people after another day's ride north. There would certainly be others traveling south to Lastrad, but that was part of the normal traffic from this area. Several roads led there, and he expected to encounter someone very soon. The moon was sinking into the earth, and he felt that his adventures in Lastrad were finally over.

It had been a trying experience, concluding in a fashion that he would never have dreamt possible. It was still difficult to believe everything that had happened. He was bitter over his humiliation by the Gran Barshara, and vowed to himself that he would get back at the man. The knowledge that he now possessed was such an obvious course of action, but he needed to think things over. There was more going on here than his personal vendetta. True, Lastrad did have much to offer him, there was no question there, and the more he thought about it, did he really want to throw that chance away? Yes, his loyalty to Trencit and the Homeguard meant everything to him, but he recalled the words of both Klellan and Questron, chiding him about his false sense of duty. They had believed him to be no more than a pawn, carelessly moved about by the hands of the powerful. They considered themselves opportunists, choosing the pursuit of their own status above all else. Was the notion really that difficult to comprehend? Well, in Klellan's case, at least, he had no sympathy. The man had aligned himself with the Dark Mage, who had no reservation in killing innocent people to achieve his own ends. But Trencit was different…

Or he believed it to be. Men enlisted in the Royal Legions on their own, usually, but at times of war there was no choice in the matter. If you were picked to go, then you either did so or face imprisonment or worse.

Forlern was tired, and these things weighed heavily on him. Before this trip, he would never have doubted his own commitment and allegiance to Trencit. But now, things had been thrown in a different light. He'd been sent on a mission which posed little chance for success. Yes, he had managed to survive and succeed, no small thing, but he felt no taste of satisfaction. What would be his reward once he returned to Daregil Keep? Words of congratulations certainly, and King Gregor would be pleased. And then what? Would he be sent to another area of danger, perhaps the border to the east, maybe on some harrowing adventure once more?

It was entirely possible, and at any other time he would have welcomed the challenge. Had he been too quick and placed such little value on his own preservation? Fighters like himself were tools to be wielded by the powerful. The leaders of the land moved them about like the pieces of a game. You either accepted your station, or tried to avoid such responsibility. Some chose the latter, and fled to places like Lastrad, or the farther reaches of Trencit where the arm of Daregil Keep seldom reached. Others traveled further yet.

"Ah, well."

Forlern muttered to himself, feeling anxious, confused, and weary. He needed sleep, and it would help clear the fog from his mind. Unfortunately, his experiences had taken a heavy toll, and would not be forgotten anytime soon. Forlern had never been plagued by such doubt before, and he didn't like it. He didn't like anything which might take the edge off his fighting ability and preparedness, and this troubled him the most. He needed to reconcile all of this somehow, and before reaching Daregil Keep. He then thought about the chest he'd been given and paused, his curiosity getting the best of him at last. Dismounting, he unstrapped the chest, opening the lock which held it fast, and what he saw was remarkable...

The chest was filled with trinkets and baubles, coins and tokens, the combined amount no less than a small fortune. Whistling under his breath, he knew that the Gran Barshara and Questron had carefully planned this out, knowing that it was impossible not to be impressed by such an offering. He would be a fool to leave it behind...

No, he was taking it with him, but he couldn't very well trot into Daregil Keep with this in tow. He could probably manage to get it to his quarters inside the fortress, but the idea of having this hidden in his chambers was an unpleasant notion at best. He would constantly be worried about it being discovered, or perhaps revealed by some servant of the Gran Barshara who had been planted somewhere inside the keep, waiting for the order to take action. It was possible, he had to admit... Well, he had another idea. He would keep the chest secreted away somewhere else. Find a place that he could bury it, and return to it if he ever had the need.

All right, fair enough, he thought to himself. That's what I'll do with it. If it was ever discovered, he would simply say that he'd kept it hidden in case he ever left the Homeguard. They were not required to serve for life, so it wasn't that hard to use this as a possible reason, but the big problem with this excuse was that they were not allowed to keep payments from anyone *other* than their own leadership in the form of their allowance. This idea bothered him a lot, but he was also unwilling to give up such a large amount of valuables either. It truly was a fortune.

Forlern mounted up once more, deciding to go further before finding a place to rest. He was no longer concerned about pursuit, since the guards would never catch their horses while on foot. No, they would have to return to Lastrad and face the wrath of their leaders.

He didn't envy them.

So with a clearer mind and purpose, Forlern rode ahead, knowing that he had come to terms with his situation, at least for the moment. He could focus again on what lay ahead instead of looking behind. Or at least he hoped.

And thinking such things and being lost in his head

was why he never saw the shadow following him some distance from where he had come…

Forlern rode into the night, making good time and placing miles between himself and the guards from Lastrad. He felt drained in both mind and body, his injuries still mending. He knew it was time for some much needed rest, so he looked about, deciding to enter the woods to his left and find a suitable spot to hole up for the remainder of the evening. Barely able to keep his eyes open, he led his horse deeper into the forest, coming upon a small brook sheltered by tall oaks on both sides of the lazy current. He tied the animal, giving it ample room to drink, and then he slumped onto the ground, pulling his cloak from his pack and trying to get comfortable. His recent ordeal weighed heavily on him and he fell asleep almost immediately.

Forlern stumbled in that twilight realm for a while, unaware whether he dreamt or was awake, but some inner sense nudged him from the darkness and he opened his eyes, finding a cloaked figure sitting across from him where a small fire was burning, one which had not been there before. It only took him a moment to realize his danger and his mind unraveled the bindings of sleep, his fighting instincts taking over.

"Peace, Forlern. If I had wanted to kill you I would have done so. I'd rather not fight a pitched battle at the moment either."

Forlern was on his feet in an instant, knife in hand. It seemed his adventures from Lastrad were not over yet…He didn't recognize the stranger who obviously knew *him*, and he wasn't one of the guards he had left behind. Then who was he?

"Yes, I'm from Lastrad of course, not some highway robber. That's your initial question."

"Who are you then?" Forlern's weapon never left his hand.

"I'm one of Questron's men. Does that make you feel better?" The man chuckled; a low, monotone sound which was more cynical than humorous. Forlern's eyes narrowed.

"Another escort for the road to Daregil Keep?"

"Come now, you're not that much of a fool. My purpose is a bit more complex than that."

"Explain yourself then, or we will have that promised fight," Forlern shot back.

The man shrugged, standing up causally, stretching his arms, throwing several twigs into the flames. "I wanted to get the chill out of the air. It's in the deepest part of the night when the bones feel coldest."

Forlern said nothing, bothered more than a little by the stranger's composure. Who was this man?

"My name is Ganavin. You don't know me, so save yourself the effort."

"And I'm supposed to believe that?" Forlern asked.

"Well, then call me something else if you like. It matters not."

Forlern grunted, easing himself into a sitting position, still uncertain how to proceed. "I take it you're under orders to follow after me, perhaps to take action as well."

"You were careless in thinking those other fools were the only ones sent by Questron."

Forlern bit back an angry retort, but knew the man was telling the truth. He should have backtracked and made certain no other was following. Foolish…

"I know what you're thinking. Ah, but you didn't check, did you? And now, here I am." Ganavin laughed again. "Take comfort in the fact that it wouldn't have made a difference. You would not have seen me regardless."

"Oh, you think so? No small amount of confidence. It seems Lastrad has much of that to spare these days," Forlern mocked.

"Indeed it does. And confidence has many faces. Many claim it as their own while being undeserving of such."

"But not for yourself?" Forlern nearly laughed at the man's arrogance.

"Well spoken. Maybe we're getting somewhere finally, eh?" Ganavin reached into a pack at his side, pulling out a large drinking sack. "Lastrad wine is the finest. One of the city's more notable qualities. You've hardly been there. So much to see and partake of...Many of those fools become lazy and complacent. We'll see how they fare against those devils. I hear you went some rounds yourself. Looks like you came out on top."

"Have you ever fought the Devlents?" Forlern was skeptical, and made no attempt to disguise his tone.

"Certainly. They're fools as well. The entire nation of them." Ganavin shook his head, taking another swig.

"This grows tiring. It's time to conclude our conversation and for us to depart on our separate ways." Forlern said. "For myself, there's been enough bloodshed lately. If you agree to leave and return to Lastrad, we can forget this meeting. You can tell Questron you never caught up to me. He knows I'm fairly capable of avoiding capture."

Ganavin inclined his head. "I'm sure he does. Unfortunately, he also knows I'm equally *incapable* of losing you. So we have a dilemma now, don't we Forlern? I'm traveling north with you."

Forlern eyed him suspiciously. It appeared there would be no way to extricate himself from the situation without a fight, and just when he was beginning to think he was finally moving away from all the chaos and madness of Lastrad. He sighed, raising himself casually from the ground, but Ganavin seemed disinterested by both his words and actions.

"You would prefer to quarrel as opposed to a peaceful compromise?" Forlern tried one last time. "Must I remind you that I'm an envoy from Trencit, a Captain of the Homeguard, and an advisor to King Gregor?"

"And perhap's the new King's Champion and butler of his wineries as well?" He laughed loudly, Forlern scowling at the stranger. "Quarrels and disagreements faze me not." Ganavin kept laughing. "And I have little care for titles and such. Curiously, you don't strike me as someone who needs to hide behind lofty names. Have these recent promotions affected your confidence, perhaps?"

Forlern had heard quite enough by now, and the man was deliberately baiting him further. Why, Ganavin seemed as audacious as the Gran Barshara himself, the Lastrad leader lacking the black humor, however. Insolence appeared to be in great abundance in these parts.

"You've tried my patience with your insults." Forlern inched forward. "It's a wonder you still have a tongue left. Do as I say and leave *now*."

Ganavin shook his head. "You'll do as *I* request, rest assured."

"You think so?" Forlern smirked, one hand on the hilt of his blade.

Ganavin reached into his pocket, pulling something

out. Forlern was ready for anything, balancing on the balls of his feet as he coiled to spring, but it was no weapon that Ganavin brought forth. The man held something small and shiny in his fingers, making no attempt to conceal it. Forlern squinted a moment, recognizing it immediately as Ganavin placed it on one finger.

It was a ring bearing the symbol of a Ja-Ravel assassin...

"I don't usually wear it. There are some who know what it is."

"So," Forlern hissed, pulling himself straighter and backing away a step. "It seems Klellan wasn't working alone then."

"No he wasn't. But don't mistake me for one of his allies. My purposes are not the same."

"And I should trust one such as yourself?"

The situation had now changed drastically, Forlern trying to figure out the best way to deal with his unwanted visitor, one who now appeared in a much more dangerous light. Confident only moments ago, he now felt less certain of the outcome if he had to fight against Ganavin.

"I see you're not afraid of me in the slightest. Wary, but not frightened. That's admirable. But there is no need to draw weapons. We do not have to fight. You actually know very little of the Ja-Ravel, and what you do know is likely false, for the most part. We are not all assassins."

"Indeed? Do you care to enlighten me?"

"Yes I do," Ganavin answered. "Why don't you sit and we can talk this over like men."

Forlern hesitated, unwilling to fall for any treachery. Admittedly, he was very curious to hear the man out at this point, and perhaps there was still a chance to avoid a confrontation. He backed away to his previous spot and sat down once more.

"Good move," Ganavin said. "A reasonable man knows when to fight and when to talk. You already know that I could have killed you while you slept, or do you propose to challenge such an obvious fact?"

Forlern couldn't deny it. He had been vulnerable while he slept alone, yet here he was, awakened by this intruder, unharmed and left with all his weapons. He shook his head. "True, but that doesn't automatically gain my faith to your motives. I don't trust you or your brethren. Klellan was in league with the Dark Mage. You might be as well yourself, and even if you aren't, my skepticism remains strong."

"See, this is exactly what I told you. Such generalities are founded in fear and rumor. You have much to learn about us."

Forlern said nothing.

Ganavin shrugged. "Ja-Ravel are free to do whatever they like. Klellan was a fool, but one of his own choosing. His greed and lust for power destroyed him. He aligned himself with dark powers that would probably have betrayed him in the end."

"I won't disagree with you. Did he know who you were?"

Ganavin shook his head. "No. Klellan chose to reveal his background to some in the pursuit of gaining a position. And it did help him in part...Again, this is something he did of his own freewill. As Ja-Ravel, we are not bound by any laws or authority. We are above everything."

His words struck a nerve in Forlern, and it only put him more on edge. "Above everything? Well, that has the ring of supreme overconfidence if I ever heard it."

"I merely state facts, nothing less. But how is this different in comparison to any other man's life? You make your own choices, do you not? Some choose to be free, others to be enslaved. Why is this so strange?"

"I don't know what you're getting at, and it makes me feel no less suspicious," Forlern replied.

Ganavin sighed. "Listen then. What people know of us originates from tales involving assassinations and betrayals. Opinions get passed along, beliefs are grounded firmly among the recipients of such stories, and behold, a general consensus is created. It's not so hard to understand. I'll go further…People then conclude we are *all* assassins, hired mercenaries trained to poison and kill, all at our master's bidding, whomever chooses to pay us to make it worth our while. And so the Ja-Ravel are universally viewed as being inherently evil by nature, our sole purpose to spread such across all the lands." Ganavin laughed louder, slapping his leg. "Now why in the world would that be the entire truth? Why is the gain only recognized in these types of despicable acts? Tell me that!" He pointed a finger at Forlern. "So these stories get retold, and the worse culprits become the face of the Ja-Ravel. The assassins and murderers represent all of us, and we are hopelessly evil." Ganavin patted his chest for emphasis. "It's not the entire story. There you have it."

Forlern chewed on his lip, thinking things through. At this point, he really didn't know what to make of it all. Could the man be telling the truth? Everything he'd ever heard spoke the contrary, but as he pondered Ganavin's words, he also could see why it might be possible. Little was known about the Ja-Ravel except that the sect was considered long lost, and in their time, members had been responsible for evil acts. Or at least suspected to be behind a number of them…was it that far of a leap to think that not all of them were assassins? He didn't know, and wanted to hear more.

"You have me considering my knowledge of your sect, I'll admit. I need to understand more, though."

"Fair enough. Glad to see you have an open mind, Forlern."

Forlern shrugged. "Now tell me what your purpose was in following after me. What did Questron have in mind?"

"My orders were to shadow your company and make sure nothing threatened. He was interested in what you were going to do with the chest, *and* his men. He told me of the Gran Barshara's proposition. Ultimately, I was to enter Daregil Keep and be his eyes and ears."

Taken aback by Ganavin's words, Forlern was at a loss. The Ja-Ravel might very well have been the one to be planted at Daregil Keep, his purpose to spy on Forlern in particular. It was an unnerving possibility, but Questron had made no secret of it, boldly telling Forlern their plans.

"And what else?" Forlern asked.

Without hesitation, Ganavin responded. "To kill you if the story of Klellan's treason was told."

The silence was like ice, and Forlern didn't move as he sat there watching the other. Ganavin's face bore no expression. It was impossible to read the truth behind his words.

"Tell me this," Forlern said. "Are there spies in Daregil Keep already? Other Ja-Ravel?"

"Ah, you ask something of which I do not have knowledge about." He held up one hand at Forlern's look of disapproval. "I'm one of Questron's chief fighters, handpicked for clandestine errands. I'm not a close confidant of either the Lastrad Captain or the Gran Barshara, I'm afraid. He is a powerful and rich leader, and his influence stretches into every corner of Trencit. I would be surprised if he didn't have men in Daregil Keep. Fair enough?"

Forlern frowned in response, letting Ganavin continue.

"You'll either accept my words or you won't. I see where this poses a greater dilemma for you. My excuse offers me cover in both matters, does it not?" Ganavin grinned. "By coming to Daregil Keep, I could still be watching you, staying in place as I wait for a signal to act."

"You seem to have the future well in hand, I see," Forlern mocked. "Are you so certain that it will work out this way?"

"Not certain at all!" Ganavin laughed. "I deal with the present. That is trouble enough! I told you we are free to do as we wish."

"Then your allegiance to the Gran Barshara is false?"

"If I wish it to be, then yes. And if not, then I stay true." Ganavin opened his palms for emphasis.

"You speak in riddles. None of this has reassured me of your intentions." Forlern replied evenly.

"If I want to reassure you, then I will do so," Ganavin quipped.

The exchange was maddening. Forlern had no idea of the man's true motivation. If anything, Ganavin was proving to be the most frustrating person he had ever met. "The only thing I'm convinced of is that you're doing your best to thoroughly confound me. I'm tired of this game of words. Ja-Ravel or not, I have no fear of you."

Ganavin nodded. "I see this to be true. I have no wish to fight you as well, Forlern. And like yourself, it's not from fear."

"Enough of this, man. Speak clearly or not at all!"

"But I have been...Forlern, I know you grow tired of this discussion. It was not my intention to anger or confuse you, but in my own way to let you understand me better. All I have told you is true, you have my word, trustworthy or not." He winked at Forlern. "And I will continue to enlighten you. My plan is to travel to Daregil Keep, but for my *own* purposes, not Questron's or the Gran Barshara's. I have no intention of spying on you, or even slicing your throat at some point in time." He grinned wickedly. "Thus, I cut my ties with Lastrad and bid farewell. Truth be told, I grow stagnant within those high walls, parrying and dodging all the politics and subterfuge. Lastrad is a grand city, but you have only seen a tiny bit. Dig only a little, and the layers peel off, running deeper and deeper. There exist many challenges there, but no more for me. I've left the city behind, perhaps for good. Certainly Questron won't be pleased." He shrugged.

"So you're telling me that it's not a challenge to you anymore? That's why you're leaving?"

"Exactly so. I grew bored there. I need more to do. And that's where *you* come in."

Forlern could only shake his head in stunned amazement, unable to reply.

Ganavin spoke before he could formulate a response. "There is a great war brewing. The first blows have been fought, and terrible things are rising from their hidden lairs, summoned by this dark enemy. You're in the midst of this battle, one of those who have a part to play in it all. That is what *I* seek."

"What? You want to fight for Trencit and King Gregor?"

"It might come to that, but I bear no love or loyalty for either. I sought out the training grounds of the Ja-Ravel to see if I could find my limits. And let me tell you this, Forlern." His face was expressionless. "I've never been bested in combat."

They locked eyes, and Forlern looked at him, stunned. He'd never met someone so perplexing, and although he had zero proof of what Ganavin said, he believed him…

"I'm also no assassin. Spilling the blood of other men is not my taste. Oh, I'll do it if necessary, if I'm threatened. But not just for the sake of it. I've never considered myself evil, either. I hope you're not disappointed." He grinned wickedly.

Forlern shook his head slowly. "Your words are impossible to prove either way."

Ganavin continued, leaning forward, his eyes and

face possessed with an animation that spoke more than words. "I'm after a challenge, in whatever form it comes. Your King would be wise to accept my services."

"And if he refuses?"

"He won't. Why would he turn down someone with my skills? He needs all the help he can get in this fight."

But which side will you ultimately be fighting on? Forlern asked himself.

"So there it is. Let's travel together to the Keep as fellow companions and see what we will. Do you trust me in that matter, Forlern? You may tie me up at night if you like. Search me and take my weapons." Ganavin held his hands together, standing slowly and turning around. "You can even strike me down now if you wish."

Forlern paused for a long moment, thinking of doing exactly that. What a dilemma he now faced. He could be telling the truth, or lying through his teeth. Which was it? Silently debating, he made up his mind.

"Very well," he said. "We'll go to Daregil Keep together. But don't think you've gained my entire trust, Ganavin."

The Ja-Ravel turned about and smirked. "I would be very disappointed in you if I had…"

The two companies stood before the gate, few words being spoken amongst them. Sarion's companions had quickly been ushered to the main courtyard, and he only had moments to tell them what had happened.

Despite everything they had been through, they were still stunned by the news. Their faces said it all…Geld

Rinn's eyes were wide, and Sarion believed that something had been changed permanently inside the young fighter, perhaps a faith in his fellow man that had been broken, perhaps never to heal. Lassel looked as determined as ever, and if she had been shaken it was not visible in her unrelenting demeanor. All of them had seen the ogres and the Ravenor. How could they hope to be victorious against such power? It was a grim moment as they knew a terrible battle was only minutes away, and one in which many, if not all, of their lives would be taken.

Above the gates, a herald called out to the waiting enemy below, giving voice to Lord Berillon's word. The gates began to swing open.

Sarion leaned towards Thustan. "Our only hope is to find Chardoom. He controls the Ravenor. Without him the beast will lack guidance, perhaps leave the area and give us a chance."

The prince nodded. "My men will attack the ogres directly. I don't think they will expect an outright assault."

"I'm not so sure of that…" Sarion replied.

"Once battle begins, I want you and your men to seek out this Chardoom. For the sake of us all, I hope you find him."

Sarion shook his head. "I will stay and fight with your men. Valadire will sneak away and try to come around from the lower woods." Valadire and Chertron were close by, listening to every word.

"Sarion, I would rather you leave with them. You have the most experience and greatest chance of finding Chardoom." Thustan held his shoulder tight.

"No, I trust them to succeed. I wish to stay in the front of the battle. He will send the Ravenor to finish us off as soon as he realizes your men stand with us. We will only have a short time to press the ogres."

"But what can we possibly do against the monster?" Thustan asked.

Sarion shook his head. "Keep moving, don't let it trap us. Don't forget, we have the rod."

"And the rod is exactly what you do not want us to use."

"We *will* be using it though...If the Ravenor is a magical creature, the rod will negate whatever magic it carries, making it vulnerable to our weapons."

Chertron grumbled. "It is too large, too powerful, my friend. I'm afraid this really is our last adventure."

Sarion clapped him on the shoulder. "There is always hope. Perhaps we can find something to our advantage yet."

The gate was fully open now, the hinges creaking eerily in the gloom.

Sarion spoke again. "Let's try and keep the ogres between us and the Ravenor. In the confusion, it won't be able to strike out as it would like."

"And if things become desperate, I want you to flee into the woods. Some of us must escape the battle. That's my command." Thustan said.

Sarion nodded. "I agree. But it's also time for us to find a way to destroy the danger of Chardoom and the beast. If we fall here, they will attack us at Nighton, or further into Trencit if we don't find a way to kill the Ravenor now. And beware the woods, Valadire. Chardoom will anticipate us trying to flee. I'm sure the Crage waits below, protecting him."

"The Crage..." Valadire cursed. "I had forgotten about the monster."

"Try and skirt the woods when you're able to, Valadire. It lurks somewhere in there, I'm sure, and it will be guarding its master."

"Then how do we hope to kill Chardoom? We need you with us, Sarion."

He shook his head gently. He was needed here as well, and there was no time for further argument. It was time to go.

"This is our plan. Let us stick to it and have faith. You have the strength of arms to do what is necessary. All of you." Sarion looked over at Geld Rinn, Lassel, Piril, and Bertilik. He was asking a lot from them, but fate was asking a lot from them all. Sarion knew the odds were terribly stacked against their favor, and he knew with chilling certainty that some of those he looked at now would not see the new dawn…

"It's time." Thustan gave the signal to move out to Garvin, his captain, who had also stood by, knowing what needed to be done.

Sarion rode out first, Thustan and his men next to him. Valadire and the rest would slowly fall back in the ranks until the battle ensued, when they would follow through with their plan. They had no idea where Chardoom was, but Sarion knew that he was probably hiding somewhere close by. The ogres and Morlek were dozens of yards before them. There was no sign of the Ravenor, and the last they had seen, it was near the dam breast, lost in the distance. Sarion knew that things would happen very quickly, and the chaos of battle would cast its pall over clearer thinking. He needed to stay close with Thustan so they could react to the changing field.

The gates closed ominously behind them, and immediately the fighting began…

Archers threw up a volley of arrows at the ogres, the brutes already in formation with their shields held protectively before them. More ogres had been added to their ranks, doubling their numbers. Sarion recalled the fierce fighting against them on their hunt to Grammore, not relishing the coming fray.

The lead horsemen reared up against the brutes, who seemed unaffected by the rain of arrows. Some hit their mark, but these creatures had tough hides and could shrug most of them away with little or no injury. A dozen warriors fell in the initial assault, the ogres refusing to give ground. Now spearmen came forward, hoping to find a target with their heavier weapons. Sarion had grabbed a pair for himself, and he rode dangerously close to one of them, the ogre wielding a heavy club, sweeping it outwards in a broad arc. Coming too close, Sarion urged his mount backwards, thrusting his spear and throwing it at the last second at the monsters exposed foot. The long shaft found its mark, and the creature howled in pain. Injured, but still deadly, it backed away several yards while other fighters pressed it further. Numerous archers, seeing the creature's dismay, poured dozens of arrows down on it, several finding a home. The brute stumbled, tripping backwards, and a dozen swordsmen charged, pinning it to the ground and finishing it off.

They had killed one of the enemy.

But all the rest remained…

The fighting grew frantic as Thustan's men pressed the ogres at every angle. These were not new recruits, or inexperienced fighters from some outlying province. These men were fighters of the Royal Legions of Trencit, disciplined and well-organized, but they fought against deadly Grammore predators of which they had no combat experience. A single ogre had the strength of twenty men, and fought with a ferocity that had never been seen before in civilized lands.

Sarion stayed near Thustan and Barimon, the three of them encouraging the fighters where they could, lending their direct help when possible. Thustan was heir to the throne of Trencit, however, and would not place himself directly in the fray. After Sarion's initial assault on the fallen ogre, he had commanded him to pull back and remain with him. Sarion was unwilling to remain totally out of combat, and he held his bow ready, firing volleys whenever he saw an opening. The battle continued for long minutes, another pair of ogres meeting their death at the hands of the skilled Trencit fighters. Dozens of Thustan's men had already fallen, with just as many injured. The ogres were relentless and brutal, a savage race of Lowland predators that had managed to survive in Grammore as one of the dominant races, and were not to be easily defeated. Sarion looked in the distance, wondering what Chardoom would do next, fearing the worst. Valadire had led the others away, and would be trying their best to move south in the attempt to find Chardoom and strike directly against him.

Thustan pointed to his right, where another ogre crumbled to the ground, felled by one of his men's spears. "They fight a valiant battle. The ogres are reduced in force."

Sarion nodded. Despite the savagery of the brutes, they faced a huge disadvantage in numbers. If these had been the only combatants, then they would ultimately lose. He knew that Chardoom was watching from nearby, and it was only a matter of time before he called in his ultimate weapon, the dreadful Ravenor. But the man had to know that they would be searching for him, especially with these greater numbers. Chardoom needed to be careful if he revealed himself and they were able to attack him directly. The Crage was a terrible predator in its own right, but it was flesh and blood, and could be killed.

Thinking such thoughts, Sarion's skin grew cold when he heard the blasting of a horn in the distance. Chardoom was calling forth the Ravenor at last…

Thustan's men paused, all of them hearing this battle cry and knowing what it meant. They continued their thrust, Thustan's men maneuvering more to the south now, trying to keep the ogres between themselves and the approaching beast. Sarion's keen eyes looked deeper into the valley, probing the mist for signs of movement, and moments later he spotted something massive making its way for the battle.

The Summoning

The Ravenor was coming…

"Shades." Thustan pointed. "What a beast. Barimon, do you have knowledge of anything which we can use to confront this monster?"

"I'm afraid not," the mage answered. "We will all meet out doom. We have one weapon at our disposal, and one alone."

"Yes, the one thing we should be most reluctant to use."

They watched as the creature drew near, bellowing its hatred at the men. Its mighty roar echoed up and down the valley, placing fear in the hearts of everyone, filling them with dismay. Regardless, the fighters continued, now battling against a renewed foe, the ogres gaining confidence as their master added his greatest emissary to the fight.

"Look! They've split into two groups to give the monster room!"

Sarion shouted, all of them watching as they ogres separated, trying to give the beast an opening through which it could attack them directly. Thustan's men followed suit, half going to the south, the other to the north, attempting to keep the ogres in front of them. There was a lot of movement on the battlefield, and for the moment, the Trencit fighters were able to avoid getting too close to the Ravenor, the beast pushing its bulk forward, but also avoiding trampling the ogres. Two more of the brutes fell, but time was against them, for the more ogres that died, the more room for the Ravenor to strike. It now spun about, sweeping its tail against some of the Trencit riders, tossing men and horse through the air like they were weightless. Growing impatient with the game, it thundered forward now, heedless of the ogres in its frenzy for blood. Despite its mammoth bulk, it moved surprisingly quickly, and with its deadly talons found more victims. It rushed into their ranks, coming directly towards Sarion and Thustan.

Barimon was swift in turning his horse while Sarion hesitated, shooting multiple arrows at the monster with all of them finding their mark, but none of them having any effect. The beast had a hide of skin and scales which protected it from such harm. The creature had no eyes, and thus was not vulnerable in this way. He still was unsure if it had magical properties, although the mere fact that it *existed* seemed proof enough to him…

The ogres numbered only four now, all of them injured to some extent. They backed off several dozen yards, content to let the Ravenor finish off the enemy. It was a hopeless battle now, with Thustan's men trying to get close enough for their arrows and spears to strike the beast, but with each thrust, more of the fighters fell beneath either the monster's tail or one of its crushing talons. The Trencit force had suffered terrible losses, and Sarion estimated that over half of Thustan's men lay dying or were already dead. The Ravenor moved to its left, rushing forward and catching a few more men. The fighters not only had to beware the beast, but many of the horses grew frightened, tossing their riders at the worst possible time and leaving them on foot.

The situation looked desperate, and Sarion wondered how Valadire fared.

"Thustan, we can wait no longer. Either we flee or lose our own lives here. Or we choose another option…"

Sarion stared at Barimon. Clearly he referred to using the rod against the Ravenor. Try to awaken its magic and use it as a weapon. He looked at Thustan, who returned his gaze.

"If we flee, then as Sarion said, the Ravenor and Chardoom will have scored a major victory against us, giving them greater confidence and securing the southern part of our western border. Nighton will fall next. I also fear that Sharield will be destroyed. Surely Chardoom will throw the monster against it, and thousands of innocent people will die." He faced Sarion as if in appeal.

"I understand the consequences, believe me. But it's an unknown talisman filled with power beyond our knowledge. We don't know what it can do."

Barimon spoke. "Do we have a choice? We are not defenseless at Daregil Keep, but that does us little good if the rest of Trencit is overrun. Thustan, we must act now. There is no time for debate, only action."

Thustan nodded. "I fear he's right, Sarion."

They were all wary of the Ravenor, but the creature was still focused on the men on the far side, who looked to be only moments away from a complete rout. Some of them were already riding off, heading towards the forest to save themselves. And when they were all scattered or dead, the Ravenor would come for Thustan's group last...

The prince pulled out the rod, holding it in his hand. "By fate or fortune this talisman has come into our hands, and it is *my* choice to try and use its power to save our people."

"Wait!" Sarion held up a hand. "If this is your command, then let me wield it. I've used it before, and am partly responsible for what has happened. I also never had the chance to tell you of my experiences in Sprechyd Wood."

"What do you mean?" Barimon snapped. "Quickly."

He told them briefly of his encounter with the strange creature known as the Keeper of Sprechyd Wood."

"Fascinating." Barimon said. "I've heard tale of such a thing, yet you have encountered it yourself. It said the rod can be our salvation."

"Or destruction..." Thustan replied.

"Maybe both," Sarion added.

"Well, the time has come now to discover the truth, and I will be the one to do so." Thustan nodded grimly, waving Sarion off. "I will approach the monster directly and I need you both to ward my back."

"Thustan, hold a moment. I should be the one to attempt its use." Barimon moved close. "I am the only one with the lore and knowledge of such ancient talismans and have studied this craft for long years. My experience might make the difference in unleashing its power, and also controlling it." Barimon spoke, his voice intense, but Sarion did not like the look in the man's eyes. It was a look of hunger...

Thustan paused, considering the matter for a moment, but remained silent. In the background the Ravenor roared, pushing against a small group of perhaps twenty men who attempted to encircle it. Thustan's own group held their position, still pressing the ogres while protecting their leader.

"You're right, Barimon."

Sarion was stunned at the man's quick change of heart.

"You are the mage of Trencit, and closest councilor to my father. If anyone can unlock its secrets, you are best equipped to do so. Good fortune with it."

Thustan handed the talisman to Barimon, who gazed at it in marvel, nodding to himself. The mage never hesitated, closing his eyes and focusing on the rod, guiding his horse forward towards the ogres.

"Now we will see what lies within..." He whispered.

Valadire glanced behind him at Chertron. "If we don't find Chardoom soon, there will be no one left to save."

The durable fighter muttered beneath his breath,

motioning his head for them to continue. Visibility was still limited, and they dared not light any lanterns. The forest edge was only a few yards to their right, and that had come a good distance already with no sign of the Dark Mage's emissary. Time was running out, and behind them they caught snatches of men yelling and steel clashing, as a frightful battle was underway.

"He can't be that far off." Valadire gritted his teeth, shaking his head in frustration.

Piril and Bertilik took up the rear while Geld Rinn rode by his side, Chertron riding behind him alongside Lassel. Six of them to stand against Chardoom and whatever else lurked with him. Certainly he would be guarded, but whether they found the Crage, ogres, or both, was yet to be seen. None of the possibilities were pleasant…

The company froze as a horn erupted into the night, coming from the woods directly ahead of them.

"That's it," Valadire said, his voice low and dangerous. "Chardoom summons the Ravenor, but he also gives away his position. We need to take him out quick before any of his creatures can prevent us."

"And also before the Ravenor kills our friends." Chertron added.

They moved swiftly and silently, the horses' hooves muffled against noise. The last echoes of the horn died away, but there could be no mistaking it – the sound had come from just ahead. The light was growing stronger, although the mist and rain still obscured most of the landscape. Suddenly Geld Rinn stopped, pointing ahead.

He had seen something...

Chertron had also seen movement.

Valadire knew that the time for action had come, and he kicked his steed into a full run, heading for the spot Geld Rinn had pointed to. The younger fighter a length behind him, the company rushed ahead, knowing that their elusive quarry was finally within reach.

Valadire stopped at a small opening in the woods where the brush was thinner, the trees more open. It was here that Geld Rinn and Chertron had seen the movement. Chardoom had to be just within the eaves of the forest...

There was room for the horses, so Geld Rinn led them now, spotting fresh tracks, and they plunged into the woods, the next few seconds dragging by, all of them anticipating a confrontation. They'd only gone a few yards when the forest opened up, and they spotted a dark, hooded figure on the far side of a small clearing, only a few dozen yards away. Valadire never hesitated and maneuvered his horse in a direct line straight at the figure, who pivoted to face the advancing threat, a staff held before him.

It was Chardoom...

Wharla was also there, slumped down and bound to a tree, her mouth gagged. She wasn't moving, so there was no way of knowing if she was alright.

Valadire was almost upon him now while Chertron held his bow aloft, determined to strike their enemy first. Too late to stop the thundering Valadire, Chertron cursed beneath his breath. There were too many shadows, too many places to hide.

Just before Valadire reached Chardoom, his sword drawn, two things happened...

First there was a noise from the trees at the right side of the clearing, and a large figure leaped from concealment, heading straight for Valadire. The Crage had revealed itself at last!

In the same instant Chertron's arrow found its mark, and Chardoom screamed in anguish as the dart imbedded itself deeply into his left arm. He never let go of the staff though and he stumbled backwards, trying to put the Crage between the attackers and himself. Geld Rinn yelled in warning as things happened too quickly. The Crage bowled into Valadire, all muscle and talons, knocking the Forester from his horse, although he managed to lash out with his sword before rolling with the fall. He struck the Crage in its abdomen, and the creature seemed stunned for a moment before catching its balance and pivoting towards the others as they now moved to engage it.

The fighters all understood the stakes here, and they were high. Only one side could emerge as victor, and death was the reward for the loser. They had battled the Crage back at the outpost, but only in a limited way. This was direct hand-to-hand combat...

Piril and Bertilik closed, while Lassel held a spear in front of her, effortlessly guiding her horse and looking for an opening. Chardoom disappeared into the woods, and the Crage stood between him and the fighters. They could not reach Chardoom without killing the monster.

Valadire regained his feet quickly, although his horse had fled in terror. The fighter slashed to and fro with his sword, unwilling to leave himself open to attack. He sensed they had a possible advantage here as he believed the Crage would protect its master at all cost, and *that* meant it would have to defend its ground.

"Press it from all sides," he yelled. "It tries to protect Chardoom."

Lassel was a flash of lightning on her horse, confident and focused. Spear held in front, she held the Crage at bay while the others rained arrows on it and moved into stronger positions. The beast appeared slower than before, and Valadire wondered if it had sustained multiple injuries, both from the outpost and perhaps afterwards, while the men of Sharield hunted it. Piril brought his spiked metal ball out now, swinging it over his head and towards the Crage. The creature stumbled, faltering, and the fighters moved closer, but it was a ploy, for the beast feinted to its right, then charged to the left, springing forward in a great leap and landing behind Piril and Bertilik. All of them turned to defend but it was too late, the monster too strong. It slashed out with its talons to either side, crushing the pair of brave fighters to the ground where they both collapsed, unmoving.

Just like that, both of them were dead...

Valadire screamed in fury, and Lassel let go of her spear at last, piercing the Crage in its side. It shrieked in rage, clearly hurt, but still not out of the battle. Chertron swiped at it with his blade, careful lest he meet the fate of the others. The beast nearly had him, but he ducked at the last second before the creature's claws could behead him. Geld Rinn jumped off his own horse, the animal frightened, and the young fighter had a pair of long knives in his hand, letting one fly, which the Crage dodged. The fighting was close, and the Crage conceded nothing. Valadire stood his own ground bravely, wielding his sword and looking for an opening. Chertron had taken his own sword in hand, knowing that this was no fight for arrows. They had to strike the creature down with blade or spear in order to gain victory.

The Crage was quick and agile, feinting in both directions, trying to keep the fighters off balance, but these were highly trained men and women, some of the finest in their ranks, and they would not succumb so easily. Valadire was hoping that the Crage would grow impatient, expose himself to a close strike, but as yet, it held its own, as if daring them to come too close.

And then Geld Rinn did just exactly that...

It didn't take long...

Barimon held the rod before him, raising it high, and the talisman glowed with an inner fire, steadily burning brighter.

The Summoning

"He's awakening its power!" Thustan pointed, but Sarion needed no guidance to watch as the mage seemed to grow in height, sitting even taller on his horse. Around them, the sounds of battle seemed to diminish and fade away, as if time itself paused as the ancient weapon stirred to life.

Sarion looked at the Ravenor, and even the great beast hesitated, its eyeless face now pointing in their direction. It waited there for several long moments, motionless, but then it took action, lumbering directly towards the mage.

"Does it sense the power of the rod?" Thustan asked.

"I don't know," Sarion answered, watching in both awe and horror as the great predator closed in on Barimon. The Ravenor would be on him in seconds.

The mage never backed away, hands gripped tightly on the rod, and then something incredible happened...

The air before Barimon seemed to shimmer, and they heard a tremendous noise, almost like the pounding of water falling over a deep summit. The air crackled with power, and Sarion felt a rush of energy from within his own memory, a terrible allure to wield the rod as his own. He shook his head, staring at the mage, unable to shift his gaze. Barimon shouted, and before their eyes a blackness materialized, a total and complete absence of light as if they now looked into the deepest abyss of time and space – the air around them growing stronger, whipping into gale force winds.

"What's he doing?" Thustan shouted but Sarion barely heard him, at a loss to comprehend what was going on.

The remaining ogres stood rooted in their tracks, unable to decide whether to attack or retreat. The Ravenor, however, had continued forward with jaws gaping, and it appeared as if Barimon would be swallowed whole.

Moments before the monster could strike, the disturbance in the air took form, combining itself into a funnel of sheer power, and Barimon waved the rod, directing its movement. The vortex of air smashed into the mighty creature, and they watched in amazement as the Ravenor was pushed back, facing a force to match its own.

"I don't believe my eyes!" Thustan yelled. "Barimon has discovered the power of the rod and can defeat the monster!"

The mage shouted something, but the words were lost in the wind. The fighters below reformed their ranks, but they moved backwards, away from the vortex. Beneath the sound of the wind a new sound emerged – a high, ear-piercing shriek as if hundreds of creatures were hissing and roaring in great torment.

Sarion looked on in both horror and fascination. The vortex grew in size, and Barimon moved forward, seemingly unaffected by its force. Sarion and Thustan were barely able to restrain their mounts, Sarion yelling, trying to get Thustan's attention.

"Something is happening! We must back away!"

Thustan nodded, a look of worry on his face. "Barimon! What are you doing?"

The mage seemed unaware of their presence, the vortex growing in size and ferocity, and he entered the churning maelstrom, disappearing from view. They could still see the light of the rod, immersed within that terrible disturbance, but nothing else. The Ravenor was beaten back and the ogres were in full retreat, realizing that there was power at work here that dwarfed their own. The vortex thundered ahead and followed after them, catching up to the Ravenor and thrusting the monster on its side as it rolled over, stunned, the ground quaking. The ogres were next, the whirlwind now hundreds of feet high, the wind buffeting them about helplessly. Thustan and Sarion had placed some distance between themselves and the fray, but the valley was under full assault; trees bending and whipping, the water from the stream churning and foaming, the remaining fighters galloping away for their lives.

The vortex battered the ogres, and the remaining brutes scattered, trying to escape. The Ravenor was back on its feet now, staring sightlessly at the vortex, focusing on the light. The whirlwind doubledback on itself, now heading toward the dam.

Sarion spotted movement to their right, and a solitary horseman approached. It was Glorafin. He had forgotten about the Sharield Captain, who had chosen to forsake his people and put his life in extreme danger to stand with Thustan and Sarion.

"Shades! What's happening here? Is the world ending?"

Sarion listened to his words, wondering the same thing himself...

"Barimon attempts to wield an ancient weapon against our enemy, but I fear he doesn't realize what he created." Sarion pointed as the vortex now slammed up against the dam itself. The stone held, but the vortex continued to grow in both height and mass.

"What can we do?" Glorafin asked. "Does he try to destroy the dam? He must be stopped."

"I don't think he *can* be...look, the Ravenor pursues him!"

It was true. The mighty creature headed straight at the vortex, somehow keeping its balance as it sought out Barimon. Sarion understood then that the monster knew Barimon had unleashed the power, and it acted to try and reach the mage and destroy him. The vortex hovered at the same spot before the great dam, and Sarion feared that the worst had now happened to Barimon – the mage had fully awakened the talisman and was unable to control it, lost in its power and violence. The vortex shifted, carrying the Ravenor with it dozens of yards, the beast once again thrown to the side. The maelstrom then came toward the dam again, this time with greater force. The dam shuddered, stones beginning to loosen and tumble below. Sarion glanced up at Sharield fighters as they stood on the walls, pointing and yelling. The vortex continued to increase in power, the funnel spinning faster and faster. Water gushed out at several spots, and within moments, the impossible happened, as a huge section collapsed and the Brightening became a raging torrent, the full weight of the lake pressing against the stone and looking for release.

"He's mad! We must leave or we'll be swept away in the flood!"

There was nothing they could do but gather their reins and head north, further away from the coming violence. They galloped away until Glorafin pointed towards a small rise. "I think we'll be safe there."

They pushed to the summit of a small hillock, which gave them a good view of the valley, a gloomy dawn breaking through the mist as the rain stopped. In the distance they watched the chaos as the dam broke asunder, the lake unleashing its fury. Incredibly the Ravenor held its ground, and it moved further along the rest of the dam which had remained unbroken. Its great claws dug into the earth and it waited, braced against the onslaught. The vortex churned ahead, going directly into the lake and forming a massive waterspout, a tiny light illuminating the middle where Barimon must still be.

"Shades, what has he done?" Thustan asked.

"What I warned you about," said Sarion. "You wanted to tap into the power of something ancient and beyond our comprehension. Now you see the result."

The waterspout was so strong that it separated the water to either side, moving along the lake bottom, muck and rock boiling in its wake. Colored brown from the silt and debris, the vortex reached ever higher, the water sizzling and steaming from the output of raw energy. The screams of invisible creatures filled the air in a deafening cacophony of madness and chaos, all of it coming from the heart of the vortex; a hybrid abomination of power and ancient magic. To their horror the waterspout changed course, heading directly for the city now, crashing into the nearest docks and tossing buildings aside like they were weightless. The lake grew narrower as more water rushed out, and the Ravenor loomed in the distance as it reached the far side, clambering its bulk upwards by gouging its claws into the dam and soon gaining the top. Pausing above the water, it lowered itself into the newly surfaced mud, and heaved itself forward. Sarion thought the creature must surely sink into the soft bottom, but there appeared to be enough solid mountain rock to give it access.

Sharield was in complete chaos...Warning horns echoed from above, and the din from the vortex and its horrible screams was almost rivaled by the sounds of people dying. The waterspout had lost most of its water now, becoming almost a wall of solid, impregnable air. The Ravenor disappeared from their view, and they could only catch glimpses of the terrible vortex as it laid waste to Sharield. The gates opened and people poured through, rushing out of it in chaotic droves, a mix of both citizens and fighters.

Glorafin shook his head, his face a mask of stunned amazement. "Sharield is destroyed, cursed for abandoning those who came in friendship."

Sarion responded. "Curse or not, a great evil has been unleashed here. Barimon directs the vortex, but I fear he has lost himself. We are powerless to stop him."

"I need to see what's happening in there." Thustan moved his horse down the hill, the others hesitating. "No one else has to come. This was my fault for attempting to use the rod."

Disregarding his words, Sarion and Glorafin followed him, soon making their way through a scattering of people running through the gates. Once inside, they were greeted by turmoil. Most of the guards had left their posts, either fleeing the city or perhaps moving deeper inside to save family and friend. Despite the harsh treatment by Lord Berillon, Sarion felt nothing but a sense of overwhelming compassion and loss. How had they come to this?

They made their way toward the lake, trying to gain sight of what was happening. Reaching the docks and the main pathway, they galloped ahead, growing steadily closer to the heart of destruction. They soon rounded a bend which overlooked the lake and then spotted the vortex further east, in close proximity to the mansion grounds. The vortex seemed to be smaller in size but no less intense. Battering itself against buildings, it left behind a path of unimaginable destruction. It turned and weaved, moving randomly now, a creation of violence that had no conscience or direction. Sarion still saw light from within, but it was brighter than before, much brighter. What was happening?

Without warning the Ravenor appeared, raising itself up from the lake and following after the vortex. Sarion was amazed that the creature had still managed to survive everything. How could they ever hope to defeat something so powerful?

The vortex/Barimon seemed oblivious to the creature's presence as it continued swirling about and leveling everything in its path. The Ravenor approached without hesitation, making directly for it, and as it came close it paused for a second, rearing back as it gathered strength before finally colliding with the whirlwind, two juggernauts of tremendous power clashing head on. The screams from within the vortex reached a new level of shrillness and the air exploded around them, flashes of green light coming from the spinning depths. The ground shook and Sarion had to leap off his horse, the animal whining in terror. His companions were no better off,

The Summoning

Thustan falling from his steed and Glorafin somehow managing to stay mounted.

The sound was deafening, and Sarion covered his ears, wondering if it truly were the end of the world…

❁ ❁

Geld Rinn dove toward the creature, seeing an opening, both knives flashing as he whipped them in a daring attack. It appeared the Crage had not expected the move and faltered for a brief second, but then like a massive snake it recoiled, its body shrinking back, and then it acted in a completely opposite fashion, leading Geld Rinn in close before flinging itself upon the startled fighter, its powerful limbs heaving upwards and knocking both of Geld's arms away. It never stopped and dove headfirst into the young fighter, hitting with all the force of its body and sending him flying against a tree where he crumpled to the ground, where he lay without moving.

Valadire was stunned by the ferocity of the attack, and knew that the Crage was more than a match for them, injured or not. Chertron held his sword before him, attempting to prevent the Crage from advancing while also protecting the fallen Geld Rinn. Lassel, again showing her mastery of horsemanship, brought her own weapon to bear, striking the monster with the edge, cutting into its shoulder. The Crage snapped at her in anger, but backed away for the moment, repositioning itself. Valadire did his best to keep the creature at bay, making sure that it didn't ignore him and attack his companions. His heart sunk at the sight of Geld Rinn lying motionless on the ground, and knew they had to do something quick or they might all share the same fate. They were only three now, fighting against a relentless creature from the Grammore Lowlands, an adversary which had proven time and again that it was not to be underestimated, and nothing seemed to stop it.

Valadire considered their options, and none of them looked good... Chardoom was surely doing his best to make good his escape, and almost certainly had a horse somewhere nearby. And then, adding to the chaos, Valadire heard something loud from the valley behind them, and a rushing noise. He hesitated for one moment before realizing what had happened.

"The dam has broken! A flood comes our way!"

They were close to the river which flowed out of the dam, and if the Ravenor had succeeded in destroying the structure, then the waters of the great lake would unleash a devastating fury into the valley below and they would be directly in its path, in grave danger of being swept away. The noise grew louder, and Chertron called to him.

"We need to climb the trees. It's our only hope!"

Lassel never took her eyes from the Crage, the monster sniffing the air, looking to the north.

"What of Wharla and Geld Rinn?" Chertron yelled.

Valadire was already off his horse, smacking the beast and sending it off. He hurried over to the young fighter, lifting him over his shoulder and searching the canopy overhead, looking for a spot to climb. Lassel also dismounted warily, her weapon never lowering. The Crage now moved, angling over towards Wharla, ripping the ropes binding her and lifting the helpless woman over one muscled shoulder.

"Look! The monster seeks to escape with Wharla!" Lassel called to her companions, but Valadire was already climbing, Chertron moving towards him now.

"Save yourself! Lassel, hurry!"

The noise seemed to grow with every passing second, and they heard trees and rock crashing behind them as the flood increased in size and power. They only had seconds to act…They watched as the Crage leaped effortlessly into a tree, moving higher and disappearing in the foliage. Both Lassel and Chertron were in the lower boughs of the ancient oak tree where Valadire held Geld Rinn, the Forester finding a spot which permitted him room to support both himself and the young fighter.

"Get ready!" Valadire yelled. "Climb higher and hold tight! If this tree falls, we're all lost!"

The three of them were nearly halfway up the great tree now, holding on and bracing themselves. They looked to where the Crage waited, quickly spotting it less than midway up its own tree, its head staring directly at them. Its bulk prevented it from going too high, but it was a creature of cunning and instinct, acting to protect both itself and its charge.

"What of Chardoom? He cannot have gone far." Chertron said. "This flood will spell his end."

"Let's hope…" Valadire had barely spoken the words when the water rushed towards them in a rage of mud and tree branches, crashing into the oak with crushing force, the huge trunk shuddering like an ancient giant awakened from deep sleep. They held on for their lives, the entire forest under a merciless assault, the angry waters knocking both rocks and trees aside like they were weightless, ripping many from the ground. The oak withstood the initial burst, and there was nothing they could do but wait it out and hope that its roots would hold.

Foam and mist were everywhere and it was a scene of chaos and destruction, the water threatening to sweep away everything in its path. Suddenly they heard a loud crack, and the tree which held the Crage and Wharla buckled and swayed, the monster desperately holding on to both the tree and his charge. But this was one time where its bulk worked against it as the tree snapped completely, the beast howling in rage as it tumbled into the water, taking Wharla with him. They saw her struggle but could only watch in horror as both Wharla and the Crage crashed into the torrent, the monster forced to loosen his grip as it attempted to save its own life. They both instantly disappeared into the churning flood and were gone.

The three fighters stared at the carnage in stunned silence, all of them thinking the same thing.

Neither man nor beast could have survived such an onslaught.

Nothing could...

They waited there for long minutes, never knowing if the tree would also succumb to the flood like the other one. Around them, trees which looked no less sturdy fell victim to the raging waters, creaking and breaking, becoming another piece of debris to the growing deluge which eagerly swallowed them up. They lost track of time, the day growing brighter, and at some point they noticed a lessening of the water, the flood finally receding. It happened quickly when it did, and soon the water was little more than a haphazard overflow lapping against the oak.

It was over.

Breathing a huge sigh of relief at last, Chertron looked towards Valadire, a question forming on his face.

The Forester stared down at him, his eyes haunted, and Chertron felt chills go up his spine, the fate of the brave young fighter unknown...

Chertron and Lassel searched below quickly, looking for signs of Wharla, the Crage, or Chardoom, but found nothing. The destruction was severe and the woods were silent -- a soggy, disheveled grave which was still shaking off the effects of the catastrophic flood. There was nothing to do but give up the search, knowing that all three had been lost.

They returned shortly, finding Valadire stooped over Geld Rinn, who lay on the ground unmoving.

"Nothing," said Chertron. "Not a trace."

"Even on horseback, Chardoom would not have gone far. Injured, he might have climbed a tree, I suppose, but I don't think he survived." Valadire said, his voice low.

"How fares Geld Rinn?" Lassel asked, approaching close and examining the young fighter.

"At first I feared the worst, but his breathing has steadied. I think there is hope that he will come to soon. We need to get help for him. It's time to return and see how Sarion and the others fared. The forest is quiet, and no sound issues forth from Sharield. I know not what this foretells."

On foot, they moved through the mud and puddles, making their way eastward towards the valley, Valadire carrying Geld Rinn across one shoulder. The day was growing long, and all of them walked with heavy hearts. They had fought a valiant battle against a powerful creature, and paid dearly for their struggle. It seemed like an eternity, but finally the woods opened up and the valley sat in front of them once again, but they were not prepared for the sight which lay before their eyes…

They looked upon a desolation. The dam was almost completely gone, the new river running forth in a strong current, with much of the lake now emptied. The wall surrounding Sharield was also severely damaged, large holes cut away into the stone as if gouged away by the hands of a monolithic titan. Men lay dead everywhere, victims of the Ravenor and ogres, and the city of Sharield was a smoldering ruin.

"Shades…" Chertron swore. "I've never seen such destruction."

A pair of riders appeared due north of them, spotting them as soon as they emerged from the treeline.

Valadire watched as they drew near, recognizing them as Thustan's men. The three companions looked at each other, no one daring to speak, uncomprehending as to what had happened while they were gone, and none of them cared to speculate on what dreadful tale they would soon hear...

Four of them sat on the ground awhile later, warming themselves around the fire.

Sarion looked around him, Chertron and Valadire to either side. Devastated by their story, he still couldn't make himself believe that Piril and Bertilik were dead. Another terrible loss for Nighton and the westland. The pair of brave fighters, chosen by Chensel to be his personal bodyguards, had fought against terrible creatures and traveled hard the past few weeks, only to find their doom in the most unlikely of places. Another tragedy among many others.

One good stroke of fortune was that Geld Rinn appeared to have escaped serious injury and was now being tended by healers. Gaining consciousness a short while ago, they believed he would fully recover, and Sarion felt a huge sense of relief at the news. Enough of his men had already paid the ultimate price.

Thustan approached, beckoning Sarion to follow him as he moved away from the others. Neither of them spoke for awhile, the prince leading him further off. His guards shadowed him from every direction but gave him enough room for privacy.

Thustan stopped and turned to him at last, fatigue and loss showing in his face. "You were right." His voice was low, and Sarion heard the pain in his words. "I failed to listen to your warning, and now Sharield is destroyed.

Barimon is dead, along with many of my men. Countless numbers of innocent people are gone as well."

Sarion said nothing. How could he disagree? But it wasn't the entire truth, the full summation of what had transpired here. Thustan could not place blame on his own shoulders. Hadn't he done the same thing to himself so often?

Sarion replied, his voice steady. "We were desperate. Were my own choices much different at Nighton against the Killworm? Our situation was dire, and I also attempted to use the rod then, barely able to wrest myself away from its grip. It was close. Very close. This – he swept his arms wide for emphasis – all this, could have been done by my own hands."

Thustan stopped, staring back towards the ruined city. The loss of life had been tremendous, including Lord Berillon himself and most of his councilors. The people of Sharield were now leaderless and for the most part homeless. The city with its great dam could not be rebuilt. There simply was not the manpower left. It would take a sizable force years to complete the monumental task. The ageless grace, beauty, and protection of the mountain city was now lost. The citizens would be uprooted, lacking the numbers or will to rebuild. No, they would move onward to the settlements or take up again in other lands.

And Sharield? It was now a dead city…

"Barimon gave into the allure of the rod. I should have *seen* it." Thustan shook his head, slamming a gloved fist into the palm of his other hand. "He became trapped, overwhelmed by its power."

Sarion nodded in agreement, still stunned by what had happened. "Well, we've learned useful information at last, although the cost of our enlightenment has been staggering. We now realize some of the other properties it contains. Besides negating the magical nature of these creatures, it's also a rod of summoning. And the scope of such power…" His voice trailed off as he attempted to put things into some type of perspective. "The vortex was raw energy, perhaps created by the ancient giants themselves. Uncontrollable, it destroys everything in its path until the wielder is destroyed as well. A frightening paradox."

Thustan rubbed his beard. "Yes, to have such might in your hands, but also realizing that if one attempts to use it, the wielder will be destroyed too, along with any others unfortunate enough to be close by. But wherein lies the purpose of creating such a destructive talisman? Did they manage to control it somehow? And I don't understand the actions of the Ravenor."

Sarion thought he knew some of that answer, but was still trying to reason it out. "There's no easy explanation, I'm afraid. Clearly, the creature was aware of the magic it contains, and realized the extent of its threat. It tried to confront Barimon, and I think he was so lost in its power that he didn't know what he was doing anymore. In the end, it took the strength of something *like* the Ravenor to neutralize the power of the rod. In the clash of such terrible force, they destroyed each other."

"And what would have happened if it were not *for* the Ravenor?"

Neither of them wanted to elaborate on the question…

But the monster was gone, and that was surely the one good thing to come of all this, Sarion understood. The Ravenor *had* been destroyed, and could threaten them no longer. It was a formidable foe, and could have wreaked havoc against the armies of Trencit. In his heart, Sarion felt that the Ravenor had been a creature magical in nature and had thrown itself against the energy of the rod, in the end dooming both itself and Barimon. Amazingly, they had retrieved the rod intact, the talisman unharmed. Thustan and Sarion were both shocked after they had spotted it lying there on the ground like nothing had ever happened, the vortex banished, the clashing adversaries mutually destroyed.

Thustan placed a hand on Sarion's shoulder and drew him close. Looking at his men, he saw they were all focused outwards, keeping vigilant. Thustan reached carefully into his tunic, bringing out the rod. "You are to be its keeper once again, Sarion. Take it."

Sarion looked at him in silence, stunned by his action. "What?"

"I want you to be its bearer. You have been wise in its use, defending the land against the evil of the Dark Mage. I'm sure my father will approve, especially after the fall of Barimon."

Sarion hesitated, his mind awash in mixed emotions. He knew that the rod was an equalizer against the servants of the Dark Mage, and was the tool they needed if they were to have any chance in a confrontation, but the rod was also tempting to use as a weapon, despite what it had done to Barimon and Sharield. Part of him entertained the notion that perhaps it could be harnessed in some fashion, maybe in a show of tremendous willpower. But no…he told himself. That path led to darkness, and would destroy him if he pursued it, no matter how desperate the situation. Barimon had been a powerful and knowledgeable man, a necromancer in his own right, and in the end he had failed to wield the talisman as his own. Failed, and perished because of it.

Dare he accept Thustan's offer, knowing all this? If the strongest mage in Trencit had fallen because of it, what chance did *he* have of ultimately prevailing?

Thustan was unwavering. "Take it," he insisted.

But Sarion hesitated. The last thing he had wanted was to lose the rod and have it taken back to Trencit where an attempt might be made to use it. And now, knowing what power it truly contained, how could he trust himself to hold the talisman in his possession, knowing it held both victory and defeat within its mysterious depths? Yet, who else could be trusted? He'd already taken on the weight of responsibility many times over the past few months, unwilling to let such terrible risks fall on any other. Could he do no less now?

Sarion slowly took the rod from Thustan, misgivings eating away at him as he touched its polished surface. He sensed the latent energy inside it. Sensed it, and was daunted. To be the bearer of the rod again, an ancient weapon which held such power…

Thustan stared at him for a moment, and then spoke. "For now, we need to talk of the immediate future. Pressing matters demand our attention, and things have rapidly spun out of control. I know you wish to stay in the westland, protecting Nighton against any new threats, and that's the main reason for you to act as bearer of the rod. Chardoom and his emissaries are destroyed, and more will certainly follow, but it is long past due for you to come before my father at Daregil Keep. We need to return there where he will speak with you directly and hold counsel. Too many events are playing out around Trencit, and too quickly. We need to coordinate a larger strategy."

Sarion frowned, a look of uncertainty on his face. "Things have happened more swiftly than I could have dreamed, and more will still come. My place should be to remain here, in the westland."

Thustan held him off. "I give you my word that you may return as soon as possible. I understand that you are best suited to fighting for Nighton, where Trencit needs you the most. Nevertheless, my decision is made. Will you come on your own volition? I would rather not command such."

Sarion was touched by the man's honesty, and could not have refused him regardless. He nodded in reply. "I will, but I also have a request. I would like Chertron to remain with me for as long as he so wills it, and for him to be let go of his commitment to the Hybril Legion. He has proven himself invaluable as both friend and warrior in our travels."

"It is done."

"And what of Forlern? I haven't even had the chance to inquire about him. He was reluctant for us to separate."

"Ah, let's go back to the camp and I'll fill you in." Thustan gestured. "We are both weary and I need the warmth of the fire with some food and ale to strengthen my heart. Come."

They returned, the others watching them approach. Sarion looked at their faces, seeing the wash of emotions within their orbs. Valadire was expressionless, but his eyes burned with an inner fire of determination. He had proven himself exceptionally well on this venture, worthy of his new promotion. Sarion was glad the man was on his side, and knew he would make a dangerous enemy to anyone opposing him.

Glorafin and Barthaniel huddled together, both of them devastated at the loss of their city. What would they do now, Sarion wondered?

Lassel sat on the ground, drinking from a small goblet, her eyes downcast, her face thoughtful and unreadable. She was like granite, Sarion thought. Even back at Nighton they had failed to grasp her full potential. Nothing seemed to faze her. What had made her so unyielding?

She looked up, standing as he approached.

"Any more word on Geld Rinn?" Sarion asked.

Lassel nodded, Sarion watching as her eyes reflected her relief. "He has awakened, and should recover. We are all glad at heart."

Sarion breathed deeply, nodding. "That is one piece of welcome news at last, and not the least. I'll check on him myself shortly, but I'm sure rest is the best thing for him now."

He looked around, his gaze falling lastly on Chertron. Reliable and brave, Sarion felt a strong kinship with the fighter, one as powerful as any bond of blood or oath. They had faced harrowing experiences together, and both had come out unscathed. Perhaps not unchanged, but they were survivors, having prevailed through danger and terrors which had claimed numerous other lives.

Would their fortunes continue to follow this path, or would they also find themselves falling victim to the Dark Mage? There were too many questions which couldn't be answered, and Sarion was no stranger to thinking such thoughts. The past few weeks he had been overwhelmed by constantly unfolding events which hurled him in new directions without warning. Where would they lead him next?

Well, some if it was laid out before him now. For the near future, it seemed he would finally travel to Daregil Keep and meet with King Gregor. It was true that they needed to discuss their strategy and formulate plans against the threat of the Dark Mage and the creatures from Grammore. They had learned much, and needed to draw on their experiences; make the sacrifice of others meaningful to the survival of the living. Sarion's heart was heavy with loss, and he wouldn't feel the weight lifting anytime soon, but there *was* one thing which had not changed in him.

He knew that the day would come when he faced the Dark Mage directly, and *then* he would have a chance to avenge the loss of his friends and companions, and all the innocent people who were no longer there.

That day would arrive, but until it did, Sarion needed to do his best to make sure he survived long enough to see it.

The End

This concludes Book Three of the Trencit Legacy. Book Four, follows the adventures of Sarion and his companions as they set out once again hoping to find answers in the epic battle against the Dark Mage.

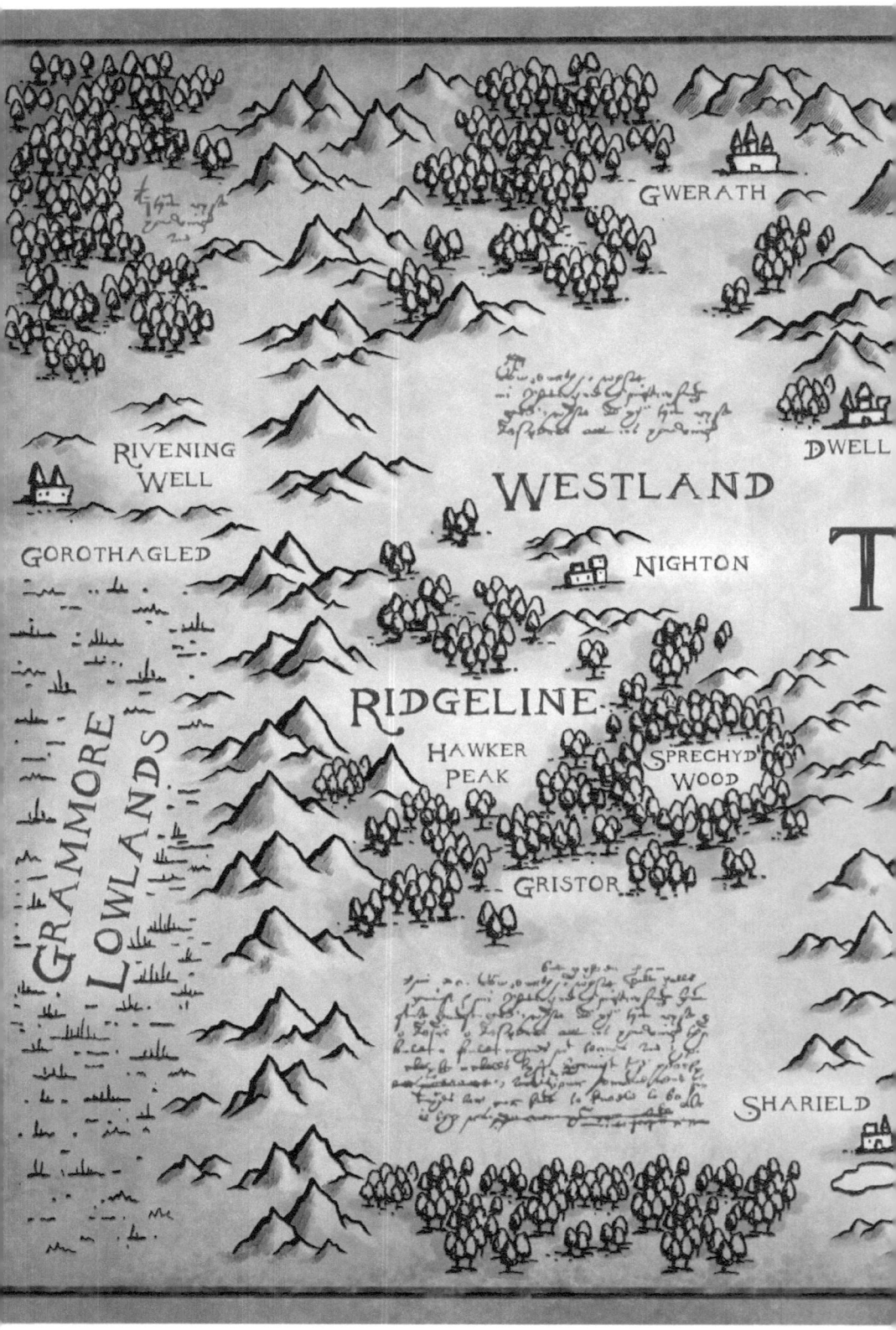

www.ingramcontent.com/pod-product-compliance
Lightning Source LLC
Chambersburg PA
CBHW022145010726
47493CB00002B/352